MOLLY GREEN has travelled th suitcase in a score of different became her new place of work. On returning to England, she set up an estate agency business which she ran and expanded for twenty-five years. Eventually, she sold her business to give herself time and space to pursue her dream to write novels. Last year she moved to a village near Lewes in East Sussex and has recently adopted Bella, a senior white and black cat, who she hopes will assist her in her writing, as her beloved rescued cat Dougie ably did for so many years.

## Also by Molly Green

The Dr Barnardo's Orphanage series:
*An Orphan in the Snow*
*An Orphan's War*
*An Orphan's Wish*

The Victory Sisters series:
*A Sister's Courage*
*A Sister's Song*
*A Sister's War*

The Bletchley Park series:
*Wartime at Bletchley Park*
*Winter at Bletchley Park*

# Wartime Wishes
## at
## Bletchley Park

# MOLLY GREEN

Published by AVON
A division of HarperCollins*Publishers* Ltd
1 London Bridge Street
London SE1 9GF

www.harpercollins.co.uk

HarperCollins*Publishers*
Macken House, 39/40 Mayor Street Upper,
Dublin 1, D01 C9W8, Ireland

This Trade Paperback Edition 2024
1
First published in Great Britain by HarperCollins*Publishers* 2023

A catalogue copy of this book is available from the British Library.

ISBN: 978-0-00-859938-6

This novel is entirely a work of fiction. References to real people, events
or localities are intended only to provide a sense of authenticity, and are
used fictitiously. All other characters and incidents portrayed in it are the
work of the author's imagination.

Typeset in Minion Pro by Palimpsest Book Production Limited, Falkirk,
Stirlingshire
Printed and bound in the U.S.A. by Lake Book Manufacturing, LLC

*To my father, Hatherleigh Percy Harold Barnes, an enthusiastic ham radio operator for much of his life.*

'Happy are all free peoples, too strong to be dispossessed,
But blessed are those among nations who dare to be
strong for the rest.'

Elizabeth Barrett Browning (1806–61)

# Before . . .

*London*
*9th September 1926*

Her father's shack, as he'd named it the day they'd moved in a year ago, was sacrosanct. Not that Maddie had really understood the meaning of the word when he'd reprimanded her the first time she'd entered without knocking.

'It's out of bounds if I'm not here, Madeleine,' he'd added firmly.

But today she'd turned nine – next year double figures, she kept hugging to herself – and was determined to find out what kept her father stuck in his room for hours on end, infuriating her mother. She knocked, and hearing no reply opened the door. Her father swung round in his chair, frowning at his daughter.

'Can I come in and watch?'

His expression softened. 'All right, as it's your birthday. If you're really interested I'll show you how I talk to people in this country and on the Continent and even as far as America.' He lit his pipe and puffed at it before it finally caught alight.

1

'Is it that tapping thing you do that Mummy gets cross about when she's calling you for lunch?'

Her father grimaced, then laughed.

'What's it for?'

'Sit down a moment.' He pulled up a chair for her and reached for a small instrument, about the size of her hand, with a little metal hammer. 'This is called a Morse key. Look. I'll show you how it works. Every letter in the alphabet is made up of dots and dashes in different ways. The letter "e" is only one dot and the letter "o" is only one dash but the others have multiple dots or multiple dashes or a combination of both. You have to tap the key like this –' he gave a short sharp tap '– which makes a dot, and a longer stroke like this, to make a dash. The dash sounds as a "dah" and the dot sounds as a "dit". Then when the person at the other end taps their reply you understand what they're saying because you've memorised the different series of dots and dashes – dits and dahs. If you wrote each letter in a notepad you'd soon have words and eventually a proper sentence. And that's called communicating with someone over the air in Morse Code.' He paused to make some popping noises with his pipe to get it going.

'When I want to speak to someone using Morse, I have to tap out my call sign "2BV" and that tells anyone who's listening that it's me, Walter Hamilton in England. Then whoever's about will tap *their* call sign and I can look it up on the list and see who it is. It might be someone I know quite well, or it might be a new chap who's appeared.' He adjusted his headphones. 'We'll see if someone's about in America first.'

She watched, fascinated, as her father fiddled with the knobs of his radio – to get the right frequency for America, he explained. After several moments of crackling he tapped his Morse key and wrote something down in the special notebook he used.

'Ah, someone's responding.' He nodded as he then jotted down some letters. 'I recognise it. It's Brad Jackson from Oregon – that's on the west coast of America. Nice chap. I'm now going to ask him if he's receiving me.' He tapped some more and waited, then turned to Madeleine with a satisfied grin. '"Loud and clear," he says.'

She stood several more minutes while her father sent his message and this Brad person answered. How could tapping that little machine possibly make letters that became words and even sentences? And to America? It was thousands of miles away so how was it possible her father and this man were able to talk to each other in that funny way just by tapping? She wanted to have a go.

'It's like being in a secret club.' Madeleine's voice had dropped to a whisper.

'Exactly like that.' Her father smiled.

'Then that's what *I* want to learn.'

'I don't know any girls or ladies that do Morse Code – at least I've never heard of one.'

'Why don't they?'

Her father took a few puffs of his pipe.

'Beats me, now you mention it.' He chuckled. 'Maybe you'll be the first.'

A thrill shot through the child. She would be the very first girl to learn Morse Code and make her daddy proud.

'Will you teach me?'

Her father nodded. 'I will if you're serious. But you'll have to learn every letter in Morse Code by heart. It's not easy at first – like learning another language. But it gets easier and becomes a rhythm – then it's like playing an instrument.'

'That's all right, Daddy. I'm good at reading notes in music in class. I'm sure I can learn dots and dashes of the alphabet. And I'll be the first girl in the whole world to do Morse Code!'

# PART ONE

PART ONE

# Chapter One

*Munich, Germany*
*Early September 1938*

Madeleine glanced at the wall clock, then over to the shiny bent heads of the twins.

Lotte was reading in her confident tones. She didn't always pronounce the words correctly but she was game, Madeleine thought, hiding a smile. Erich was more hesitant; he was determined to say everything perfectly even if his delivery was slower. As Lotte read, Erich ran his forefinger along the line, silently mouthing the words:

Lotte looked up. 'Maddie, I have . . . zirst.' Although she showed the tip of her pink tongue, she was still unable to pronounce the 't-h' sound her twin had mastered.

'Better to say: "I am thirsty".' Madeleine smiled. 'All right, children, we'll finish the chapter tomorrow. But don't forget you've both got homework to do ready for school Monday morning, so it's not all play.'

She'd hardly finished her sentence before her eight-year-old charges clapped their hands with glee and put their books to one side.

'Please may we be excused?' they said in unison.

7

'Yes, you may. *I'll* be excused, too.' She grinned and the twins giggled. 'You've done well today so we'll pack up and I'll make you both a drink in a few minutes.'

Madeleine ushered them out of the small schoolroom her German hosts, Herr and Frau Weinberg, had had remodelled from one of the pine-panelled bedrooms for their children's English lessons. Her gaze fell on the huge tiled stove in one corner which Frau Weinberg had assured her they'd be glad of in winter, the hand-painted flower borders on the chest of drawers where the twins kept their lessons and other paraphernalia, and the photographs of the family on every available flat space, juxtaposed with houseplants and books. But the effect wasn't at all cluttered; it was merely interesting and homely.

The children were delightful, sometimes surprising her with their level of maturity. Once again she thought how lucky she was compared to her friend Gwen who was a nanny to a baby and a fractious toddler in a family where the parents treated her like a servant instead of a member of the family as the Weinbergs did.

An hour later and humming a tune as she walked towards the restaurant where she was to meet Gwen, Madeleine relished the rest of the day where she was free until the following morning, Sunday, although she was still thinking about the twins. She loved the good-natured competitiveness between them and so far they were making good progress in English, so much so that she'd adapted *The Secret Garden* into a simple and condensed play she thought they'd enjoy enacting. She'd run through the first scene with them this coming weekend, thinking how much she was going to enjoy taking them through the actions with the dialogue to help with their understanding of the story.

Both children were intelligent with a mischievous sense of humour of which she was sometimes the brunt. She grinned, remembering the white rat they'd put in her bedroom two days ago hoping it would scare her, and their disbelief when she'd picked up the little creature and casually handed it to Erich.

'Your new pet, I believe, Erich,' she'd said, managing to contain her laughter as Lotte broke into a burst of giggles.

As Madeleine strolled along the street, she noticed how some of the women with their shopping baskets kept their heads down as though afraid to be conspicuous. Why was that? she wondered. Feeling the sun too hot on her face, she pulled the brim of her hat a little lower as she passed a parade of shops. It was then that she heard shouts coming from one of them. She froze. Two men, who couldn't have been much more than her own age, were dragging a loudly protesting elderly man from his premises. One of them butted him in the stomach with a rifle. What on earth . . .? She blinked. Dear God, it was Herr Cohen, one of Herr Weinberg's business friends. She noticed men and women who'd been chatting together only moments before suddenly melting away.

Before Madeleine could gather her wits the two men shoved Herr Cohen into a van, jumped in themselves, and immediately roared off. No one even glanced up when a woman whom she recognised as Herr Cohen's wife rushed out of the same shop but was swiftly intercepted by a man stepping in front of her, his rifle only inches from her face. She blinked. Judging by his green-grey tunic, he was a member of the Gestapo.

'*Halt! Zurück ins Haus!*' the uniformed man ordered.

Hardly realising what she was doing, her heart thumping

in her chest and ears, Madeleine flew towards the scene, brandishing her handbag at him.

'Lassen Sie diese Dame in Ruhe!' she shouted.

Two more Gestapo swaggered towards her, their eyes like pebbles, their mouths hard.

*Dear God, what had she started?*

'Back, *Fräulein*,' the older of the two ordered her in English. 'It is not your business. Do not interfere with things you do not understand.' He pointed his rifle at her.

Out of the corner of her eye, Madeleine saw the first Gestapo manhandle Frau Cohen back into her husband's shop and ordered her to stay inside or she would regret it.

'You're nothing but cowards – the lot of you,' Madeleine addressed the older man, her lips tight with rage. She made to go towards the shop. She would tell Frau Cohen how sorry she was and ask if there was anything she could do.

But he caught her arm in a vice-like grip.

'Ihre Name.'

For an instant Madeleine thought of refusing to give her name to this callous man. But his ice-cold stare brought her to her senses.

'Madeleine Hamilton.'

'Spelling?' he barked.

She told him, enunciating the letters in the German way, forcing herself to keep calm, though her heartbeat pounded in her eardrums.

He wrote it down in a notebook.

'You are English?'

'Yes.'

'Why are you in München?' His eyes were steel as they penetrated hers.

'I teach English.'

His gaze turned to suspicion.

'*In der Schule*?'

'No, in a private family,' she answered in English.

*Please don't ask me their name.* Madeleine pressed her lips together.

'And the name of this *private* family?' The man's eyes narrowed.

*Dear God.*

She looked at him unflinchingly, the lie springing easily to her lips. 'Herr and Frau Schmidt.'

Cold grey eyes bored into hers. She would *not* let herself lower her gaze, no matter what it cost her. Did he suspect she was lying? Would she be taken off like poor Herr Cohen? She tried to swallow but a lump had formed in her throat. He didn't write anything down. He knew she'd lied. Then to her astonishment he jerked his head back and laughed. It was more of a mirthless bark, sending a shiver across her shoulders.

'You think I am stupid, *nein*?' When she didn't answer, he said, 'You have your papers to return to England?'

She reached in her bag and pulled out her pass then handed it to him. He studied it carefully, glancing at her now and again. Finally, slowly, he gave it back to her.

'You have four months still,' he said, as though he thought she might not be aware. 'See you do not—' he broke off, searching for the word he wanted.

Madeleine's stomach churned.

'. . . *interfere* with our customs.' His eyes glinted with warning as they met hers. 'I wish you enjoyment for your stay in the *Vaterland* and say your friends at home of our splendid country.' He gave a tight smile, nodded and clicked his heels together, then the two of them marched

11

off, scattering a few curious bystanders who had by this time silently gathered.

Madeleine bit her bottom lip hard, mainly to stop the sour acid rising from her stomach into her mouth. She shuddered. It wouldn't have taken much more for him to have arrested her.

*Stop it, Maddie. You're being ridiculous.*

She was perfectly entitled to be here. And she was glad she'd given that hateful man a false name that didn't sound Jewish for her hosts. There were so many Schmidts, the Nazis would never be able to check them all. Thank goodness he hadn't asked her address.

Her heart would not stop pounding. Aware that the two Gestapo had turned round and were still watching her, Madeleine forced herself to walk slowly, as if on a Sunday stroll, towards the restaurant where she was to meet Gwen, though she longed to rush back to Herr Weinberg's shop and tell him what had happened. To caution him.

Still dazed with shock at witnessing such brutality, she kept her gentle pace, numbly placing one foot in front of the other, convincing herself she'd made too much of what was surely just a routine request to see her papers. It was simply the German way of doing things. But she couldn't forget how not one member of the public had raised an eyebrow at the way those two thugs had pushed Herr Cohen into the van.

'Cowards, the lot of them,' she muttered under her breath.

The walk steadied her heartbeat and by the time she arrived at the restaurant, she felt almost back to normal and her spirits lifted when she saw Gwen waiting outside, her anxious face breaking into a smile of relief.

12

'I was getting worried,' Gwen said. 'You're always so punctual.' Then she looked more closely at her friend. 'Are you all right, Maddie? You look as though you've seen a ghost.'

'I can't tell you in the restaurant,' Madeleine said, putting her hand through Gwen's arm. 'Let's just have five minutes before we go in and I'll tell you why I was held up – literally. I'll warn you, Gwen – it's not a pretty story.'

Gwen's eyes almost popped from her forehead as Madeleine recounted the fright she'd had.

'Oh, how horrible. Poor Herr Cohen.' She bit her lip and said nothing for a few moments. Then she said in a low quiet tone, 'I've never told you this, Maddie, but *I'm* Jewish.' She looked at Madeleine, her eyes shining with tears. 'It brings it home, rather, hearing that.'

'Oh, my goodness.' Madeleine put her hand on Gwen's arm. 'I had no idea . . . not that it matters a jot,' she added hurriedly. 'But it's not something to mention in public while we're in Germany.'

'I know. But I never realised until now how bad it would be. I'm not sure I'd have come if I'd known.'

'Well, they're not going to take any notice of a Jewish English girl,' Madeleine said firmly. 'It's the German Jews that are going to be in for a rough ride.'

'Will you tell the Weinbergs?' Gwen said.

'I must. I have to warn them.' Madeleine paused. 'When we're in the restaurant, Gwen, don't mention anything at all about what I just witnessed or your religion – nothing that might get us noticed in the wrong way.'

'No, I won't. But I'm beginning to feel uncomfortable here and I'm seriously thinking of going home before my year is up.' She looked at Madeleine. 'I didn't tell you but

13

the other evening the Schertenleibs gave a dinner party and they invited me. I don't know why, because they never have before. I'm always treated politely but like a servant.' Gwen gave her friend a rueful smile. 'They're not like your lovely family.' She paused. 'Anyway, there were three couples – the women dressed to the nines like they always do – and the men talking amongst themselves. I understood enough of their conversation to know they were –' she looked round then whispered '– all Nazis.'

Madeleine gave a start. 'How do you know?'

Gwen bit her lip. 'They mentioned the Great War – how they'd lost everything including their pride. And worse for them that they're not allowed to build an army. Apparently, Hitler's never got over it. One of the men said Hitler's the only leader who can make Germany a great country again and his goal is for the Third Reich to rule the world.' She looked at Madeleine. 'I wish you'd been there, Maddie. Another man said in such a quiet tone I could hardly hear him, "Our Führer has great plans – but slowly does it." That's my rough translation but it makes my blood run cold just to think of it.' Gwen took in a breath.

'Jews were mentioned more than once and you should have seen their lips curl. I wish I'd been brave enough to tell them I was Jewish but I was too terrified. Can you imagine their horrified expressions if I had?' She glanced at her friend. 'I don't think they realise how much German I understand because I don't speak it nearly as well as you.'

'Hadn't you noticed this before, Gwen?'

'No, their guests never mentioned politics but this was a different set of people.' She stared miserably at her friend. 'It really upset me, Maddie, and now I don't know what to do.'

Madeleine tried to think calmly but it wasn't easy after the scene she'd witnessed a few minutes ago. 'It might be best for you to pack up quietly and go home.' She paused. 'You know, Gwennie, this is making me worry even more about the Weinbergs, especially the twins. I couldn't bear anything to happen to them.'

# Chapter Two

After she had said goodbye to Gwen, who needed to do some shopping for her young charges, Madeleine wandered over to Munich's *Englischer Garten*, thinking about her conversation with her friend. There she found a hard bench and closed her eyes against the still-warm sun, peaceful even with the sound of children's shouts and laughter in the distance, but it did nothing to dispel her inner feelings of discomfort.

Up until now she'd been content with learning a new culture, deepening her knowledge of the German language, and teaching the twins in the family she lived with. And meeting Gwen, who lived in a neighbouring district, provided the much-needed opportunity to have some fun when their days off coincided. Now, it seemed, a darker element had crept in.

So the Schertenleibs were Nazis. Madeleine turned over this revelation in her mind, nausea spreading into her stomach. Even though Gwen's family lived in one of the grand houses overlooking the English Garden – where they'd first met when Gwen was taking the baby out in the pram and had struck up a conversation – she didn't envy her friend one bit going back to such a household and trying to keep it a secret that their nanny was Jewish.

But maybe Gwen's eye-opener and Herr Cohen's abduction were simply a couple of isolated incidents that had happened in a short space of time, and things would now settle. But even as she told herself that, she knew it would never settle. Hitler was too arrogant to change his mind on his grandiose plans. She sighed and glanced at her watch. Ten past three. She should go back to the Weinbergs to be in time for the children coming out of school.

As Madeleine stepped through the front door she thought she heard the faint sound of weeping. Hurrying to the orangery she found Frau Weinberg sitting in a corner by the garden table, her head buried in her hands.

'Oh, my goodness, whatever's the matter?' Madeleine said, rushing towards her.

Frau Weinberg looked up, her eyes streaming. 'I cannot tell you.'

'Please, Frau Weinberg . . .'

There was such a long pause, Madeleine wondered if she'd attempted a step too far into her hostess's privacy. Frau Weinberg pulled in a long jerky breath, speaking in rapid German. Madeleine put up her hand.

'*Langsam, bitte schön.*'

Frau Weinberg nodded.

'In the market this morning the stall-keeper where I was queueing said he was not going to serve Jews any longer,' she said more slowly. 'I needed some vegetables but I left before he saw me. He knows I am Jewish. If that is not bad enough, my husband found a notice on his shop window yesterday telling people not to shop there.' She looked up at Madeleine, her eyes imploring. 'Do you understand my German?'

17

Madeleine nodded. 'Yes, so long as you don't go too fast.'

'How will we survive if the customers no longer come? We depend upon everyone, Jewish or not, to keep the business running. But it's partly my husband's fault. I get so upset because he is not discreet. He says what a dreadful man Hitler is and refuses to give the Nazi salute when he passes an officer. Instead, he dives into a nearby doorway. I tell him to keep his opinions to himself or he is going to land us in trouble.' She took a spotless handkerchief from her skirt pocket and dried her tears. 'It is not the first time we have been exposed to such hatred but I have tried to keep it from you. I do not want to spoil your time here.' She looked up at Madeleine with a wobbly smile. 'We like you very much, my dear. You are almost like one of the family.'

Madeleine swallowed, her eyes pricking with tears. Herr Weinberg was taking a risk in his behaviour. No wonder his wife was so upset.

'I do not mind about me but I do mind about my husband. He cannot take much more than this, but it is going to get worse with that madman in the Chancellery.' She paused. 'The Nazis are ruthless and hate the Jews, particularly those with their own businesses. They want to destroy us – all of us. But my husband doesn't believe it. He fought in the last war and was decorated as a war hero. He says he is a loyal German. That comes above everything. But I tell him loyalty will not help him.' She looked at Madeleine, her eyes streaming. 'There will be another terrible war . . . and the Nazis will win!'

Madeleine gave a start. This wasn't a casual conversation between her and Gwen who were mere observers from another country. This was a sensible and kind German

18

Jewish lady who was desperately worried about her family, stating something she saw as obvious.

As though Frau Weinberg had picked up her thoughts, she continued:

'I dare not tell him but I can tell you.' She licked her lips. 'I am worried sick about the twins growing up under such a terrible regime but I know my husband will never leave the shop he built up from nothing. He loves mending the instruments and talking to the customers about his beloved music. It is his life. Besides, he is too proud.' She glanced at Madeleine. 'He insists he will remain in his home – the land that he loves.'

This was far worse than Madeleine had realised. She tried to swallow but a lump had formed in her throat. She didn't know how to answer. What was the right thing to say?

'I'm sure it won't come to war,' she managed. 'No one can want another one after only twenty years since the last.'

Frau Weinberg threw her a pitying look.

'You will see that I am right,' was all she said.

Two days later Frau Weinberg confided to Madeleine that her husband had scrubbed off the notice pasted by the Nazis from his shop window. Consequently, most of their regular customers, Jews and Gentiles alike, were still bringing in their instruments for him to repair and asking his advice on which make of violin they should buy or arranging an appointment for him to tune their pianos. More importantly, they were spending money. But Madeleine could tell from Frau Weinberg's tone that her employer didn't believe for one moment it would last.

19

Madeleine turned the question of returning home over in her mind before going to bed that night. But in the morning when the household sprang into action and she heard the twins laughing, she told herself she'd be turning her back on the family who'd been so kind to her. Besides, she wouldn't be carrying out her plan to stay a year. She'd be giving up. Once again, she'd see the expression on her parents' faces that said she never stuck at anything. Madeleine sighed. She couldn't bear that. How often she'd tried to vie for her mother's attention and approval. But her gaze was always firmly directed towards Maddie's two older brothers and Maddie had grown up with the idea she would never be successful like them.

But if she'd been allowed to do what she'd always dreamt of – to train to become a professional actress – she was sure that with hard work she would have eventually become successful too. Surely being given the lead parts in school plays proved she had some talent. And to show how serious she was, she'd applied and had been accepted at one of the most reputable drama schools, but her mother had refused to sign the papers and had persuaded her husband to do the same. And at only eighteen she needed parental permission. 'It's not a proper career,' her mother said scathingly, 'and it's very unstable unless you're one of the few big names.' Madeleine had had to bite her tongue that a romantic novelist, as her mother was, didn't seem any more stable as a career choice, though she had to admit her mother was very successful. She grimaced. She'd given up reading her mother's lightweight novels by the time she'd turned sixteen and realised life wasn't the way her mother portrayed it with everything tied in a neat bow at the end. And as for now, being an actress would have to remain a dream.

She'd stay with her Bavarian family a few months longer and see how things went. Keep up her German that she'd worked so hard at, both at school and college.

*Except you gave it up – you didn't finish your degree.*

Madeleine shook her mother's words away. Frau Weinberg often talked to her in German and she was improving fast. So whether she stayed in Germany or not, if the present situation worsened, she might find the language useful one day.

# *Chapter Three*

'I've given in my notice, Maddie,' Gwen said. 'I'll be on my way home at the end of this month.'

Several days had gone by since they'd last met and the two girls were walking alongside the Isar River which flowed through the middle of the city, Gwen with two-year-old Beatrix in her pushchair.

Madeleine wasn't surprised at her friend's announcement. Gwen's nervous tension was palpable today.

'Have you learnt anything more at the Schertenleibs' that's made you decide this?'

'Yes.' Gwen stopped and faced her. 'I think there must have been things going on that I didn't notice, or maybe I chose not to, but yesterday I saw an envelope on the hall table with a swastika. It gave me the creeps. That's what made up my mind.'

'Then you've made the right decision,' Madeleine said.

'I wish you'd come with me. But it's no good trying to persuade you if you're determined to stay. I know what you're like. But I just don't want you to get caught up in any war, that's all.'

'I can't believe we're talking about the likelihood of a war, and yet I suppose it really *is* possible.'

'You haven't been here as long as me,' Gwen said, 'and you've already witnessed that horrible scene with Herr Weinberg's friend, and the threatening way that hateful Gestapo man spoke to you.'

Madeleine's heart thumped as she pictured the two scenes again. Was it just a preview of what it would be like living here under Hitler? She set her jaw. She would not be intimidated. No. She would go in *her* time, not Herr Hitler's.

'If I can I want to complete the year as I set out to do.' She paused. 'But I'll really miss you.'

'I'll miss you, too,' Gwen said fervently, 'and Beatrix – she's such a darling, though I hate to think of her growing up in a family where there's such a beastly undercurrent below all their charm.'

Madeleine bit her lip. Herr and Frau Schertenleib's enthusiasm for the Nazi party were obviously affecting her friend badly. She was about to say something when Gwen's expression brightened as she looked down at Beatrix. 'You know, Maddie, I'd love a daughter like her . . . one day – though she probably wouldn't have the same blonde hair,' she added lightly.

At that moment the child twisted her head round and stared up at Gwen, then for no apparent reason screwed up her face and let out a wail.

'Even when she's like that?' Madeleine said, grinning.

'I think she's too hot, aren't you, my love?' Gwen stopped and put the brake on. 'Frau Schertenleib insists she has to wear a bonnet and jacket even though it's so warm. Would you like an ice-cream, Beatrix?'

The little girl didn't respond, though she immediately stopped crying.

'*Möchtes Eis*?' Gwen said in a strangled accent.

'*Möchte Eis*,' Beatrix repeated, tears standing in her eyes.

'Isn't it strange when a little child speaks in another language?' Gwen said, chuckling. 'They always sound so clever.' She lifted the brake off the pushchair. 'All right, then, let's go and find some ice-cream.'

'There's a stall over there and by the looks of things they're selling drinks.' Madeleine pointed. 'I'm sure they'll have ice-cream as well. And it's my treat.'

They strolled over to the open stall, Beatrix grizzling until Gwen removed her bonnet and jacket. There were several people in the queue, mostly mothers with children, and two young men in front of them. One of them, the blond one, turned round when Beatrix gave another wail. Madeleine couldn't help noticing his refined features and penetrating blue eyes, as if they missed nothing.

'*Bitte schön*,' he said, waving for the girls to take their place in front.

'*Danke schön*,' Madeleine said, giving him a grateful smile. The sooner Beatrix got her ice-cream the better.

He gave a slight bow.

'Will Beatrix eat one on her own?' Madeleine said, turning to Gwen.

'I'm not sure. But if she doesn't finish it, I'll do her the honours.' Gwen giggled.

Madeleine heard the two young men behind them mutter something she didn't catch. Then she felt a light tap on her shoulder. She swung round. The blond one was smiling.

'Excuse me, but you are English,' he said. 'We would like to buy you an ice . . . for all.'

'That's very kind of you, but really—' Madeleine started.

24

'We insist,' said his taller, auburn-haired friend, gazing at Gwen as he spoke.

'Thank you,' Gwen said. 'I'll have strawberry. . . *bitte.*'

'And for your little girl?'

'Oh, she's not mine,' Gwen said quickly. 'I'm her nanny.'

'*Ach so* – an English nanny.' He kept his gaze upon her. 'You must live with a good family.'

Madeleine shook her head at Gwen to try to stop her from saying any more. The boys seemed friendly enough but they'd never set eyes on them before.

But Gwen simply smiled and nodded towards Beatrix. 'She'll have a small strawberry ice-cream as well, please.' She paused. 'I'll just be standing over there.' She guided Beatrix out of the queue.

The blond one watched her go with raised eyebrows and an amused smile playing on his lips.

'And for you, *Fräulein*?' he said, turning to Madeleine. 'What flavour would you prefer?'

'Vanilla, thank you,' Madeleine answered as graciously as she could muster, not really understanding why she felt slightly uncomfortable.

He stepped past her saying, '*Entschuldigung*' and turned his smile onto the prim middle-aged woman serving the drinks. A minute later he handed Madeleine a vanilla ice-cream, then he strolled over to where Gwen was waiting with Beatrix in her pushchair, leaving his friend at the counter. Soon the little girl was delicately licking the ice-cream with her small pink tongue, letting it dribble down her chin as it immediately began to melt.

'Where do you live?' Madeleine heard the blond one asking Gwen as she joined them.

'Not far from here,' she interrupted before Gwen could

answer. She felt embarrassed eating the ice-cream he'd bought her and sounding so short but he seemed to be taking the new acquaintance too much for granted. She didn't even know his name.

'Are you a nanny also?' he asked, turning to her.

'No,' Madeleine said, reluctant to say more. But she could tell he was waiting for her to expand. Well, there couldn't be any harm in it. It wasn't a secret and she had to be here for a reason. 'I teach English to German children.'

'*Ach so.*' He looked at her with interest. 'In a classroom or in a family?'

There he was, firing questions again – almost the same questions as the horrible Gestapo man last week. Thankfully, Madeleine was saved from giving him any more details when the friend came up holding two mugs of beer and handed one over.

'*Danke schön.*'

'Do we sit at that table?' He nodded towards an empty wooden trestle with several chairs just a few yards away.

'Good idea.' The blond one strode over and pulled back two of the chairs, gesturing for Madeleine and Gwen to take a seat, leaving enough space for the pushchair. Once they were all seated, he continued. 'We are pleased to have such an opportunity to talk to two charming English ladies.' That smile again as he pointed his forefinger at his chest. 'I am Rolf and my friend is Otto.' He gazed at Madeleine and Gwen. 'We know the little one is Beatrix. So will you tell us *your* names?'

Why did she feel so uncertain – even wary? But she'd felt wary ever since poor Herr Cohen had been dragged off. And any rate these boys were much too young for her to be in the least interested although Otto seemed

26

genuinely nice. But Rolf . . . with the sun catching his blond hair . . .

She couldn't stop a prickle of apprehension. She'd heard that Hitler preferred blond-haired boys for his Hitler Youth training programme. Rolf was probably still young enough to belong.

'When do you come to Germany?' Rolf now enquired, turning towards her, then taking several gulps of his beer.

'At the beginning of this year,' Gwen said before Madeleine could answer.

'And how long do you stay?'

Gwen hesitated. With his eyes fixed on her, Madeleine felt she had to give him some kind of reply.

'We're not sure . . . a little longer, perhaps.'

'And where other have you seen in my country?'

'Just Munich really.'

'That is good, but not enough.' He threw her a smile. 'Would you like us to show you more of Germany?'

'Aren't you at school?'

Rolf smiled. '*Nein*. I am on holidays from university. We go back very soon. But tomorrow morning Otto and I go to Nürnberg.' He glanced at his friend who nodded. 'We would like you to accompany us. You will see something of the greater Germany.'

Madeleine blinked. *What on earth did he mean – the 'greater' Germany?*

'What do you think, Maddie?' Gwen said, her eyes lively with enthusiasm. 'It's Sunday tomorrow and I have the day off.'

'I usually work Sundays.'

'You said you had to work yesterday on your birthday so maybe they'd let you off tomorrow.'

27

'I'd have to see.' She wouldn't tell Gwen in front of Rolf and Otto that she'd been given Sunday off. She needed to think.

'We are from good families,' Rolf broke in. 'You will be safe with us.'

'How far is it?' Gwen said.

'On the train? One hour and half.'

Gwen turned to Madeleine. 'It would be nice to see somewhere new in Germany . . .'

Otto pulled out a card from his jacket pocket.

'It is my student identification,' he said, showing it to Gwen who passed it to Madeleine. 'Rolf has the same.'

Madeleine glanced at it, then at Gwen.

'I suppose it would make a change,' she said slowly.

'*Gut. Sehr gut.*' Rolf swallowed the rest of his beer. 'We meet you at the *Hauptbahnhof* tomorrow morning at eleven.' He jumped to his feet. 'For now, we must go. It is good to meet you.'

'Goodbye,' Otto said, shaking hands with them. 'I look forward to seeing you tomorrow.'

They both bowed, brought their heels together, and strode off.

'That was a sudden departure,' Gwen commented as her gaze followed the two boys. She turned back to Madeleine. 'You didn't seem too sure, Maddie.' She pressed her friend's hand. 'We don't have to go.'

'I know we don't.' And then it struck her why she'd been reticent. She'd heard the announcement only yesterday on the wireless and seen how grim Herr Weinberg's expression was when it had finished. He'd risen and switched it off with an angry click.

'Damn the Nazis,' he'd said and slammed out of the door.

'What's the matter, Maddie?'

Gwen's question shook her into the present.

'Do you know where I bet they're going in Nuremberg?'

Gwen shook her head.

'They're celebrating the Anschluss – the so-called unification of Austria with Germany in March.' Madeleine shuddered. 'Some celebration – it was a deliberate takeover.'

'The Austrians seemed happy enough,' Gwen said.

'That's what they reported in the newspapers. And who has control of the newspapers?' Madeleine challenged.

'The Nazis.' Gwen bit her lip. 'Oh, I see what you mean.'

Madeleine thought quickly. 'Perhaps we *should* go and see for ourselves how the little Austrian runt persuades thousands he did the right thing. I saw a few seconds of it on Pathé News before I left England – it was incredible how his screaming and shouting appeals to the Germans and we'd be witnessing history right in front of our eyes.' When Gwen hesitated, she added, 'We can always leave if we don't like it.'

'All right, we'll go if you think it's important.'

'But I want to avoid those two boys.'

'Any particular reason?'

'Yes, dear Gwennie. You can bet your life they're in the Hitler Youth!'

The *Hauptbahnhof* was crowded with people shouting, jostling, laughing, pushing good-naturedly into each other, and obviously bent on having a good day out. For a few seconds Madeleine envied the jabbering Bavarians with their wide smiles showing white teeth in contrast to their tanned faces, many of them clad in shorts or *Lederhosen*,

29

showing off their firm golden legs that looked as if they'd been mountain-climbing all summer, shaking hands and kissing cheeks and pushing through the doors of the waiting train to Nuremberg. She looked round. No sign of Rolf and Otto. Good. But even if they were here, she and Gwen would probably never spot them amongst the masses. She slipped her hand in Gwen's arm.

'Come on, Gwennie – brace yourself for an adventure.'

The train was packed but Gwen spotted one empty seat. Madeleine nodded for her to take it. A young man sprang to his feet.

'*Bitte.*' He motioned for Madeleine to take his seat. '*Setzen Sie sich bei Ihrer Freundin.*'

For an instant Madeleine's instinct was to refuse. She couldn't bear the thought of sitting in the space so recently occupied by a youth who was probably a Nazi. The seat would still be warm from his behind. *Stop this*, she told herself. She was getting carried away with suspicion. They couldn't *all* be Nazis.

'*Danke sehr*,' she replied as calmly as she could muster.

He nodded, giving her a slight smile.

Madeleine tuned her ear towards her fellow passengers. She'd become used to the strange Bavarian twang, so different from the pronunciation she'd learnt at school, but it was hard to follow the fast and furious delivery of her fellow passengers. After a while she followed Gwen's example and closed her eyes.

'Nürnberg,' the conductor called.

Madeleine sprang up and tapped Gwen's arm.

'Come on, Gwen. We're here.'

Almost everyone alighted. The two girls were pushed

from behind by impatient passengers as they jostled to get to the door.

'Germans certainly don't go in for queuing,' Gwen said in her clear tones, as she and Madeleine scrambled down to the platform.

'Careful,' Madeleine muttered. 'You don't know who's listening and understands English – probably more than you might think.' She hesitated, watching the surge of people all going in one direction. 'We'll follow the crowd. They're bound to be going to the rally.'

It was a long walk from the railway station to the Luitpoldarena where the rally was to be held. Gwen complained constantly that something in her shoe was hurting her foot, but the crowds were so dense there was no room for her to stop and shake it out. To Madeleine it looked like thousands more people had joined them on their walk but this was only a fraction of what appeared to be hundreds of thousands of uniformed party members who were already in position, perfectly lined up and standing still as statues in the arena as far as the eye could see, ready to salute their Führer when he appeared.

'Goodness, I've never seen so many people in one place,' Gwen said, her head turning from one side to the other. 'It's incredible.'

At the far end of the parkland, which appeared at least half a mile away, Madeleine saw what looked like three monolithic columns. They were each draped with a huge flag emblazoned with the swastika emblem. Everywhere she turned were enormous flags tied onto every conceivable post and building. That terrifying hooked-cross design. She felt her stomach curdle and swallowed hard.

As though feeling just as queasy, Gwen said, 'Look at

31

all those children waving those hateful swastika flags. They have no idea what they're doing, poor little kids.'

'Keep your voice down,' Madeleine hissed, though she still shivered at the signs. 'Let's go and find a space.'

'It doesn't look as though we'll get even a glimpse of Hitler.' Gwen bent to take her shoe off and flicked out a small stone. 'Oh, that's better.' She straightened up and glanced round. 'I never dreamt there'd be this many people. And look over there –' she gestured with her arm '– there's a film crew setting up their cameras.'

Madeleine glanced at her watch. It wasn't yet one o'clock. The rally wasn't due to start until two. But the atmosphere was electric. She could almost touch the excitement and anticipation within the crowd as they waited patiently for their leader. A wave of foreboding coursed through her body.

Without warning a Wagnerian overture suddenly blared, the vibrations causing Gwen to startle and knock into her. Madeleine put out a steadying hand. Finally, the distorted sound of the overture ended. With barely a pause, a large group of Nazis began to sing Party songs in time with their marching. Their voices were perfectly in tune and the words so beautifully enunciated, it sounded almost religious – like a choir. Madeleine felt her scalp prickle.

She grabbed Gwen's arm. 'I can't take much more of this.'

'I'm ready to go, too.'

The two of them turned, battling their way through the hordes going towards the rally and ignoring several angry expletives.

'*Geh mir aus dem Weg, dummes Weib*,' one middle-aged lady who was bursting out of her dirndl snapped.

'Sorry,' Madeleine said in English.

'What did she say?' Gwen said.

'She told me to get out of her way and that I was dumb – or something like that.'

'Nice.'

They spent the next half-hour pushing through the people still coming in the opposite direction.

'Oh, I'm so glad to be out of that place,' Gwen said as they finally reached the station. 'You know, Maddie, we didn't need to hear Hitler after all. You only have to see that crowd to feel his evil presence. I just hope we don't have to wait too long for the next train back to Munich.'

# Chapter Four

'I was becoming worried,' Frau Weinberg said, relief showing in her eyes, when Madeleine stepped into the hallway that evening.

'I'm sorry, Frau Weinberg. I didn't realise how late it was.'

'Have you eaten?'

Madeleine realised she was hungry.

'Um, not exactly.'

'You have answered.' Frau Weinberg's voice was firm. 'It will be ready soon. We will have chicken and dumplings. I have made it as it is Lotte's favourite.'

'Mine, too, and it sounds wonderful,' Madeleine chuckled. 'Where are the twins?'

'They are doing their homework.'

To Madeleine's relief, Frau Weinberg didn't question her as to where she'd been, but she noticed the woman's face looked drawn and suddenly much older.

'Is anything the matter, Frau Weinberg?'

'I do not think school went very well for the twins this week. They are keeping something from me. Maybe you can talk to them.'

'I'll have a word with them,' Madeleine said, feeling guilty she hadn't noticed anything amiss.

She opened the classroom door to find two dark heads bent over their books on either side of the table which served as a desk. They looked up.

'Maddie!' Erich cried. 'You are very late for supper. We have eaten all. Nothing is left for you.'

She couldn't help smiling at his nonsense.

'It is not true,' Lotte said in a loud voice. 'We have not had supper.'

'What is your homework for tomorrow?'

'Numbers,' said Lotte.

'Mathematics,' Erich corrected. He closed his book. '*I* have finished.'

'And me.' Lotte snapped her book shut.

Madeleine took in a breath.

'How are you getting on at school lately?'

'All right.' Erich's voice sounded guarded, or was it Madeleine's imagination?

'What about you, Lotte?'

'*Freitag* was not very nice.' Lotte's voice sounded thin and flat.

Not at all like her usual strong, confident tones, Madeleine thought. She braced herself.

'Why was that?' she asked encouragingly.

'Frau Winkelmann made us put our hands up,' Lotte said.

'What do you mean – she *made* you?'

'Me and Erich.' The child hesitated, then added, 'All Jew children.'

'Oh.' Madeleine felt her insides curdle. She thought fast. 'Are there other Jewish children in your class?'

'*Ja*. Anna and Jacob and David. Frau Winkelmann write our names in her book.'

35

*Five Jewish children.* Madeleine bit her lip.

'When we finish class Gretchen says . . . said we are dirty Jews and she will not play wiz us.'

So here it was. She couldn't ignore it. Madeleine swallowed.

'Mutti does not allow us to go to school in dirty clothes,' Erich said matter-of-factly.

Oh, how could she tell them that was not what Gretchen meant? And anyway, did the child understand the real meaning herself? Gretchen was likely only parroting her parents. But it wasn't Madeleine's place to explain.

'Of course your mother doesn't let you go to school in dirty clothes,' she said briskly. 'Now, do you have any questions about your homework before you read to me?'

'*Nein.* But we are the children. You must read to *us,*' Lotte said, squealing with laughter.

'Sorry, Lotte, that won't work. You're the ones learning English. I can speak it fluently already.'

Relieved she'd managed to turn the conversation, Madeleine stayed with the twins another fifteen minutes while they read to her in English, and then she left them to pack up their books. She needed to speak to Frau Weinberg as a matter of urgency.

Back in the kitchen she noticed the slumped shoulders of Frau Weinberg and alarm filling her eyes when Madeleine mentioned how Gretchen had called the twins 'dirty Jews'.

'This is what I am afraid of.' She looked directly at Madeleine. 'This situation will not improve. It's become steadily worse these last years.' She shook her head as if to clear it from an impending bad dream. 'We were lucky the twins were let into their school at all.'

'What do you mean?'

'The percentage of Jewish children has dropped right down. Most Jewish children now have to go to a Jewish school run by their parents, but Hermann and I wanted ours to have a wider education. We felt it more healthy. Besides, as you have seen, we are secular Jews.' She paused. 'There is only one reason the teacher asked the Jewish children to raise their hands. It is to confirm them on a register. To maintain a record of the Jewish children, which means, of course, their families. Many of us do not have obvious Jewish names. It is a typical Nazi approach – to reach the children who are bound to tell the truth before their parents have a chance to conceal their identity.'

Madeleine swallowed the nausea that rushed to her throat.

'The trouble is, they're only eight, so they don't yet understand the significance of such a cruel remark but they know things aren't right.' Madeleine bit her lip.

Frau Weinberg gave a heavy sigh. 'Hermann and I will speak to them.' She looked up at Madeleine with tear-stained eyes. 'Can you call the twins for supper, Madeleine?'

'Yes, of course.'

Madeleine opened the schoolroom door but it was empty. Where on earth . . .? The twins' books were open just as they'd been when she left the room. Madeleine didn't hesitate. She took the stairs two at a time and heard Erich's voice behind Lotte's bedroom door. Gently opening it, she found Lotte sitting on the edge of her bed sobbing into her handkerchief and Erich with his arm around her. Both children spun round.

'What's the matter, Lotte?' Madeleine said, rushing to sit on the other side of the child.

'Gretchen is my best friend,' Lotte wailed. '*Why* did she

say I am dirty?' She looked up at Madeleine. 'I am *not* dirty, am I, Maddie? Mutti make us wash every day.'

'Of course you're not, darling. Why don't you wipe your tears and come down for supper. You'll feel better when you've had something to eat.'

'I do not have hunger.'

'You will when you smell Mutti's delicious chicken and dumplings. It's your favourite.'

Lotte wrinkled her nose, then blurted, 'I am not going to school tomorrow. I *hate* it.'

'We'll see how you feel about it in the morning, love.'

Supper was much quieter than usual. Late to the table, Herr Weinberg took his place at the head and asked what sort of day the twins had had. His wife sent him a warning look, which only made him frown in response. Lotte pushed her knife and fork together, hardly having touched her meal, though Erich gobbled his at his usual speed.

'You are tired,' Frau Weinberg said. 'It will be good for you both to go to bed early.'

'I am not a baby,' Erich protested. 'I will soon be nine.'

'So will Lotte,' Madeleine said, taking the little girl's hand. 'Come on, darling. I'll help you get ready and read you a story. Then you can go to sleep and dream of fairies.'

'Lotte can,' Erich said firmly, 'but I shall dream of soldiers.'

'You have a letter today, Madeleine.' Frau Weinberg handed her an envelope the following morning with her mother's unmistakeable clipped handwriting.

Madeleine's heart leapt. She'd take the twins to school, then read it in her room before she prepared their lessons for the weekend. An hour later she opened the envelope, anticipating news of home. Pulling out the two sheets of Basildon Bond notepaper, she read:

*20th September 1938*

*My dear Madeleine,*

*I hope you had a nice birthday. However, your father and I are most concerned about your safety. Before you argue that you are perfectly all right, you will know by the time you receive this letter that Mr Chamberlain visited H a few days ago in Berchtesgaden, not far from where you are in Munich. Britain and France do not want war and Mr C is possibly the only man who can talk to H and hopefully make him see sense. This is my view and I think C will be successful. Your father is much more worried about the other possible outcome. Thank goodness I have my writing. I don't know what I'd do if I didn't have that, especially when I hardly see your father these days.*

*Now, Madeleine, because of these volatile times, we must insist that you come home immediately before it is too late and you are caught up in something dangerous.*

*All the news is political at the moment and we can only keep our fingers crossed.*

*Please let us know the date you plan to leave.*

*Your father and I send our love,*

*Mother*

*P.S. Gordon and Raymond have sold the club and both joined the Royal Navy Fleet Air Arm and despite an added worry for us, your father and I are very proud of them.*

On reading the last lines, Madeleine swallowed hard. She adored her brothers, born within a year of each other and five and six years older than her. They must think there was every possibility of a war if they'd given up the flying club they'd set up together more than two years ago. She skimmed her mother's letter again. '. . . *we must insist that you come home immediately . . .*' She blew out her cheeks. There was her mother still not recognising that at twenty-one she was now an adult. Then a curl of guilt brought a flush to her cheeks and the present shifted . . .

It was last year just before Christmas when she'd stood on the opposite side of the desk to Mr Graham, the college principal, her jaw set defiantly though her legs felt none too stable.

'Perhaps you would like to explain why there was a young man in your room yesterday evening when you know the rules perfectly well.' He glared at her. 'No boys and no men *ever* to be admitted into a student's bedroom!'

'I'm sorry, sir. He's just a friend, wanting to help me with my French. I'm a bit further behind with French than with German,' she added for good measure.

'A friend, you say. Hmm. I don't think so from what Miss Williams heard as she was passing your room and decided to look in.' He stared at her pointedly. 'Not that you would've noticed.' His lip curled unattractively.

She didn't answer. What was the point? She'd momentarily lost her head with Andrew's brooding good looks and his pleading to let him be the first. The fumbling and the pain hadn't been worth satisfying the curiosity as to what being made love to would feel like. She couldn't for the life of her understand what all the fuss was about. But maybe in spite of all his bragging he was just as inexperienced as she'd been.

'I shall be writing to your parents,' Mr Graham said,

leaning back on his comfortable chair, regarding her in the smoke-filled office.

'Oh, please don't do that, sir. Let me tell them I'm leaving of my own accord.'

'I'm sorry.' He looked down at the open file. 'I'm afraid I must expel you.'

'If you'd give me another chance, sir,' she said but her words had fallen on deaf ears.

She would *not* let him see how shocked she felt. But she'd known it was coming. The starchy Miss Williams would have lost no time in reporting her.

A sliver of luck had been on her side as it was Friday. At least she wouldn't have to pretend to her parents she was going to college. She'd have the weekend to try to work things out. The postman had delivered the letter from Mr Graham first thing Monday morning. Madeleine was waiting for him and picked up the white envelope addressed to Mr and Mrs W Hamilton. She was about to tuck it into her dressing-gown pocket and then destroy it when her mother appeared.

'What was in the post?'

'Nothing much. Just something for me.'

'Then why is your face red?' Her eyes fell on the envelope Madeleine was clutching.

'Let me see the envelope.'

It was no use. Silently, Madeleine handed it over. Her mother tore it open without bothering to find a letter opener as she would normally do. Henrietta Hamilton's forehead creased with fury as she began to read.

'You'll be hearing from your father about this,' she said through clenched teeth. 'After all we've spent on your education . . . . to give you as good as your brothers . . . and this is how you repay us.' She stared at Madeleine. 'Did you let him have his way with you?'

Madeleine stared stonily at her mother. She wasn't a kid of sixteen, for goodness' sake. But her mother went on:

'I see. You obviously did. Well, you've disgraced your father and me. You've let us down in the worst possible way. I don't know what to do with you. You've always been impetuous, Madeleine. Never taking any notice of us even though we've always wanted the best for you.' She gave a heavy sigh. 'I don't know what your father will say – or your brothers.'

'There's no need to tell Gordon and Ray anything,' Madeleine said, finally finding her voice. 'They don't tell us what *they* get up to and it's probably a lot worse than me.'

'Don't you *dare* compare their behaviour with this . . . this—' She flung the sheet of paper on the hall table. 'I'm disgusted with you. You can go to your room.'

'Sorry, Mother, I'll do nothing of the kind. If you haven't noticed, I'm no longer a child.'

'Well, you're behaving like one.' Her mother glanced in the region of Madeleine's stomach. 'I just hope you're not about to *have* one.'

'Don't worry, Mother. If I was, I won't hang around to bring even *more* shame on the family.'

With that, she'd flounced out of the door, holding in the sobs until she was well clear of the house.

It was only when her monthlies finally came five days after they were due, when she'd been worrying herself sick, that she realised the risk she'd taken and how lucky she'd been. What an absolute fool. It could have wrecked her chances for a career, her future happiness – everything. She vowed never to do anything so stupid where a man was concerned ever again. No wonder Mother had been so furious. She must have seen only too well how close her daughter had come to ruining her life. It took several more days before Madeleine realised she needed to apologise.

Feeling bitterly ashamed of herself, she finally faced her mother.

'I'm sorry I was rude to you, Mother. I am truly grateful how you paid for me to go to college and I didn't repay you in the way I should.'

Her mother simply nodded. That was all. Just a nod that she'd heard. Madeleine gave an inward sigh. What would it have cost her mother to give her a hug and tell her all was forgiven, and that whatever happened she still loved her daughter?

But her mother's affection was always reserved for her two sons – although Gordon and Raymond were oblivious to the fact. They always acted as though they were one happy family and Madeleine had never hinted to anyone outside the family that the actuality was very different. She remembered when she was only fourteen that she once told her older brothers, now nineteen and twenty, they were her mother's favourites.

'Silly goose,' Raymond had chuckled, giving her hair a playful tug. 'She loves us all the same.'

'She doesn't . . . honestly. She told me once she wished I'd been another boy.' Madeleine looked at her brothers through her hated wire-rimmed spectacles, appealing to them to believe her.

'She was just ribbing you.'

'She wasn't, Ray. I wish you'd believe me.'

'Hmm.' Gordon stroked his moustache. 'Maybe she wants to be the only beauty in the house and she can see

43

her daughter growing up to be a lovely young lady . . . well, you are without those hideous glasses.' He grinned. 'You never know, Mother just might be a teensy-weensy bit jealous.'

She knew they were teasing her but it had struck her at the time that perhaps there was more than a whisper of truth in her brother's idle suggestion.

Seeing that advertisement in *The Lady* magazine for someone to teach twins in Bavaria had been like a lifeline, Madeleine thought, as she skimmed her mother's letter again in the now-familiar Munich bedroom. She took in a deep breath. Maybe her parents were right. Maybe this *was* the time to leave . . . to go back to England with Gwen. So why was she hesitating?

That evening Herr Weinberg came home from his shop looking, to Madeleine's eyes, even more drawn than usual. He nodded to her, then kissed his wife on both cheeks.

'Hitler has just announced that if the Czech Government have not ceded all the Sudeten lands by 1st October, Germany will occupy them immediately. That only gives them a few days to make such a decision.' He briefly shut his eyes, then added, 'Those poor Czechs losing such a vast area of their country to that maniac.' Wiping his forehead with a handkerchief, he looked at his wife. 'You know what that means, my dear?'

'Yes, of course I do.' Frau Weinberg's voice sounded as though it came from the bottom of a well. 'He won't stop at Czechoslovakia. Poland will be next on his list.'

'Not only that,' Herr Weinberg sighed heavily, 'but he's risking war with Britain.'

Madeleine gulped. The twins . . . putting up their hands in the classroom to be singled out as Jews would be nothing if Hitler began to invade other countries. Yet surely his advisers wouldn't allow him to go this far. But it was said that Hitler rarely took any advice. Her stomach churned. Suddenly the possibility of war with Britain now looked extremely likely.

'I think Miss Hamilton should return to England.' This time he looked at Madeleine directly. 'For your own safety, my dear.'

# Chapter Five

*Early October 1938*

'Oh, Gwen, I'm going to miss you terribly,' Madeleine said, putting her cup on the table in the café at Munich's railway station.

'I'll miss you, too,' Gwen said as she picked up her case. 'But things are hotting up here –' she lowered her voice '– and I feel vulnerable. And quite honestly, the family are beginning to get on my wick with their revolting guests.' She looked directly at her friend. 'I only wish you were coming with me, Maddie. I don't know what your parents will say when you tell them you changed your mind at the last minute.'

They'd be furious – at least her mother would be. She'd made the decision to go back with Gwen and written to her parents to tell them so, but the next day she'd gone to the post office and sent them a note saying she was postponing the date for a few weeks and would write more fully later. She hadn't yet written that letter because she knew she would find it difficult to explain to her parents her reasoning. But after some more thought she'd realised she couldn't just walk away from the Weinberg family

46

who had been so kind to her – Frau Weinberg so motherly and Herr Weinberg becoming more and more worried about trying to hold his business together as well as his family. Then there were the twins who were innocent children, too young to understand Hitler's relentless measures to make the Jewish community's life ever more wretched. Madeleine shuddered. That was an understatement. And Herr Weinberg's sudden announcement that she should go home for her own safety only made her realise how responsible she felt for the twins. Now things had started to become difficult – even dangerous – it was more important than ever she should be a steady figure in their lives, especially during the times their mother was helping her husband in his music shop and sometimes didn't get home before the children came back from school.

'If the situation becomes worse here, I'll pack up immediately,' she said now to Gwen as they found the platform where the train left for Paris. 'I have your address so I'll let you know when I'm ready. I *will* stay in touch, I promise.'

'I should hope so.' Gwen's eyes were moist. 'We're not on the telephone at home so don't lose it.'

'I won't.' Madeleine gave her a tight hug, tears pricking her own eyes. Gwen was a darling and she would genuinely miss her.

The train slowly began to move and Madeleine walked alongside, then ran, to keep up with it, as Gwen hung out of the window waving madly.

'Bye, Maddie. Bye.'

'*Gute Reise*,' Madeleine called, hoping her friend's journey would indeed go without a hitch.

The train disappeared in thick, grey, billowing clouds of

smoke. Madeleine turned and walked back through the entrance.

'I am ill,' Lotte said the next day. 'I cannot go to school.'

It was the third time she'd refused to go to school.

Madeleine took her temperature. Thirty-six point four. She did a quick calculation. It was the equivalent of ninety-seven point four at home. Normal for a child.

'Lotte, you can't keep doing this – pretending you're too ill to go to school.'

Lotte rubbed her leg and mumbled, 'I do not pretend.'

'Do you have a pain?'

'Yes.'

There was a catch in the little girl's voice. Was Lotte simply acting? Or was she just tired? It was hard to tell.

'Where?'

'In my foot.'

'Did you hurt it in games yesterday?'

'Yes.'

'Let me look.' Inch by inch, Madeleine pressed the child's foot gently.

'Ow!' Lotte squealed like a piglet.

There was no sign of any bruise or graze.

'You'd better stay home then,' Madeleine said, 'and go straight to bed.'

If the child was pretending, she'd soon become bored.

But Lotte called her bluff and seemed perfectly happy to remain in bed with her books.

'If you're well enough to read, then you're well enough to go to school,' Madeleine said firmly.

But Lotte wouldn't budge and shouted at Erich when he tried to persuade her to get dressed and go with him.

'And you do not worry about me,' Erich told Madeleine. 'I can go to school on my own.'

Madeleine hesitated. Normally, she took the twins to school but it was Frau Cygan the housekeeper's day off, and Frau Weinberg had gone to her husband's music shop that morning to do the bookkeeping. Lotte would be on her own.

'Jacob walks on his own,' Erich said, as though reading her mind. 'It is not far. I am nearly nine.'

'So you keep reminding me.' Madeleine hesitated. It must be half a mile away but she couldn't leave Lotte. 'All right. Just this once. But don't speak to any grown-ups. Just go straight to school. Do you promise?'

'Yes, Maddie, I promise.'

With a slight niggling feeling, Madeleine prepared the twins' next English lesson for the coming weekend, and the play she wanted them to act out. She glanced out of the window. Already the trees were beginning to lose their leaves. What sort of a winter was coming to the German people? Didn't *anyone* have any common sense and see what was happening?

She shuddered at the thought of the family she lived with being subject to even more injustices. What kind of example did it set to the children – *all* children, not just Jewish ones? Was she playing a risky game herself, not heeding Gwen's advice – or Herr Weinberg's – to leave? Her father always accused her of being stubborn. She grimaced. That trait she'd definitely inherited from *him*.

The telephone rang, interrupting her qualms. She went into the hall to answer it.

'*Frau Weinberg?*' A woman's firm tones.

'*Nein, hier spricht Fräulein Hamilton.*'

49

'Ah, you are English.' It wasn't a question. 'This is Frau Weilland, the teacher of Erich and Lotte.'

Madeleine drew in a guilty breath. She'd meant to write a note explaining Lotte was poorly and give it to Erich to take to her.

'I'm sorry,' she started. 'Lotte is in bed not very well—'

'It is not about Lotte,' Frau Weilland interrupted. 'It is about Erich.'

Madeleine's heart plummeted. 'Has he had an accident?'

'You could say.'

There was a silence. Had they been disconnected? What had the woman been about to say? She held the receiver closer to her ear.

'Hello? Are you still there?' she asked.

'He is with a nurse,' the woman continued. 'He will not say what happened but he has been in a fight.'

*Oh, no.*

'Is he badly hurt?' Madeleine's voice was thick with worry.

'*Nein.* But you should come to take him home for the day.'

Madeleine swallowed. Now she'd *have* to leave Lotte on her own unless one of the neighbours would keep an eye on her. But that was out of the question. She couldn't let someone into the house without the permission of Herr Weinberg or his wife, and anyway, she couldn't be sure what the neighbours' opinions were of the Jewish family. No, she'd have to drag Lotte out of bed to go with her.

'I do not want to go to school,' Lotte whined. 'I am sick.'

'I don't think you're too sick,' Madeleine said. 'We have to go and fetch your brother – he's had an accident.'

'Is he going to die?'

50

'No, love, but he might need to rest. The nurse at the school is looking after him.'

Madeleine looked at Erich's white face which was badly scratched but was horrified at the bandage on one of his knees and that his right arm was in a sling. It was a very different little boy who'd left home this morning.

'He has a sprained wrist,' the nurse said in a strong Bavarian accent. 'But it is not broken. He can remove the sling at bedtime or when he is in the bath. It is a reminder not to use it too much for a few days.'

Both children were silent as they walked home. Erich limped and clutched Madeleine's hand. Once inside, she made them a hot chocolate and one for herself.

'What happened, Erich?' Madeleine asked him as he sipped his drink.

The boy shook his head.

'Sometimes it's best to talk about things,' Madeleine said.

'Wolfgang said horrible things.'

'What kind of horrible things?'

'He said me and Lotte are *schmutzig*. That we should move away from München. He said the whole family was *schmutzig*.'

*That word again. Dirty.* Madeleine swallowed hard.

'Then what happened?'

'I punch him on the nose.'

'Oh, dear, that wasn't very nice.'

'He was not nice to say such a bad word. Then we fight.'

'Sometimes it's better if you just walk away before any fighting and someone gets hurt – as you did.'

'He got it worse,' Erich said proudly.

\*   \*   \*

That evening, after supper, when the twins were asleep, Herr Weinberg asked Madeleine if she would join him and his wife in the drawing room. Frau Weinberg brought in a tray of coffee and some biscuits.

'Make yourself comfortable, Miss Hamilton,' he said, as usual in German. 'We have something serious to speak to you about.'

They were about to insist she leave them, Madeleine thought miserably. She would miss those twins more than she'd ever thought. But the last thing she wanted was to bring extra worry to her hosts. Well, she would tell them she'd go to the railway station and buy a ticket for England. Before she could speak she saw Herr Weinberg throw a glance at his wife.

'Maybe you will tell her,' he said.

'Madeleine, my dear, you know you have become like one of the family. We are very fond of you and the children adore you. My husband and I must ask you a difficult question and we will quite understand if the answer is no.'

Madeleine drew in her stomach, bracing herself. This sounded more serious than just advising her to go home.

'You know we are most worried about the twins. But we have a solution. We want them to be safe. And we want *you* to be safe. So you must prepare to go back to England.' She paused. 'And we want to send the children to England also!'

Madeleine felt her heart miss a beat. No, no. Much as she loved the twins, she couldn't take such a responsibility for them. Oh, it was too much. No, she couldn't. She . . .

'I-I'm sorry, Frau Weinberg, it's not possible. I—'

'No, no, you don't understand,' Frau Weinberg quickly intercepted. 'We are asking if you would take them only as far as Berlin and then you can catch your train there to England. I have an English friend in Berlin called Fran. We have known one another since we did an exchange for three months after university – I to England and she to Munich. She is married to a German – Frederick Scholl. He is not a Jew but we are all long-time friends. Frederick wants her to go to England to be safe and he will follow when he can. She has written to us with her plans and has offered to take the twins to stay with my husband's brother and his wife in London until we can join them one day soon.'

As far as Berlin. They weren't asking her to take them all the way to England. And there wouldn't be any problem with a train journey from one city in Germany to another. Surely she could do that. A return for all the kindness they'd shown her.

A thought struck her. 'What about passports? They won't be able to travel to England without them.'

'Things have been progressively difficult for Jews in the last five years and we were anxious about the twins so we applied for them to have separate passports when we renewed ours last year.' Herr Weinberg removed his glasses. 'So what do you say, Madeleine? Or are we asking too much?'

It was the first time he'd used her Christian name. Madeleine glanced at Frau Weinberg's tear-stained eyes, red with recent bouts of crying, worrying about Erich and Lotte. Of course it wasn't asking too much. She'd get a train to London just as easily from Berlin as Munich. Then why was she hesitating? It was just . . . oh, supposing something went wrong.

But those precious children. Innocent. Bright as buttons,

both of them. If she ever had children she'd want them to be just like Erich and Lotte. They would have a future in England. And all she'd have to do was drop them off at this Fran's house, knowing they would be safe and taken to England where they'd be cared for by their own blood relations.

She swallowed hard.

'All right,' she said, 'I'll take them to your friends in Berlin.'

She noticed the look of relief that passed between husband and wife.

'We must not waste a moment longer,' Herr Weinberg said. 'You must take them tomorrow.'

Madeleine's eyes widened. Tomorrow!

'There is one more request,' Frau Weinberg said. 'We do not have a fortune. We had quite a comfortable living with my husband's shop but things are becoming more difficult, as you know. We have had to use our savings for some time. But I have some jewels and would like you to take them to Fran. It will help her to pay for the children's fare to England and also to my husband's relatives who will see that they're looked after and educated until Hermann and I can follow – if I can persuade him to leave.' She gave Madeleine a wan smile. 'Would you also do this favour, my dear? There are just a few good pieces. One is this – my beautiful engagement ring.' She tried to remove the ring but it wouldn't go over her knuckles.

'Already I have arthritis in my fingers,' she said with an apologetic smile.

*She's willing to casually hand over her precious ring which she must know she might never see again if she and her husband are not able to get out of Germany.*

54

Madeleine's throat ached at the thought.

'Do keep your ring, Frau Weinberg. It's got too much meaning for you.'

Frau Weinberg shook her head.

'No, I have a special locket I'll keep back. The ring is more easily sold. I want you to take it. I'll get it off with some soap.'

She was back in two minutes, triumphantly holding out the beautiful sapphire and diamond ring.

'I'll worry I might mislay it,' Madeleine said.

Frau Weinberg smiled. 'You won't if you put it onto your own engagement finger, my dear. Then it will be perfectly safe. Regard it as your own while you're travelling and then you won't let it slip that it has ever belonged to another woman.'

Their eyes met in mutual empathy.

# Chapter Six

The following morning Madeleine stood on Munich's *Hauptbahnhof* platform, Lotte holding a cloth bag with some snacks in one hand, the other firmly in her own, and Erich by her side clutching his and his sister's leather bag. The twins were always game for an adventure so she'd decided that's what this would be. School had lately become a place in which they were bullied, so they'd been easily persuaded to go with her to Aunt Fran and Uncle Frederick's house in Berlin for a holiday. Frau Weinberg asked her not to mention anything about Aunt Fran taking them to England. They needed time to digest such changes.

'It is a reserved seat in First Class,' Frau Weinberg had said as she handed Madeleine the three tickets, 'so you will be very comfortable. There will be a dining car and we have reserved you a table. But if anything should go wrong—' She broke off and gulped. 'I have packed enough food for all of you.'

'We'll be fine,' Madeleine assured her. 'Please don't worry. I'll send you a telegram when we've arrived at the Scholls.'

'These times are not normal,' Frau Weinberg said. 'It is

best you do not send a telegram. Fran will write to thank me for the two ducks I have sent her.'

A frisson of apprehension fizzed through her. Frau Weinberg was right – these weren't normal times. Madeleine bit her lower lip. She wanted to be a professional actress, didn't she? Well, here was her chance. Her actions must all appear to be ordinary. Straightforward. Nothing must go otherwise. She would play her part to perfection.

Now on the platform people were beginning to board the train. She smiled down at Lotte.

'Isn't this exciting?'

'Yes,' Lotte said, sounding a little uncertain. 'But we have not seen Aunt Fran for three years when she comes to us. We were only little then. Maybe we forget her face.'

'You needn't worry. The taxi will take us straight to their house.' Madeleine turned to her brother. 'Erich, you lead the way.'

Erich found the carriage and waved to them to catch up. By the time she and Lotte opened the compartment door, he had already squeezed himself in the row opposite between a grey-haired man in a dark-blue raincoat in the window seat and an elderly woman wearing a large green brimmed hat with a tall feather, who smiled at the boy in a motherly fashion. A young couple sat opposite the grey-haired man, having no eyes for anyone except for each other.

'Well done.' Madeleine found their other two reserved seats by the door. 'Lotte, come and sit next to me. Erich, give me your bag.'

At the same moment the train slowly rumbled away from the station, the door swung open. A tall man stepped in, removing his hat as he quickly glanced round. His eyes caught Madeleine a full three seconds before he placed his attaché case on the luggage rack above the seat opposite marked '*Reserviert*' and tossed his hat on the top, just as she'd been about to haul her own suitcase up. He took it from her.

'Allow me.'

*An English voice. A rather nice voice.* With perfect ease he laid the case flat, then smiled at her.

'Thank you,' she said. 'You're very kind.'

'Not at all.' He sat down and regarded her with steady brown eyes. She noticed their colour exactly matched the lock of hair which had fallen over his forehead. And that his dark eyebrows almost met in the middle.

Feeling strangely unnerved under his gaze, she gripped the bag of food even more firmly between her shoes. His eyes fell on her left hand where Frau Weinberg's sapphire and diamond engagement ring now rested on her own fourth finger. It was a little loose and kept slipping round, now showing only the plain gold band. She looked up. Was there a trace of disappointment in his eyes? Inwardly, she shrugged. Let him think what he liked.

'Are you going all the way to Berlin?' he asked.

This was awkward. She'd agreed not to get into conversation with anyone or to draw any attention to herself or the twins. In fact, Herr Weinberg had been most emphatic about it. But this man was British. And well educated by the sound of him. He was dressed in a navy pin-striped suit with immaculate white shirt, his gold cufflinks peeping out from under his jacket sleeve. She desperately tried not to stare but he smiled, catching her unawares, making her chest tighten. It was as though the sun had suddenly come out on this dull, drizzly October day. Lotte touched her arm and the moment was broken.

'I would like my colouring book . . . please.'

'All right, love.'

She stood to reach the twins' leather bag but it had been shifted to the back at an awkward angle. Without saying anything, he sprang up and retrieved it. Did his fingers touch hers by accident as he handed it to her? Ridiculously, she hoped not.

Lowering her head to hide what she knew was her flushed face, she found the book and a pencil box with some crayons and put them on Lotte's lap. She noticed Erich was staring at her. She looked up and smiled.

'Do you need anything, Erich?'

He shook his head. 'No, thank you.'

Madeleine managed to shove the leather bag back on the rack above Lotte's head before the man opposite could offer again.

'Shall I move so your son can be nearer to you?' the elderly woman asked. She spoke perfect English.

Madeleine was about to correct her when she remembered not to draw attention to herself. Thankfully, Erich already had his head in his book.

'That's very kind of you,' she said.

'Are they twins?' the woman said, as she tapped Erich on the arm and staggered to her feet to change seats. After she'd sat down heavily next to the man by the window she fumbled in her handbag.

'Yes.'

'Good-looking children, and in such contrast to you, being so dark and you much lighter, but I expect your husband is dark-haired.'

Madeleine felt a flicker of . . . not fear, but a curl of disquiet.

*Just my luck to be questioned by someone who is probably only being friendly.*

She gave a nervous glance at the man opposite. He was reading his newspaper, seemingly oblivious, but even though his face was partially covered, Madeleine got the distinct feeling he was fully alert.

'Are they allowed to have one of these?' The woman brought out a small bag with what looked like boiled sweets.

Lotte turned to her with wide shining eyes.

'All right,' Madeleine said. 'Just one.' The woman twisted her neck to Erich. 'Would you like one, too, dear?'

Erich looked up from his book, mumbled a 'No, thank you' and buried his head back into it again.

The woman unwrapped one and popped it into her mouth, making little sucking noises as she rolled it around, her eyes darting to all her fellow travellers in the compartment. Her glance fell on Madeleine and she smiled, showing large yellow teeth.

'Are you here in Germany for holidays?'

Madeleine hesitated. 'Um, yes, but I'm going home in a few days' time.'

This was awkward. Oh, why hadn't she been like Erich and got her book open already. The man opposite lowered his newspaper a fraction.

'We go to see Aunt Fran and Uncle Frederick,' Lotte announced, looking up from her colouring book.

'How lovely, dear. Perhaps they live near me so you could visit me while you're there.'

'I don't think we'll have time,' Madeleine said, grabbing her handbag. She removed her book and opened it, but not before the man opposite leant forward.

'Very wise,' he remarked. 'It's best not to get too involved with anyone until you get to the relatives.' He spoke so quietly only she could possibly have heard above the noise of the train as it gathered speed, steam belching out in thick grey clouds beyond the window looking almost as if the train were on fire.

Madeleine gave a start. Who was this man? Why had he said something that sounded very like a warning? How had he guessed she was English when he'd first spoken to her? She supposed he must have heard her speak to Lotte just as he opened the door to their compartment. But there were still too many questions and not enough answers. Or was her imagination running riot and he was nothing but an ordinary Englishman on his way to Berlin? If so, what was he doing in Germany? She allowed herself a surreptitious glance. He was leaning back in the seat, his eyes closed but by the tense lines around his mouth and the firm set of his jaw, she was quite certain he hadn't fallen asleep. No. With that authoritative air about him he was far from ordinary. As if he knew she was watching him, he opened his eyes and gave an almost imperceptible nod. She hastily looked away and turned some pages in her book, pretending to find the right place.

'I am hungry,' Erich said an hour later.

'It'll be two more hours before lunch,' Madeleine told him. 'But I have something to tide you over.'

She gave them both a small cheese sandwich and tried to immerse herself in her book. But it was useless. She was too aware of the tall man opposite. She told herself it was because she mustn't trust anyone. She must act like a very ordinary young woman doing a simple task of taking the twins to see their aunt and uncle. But all the while was the nagging worry that she was solely responsible for two precious children who were, through no fault of their own, destined to be punished just for being of a religion that the Nazi government would never accept. That was, unless she got them safely to the Weinbergs' friends and the Englishwoman managed to get them out of the country.

To her acute embarrassment, she heard her stomach rumble loudly. Automatically, she glanced over at the Englishman but this time he didn't flicker an eye. She realised no one in the compartment could possibly have heard over the noise of the engine. She relaxed and continued reading. An hour must have passed when the man opposite broke into her concentration:

'Would you and the children care to join me for some lunch in the dining car?'

No! It was the last thing she wanted. He would ask questions she wouldn't be prepared to answer. She could say she had brought their food. But she was in First Class. There was a reserved table waiting for them.

Before she could think of a reply, the door slid open and a uniformed guard stepped in, seeming to dwarf the entire space. The young couple, who until now had been almost silent, suddenly jerked up, their startled eyes fixed on the guard's hard expression.

'Ausweis, bitte!' he barked. 'Und Fahrkarten.'

Heart beating furiously at the sudden tense atmosphere, Madeleine opened her handbag where she'd placed the jewels in a hidden compartment. Her passport was on the top, together with the twins' passports. Everything was in order but it was Frau Weinberg's jewels that could

62

cause trouble. The guard might think she had stolen them. Too late now. She drew out the passports and the three tickets, praying the guard wouldn't notice her hand trembling.

The grey-haired man by the window who'd slept most of the journey handed over his documents. The guard briefly scanned them and gave them back. The elderly woman passed hers over and the guard did the same. It was Madeleine's turn. He flipped open her passport, stared at her for a few seconds, then nodded and handed it back. Relief surged through her. Then he looked at one of the twins' passports, then the second one, and demanded in German:

'Why are you taking these children from their home in Munich to Berlin?'

'They are going to stay with their aunt and uncle for a holiday.' She kept her German as simple as possible so she wouldn't have to answer anything in too much detail.

'But you are not their mother?'

'She is our teacher,' Lotte said, her eyes wide.

The guard didn't take his gaze away from Madeleine.

'Show me the letter from their mother and father to give permission for you to take them away.'

'I don't have one. I didn't know—'

'What is the address of these. . . relatives in Berlin?' he cut in, his tone coated with suspicion.

Madeleine's heart thudded in her ears. She must keep calm. She couldn't. . . *wouldn't* give the guard their address. She swallowed hard. Oh, why hadn't the Weinbergs thought she would need written permission to take them to Berlin? Probably because everything had happened in such a rush. Unconsciously, she twisted Frau Weinberg's

63

ring so the sapphire and diamond stones were uppermost. As she did so, a ray of sunlight bounced off the faceted jewels and danced around the compartment. Without warning, the Englishman sprang to his feet. He unfolded a small leather cardholder and keeping a firm grip of it, put it under the guard's nose. The guard peered at it, then raised his head and studied Madeleine.

'This lady is my fiancée,' the man said, gesturing towards Madeleine. 'I know the children's family well. We're taking the twins to their relatives for a holiday, just as my fiancée explained.' He gave her an almost imperceptible shake of his head.

Out of the corner of her eye, Madeleine noticed the elderly lady eyeing them.

'*Ach so.*' The guard's cold grey stare unnerved her. '*Herzliche Glückwünsche* – Con-grat-u-lations,' he added in English with mock sincerity, pushing the twins' passports into Madeleine's unsteady hand. Then he turned to the young couple by the window. Stretching out his hand, he demanded, 'Your papers.'

The young man rose from his seat and handed over two documents. The guard took his time to read them, then handed them back. With a click of his heels and a 'Heil Hitler', he left.

Immediately, the very air in the compartment changed. Madeleine couldn't help watching as the young man took his girlfriend's hand and pressed it to his heart. The girl smiled at him so lovingly as though she'd never doubted he would take care of her. Madeleine quickly looked away, thanking God the guard had returned their identification papers.

Half an hour later they stopped at Rothenberg and

immediately two guards appeared and entered the compartment, one of them the same as before. They both stared at the couple.

'You will come with us,' the second guard snapped in German.

Madeleine gasped. The elderly woman who had taken up some knitting began counting her stitches, and the businessman continued reading his book. Only the Englishman stirred. He put his newspaper aside and made to stand up but the guard waved him back down.

The girl had turned ashen, gripping her armrest. The young man muttered something in her ear. Slowly, both of them rose to their feet. He put his arm round her but the guard roughly pushed between them as they were marched out of the compartment, the young man protesting and the girl weeping.

It was all over in less than a minute.

'What had they done wrong?' Madeleine said, her voice cracking.

'They were Jews,' the elderly woman said under her breath. 'They didn't have to do anything.'

Tears pricked at the back of Madeleine's eyes as the injustice hit her. Thankfully, the twins had both fallen asleep, Lotte leaning against the elderly woman's arm.

'Let me ask you again,' the Englishman said. 'May I escort you and the children to the dining car? I think we could all do with something to eat.'

Her stomach clenched. She felt sick. She didn't think she could eat a thing.

'I'm not hungry. But thank you for the invitation. It's very kind of you.'

'It would be a natural thing for us to be seen together,'

he said in a low voice as he leant forward, 'especially where that guard is concerned.'

He was right. Besides, her legs were cramped from sitting for so long.

'Wake up, children.' She gently tapped Lotte who shot up immediately, but Erich blinked tiredly. 'We could all do with something to eat,' she said, unconsciously repeating the Englishman's words.

He sprang up and opened the compartment door, then with the twins in tow he cupped her elbow with his hand and guided her towards a carriage from where enticing smells made her mouth water. Maybe she could eat something after all.

The dining car was almost full of chattering people raising crystal glasses in toasts, their silver cutlery sparkling in the sunlight coming through the windows.

'I have a reservation,' Madeleine said, giving her name to a passing waiter.

He glanced at his list. 'I'm sorry but you are late. I only have those two tables.' He jerked his head towards two vacant tables, one behind the other, but they were each for only two people.

'The children can go in front,' the Englishman told the waiter, then turned to Madeleine and muttered, 'So we can keep an eye.'

'I'll settle them first and ask what they'd like to have,' she said.

After the waiter had taken the twins' order, his attention turned to Madeleine, making sure she was comfortably seated with a linen napkin on her lap and a menu in her hands.

'Whatever you say, speak very quietly,' the Englishman said when he'd gone. 'You never know who's listening.'

*Dear God.* Madeleine was aware of her heart pulsing in her throat.

'But I'm glad we can talk in private and not in front of the children,' he went on. 'They don't need to hear what I have to say.'

Madeleine swallowed. 'Can I first ask you something?'

'Go ahead.'

'Why did the guard's attitude change when you showed him what I presume was your identification?'

'I'd better introduce myself.' He placed a cream-coloured business card on her place setting.

She looked down at it.

### James Mark Sylvester
### Cultural attaché
### British Embassy

### Berlin

*Mmm. Nice name.*

He looked across at her. His face was even closer than it had been in the compartment. She could see gold flecks in his brown eyes.

'So he backed off just because you work at the British Embassy?'

'Yep. It's a rule. They don't interfere with us. And we don't interfere with them. That's how it works.' He glanced at her left hand. 'You know, it might help if I knew my fiancée's name.' His eyes sparkled with amusement.

'I really wish you hadn't said that I was your fiancée,' Madeleine said, her voice cooler than she'd meant. 'It could get me into trouble if the guard finds out it was a lie.'

'Don't worry – he won't be able to find out anything of the kind,' James Sylvester said. 'It was all I could think of at the time when I spotted your ring wasn't a wedding ring after all, but an engagement ring.' He picked up her hand as he peered more closely at the stones, causing a tiny quiver to race up her arm. 'Mmm. It's a beautiful ring.' His warm brown eyes looked directly at her. 'Well, at least *that's* not a lie – you're engaged, so you have to admit my ruse worked.'

Madeleine bit her lip. What would he say if she told him it *was* a lie – that she *wasn't* engaged? He'd start asking questions about why she was wearing such a valuable ring. No, the less he knew about her the better.

'I had a feeling you were getting yourself tied up in a sticky situation.' He gazed at her. 'Were you?'

'I don't know what you're talking about.'

'Oh, I think you do. I think there's more to simply taking those kids to their relatives for a holiday.' He lowered his voice even further. 'I'm guessing they're Jewish. Am I right?'

Madeleine hesitated. Was this James Mark Sylvester all that his card said he was? And what exactly was a 'cultural attaché' anyway? She told herself she must be very careful.

'Your silence has answered my question.' He scanned the menu. 'Come on, let's order.' He looked up. 'May I offer you a glass of wine?'

'It's tempting, but I need to keep a clear head – especially where that guard's concerned.'

*Or you.* She irritably pushed the thought away.

He nodded and ordered her a tomato juice and a beer for himself and soon she was tucking into poached trout, green beans and potatoes, relieved he had lightened the conversation, chatting about how he missed fish and chips and cricket and the British Library, in between asking her about her own hobbies. To her surprise she found she was enjoying not only the meal but his company.

When she'd finished he leant over the table. 'You still haven't told me your name.'

'It's Madeleine Hamilton.'

'Miss Hamilton—'. He cleared his throat. 'I think I ought to tell you a few things you might not be aware of.' He swallowed the last of his beer.

She was suddenly alert. He sounded serious again. She watched as he pulled out a packet of cigarettes.

'Do you mind if I smoke?'

'Please go ahead.'

He lit a cigarette with an expensive-looking silver lighter. She caught sight of a small inscription. A present from a girlfriend? Wife? And if it was, so what?

'These are strange times in Germany and as you've already seen, things can turn nasty at any moment. Just be aware of everything you say and do and keep your head below the parapet.'

'Do you think there's going to be a war?'

'Oh, yes.' He drew on his cigarette. 'There's no doubt about that.' He looked directly at her. 'I haven't heard you speak much German. How good are you?'

'Fairly fluent.'

'Keep it up. I think you're going to need it in the not-too-distant future.'

'I'll try, though it'll be more difficult when I'm back in England and not practising every day.' Madeleine glanced at her watch. 'Thank you for encouraging me to eat something. It was very good. And we didn't hear a peep out of the twins, so I know they enjoyed theirs.'

He gestured to the waiter for the bill, and then she and the twins were following him as he strode along the jolting, shuddering corridor to their compartment.

Just as they arrived at their compartment, he said under his breath:

'We still have stops at Dresden, Wittenberg and Potsdam before we get to Berlin so there could be more checks. Just keep calm and I'll deal with it, but I may have to use the fiancée trick again. . . keep to the same story.'

There was no time to thank him. He'd already slid open the compartment door.

# *Chapter Seven*

Madeleine thought the journey would never come to an end. The businessman got off at Dresden and the elderly lady, who introduced herself as Frau Müller, slept most of the time. She never went along to the dining car but instead ate noisily from the various contents of her string bag, the salty odour of sausage lingering in the stuffy compartment. The twins became bored and fractious until James Sylvester played some word games with them and managed to keep them amused for several half-hours, leaving Madeleine to wonder if he had children of his own. Wittenberg came and went with no guard passing through the train. *Only Potsdam now*, she thought, mentally keeping her fingers crossed.

She was grateful the journey was broken up by the four of them visiting the dining room for afternoon refreshments and again at supper, this time all at the same table. She'd had no privacy to caution the twins not to ask James Sylvester any questions, and thankfully they were more intent on their food – that was until Erich put his knife and fork down before anyone else had finished and stared at him.

'Do you know what "Silvester" means in German?'

71

'No, you tell me.'

Madeleine caught James's eye. He sent her a wink.

'It means "New Year's Eve",' Erich said triumphantly. 'The thirty-first of December.' He gave a sly grin. 'Is that not a silly name?'

'Now I know what it means, it's a ridiculous name,' James said, keeping a straight face. 'I will have to have a word with those who named me when I'm back in England.'

Madeleine's heart jumped. So he planned to go back to England. But when? And why was she so interested anyway in his plans?

'I will call you Mr New Year's Eve,' Lotte said, squealing with delight.

Madeleine couldn't help laughing and she was relieved that James was chuckling. The twins' nonsense seemed to create a bond between all of them. *So this is what it would be like to have a family,* Madeleine thought, then brushed the fantasy away. There were far more important real and possibly dangerous things to dwell on.

'Potsdam!' the conductor called out as they approached the city.

Madeleine's heart beat fast. Would there be a final check? It would be too good to be true if there wasn't one before they arrived in Berlin.

'We're nearly there now.' The Englishman's calm voice soothed her nervousness. 'Only another twenty-five kilometres. It's a pity we can't stop and see it. It's a very old city, with palaces and lakes. I think you'd like it.'

For a fleeting moment she pictured the two of them walking round Potsdam admiring the architecture and the gardens, enjoying the peaceful atmosphere as though they were on holiday. Stop being so ridiculous, she reprimanded herself. You have a very important job to do. Then in two days' time you'll be on the train heading for London.

*And you'll never see James Mark Sylvester again.*

So what? she told herself irritably. It had merely been a brief encounter with a man she couldn't deny was extremely attractive. But it was nothing more.

It was almost an anti-climax when the train steamed and clanked and grumbled into Berlin's huge central station. Frau Müller had written her address and given it to Madeleine, who, with the twins, was ready with their luggage. James Sylvester was the first to alight, setting everyone's cases on the platform.

Even though it was getting dark, and the smoke and steam from other trains arriving and departing left a thick fog making it difficult to see clearly, Madeleine's stomach turned at all the flags bearing swastikas adorning every available post and railing, as though they were balloons for a child's birthday party.

'Stay close to me,' James told the little group, 'and I'll find you all a taxi.'

'My husband meets me,' Frau Müller said unexpectedly. She gave him a stern look. 'You must see this young lady and the children are safe on their way.'

At the gate a rather bent gentleman appeared and took Frau Müller's arm. They disappeared into the dusk and James – as Madeleine had begun to think of him – guided her and the twins towards the taxi rank. Every time a taxi came and the queue shortened, she couldn't help thinking it would only be a matter of minutes and then she'd never set eyes on him again. She didn't like that idea. Even though she knew practically nothing about him, he now seemed so familiar to her. As though he knew what she was thinking he took her arm, and the solid warmth of his touch comforted her.

They were now at the head of the queue. A taxi rolled in and the driver jumped out to put their luggage in the boot. The twins scrambled in the back.

'This is it,' James said. 'Tell me the address and I'll have a word with the driver.'

Too tired to argue, she passed him a piece of folded paper with Frau Weinberg's precise directions. He glanced at it and spoke to the driver who was standing a few feet away, tapping his feet impatiently, then handed the paper back to her, brushing her fingers as he did so, the touch of his skin causing a tiny electric shock.

She stared at him. This time she was sure it had been on purpose.

'It's not that far,' he said. 'You should be there in twenty minutes or so.' Brown eyes flecked with gold held hers.

Was he, too, reluctant to let her go?

'Madeleine, if you get into a bad situation while you're in Berlin . . . if you need help . . . just come to the embassy. Or phone. Ask for Jack.'

She felt a trickle of disappointment. It would have been nice if he'd invited her to ask for *him*. But maybe this Jack he'd recommended was the right person if she ever needed help.

*Please God, don't let it ever be necessary.*

'Maddie, come on!' Erich called through the taxi window.

'Good luck,' James said. 'I hope all goes well with the twins. And soon you'll be safely on your way back to England . . . and that lucky man of yours.'

He put both his hands on her arms and gazed at her.

For a mad moment she thought he was going to kiss her on the mouth. But instead he gave her arms a little squeeze, then kissed her lightly on her cheek, so lightly she couldn't swear that his lips even touched her skin. The driver opened the taxi door and she stepped in, then turned to look out of the window. The last she saw of James was a tall lone figure standing on the pavement waving.

She swallowed hard. She had more serious things on her mind now.

'We're going to see Aunt Fran and Uncle Frederick,' Lotte chanted, seeming to have found a burst of energy.

'We are entering the city through the Brandenburg Gate,' the taxi driver said in German. He pointed out other sights. 'We are now driving down *Unter den Linden.*'

Madeleine looked out of the cab window. Along both sides of the boulevard were huge Nazi flags, and in the distance, to her amazement, was a double-decker bus. She couldn't read the words on the poster painted on the side, but the red English double-decker bus juxtaposed with the ominous swastika signs made her flesh creep.

The taxi wound its way through the traffic, finally leaving the city centre, and slowed down in a tree-lined avenue where houses were placed well apart from their neighbours. Number 21 had a gated entrance and a long drive up to the front door with an outside light. There was only one other light showing from a first-floor window.

*Strange*, Madeleine thought. It wasn't yet eight o'clock.

The taxi driver took the luggage and set it in the porch. He shook his head when she tried to pay him.

'*Alles gut,*' he said. '*Ihr Mann hat die Rechnung bezahlt.*'

Hmm. Now James was her husband. Madeleine couldn't help a wry grin at her new elevated status. James had had

75

a cheek with the 'fiancée' bit but she had to admit it had got her and the twins out of what could have been a nasty situation. And how very kind and thoughtful he was to have paid the cab fare.

The driver swung into his taxi and drove off before she could ask him to wait until someone opened the door.

'Can I ring the bell?' Lotte squealed.

'All right.'

But Aunt Fran beat her to it. A light came on and she appeared at the entrance – a statuesque figure with light brown hair all awry as though she'd just been out in a strong wind. Madeleine noticed her eyes were red and swollen as though she'd been crying.

'Hello, my dears. Come in, come in.' She hugged Lotte and kissed her, then shook hands with Erich. 'My, how you've both grown. You were only five when I last saw you.'

'We're eight now,' Lotte said. 'And we have come all the way from *München* with Maddie.'

'Miss Hamilton.' Fran turned towards her. 'I must thank you for bringing the twins. You must all be very tired. Are you hungry?'

'Not at all,' Madeleine said. 'We've had supper on the train.'

'I would like a drink – please,' Lotte said.

'I'll make a pot of tea and there's some orangeade for the children.' She smiled tenderly at the twins. 'Go and sit down, all of you.' She opened a door to a large sitting room and switched on a couple of lamps. 'I'll bring a tray in.'

'Where's Uncle Frederick?' Erich asked.

Fran glanced at Madeleine, her eyes troubled. Something was terribly wrong.

76

'He's not here at present,' she said. 'He'll come as soon as he can.'

'But he knows we visit,' Lotte whined.

'I know, darling. He hopes he won't be long but it might be a day or two.'

She disappeared and was back in five minutes with a large tea tray and handed the twins their glasses.

'Drink this and when you've finished I'll show you your room,' she said, then glanced at Madeleine. 'Do you normally put them to bed?'

'No, we are not babies,' Erich said.

'But Maddie still comes to kiss us goodnight,' Lotte put in.

'Then that's what she'll do while she's here,' Fran said, smiling.

Half an hour later Madeleine sat with Fran on a sprawling sofa, this time with a liqueur. She took a sip. Mmm. Lovely and fruity.

'I'd much rather have a sherry but we can't get it these days, so this is *slivovitz* – it's a plum brandy so I hope you like it.'

'It's delicious.' Madeleine held up the glass. 'And what a beautiful ruby-red colour.' Then she looked at Fran's tense expression. 'What's up, Fran? – if you don't mind my calling you by your Christian name.'

'Not at all. And you're Madeleine.' Her chirpy manner suddenly changed. 'My dear, I couldn't say anything in front of the children but something rather alarming has happened. My poor Freddie was taken off by the Gestapo this morning!'

Madeleine gasped, spilling some of the brandy down her blouse. 'Oh, no! What happened?'

'He runs a printing press. The Gestapo obviously think he's printing false papers – passports and suchlike. The truth is – they're right. But he hides his work extremely well so I don't think . . . hope anyway . . . they'll find anything. But if they do—' Tears fell silently down her cheeks. Impatiently, she brushed them away. 'If they do,' she repeated, 'then we're in very deep trouble.' She turned to Madeleine. 'They took me as well but let me go after a couple of hours' questioning.' She shuddered. 'What cold-blooded murdering brutes they are. I can't bear to think how they might be treating him.'

Madeleine took another sip of the plum liqueur to still her trembling body. Frau Weinberg had told her neither Frederick nor Fran were Jewish, but the Gestapo were obviously also locating people who were thought to be anti-Nazi – as Frederick plainly was.

As if she knew what Madeleine was thinking, Fran said: 'I can't leave Freddie to face this on his own. If he won't answer their questions the way they want him to – and I know he won't – I dread to think what they'll do to him. I have to be here when he's back. If they let him out, that is.' She turned a tear-stained face to Madeleine. 'You do see that, don't you? I can't leave him. So I can't take the children to England. But I made a promise to Renate – Frau Weinberg – I would.'

Madeleine tried to swallow. She couldn't. Her mouth had gone dry.

'I've thought all afternoon what can be done,' Fran continued, 'and the only person my dear friend would trust would be *you*.'

Shock waves rolled through Madeleine's body. She'd already had a bad fright on the journey and she felt she'd

78

gone as far as she could go for the twins. This new journey would mean checks for certain at every border as well as in between. Mentally, she traced the journey she'd taken from England to Germany. There'd be a border into Luxembourg and another check at Paris. She'd had no letter of permission to allow her to take the children on a journey in their own country, let alone going all the way to England. She couldn't trust herself to carry it off. Then she shook herself. They'd be travelling with German passports which were perfectly legitimate. She'd have to take the risk of no letter of permission. There was simply no other option.

# Chapter Eight

The following morning Madeleine opened her eyes to a strange room with its heavy oak furniture and plain linen curtains at the window, not at all like the cheerful patterned curtains and light pine Bavarian furniture stencilled with flowers in her bedroom at the Weinbergs'. For a few seconds she wondered where she was. And then it all came back to her. Tomorrow she'd be on the train to England, not on her own as she'd imagined, but with the twins. Well, she'd had some experience now of Nazi guards.

*But this time there'll be no James to help me if something goes wrong.*

*Don't be such a weakling,* her inner voice snapped. *You say you want to be an actress, so act!*

She quickly washed and dressed and peeped into the twins' bedroom. There were two single beds at right angles, and they'd chosen to lie with their heads together and were sound asleep. They'd had a long, tiring journey – she'd leave them for another hour.

Fran was in the kitchen making porridge and looked up.

'There you are. Did you sleep?'

'I'm amazed, but I did,' Madeleine said, searching Fran's

face, her puffy eyes. 'You don't look as though you managed very much.'

'I didn't,' Fran said brusquely. 'But there's not much I can do at the moment for Freddie except wait – and hope.' She gave a wan smile. 'Are you ready for breakfast?'

'Yes, please.'

'I thought we'd eat in here,' Fran said, putting a bowl of porridge on the table. 'Here's the honey.' She put her own bowl on the table, then turned on the wireless. 'We might as well listen to the news even though every day seems to be more awful than the one before.'

They didn't have long to wait before the newsreader read the German headlines:

'From today, this fifth of October, passports of all German Jews are invalid. They must apply for new ones marked with the letter "J".'

Madeleine's spoon was halfway to her lips as she heard Fran's sharp intake of breath. They both stopped eating and stared at the wireless.

The newsreader went on: 'After a meeting between Heinrich Rothmund, the head of the Swiss Police, and Nazi leaders in Berlin, it was agreed that all German Jewish citizens must surrender their old passports which are now invalid. They will become valid *only* after the letter "J" has been stamped on them. This is by order of the Reich Ministry of the Interior.'

He droned on another minute or so but Madeleine felt dazed. Had she translated it correctly? She looked at Fran whose face was drained of colour. Oh, dear God. The twins no longer held valid passports. They would instantly be spotted by the first guard who checked. All he had to look for was the letter 'J' stamped. If it wasn't there, they would

81

be sent home. And she would have to accompany them, landing herself in potential danger. Worse, the Weinbergs would be questioned – no doubt about that – and heaven knew where that would lead.

'Oh, Fran—'

'It's shocking. And no warning. Not even a few days. This is the way the Nazis work. The trouble is, "Weinberg" is such an obvious Jewish name.' She broke into tears. 'If Freddie was here he'd get false passports printed for them.'

Madeleine jumped from her chair and put her arm around the woman's shaking shoulders.

'Don't even talk about false passports. It's too dangerous.' She bit her lip hard.

'We have to think of something. Maybe not all the guards will know immediately of this latest order.'

Fran sent her a sorrowful look.

'You don't understand the Nazis' super efficiency. Every single guard will be on the lookout – and be rewarded in kind for every child and adult they find trying to beat the system.'

Madeleine felt her blood run cold.

'But we've got to get them to England somehow,' Fran said despairingly.

There was only one possibility. What had James told her to do? If you're ever in any kind of trouble, go to the British Embassy and ask for Jack. Well, she would do it. It was the twins' only chance.

Two hours later the taxi swept by the Brandenburg Gate and pulled up outside the British Embassy. The driver leapt out to open the door for Madeleine and she paid him with a large tip, so grateful he'd got her there swiftly without asking any questions. She walked past the stone-faced Prussian policeman. Mounting the few shallow steps at the imposing neo-classical columned entrance, and hardly aware of the grandeur of the reception hall, she hurried over to the desk. A uniformed clerk was speaking on the telephone. He ended the call and smiled at her.

'What can I do for you, miss?'

*Oh, how wonderful to hear an English voice.*

'Good morning. My name is Madeleine Hamilton. I wonder if I could have a word with Jack.'

The clerk frowned. 'What is the surname?'

She could have kicked herself for not asking James.

'I'm sorry, I don't know.'

The young man gave her a sympathetic glance.

'Then I probably won't be able to help you – we've got more than one "Jack".'

'A James Sylvester told me to ask for Jack,' she said, hearing her voice crack.

'Oh, that explains it.' He riffled through a sheaf of papers while Madeleine tapped her fingers on the desk. 'Ah, this is the chap you need to talk to.' He dialled a number. 'Who shall I say is asking for him?'

'Madeleine Hamilton.'

'Miss Hamilton to see you, sir.' There was a pause. 'Right you are.' He turned to Madeleine. 'I'll get someone to take you to his office.'

A girl of about her own age with short brown curls and a warm smile appeared. Madeleine followed her up the ornate staircase and along a wide passage with various doors leading off. The girl knocked on one of them and waited to enter. She opened the door to let Madeleine go in front.

83

'Miss Hamilton, sir.' She disappeared.

A man stood up from behind his desk. Madeleine's heart missed a beat.

*James!*

He came round to her side and took her hand in his, then leant to give her that same butterfly kiss on her cheek. Her skin tingled where his lips had touched it. She swallowed hard.

'How nice to see you so soon.' He looked down at her. 'Here, let me take your jacket.'

'I thought I was supposed to be seeing *Jack* if I had a problem,' she said curtly, conscious of his fingers on her shoulders as he helped her remove it.

'Yes, that's me.' He looked startled. 'Oh, I'm sorry – didn't you realise? That's what everyone calls me here.'

'I thought it was a different person.' She fought down her irritation.

'Look, come and sit down. You're not here on a social call so you must have run into a problem.'

He went back to his desk and she sat on one of the visitors' chairs, the desk feeling like a barrier between them.

'I gather you've heard the news this morning about Jewish people and their passports,' he said.

'Yes.'

'I guessed as much.' He looked directly at her. 'I'm not really surprised to see you here this morning. But whatever's the problem, we'll get it sorted. Just take your time.'

Not realising she'd been holding her breath, she breathed out.

'You were right when you guessed the twins were Jewish.'

She slid Erich and Lotte's passports over the desk.

He put on a pair of horn-rimmed glasses to examine

them. She couldn't help thinking he looked just as attractive. 'Hmm. The name Weinberg is the giveaway, I'm afraid.' He looked up. 'They're intending to stamp the left-hand side with an enormous red "J" and will be onto it like wasps round a honeypot.'

Quickly, she explained what had happened to Frederick and Fran yesterday morning. He sat quietly, his expression intent, not interrupting until she finished.

'It's a pretty bad business,' he said. 'The Gestapo are just as keen to winkle out any resisters as they are the Jews, as they're often one and the same. Let's just hope this Frederick can talk his way out of it. I wish we could help him but that's impossible, him being German. In the meantime you need to get the children to England but not on their present passports.'

He took out a packet of cigarettes, holding it out to her.

'No, thanks, but you go ahead.'

He lit his cigarette and inhaled deeply. 'It will take a couple of days. Will you be all right staying with this Fran?'

'Yes, I'm sure that won't be a problem.'

'Is she on the telephone?'

'Yes. I have the number here.'

He jotted it down, then looked at her and smiled.

'Try not to worry. Just leave this with me and I'll be in touch as soon as we have some news.'

His smile made her feel as though everything would be all right. He, personally, would deal with it – she was certain.

'Can I get you some tea?'

'No, thanks. I should be getting back. Fran might have heard some news about her husband and won't be able to leave the house because of the twins.'

85

He nodded. 'All right. I'll ring you – I hope within a couple of days.'

He got up and removed her jacket from the stand.

'The Weinbergs will be forever grateful,' Madeleine said, rising to her feet. 'As I am.'

He shook his head. 'Let's hope we can get them done quickly.' He paused and gazed down at her. 'But if you *had* to run up against a problem, at least it's allowed me to see you again.'

He hesitated as though he wanted to say more, but instead helped her on with her jacket. She felt his hands through the material, strong and warm. Her pulse quickened. When she turned, as though in a trance, she was in his arms, so close she could see the gold flecks in his eyes spark. He was going to kiss her. She knew it for certain this time. Her lips parted slightly. She felt a whisper of his sigh on her forehead. And then he let her go.

'I'll see you out,' he said.

Feeling rather foolish, she said, 'Please don't bother. I know you're busy.' To soften the words she smiled at him. 'Really, James . . . or if you prefer, Jack . . . I can see myself out. And I can't thank you enough.'

'Your Jack sounds nice,' Fran said as the two women sat facing one another in the comfortable armchairs in her sitting room. She poured two cups of tea and handed Madeleine one.

'He's not exactly *my* Jack.' To hide her flushing cheeks, she bent her head to take a sip of tea, nearly burning her throat.

'Maybe – but he seems very willing to help you.'

'That's his job, isn't it?'

'Mmm. I suppose so. Though he's probably taking a risk for the twins, being German Jews. If he's caught he could lose his job. But something tells me he thinks you're rather special and he's willing to take it.'

A warm glow spread through Madeleine. Was Fran right? And if so, how had she picked that up? She didn't think she'd said anything that would make this charming Englishwoman latch on to something that probably didn't even exist.

To take the conversation away from herself, she said, 'He also seemed genuinely sorry he wouldn't be able to help your husband.'

'Again, it's because he's German.' Fran's face creased with anxiety. 'The only thing I can pray for is that they haven't found any evidence. I'm hoping they just want to give him a good fright in case he ever thinks of using his printing press for other reasons. Maybe somebody hinted that he wasn't a Nazi sympathiser though God knows what kind of a person would be. That's what I'm hanging on to anyway.' She looked at Madeleine, the lines on her face softening. 'But this Jack sounds to me as if he's taken a real shine to you.'

'That's nonsense. He thinks I'm engaged and I haven't told him anything different.'

Fran glanced at Madeleine's left hand. 'I didn't want to ask, Madeleine, but isn't that *Renate's* ring you're wearing?'

'Yes.' Madeleine spread her fingers. As it twinkled up at her, she admired the ring once again. It was a beautiful piece. 'She wanted me to give you some jewels to take for payment to the twins' relatives in London and suggested I put this one on my finger so I didn't have to hide it. The other pieces are in my handbag in a concealed pocket.'

'Just be very careful,' Fran warned. 'There are bound to be more checks at the borders.' She paused, then gave a mischievous grin as she glanced at Madeleine's left hand again. 'You know, by wearing that ring in full view you may have scuppered your chances with Jack if he thinks you're engaged.'

'He's probably married anyway,' Madeleine shot back.

As she lay in bed that night she wondered if there was some truth in Fran's words. Did Jack like her more than she realised? Madeleine pondered over the questions. She couldn't deny she was attracted to him even though she'd tried to put Fran off the scent. But she couldn't tell him she wasn't engaged – that it was her way of trying to hide the jewels. He didn't know her well enough not to have a sneaking doubt that she'd stolen them. And even if he *did* believe her, he would certainly warn her what a huge risk she was taking to smuggle them out of the country. And that would make her lose her confidence that she could pull it off. Even so, it would take all her acting skills.

No, it was best to keep up the façade – for now, anyway.

Decision made, she turned over in the bed, tucking the blanket closely around her, even though she wasn't cold.

# Chapter Nine

Just as Madeleine was tidying her hair, ready to go downstairs for breakfast, she heard the twins begin arguing in their bedroom next door. They often bickered but this was unusual. She glanced at the clock. Five past six. She marched into their room where they were sitting up in their beds and just caught Lotte about to throw a book at her brother.

'Stop this!' she ordered. 'You'll wake Aunt Fran.'

The twins fell silent. Then Lotte pointed to Erich. 'He started.'

'What did Erich start?'

'He said Uncle Frederick is not arriving. The horrid men took him.'

Heart sinking, Madeleine glanced over at Erich who was chewing his nail.

'Erich?'

'It is true. I heard you and Aunt Fran talking.'

'You shouldn't be listening to grown-ups' conversations.'

'I want to go home,' he stormed. 'So does Lotte.'

The moment she'd been dreading. Madeleine swallowed hard.

'Come to my bedroom, both of you,' she said.

89

When she and Lotte were in bed and Erich was sitting on the eiderdown, swinging his legs, she said:

'I'm afraid Erich is right, darling.' She put her arm around Lotte. 'The bad men *did* come and take Uncle Frederick. But they only want to ask him some questions. They'll let him come home in a few days. But your mama and papa want you two to be safe. I'm going to take you with me to England. You're going to stay with Aunt Ruth and Uncle Joseph in London. And you'll be able to play with your three cousins.'

The twins' eyes were wide. Lotte burst into tears.

'I do not want to play with them,' she sobbed.

'We don't even *know* them,' Erich added. 'They went to England two years after we are born.'

'Well, they're looking forward to getting to know *you*.'

'When will we see Mutti and Papa?' Erich's face was white.

'They're going to follow us as soon as they can and live in England too.'

'All of us together in England?'

'Yes.'

'Will we see you, too?' Erich's voice trembled.

'Yes, as often as I can.'

'We will be safe, Lotte, if we go with Maddie.' He patted his sister's arm. 'We will make it an adventure.'

Tears pricked Madeleine's eyes. How terrible for children to face this. Trying to work out what dreadful things people were doing to innocent others. And why . . . when there was no earthly reason.

'Come on,' she said to them. 'Let's all get dressed.'

'You will not leave us, will you, Maddie?' Lotte said, clutching her hand.

90

'No, I won't leave you, darling. It's a long journey but I'll be there with you all the way.'

Madeleine decided to send a telegram to her parents while Fran said she was going to the Gestapo headquarters to see if she could find out anything about her husband. She'd offered to accompany her, but Fran said no, she'd rather go on her own, telling Madeleine where there was a local post office just ten minutes' walk away.

While the twins were inspecting all the different envelopes and packages in the post office, Madeleine wrote out the telegram:

IN BERLIN STOP CATCHING TRAIN IN 2-3 DAYS STOP LET YOU KNOW WHEN I ARRIVE LONDON STOP M

It would have to do.

Once they'd returned to the house, Madeleine prepared a light lunch for the twins. She nibbled at some bread and cheese and gherkin but wasn't really hungry. Her stomach had remained tense ever since she'd heard the news about the letter 'J' to be stamped on passports for Jews. By teatime, she'd begun to worry about Fran, wondering why she was taking so long. Maybe it was good news. Maybe they were letting her speak to Frederick – even allowing him to go home with her. But that last thought seemed a bit too good to be true.

Just as the clock struck five she heard the key turn in the lock. Her heart accelerated. But only Fran walked in, looking white with exhaustion.

'I waited for hours and then they only let me see him

for ten minutes,' she said, throwing off her hat. 'And that was with someone standing close by, listening to every word. It was awful. He said he'd had an initial beating after he denied everything they accused him of, and he's heard nothing since. It's difficult to gauge whether that's good or bad.' She let out a long sigh. 'They haven't mentioned when they're going to give up and let him go.'

'I'll make you a cup of tea,' Madeleine said.

'The English panacea, no matter how horrible.' Fran gave her a weak smile. 'By the way, I didn't feel like cooking, so I bought supper at the deli. But the owner, Herr Hoffman – such a nice kind man whom I've known for years – told me he hasn't got half the trade he used to.' She sighed. 'Everyone's been affected, and this is only the start.'

After a light meal of cheese and sauerkraut, potato salad and pumpernickel bread, and Madeleine had settled the twins in bed, the telephone rang on the table by Fran's chair in the sitting room.

'For you,' Fran said, holding out the receiver.

*It must be Frau Weinberg asking if we've arrived.*

But the voice wasn't female.

'Madeleine?'

Unconsciously, she put her hand to her heart as though to calm the sudden flutter at hearing Jack's warm voice.

'Yes, it's me.'

'Is it too late for me to come over now?'

'Let me have a word.' She covered the mouthpiece with her hand, willing her heart to slow down. 'Fran, Jack says he knows it's late but could he come over now?'

Fran grinned. 'Yes, of course he can. It doesn't matter what time.'

92

Madeleine took her hand off the mouthpiece but before she could speak she heard crackling along the line. Then silence. 'Jack – are you still there?'

She waited a few moments. Damn! They'd lost the connection. And then she heard his voice edged with impatience.

'Hello! Hello, operator, we've been—'

'Jack, it's me again. Fran said for you to come however late.'

'I'll be along in half an hour.'

She was going to see Jack again – and very soon. Madeleine slowly put the receiver in its cradle, immersed in a warm glow.

'You'd better go and tidy your hair, Madeleine.' Fran grinned. 'And put a bit of lippy on while you're at it,' she added mischievously.

Back downstairs, with Fran's nod of approval at her freshened look, Madeleine stole a glance at the mantelpiece clock, directly in her line of vision. Only twelve more minutes and he would be stepping into the room. Her body tingled. To stop herself having such ridiculous feelings, she tried to engage in conversation with Fran but her hostess yawned several times, though each time attempting to disguise her tiredness. Madeleine felt a rush of guilt. She'd been concentrating so much on the twins' problems and now Jack – though whether he was a problem or not, she hadn't quite worked out – that she'd almost forgotten poor Fran. She doubted her new friend had had much sleep lately for worrying about her husband.

Almost to the minute, at half-past eight, the bell rang. Instinct made her half rise in her chair but Fran shook her head.

'Let me go,' she said. 'You just sit there and look gorgeous.'

In the hall, Madeleine heard her say: 'Do come in. I'm Fran. And you're obviously Jack. Madeleine's told me about you.'

She heard male footsteps in the hall. Nervously, she moistened her lips.

'All good, I hope,' he said as he followed Fran into the room.

And there he was, smiling at her as he strode over. Suddenly feeling shy, Madeleine rose from the sofa and put out her hand to greet him. He took it and held it, drawing her towards him as he kissed her cheek. His sudden proximity made her senses reel. She noticed Fran watching with an amused expression. Well, anything to take her mind off Frederick.

'May I offer you a drink?' Fran asked him.

'Thank you. Just a cup of tea if it's not too much trouble.' He glanced at Madeleine, then took an envelope from his briefcase and put it in her hands before sitting on the seat beside her.

She looked at him questioningly. He simply nodded.

She removed two passports. They were navy blue with gold lettering and the gold royal coat of arms. Two passports identical to her own.

'But I thought you were just going to get their own passports stamped with a "J",' she said, confused, flipping one and then the other open to find that Lotte was now 'Lotte Renate White', and her brother Erich was 'Eric White'.

'It's far safer for them to have British passports. They'll be your niece and nephew so you shouldn't have any trouble at all taking them over the borders and crossing the Channel.'

'I can't thank you enough,' she said, relief pouring through her body.

'But I must tell you something, Madeleine.' He looked at her intently. 'Faking the twins' passports is a pretty serious matter and if it ever came to light, the consequences would range from a severe reprimand and warning to a demotion. It could even lead to my dismissal. At best it will be a black mark against my service record.'

So Fran was right. She swallowed.

'Oh, Jack, I'd feel terrible if I've compromised you in any way. But you can be sure of one thing – I will never breathe a word of this to anyone, *ever*, that you were involved.'

'I know you won't. But let me tell you this – if anything unforeseen happens, *you* are not to blame in any way. I take full responsibility. The twins are in danger at this minute but these passports have been forged by an expert, and if it gets them to England safely, I'm more than satisfied.'

'How can we ever repay you?'

Jack gave a wry smile. 'Beating the Gestapo is reward enough in itself.'

What a very nice man he was. He'd put his career at risk for the sake of two children he barely knew. Their parents could never repay him. Nor could she.

'Don't forget, Madeleine,' he continued, 'it's not just the twins, if the Kraut guards got suspicious of their passports, you'd be accused of aiding and abetting a crime just by being in charge of them, and things could get tricky for you, too.'

95

'I'm prepared for that possibility.'

'I'd never forgive myself if anything happened to the twins . . . or you.' His voice cracked.

She gave him a sharp look. Was he remembering how he'd almost kissed her in his office? Did he regret not doing so? She was grateful when Fran appeared with the tea tray and conversation resumed as normal.

But try as she might, Madeleine couldn't help giving him a sidelong glance as often as she dared. She liked his cultured voice, his obvious intelligence and quick thinking. She liked his strong fingers as he held his cup of tea, his profile, his expressive eyes when he turned to her, the line of his jaw, the well-shaped generous mouth . . .

What would it be like to be kissed by that mouth? Really kissed. Not just a peck on the cheek. She felt her cheeks glow and he suddenly grinned as he caught her looking. She was sure he knew exactly what she was thinking. She lowered her head to tuck the passports into her handbag, feeling flustered.

'I'd better be going,' he said eventually, putting his cup in the saucer. 'I'd love to stay longer and talk but I'm afraid I have work to do when I get back.'

'But it's so late,' Fran said.

'It can't be helped.' He stood up.

'Can you show Jack out?' Fran said, 'and I'll take the tea things to the kitchen.' She sent Madeleine a wink.

Madeleine pretended not to have seen it, which made Fran's smile widen to a grin.

When she and Jack were in the hall, he said:

'There's a train to Paris tomorrow morning at ten past ten. I would take it. Things are going to get worse every day from now on and the sooner you're on your way with

96

the kids the better. But don't book First Class. It's too conspicuous with their ordinary name of "White". Second Class will hit just the right note.'

'All right.' Her throat felt tight. Any moment now and he'd be gone.

'It could be a very full train so you need to be there by nine to make sure you get seats.'

'I will.' Her voice was flat. She didn't want him to disappear and never see him again. And the way he was regarding her so seriously, maybe he didn't want it either.

'Be aware of what's happening around you. And keep the kiddies in your sight at all times.'

'I will,' she repeated. It was as though she had no more words left within her.

'I wish I could come with you.' He gently tucked a lock of her hair behind her ear.

She quivered under his touch. It seemed the most romantic gesture she'd ever experienced.

'I can see your face properly now.' He looked down at her, smiling. 'You've got my card so please write and let me know you all got back to Blighty safely.'

'Yes, of course.'

Why was he asking her to write? Was it simply because he was being polite or was he genuinely concerned about the twins? Or did it mean that he didn't want to lose contact with her? If so, was it because he more than liked her? If only she knew what was going on in that dark head of his.

His eyes held hers.

The air crackled between them.

He didn't speak.

Catching her unawares, he brought her towards him, wrapping her in his arms until she was so close she could

97

feel the thudding of his heart, the sigh of his breath on her neck, as soft as feathers.

'Maddie,' he said, his voice thick. 'Do you realise this might be the last time we'll meet?'

*Please don't say that. I couldn't bear it if it were true.*

'Madeleine – did you hear me?'

'Yes.' Her answer was no more than a whisper.

'And . . .?'

'I have thought about it.'

He looked directly into her eyes.

'And what did you think?'

'I don't know.' She hardly voiced the words.

'Nowhere will be safe – for either of us. I don't bother too much about *me*, but I bother terribly about *you*.'

She couldn't answer. The thought of anything bad happening to him was too terrible to contemplate.

'I want to leave you with this memory.' He bent his head.

The next moment his lips were on hers, gently at first, and then his kiss deepened, exploring, full of longing and passion, seeming to go on forever. She'd never been kissed so thoroughly, so sensuously, in her life, and never had she responded so completely. Catching her breath, she wanted him to kiss her again. She parted her lips, her hands sliding around his neck. But suddenly he put her at arm's length, leaving her giddy, almost overbalancing – would have if he wasn't still gripping her. She gazed up at him, trying to work out the sudden change in his manner.

'Oh, Madeleine, I'm so sorry. Please forgive me. I should never have done that. I told myself I mustn't the last time in the Embassy – even though I wanted to . . . so much. It's just that you always look so lovely and this time I couldn't resist. I forgot you're engaged to someone else and it's not fair to you or him. Or me,' he added under his breath.

Before she could answer he'd turned abruptly from her and opened the front door. Without glancing back he disappeared into the night.

He hadn't even given her a chance to explain. Madeleine gazed numbly at Frau Weinberg's engagement ring. The deep royal-blue sapphire surrounded by diamonds winked up at her mockingly under the chandelier in the hall. Her mind flew in all directions – angry with herself and angry with him. But how could he know there was any possible explanation other than she was engaged to another man? Unconsciously, she put her finger to her tingling lips. She didn't want to face Fran. Be teased and questioned. All she wanted to do was hide in her bedroom, throw herself on the bed and sob with frustration that finally a man she had to admit she was madly attracted to had just walked out of her life. And it had been no fault of anyone's except her own.

The next morning after breakfast, while the twins had dashed upstairs to collect their bits and pieces, Madeleine hugged Fran goodbye, promising to write. In such a short time the Englishwoman had already become like a friend and Madeleine just hoped with all her heart that Frederick would soon be released and unharmed.

'Are you sure you don't want me to come with you to the station?' Fran said.

'No, really. We'll be fine. You need to stay by the telephone in case there's some news of Frederick. They can't hold him indefinitely.'

'Let's hope not.' Fran bit her lip. 'But it's you I'm worried about. How you'll cope on the journey. I won't rest until I hear you're all safe.'

'You're not to worry. Jack has sorted everything for me and I trust him.'

Fran gave her a knowing smile. 'He'd be perfect for you, Madeleine. The two of you look just right together. And the way he looks at you—'

'Don't say such things,' Madeleine interrupted. 'I don't need any more complications. And anyway I doubt I'll ever set eyes on him again. He knows that as well as I do.' She saw Fran's crestfallen face. 'I'm sorry, Fran. I didn't mean to snap. It's just that I need to concentrate on getting the twins to their relatives, and then decide what to do next with my life – something useful that might help if there really *is* a war.' She looked at her watch. 'I'd better call the twins. The taxi will be here in a few minutes.'

Ten minutes later the little group were outside the front door. Erich and Lotte were kicking a stone on the pavement playing hopscotch when the taxi drew up. The driver got out and opened the boot.

'*Guten Morgen, Fräulein.*' He doffed his cap and jerked his head towards the luggage. '*Ist das das ganze Gepäck?*'

'Yes, thank you.' Madeleine turned to Fran. 'I'll be thinking of you and Frederick and waiting for some good news.'

Fran nodded. 'I'll let you know immediately.'

'I can't thank you enough for everything, Fran, when you're going through such a rotten time yourself.'

'It's me who should thank you for what you're doing.' Fran's eyes were bright with tears. 'The Weinbergs will be so relieved when they know you're all safely in England. I'll be in touch with them as soon as I hear.' She kissed

100

Madeleine and the twins in turn. 'Just be very careful, all of you.'

'*Wir solten besser gehen*,' the driver said.

There was little traffic on the roads and soon they were inside the Berlin *Hauptbahnhof*. Madeleine felt she was forever standing on steam-ridden, grey platforms, seeing people bursting from trains or trying to push their way on. The twins were quiet for a change, as she'd warned them to be.

'Remember, both of you,' she said in an undertone, although it would have been impossible for anyone to hear her words with the hissing of steam and slamming of doors drowning out every human voice, 'you must speak English all the time until we're on the ship to England. You must pretend you are English from now on but don't talk to anyone unless someone speaks to you – and then keep it short.'

Someone bumped into her.

'*Es tut mir leid*,' a youth growled as he dashed off.

'And your surname is now "White",' Madeleine continued as she gazed down at the twins. 'And let me do all the talking.'

'We know, Maddie,' Erich said. 'You said us many times.'

She smiled at them. 'You're both good children.' She gave Lotte's hand a gentle squeeze. 'Let's go and find our seats.'

Thrusting her bag onto her shoulder, suitcase in hand, she kept Lotte's hand tightly in her other, with Erich following, carrying their small cases as they looked for the Second Class carriage. She'd had no trouble getting the three tickets to Paris, where they'd have to change. *So far so good*, she thought grimly.

*Will Jack be here to see me off?*

Quickly, she shook the thought away. He wouldn't come. Not after yesterday evening. But the memory of his kiss lingered, making her cheeks hot.

*Concentrate, Maddie.* What you have to do now is far too important for any fanciful nonsense.

Once she'd settled the twins in their seats next to one another, she slid open the door to the corridor and glanced through the soot-streaked window. There was no sign of Jack. Willing herself not to be upset she returned to the compartment and busied herself with the luggage. This time a tall German boy stood up from his seat. He was dressed in the Hitler Youth uniform of black shorts and a tan shirt, with an armband displaying the terrifying symbol of the swastika. With his blond hair and cocky expression he reminded her of Rolf.

'*Erlauben Sie mir,*' he said, taking the case and pushing it onto the rack.

'*Danke schön,*' Madeleine murmured.

'*Bitte schön,*' came the polite answer.

Sighing deeply, she handed the twins their English story books and opened her own. It was going to be a very long journey.

# PART TWO

# *Chapter Ten*

Madeleine and the twins stepped off the ferry at Dover. She was mentally and physically exhausted, and amazed that the twins seemed to have found renewed energy after being cooped up in a compartment for almost a day, then changing trains in Paris at night, and finally the Channel crossing from Calais to Dover. Rain and wind had made the sea choppy but thankfully it hadn't affected the twins' appetite at all. They'd been far too excited to be out on deck in the open air, watching the waves, screaming with laugher when several pounded over the edge of the ship and splashed them, then tucking into a meal in the ship's dining room.

On the train from Berlin there had been no suspicious guards, no hold-ups, no one dragged from their seat, nothing untoward. Madeleine had kept her ears pricked for any change in the atmosphere of the compartment, anything the twins said that might have caused a curious glance in their direction . . . but there was nothing.

The passports Jack had arranged had done their job beautifully. All she had to do now was to get the twins safely from St Pancras to their aunt and uncle and cousins in Ealing, a part of London she knew reasonably well, being only five miles from her home in Richmond.

'Only one more train,' she told the twins, when they were heading for the railway station, 'and it will take us to a marvellous city called London. And you won't be far from where I live.'

'Will you come and see us in London?' Lotte said.

'Yes, darling, whenever I can. But I will have to work most of the time.'

'London is the capital of England,' Lotte said, pride rising in her voice.

'The capital of Great Britain,' Erich corrected her. 'England is only one country of four. That is why it is called *Great* Britain.' He counted off the countries on his fingers: 'Scotland, Wales, Ireland and *England*.'

Then he yawned and Lotte joined in.

Thankfully, the twins were finally overcome with tiredness – they'd been too excited to sleep much on the ship overnight. Rubbing their eyes now, they collected their bits and pieces together, preparing for the final stop in London.

'St Pancras, London,' called the guard. 'All change – St Pancras – all change.'

Fran had told her to take a taxi from the station. She'd pressed three pound notes into Madeleine's hand, telling her to use it for the fare.

'It's too much,' Madeleine protested.

'Take it. It's another journey – and well over an hour. The twins will be worn out –' she looked at Madeleine '– and so will you, my dear.'

Fran's words in her ear, and holding Lotte's hand with Erich holding his sister's other, Madeleine followed the signs to the taxi rank.

Within the warm interior of the taxi, Madeleine allowed

106

herself a spark of triumph. She'd done it! She'd taken the twins from under the very noses of the Gestapo.

*But only with Jack's help,* she told herself. *You would have come a cropper if not. Chances are you'd be back in Munich by now, most likely under armed guard, with two petrified children.*

Looking at the twins' faces, so similar to one another, she shivered at the idea.

It was heavenly being driven in a cab after all the changes of trains and the ferry. Madeleine felt her eyelids droop. She leant back on the leather seat, its smell wafting in her nostrils – luxurious and comforting. The last thing she heard was Erich's drowsy voice saying, '*Ruhig, Lotte, weil Maddie schläft.*' A minute later Madeleine was fast asleep.

'We're here, miss,' the taxi driver announced. 'Forty Windermere Road.'

Madeleine jerked awake as the taxi driver braked to a stop. He jumped out and helped the twins, then retrieved their luggage.

'Seventeen and six, love.'

She rounded it to a pound. He was worth it. She glanced along the road, appreciating the avenue of trees giving a gentle leafy appearance to the assortment of houses. Number 40 was a substantial semi-detached Edwardian house, red brick, with a short tessellated path up to the front door. The twins stood half behind her and her heart went out to them. Poor little kids – they had no idea how they would find this new family of theirs. But at least they were safe. And the Weinbergs would never have sent them to people they didn't like or trust, relatives or not.

She took a deep breath and rang the bell. The door swung open immediately.

'I'd just looked out of the window this very minute,' said the excitable voice of a plump dark-haired woman with an unusual streak of grey at the front, 'and I've already got the kettle on. You must be Madeleine . . . oh, and here are the twins. I didn't expect you to be so tall. Come in, my loves, come in. The girls have just gone to school . . . but they can't wait to meet you later today.' She shepherded them into the wide hallway.

'Have you any boy children?' Erich said.

'No.' She laughed as she looked at him. 'You'll be the only one so you'll have to keep them all in order.'

'No boys to play with,' Erich muttered, looking down at the floor.

'Shhh!' Madeleine hissed. 'Say hello to your Auntie Ruth – both of you.'

'Good morning, Auntie Ruth,' they chorused.

Ruth beamed. 'Good morning, Erich.' She put out her hand to shake his, then turned to Lotte. 'And my niece, Lotte.' She bent to kiss the little girl. 'Good morning, Lotte. I hope you'll be very happy with us. I want you to come into the kitchen and I'll make you a drink, then hear all about your mama and papa. Uncle Joseph won't be long – he's just gone to fetch his paper.' She turned to Madeleine. 'By the way, we anglicised our surname – we're now plain Mr and Mrs White, but Ruth and Joseph to you, my dear.'

Madeleine's mouth fell open.

'You won't believe this but that's the very same name Ja . . . the chap at the British Embassy used for the twins. They've now got British passports in the name of White.'

'God must finally be looking after our family,' Joseph

108

chuckled as he came into the kitchen. 'Now then, who do we have here?'

Joseph was a shorter version of his brother, though without the beard, but with what came across as a more relaxed disposition. Madeleine put it down to being in a far less nerve-wracking situation than Munich, from where he and his wife had fled. She could tell in the first hour that the twins were going to be all right. Over tea and a late scrambled egg breakfast, Aunt Ruth and Uncle Joseph had made it clear they were taking the children into their family as their own.

'That hit the spot perfectly,' Madeleine said, wiping the crumbs away with her napkin. 'Thank you so much.'

'It's *you* we need to be thanking, my dear,' Joseph said. 'I wanted my brother and his wife to come with Ruth and me years ago. We could see things were getting difficult for Jewish people, even then. But he wouldn't. He said he'd fought in the last war and was a German first and a Jew second. Said the Nazis would look at his records and acknowledge it. But I'm afraid he's living in cloud-cuckoo-land.'

His wife sent him a warning glance and nodded towards the twins who were listening intently.

'Where is cloud-cuckoo-land?' Lotte asked.

'It's not a real place, love – just an expression,' Madeleine said.

'What does it mean?'

'I'll explain later.'

'When the girls come in from school they'll show you their rooms and help to get you settled,' their aunt told them. 'There's Elizabeth, the eldest at twelve, Eliana, the middle one at ten, and Eva, the youngest, who's seven.'

'*We* are eight,' Lotte piped. 'Nine – in November.'

'My goodness, you're getting very grown up.'

Madeleine couldn't help a grin at the triumphant smile Lotte gave her aunt.

'Would you like to book a call to Fran?' Ruth said. 'It's in the sitting room. I have her number ready on the telephone table.'

'Thank you, I will. She'll be worrying until she hears from me.'

A half-hour later the telephone rang.

'That'll be for you,' Ruth said.

Madeleine sprang up and hurried to the sitting room.

'Go ahead, caller,' the operator said.

There was a crackle. Then the line cleared.

'Fran, it's me, Madeleine. We've arrived.'

'Oh, my dear, I'm so pleased. How was the journey?'

'Without a hitch.'

'So everything worked well?'

Madeleine knew Fran couldn't mention the word 'passport' in case the line was tapped. She must be very careful herself not to mention anything incriminating to either of them.

'Perfectly. Couldn't be better.' She paused. 'Have you heard any news?'

'Not a dicky bird. But I'm keeping my fingers crossed. I'll go over there again today to see if I can find out anything.'

'You have my home telephone number, so if you get some news, please let me know.'

'I will.' The line crackled. Then she heard Fran say, 'How are the twins?'

'They're going to be fine. Their aunt and uncle are a lovely couple and prepared to take them as long as

110

necessary. I'm going home soon but will leave them the payment for their education.'

'Thank you for everything,' Fran said. 'I'll never forget your kindness – and neither will their parents.'

Madeleine placed the receiver in its cradle and glanced down at Frau Weinberg's engagement ring, remembering how Jack had spotted it and used it to help her out of a tricky situation. She gave a rueful smile. She'd soon be putting it into Ruth's safe hands, along with the other jewels.

There was one more tricky situation to face – explaining to her parents why she hadn't come home immediately when they'd ordered her to. She gave an inward groan. Twenty-one and they still treated her like a wayward child who'd messed up her chances for her final year at university through her own fault. She knew she'd been stupid but when the chance to go to Bavaria had come, it had been the perfect opportunity to break away from her mother's constant disappointment in her. Madeleine was *glad* she'd taken her own decision for the first time. At least she'd seen the situation in Germany at first hand – seen the Nazi grip on the country and the repression of the Jewish people. If there *was* a war – and Jack didn't seem to have any doubts – she would help in any way she could. But who would want to employ her when they found out she'd been forced to leave the college in disgrace? Not completed her language degree.

'You should have thought of that before you got expelled,' she heard her mother's voice in her head.

'Joseph, would you bring the tea tray into the sitting room?' Ruth said, snapping Madeleine out of such negative thoughts. 'We can talk privately while the twins are sorting out their bedroom.'

Joseph wanted to know the details about his brother and the music shop and what, if anything, Madeleine had noticed of the Nazis' treatment of Jews. He and Ruth hung on to her every word about the sinister developments.

'It's worse than I imagined,' he said, pressing his wife's hand. '*Verdammt!* They've left it too late to come to England and I daren't think about the consequences.'

'Let's change the subject,' Ruth said quickly. 'Madeleine's had enough harrowing experiences lately.' She turned to Madeleine and smiled. 'Don't forget to come and see us as often as you like. The twins will feel lost at first and very homesick, but you'll be their dear familiar figure.'

Madeleine swallowed hard. 'I will . . . I promise.' Her eye caught the ring. 'I must give you Frau Weinberg's engagement ring before I forget.' She took it off her finger and laid it gently in a small glass ashtray on the side table. 'It actually got me out of a tight spot with a suspicious armed guard on the Munich–Berlin train.'

She didn't add that the ring had stopped what might have been the most wonderful relationship.

'I won't ask you what the tight spot was,' Ruth said. 'You need to put all that behind you.' She glanced at Madeleine. 'But I can imagine.'

Madeleine gave a rueful smile. 'Frau Weinberg thought it would be safer for me to wear it as an engagement ring rather than hiding it and getting caught by one of the guards. I have some other jewellery to give you.' She put the purse containing Frau Weinberg's precious gems on the little table beside her chair. 'It's for your safe-keeping and to sell it if you need to for the twins' education and clothing and anything else they need.' She smothered a yawn. It had been a tiring journey with the added stress of worrying what might happen at the borders. 'You've both been so very kind and I know the twins will be in a loving home, but I should be getting along as my parents are expecting me.'

'Of course, my dear.'

'I'll just say goodbye to the twins.'

Madeleine went upstairs to the room the Whites had prepared for them.

'When will you come and see us?' was their first question.

Madeleine's heart squeezed at their anxious expressions.

'As soon as I can. But you'll have a lovely time with Aunt Ruth and Uncle Joseph and their children.'

'All girls,' Erich said dismally.

'Can we come and see you?' Lotte said.

'It's difficult, love. I'll be looking for a job and then I'll be working all day. But I don't live far so it's easier for me to see you.'

'You will go to work and forget us.' Lotte began to cry.

Madeleine put her arm round her.

'I'll never ever forget you or Erich.' She looked at Erich. 'Come here.'

She hugged them both.

'Be good, won't you?' she said.

Both dark heads nodded.

'When will Mutti and Papa come to England?' Erich's eyes were wet with tears.

'As soon as they can, love.'

The twins came downstairs to join Ruth and Joseph to wave her off. Madeleine turned at the gate to see Lotte gripping Erich's hand. Her heart twisted. Poor little kids. All they knew for certain was that they'd been separated from their mother and father and no grown-up seemed to have a proper answer as to when they would see them again.

# *Chapter Eleven*

The closer she came to her parents' house, the more Madeleine's feet dragged. For goodness' sake, she told herself crossly, it's *my* home too. But she'd lived in so many different houses lately, and was so welcomed in all of them, that going to her real home felt awkward. She walked briskly along the once-familiar street noticing the difference in the demeanour of the people. They weren't cowed like so many she'd seen in Munich those last weeks. A neighbour, one she always tried to avoid, was about to pass her, then stopped.

'Goodness me, it's Madeleine, home at last.' The woman's small pale eyes bored into hers. 'You look thin. Haven't they fed you? I expect your mother will be relieved to see you safe and sound with what's been happening lately in Germany. I'm surprised you'd want to be in such a dreadful country in the first place. Oh, I don't know what the world is com—'

'Actually, it's a very beautiful country,' Madeleine interrupted, not bothering to hold back her irritation. 'Just a bad government.' She flashed a smile. 'I'd better be going, Mrs Deacon. They're expecting me.'

'Oh, of course, my dear. You trundle along. Give my best to your mother. Tell her I'm—'

But Madeleine simply nodded, pretending not to hear any further message, and strode on. Just a few houses down and there was the Edwardian house set back from the road with other similar detached houses. And here was her front door painted Brunswick green at the insistence of her father, who rarely got his own way. She rang the bell and moments later heard light footsteps. The door opened and there was her mother, her face still beautiful with her deep blue eyes and fair skin, standing tall before her.

*But she's looking older. Her dark hair she's always been so proud of has streaks of grey in it.*

'So the wanderer has returned,' her mother said, then laughed as though she'd made a joke.

'Hello, Mother.'

'Your father and I have been worried to death about you,' Henrietta said after she'd pecked Madeleine on the cheek. 'Why didn't you let us know you were coming today?'

Madeleine smelt a whiff of her mother's expensive perfume as she stepped into the capacious hall with its black and white chequered tiles and curving staircase.

'I wasn't sure until the last minute. But there's no need to worry – I'm perfectly fine.'

'Thank goodness you finally came to your senses.'

Madeleine rolled her eyes. Was she going to have to put up with these snipes from now on?

'Where's Dad?'

Her mother drew her mouth in. 'Where do you think?'

'In his shack, I suppose.'

'It's where he practically lives.' Henrietta's tone held a bitter edge. 'I can't understand what he does in there all day.' She gave a long-suffering sigh. 'He tells me I'm just as bad sitting in a chair with my pen and notepad all day

– of course it's not all day – and at least I'm producing something which will bring in some money.' She regarded Madeleine closely. 'You say you're fine but you don't look fine to me with those dark circles under your eyes . . . you look tired out. Lily will take your things upstairs and you can have a rest until I call you when lunch is ready.' She patted her neat coiffure. 'I'd better go and tell her to set an extra place.'

'Don't bother Lily – I'll take my things upstairs myself. And I don't need to rest,' Madeleine tossed over her shoulder as she picked up her suitcase and struggled up the thickly carpeted staircase.

For a fleeting moment she wished she was back in the more modest home of Herr and Frau Weinberg. She wondered how they were coping. They must be heartbroken, letting their children go, not knowing how long it would be before they saw them again. Hopefully, they'd be able to get new passports and allowed to travel to Britain. Well, at least Fran would have rung them by now and they'd be relieved the children were safe. That was the main thing.

She dumped her luggage and looked round the spotless, soulless bedroom. She'd been gone the best part of a year and now barely recognised it. The flowery paintings her mother loved so much were still on the wall in the same place and her bookcase hadn't been touched. So why did she feel it was so unfamiliar? Was it being away – working in another country? Her eyes had been opened to so many different people and situations from those she'd known at home – the thousands of Nazis at the Nuremberg rally, the Weinbergs in Munich, and Herr Weinberg's friend, poor Herr Cohen, who was hauled out of his business by

116

the Gestapo, leaving a distraught wife. Had they ever set him free? And was Frederick back home with Fran in Berlin? She wished she knew the answers to these questions.

And what about Jack? There was something special between them, she was sure of it. If only she hadn't put that damned engagement ring of Frau Weinberg's on her own engagement finger, then at least he would have known she was single. But was *he*? For all she knew, he was married with four kids.

He'd asked her to write to let him know the twins were safely with their relatives in England, though that was nothing to do with his liking her or not. But that kiss. Briefly, she closed her eyes. She'd never forget the feel of his lips on hers. The faint masculine whiff of tobacco on his breath. The way it had turned to a far deeper kiss than she could have imagined. A tremor rushed through her. Had he been affected in the same way? Or had it been simply an impulse of the moment?

Whatever it was, she'd promised to write. She would do it this evening in her bedroom where she had some privacy.

With a vague feeling of not really being home, Madeleine went slowly downstairs and knocked on the door of her father's shack, then walked in.

'Maddie!' He gave her a warm hug. 'It's good to see you safe and sound.' He put her at arm's length and studied her. 'How was your journey?'

'It was okay.' *If he only knew.*

'Hmm, only okay.' He shook his head. 'Well, you've certainly given your mother a fright. She was sure you'd already been captured and thrown into a Nazi prison.'

'Hardly.' Madeleine bit back her irritation at her mother's irrationality.

117

She'd already decided not to go into any details about bringing the twins to England. Her mother would go on and on about the risk she'd taken for people who weren't even her own family.

'Mother says lunch is nearly ready.'

Her father chuckled. 'We'd better go in then.'

In the dining room, when Lily had finished serving the meal, Henrietta said:

'Why didn't you come back when you said you were going to?'

'There was a bit of an emergency in the family I was staying with so I wanted to help.'

'What sort of emergency?' her mother demanded.

'Oh, about the twins' education. Their teachers are questioning Jewish children.'

'Why was that?'

'So they can keep an accurate register of Jewish families, I suppose.' Madeleine put down her knife and fork. 'They're taking away even more normal privileges from Jewish people. Bit by bit they're closing in on them.'

'Then it's just as well you're out of it,' her mother said crisply.

The rest of lunch passed quietly until her father said:

'What have you decided to do now you're home, Madeleine?'

'Go back to university and finish her degree, I hope,' her mother snapped out before Madeleine could answer.

'No, I won't be doing that,' Madeleine said. 'From what I've seen in Germany, there's going to be another war and I want to find a job where my German will be useful straight away when that happens.'

Henrietta's forehead creased in exasperation. '*When* it happens? Don't talk such nonsense.'

'It's not nonsense. If you'd seen what I've seen—'

'I don't think it's nonsense either,' Walter Hamilton cut in. 'The BBC gives us regular news bulletins. And I've read articles in the paper from people who've actually experienced the Nazis at the sharp end and managed to tell their stories.' He threw a glance at his wife. 'It's going to happen, Henrietta, whether you like it or not.'

'Chamberlain won't allow it,' Henrietta said firmly.

'He won't have any say in the matter,' her husband said. 'He can't stand up to the likes of Hitler. No one's ever come across anyone like that piece of work before.' He caught Madeleine's eye. 'Did you ever see him ranting at one of his rallies?'

'Almost.' She told him briefly what had happened and how Herr Cohen had been dragged from his shop by the Gestapo. Madeleine watched her mother's jaw drop in horror.

'You sound like you've had quite a time of it,' her father said. 'I'm with your mother and am glad you're out of all that, but don't think for one minute we haven't got anti-Semitism here because we do. We've got that dreadful Mosley bloke collecting his band of merry Blackshirts. And ignorant people are joining him every day.'

'That's why I want to do something that will be of use.'

'Hmm.' Her father stroked his chin. 'You know, the Morse Code I taught you could come in handy for picking up enemy messages. They used to do that in the Great War, and I'm sure they'll use it in the next one, so it would be a very useful string to your bow.'

'I'll have lost my speed years ago and probably forgotten how to tap out the letters.'

'It wouldn't take long to get it back again when you've already learnt it.' He paused. 'When the war starts—'

'When you two have finished talking nonsense about the war which hasn't happened and isn't going to,' her mother cut in, her voice coated with sarcasm, 'perhaps you'd like to discuss your plans with your *mother*, Madeleine.'

'For heaven's sake, Mother, give me a chance—'

'There's no need for rudeness,' Henrietta snapped.

'Let the girl settle in, Henny.' Walter sent Madeleine a surreptitious wink. 'I don't imagine she's had an easy journey.'

'You could say that, Dad.' Madeleine clanked her knife and fork together, then glared at her mother. 'I think I'll go and unpack.'

That evening Madeleine took her writing pad and pen and sat at her desk in her bedroom. Jack had helped her before. Maybe he could steer her in the right direction. But how explicit should she be? She didn't want to get him into any kind of trouble but equally she didn't want to write to him as though she were applying for a job. Sighing, she unscrewed the top from her bottle of ink and filled her fountain pen.

*Dear Jack,*

*    You will be pleased to know that the journey went without any problems at all and I have delivered the goods as arranged! The family are charming and were very welcoming – all I could hope for. I shall keep in touch with them as often as I'm able.*

She stopped writing and cupped her chin in her hand. How much should she tell him? She didn't know him well enough to tell him the truth. Well, there was no need to go into any detail. Just stick to the facts. But was it a cheek to ask . . .? 'If you don't ask, you don't get,' her brothers were always fond of saying. Drawing her mouth into a determined line, she continued:

When I saw the advertisement to teach children in a private family in Bavaria, I jumped at it. I knew it would only be short-term but I'd see for myself what was really happening in Germany in light of all the rumours flying around at home.

From what I saw, the situation looks extremely serious, but I think you know that. And now I'm back in England I feel at a loose end where work is concerned. I was wondering if you could possibly suggest something I might be able to do to use my German. It's probably more conversational than formal and I'm sure now has a Bavarian twang! But if there really is a war, maybe it would be useful in some capacity. Anyway, I hope you don't mind my asking.

Lastly, I just want to thank you so much for what you did. It would have meant the world to my 'family' and they will never forget it.

Madeleine bit her lip. How should she end it? 'Yours sincerely' sounded so distant. But he *was* distant. He was hundreds of miles away. She'd never see him again so what was the point of trying to put any more meaning into something that was over before it began. In the end she simply wrote:

A week crawled by. She didn't expect to hear right away. But on the second week when she went downstairs full of anticipation as she picked up the early-morning post, to her intense disappointment there was nothing from Jack. Surely he'd had time to answer her letter. Maybe he thought her 'forward' for asking where she might try for a position using her German. Or maybe he was simply too busy at the British Embassy. She breathed out. Yes, that would be it. But then he wouldn't be at his desk twenty-four hours a day. There'd be time to write a short note. But maybe he felt it best to leave things as they were now they lived in separate countries. But that kiss. She shook her head. The sooner she forgot it, the better, because he'd immediately regretted it. She swallowed. He might, but she would never forget it as long as she lived.

Her ever-growing worry was to find suitable work. She was resigned to teaching English children German but it seemed that was the last thing parents wanted their children to learn. As for Erich and Lotte, she decided not to visit them too soon but to let them settle in with their aunt and uncle and cousins. Instead she sent them cards and notes, though received nothing in return except from Ruth who said they were adjusting as well as could be expected.

She felt as though she was forever waiting.

'Why is the British Embassy in Germany writing to you?' her mother demanded nearly three weeks later, holding an envelope with the flash of blue for airmail.

Madeleine felt a warmth creep up her neck. She wasn't going to mention anything about Jack.

'I just needed some advice. It's probably just a follow-up.'

'Why are you being so mysterious?'

'I'm not.'

'Who is this person you are so set on asking advice? Is it a boyfriend?'

'Mother, my letter . . .'

Her mother pulled her mouth into a thin line as she handed it over. Madeleine glanced at the postmark. Thankfully, it didn't state 'Berlin'. Trying to pretend a calm she didn't feel, she changed the subject, telling her mother she was going into town. At least she could sit in the library where she could read her letter and maybe have a browse in her favourite dress shop. She gave a rueful smile; fashion in Germany had not been much in evidence.

'May I borrow the car, Mother?'

'You'd better ask your father.' She paused. 'And if he agrees, don't drive like your brothers. They think they're piloting planes the way they speed.'

Minutes later Madeleine steered the grey Vauxhall out of the garage and turned it towards the town, thoughts tumbling over one another about Raymond and Gordon. Being pilots, and if there was a war, they'd probably be in the line of fire to defend Britain. It wasn't a pleasant image but it didn't surprise her that they were keen to do their duty by preparing for the worst.

Although the town was perfectly familiar to her, it felt strange to be back, and even more strange not to feel the sense of relief at being safely back at home. But when she opened the library door she was immediately soothed by the waft of book dust in the air, the hush that emanated from the two elderly women behind the counter and the few people quietly wandering around choosing books. She found a spot tucked in the corner of the Reference Room, telling herself the contents of this letter might change the course of her life. Perhaps she'd be doing something far more important and interesting than simply finishing her studies.

There was only one elderly gentleman sitting at a desk surrounded by a pile of books, brow creased as he made notes. He wouldn't disturb her, nor she him. She sat on an upright chair and opened her handbag to find her nail file. Slitting open the envelope, heart beating wildly, though why, she couldn't put into words, she removed the thin sheet of paper covered in spidery handwriting. She glanced at the bottom of the page. 'Yours, Jack'. She took a deep breath and read:

Dear Madeleine,

Thank you for letting me know so promptly that you all arrived safely, and that the relatives were so welcoming. What a relief for you and even more so for the parents. I'm pleased you're planning to keep in contact with them as they are certain to feel homesick from time to time and you will be bringing a little bit of home to them when they hear your voice. I'm sure you'll visit them when you can so they're bound to make strides with their English studies.

Now for your question. If things develop the way we foresee – maybe sooner than some people expect or believe – I think your German could be put to very good use. Why don't you try the Foreign Office in Whitehall? You may have to take a lowly job at the beginning but I'm sure you could work your way up. And no, I don't mind your asking one bit – in fact, I'm flattered.

By the way, there's no need to worry when you write

*again as your letters won't be censored by anyone – they go*
*safely into the diplomatic bag from England to Germany*
*and vice-versa and are not tampered with. Let me know if*
*anything transpires.*

> *Yours,*
> *Jack*

The Foreign Office. A tingle of excitement swept through her. This sounded exactly the kind of place she could imagine herself working in. The very title struck her as exotic. Maybe it was where they trained spies. She shook herself. She was getting carried away. First things first. How should she approach them? Surely they wouldn't allow her to just walk in and say she'd like to see someone about a job.

A thought occurred to her. What about if she presented Jack's card and said he'd suggested she speak to someone? But he'd just given her an idea and might not want his name brought up. She didn't know him well enough to judge.

Quickly, she skimmed the letter again in case she'd missed something.

*. . . when you write again . . .*

Mmm. It was like an invitation. But she wouldn't write a second time until she had something concrete to tell him. She didn't want to look too keen. And then she remembered. Jack thought she was engaged to another man, so not only would she look keen but she would look cheap. And that was the last impression she wanted to give him.

# Chapter Twelve

*November 1938*

Madeleine picked up her father's newspapers from the mat. Without glancing at either of the headlines, she put the *Daily Telegraph* on the desk in his shack and popped the *Daily Express* under her arm to read with her first cup of tea in the drawing room. She needed to keep up with the news, particularly from Germany.

**Pogrom goes on till night**
**LOOTING MOBS DEFY GOEBBELS**
**Jewish homes fired**
**Women beaten**

Dear God, what more. Nausea filling her throat, Madeleine began to read.

**All over Germany . . .**

With mounting trepidation she read that ninety-one Jews had been killed and hundreds injured by the Nazi stormtroopers, and thousands of windows smashed in anti-Jewish riots in Germany, Austria and the Sudetenland. Synagogues, Jewish businesses and their homes burnt, schools and hospitals partly or completely smashed or burnt to a cinder, cemeteries damaged, Jews disappearing, never to be seen again . . . the horror was relentless. The Germans called it *Kristallnacht* – Night of the Broken Glass.

Madeleine shuddered. The twins. Their parents. Herr Weinberg's music shop. The words blurred as tears poured down her cheeks and she angrily brushed them away with her sleeve. She forced herself to finish the article. And then she had to face the fact that the Weinbergs might also have been taken to one of those terrible concentration camps she'd read about. Or worse – they were no longer alive. And crying wouldn't get her anywhere. She could only think of one thing – how to play her part, however small, once Britain declared war on Germany, because it was clear it was inevitable. But what was the best way to prepare herself in the meantime? And what about the twins? She swallowed hard, dreading her next visit to see them. What on earth could she tell them?

'Dad, do you have a minute?'

Madeleine poked her head round the door of her father's shack, seeing the familiar figure bent over his desk writing notes in his logbook in his illegible handwriting. She noticed the bald patch on the crown of his head. Other than that, he looked about the same – still too thin for his height. She felt the tears prick remembering how successful he'd once been. A fine, upright businessman selling adding machines and typewriters and shop tills imported from a company in the States. But then in 1929 when the New York Stock Exchange crashed, the company went bankrupt.

The Wall Street crash in turn had had a disastrous effect on Great Britain's economy and unemployment had been rife.

*He's never really recovered*, Madeleine thought. That, and going through the Great War in those dreadful conditions, has taken the stuffing out of him – especially when Mother reminds him she's the only one bringing any money into the household. She sighed. The sooner she could earn her keep, the better.

At her voice her father removed his headphones and swivelled his chair round to look at his daughter.

'I need your advice.'

'Come in then.' When she was sitting on the spare chair he said, 'Fire away.'

'A few days before I came home I met someone – an English chap who works for the British Embassy in Berlin.'

Her father sat upright. 'Oh, yes. What was he doing in Munich then?'

She didn't want to go into any details because it would mean explaining about the twins. For some reason she felt she had to keep that episode to herself. The fewer people who knew about it the better. Someone could get into trouble. Her scalp still prickled just thinking about what she'd done bringing two Jewish German children to England on false British passports, with valuable jewellery stuffed into her handbag . . . and a ring on her finger that had given the wrong impression to—

She squashed the image of Jack's face. At least the ring was now safely with Ruth along with the other pieces of jewellery.

'It's a long story,' she went on. 'Anyway, I told him I

spoke German quite well and he suggested I approach the Foreign Office to get a job – something that might prove useful if there's a war.'

'Which we both know there *will* be.' Her father sucked on his pipe. 'It's not a bad idea but you'd probably end up as some sort of filing clerk which would be a pity for someone with your brains.' Brows drawn, he tapped his fountain pen on the desk for a few moments. 'Of course, you know what you *should* do.'

'No, that's why I'm asking you.'

'Like your mother said – you should go back to Kingston College. Finish your degree.'

'No, I don't want—'

'You asked for my advice, so let me finish. Then when the war starts you'll have your degree – something solid to offer to whomever you apply – which means you wouldn't have to start at the bottom so you'd be better paid for one thing and do something more interesting to boot.'

Madeleine stared at her father. The last thing she wanted was to go crawling back to Mr Graham, the principal. She could imagine his smugness as he told her to her face he would not let her darken the college doors again. No, she wouldn't put herself through such humiliation.

'You've always told us not to look over our shoulder and that's what I'd be doing. I'd be going backwards.'

'On the contrary, you'd be gaining. Don't you see, Madeleine?' He cleared his throat. 'And what's more, you'd ease a lot of tension between you and your mother.'

Madeleine sighed. There they were again. Wanting her to do something against her wishes. But then she didn't even know what her wishes were anymore.

*That's not quite true, Maddie. What about your dream? The one you've never told anyone – except Andrew at Kingston College. The only one who encouraged you. And where did that lead you?*

'So what do you think, Madeleine?'

Her father's voice brought her back to the present. Maybe if she had that piece of paper which seemed to mean so much to employers, it really would be the answer. And as her father said, at least Mother might stop criticising her.

'I need some time to think about it.'

Her father regarded her. 'The trouble with you, love, is that you can be a bit headstrong sometimes and don't always think things through.'

'That's not true. I—' She bit her lip. Nothing must slip out.

'I'm sure you've worked hard at your German and I imagine you have a good command of it, but now you're home again you need to settle at something. And the obvious thing for you is to teach. It's what your mother has always wanted for you.'

*But I wanted to go to drama school and you and Mother pooh-poohed it without even giving me a chance. Wasting your brain, Mother had said. As though learning Shakespeare off by heart wasn't using your brain.*

She thought of the twins and how she missed them. To her pleasant surprise, she'd enjoyed teaching much more than she'd expected. But a class of thirty children would be a different thing altogether.

'It doesn't really excite me, Dad. I enjoyed teaching the twins tremendously, but it's because I got to know them so well. They were such characters and I grew fond of them. But I don't really want to stand up in front of thirty children every day.'

'Well, then, do as I suggest. Finish your language degree and then do private teaching if by some miracle the war doesn't intervene.'

'The autumn term has already started.'

Her father cracked a smile.

'Knowing you, you'd soon catch up. Then you'll have something concrete to offer the Foreign Office or any other organisation when we're at war.' He swung round to his desk and picked up his headphones, saying he must get on, then suddenly swivelled round again. 'Working for the Foreign Office is not a bad idea actually.' He gazed directly at her. 'This chap you've met who suggested it – is he special?'

Madeleine startled at the sudden change of subject. 'Why do you say that?'

'The deliberately casual way you mentioned him. The way your cheeks went pink. The "long story" you didn't want to enlighten me with.' He took a few puffs on his pipe. 'Well . . . am I right?'

Not for the first time she thought her father had more insight than her mother.

'He was a good friend when I needed one.'

'Oh! Why's that? Were you in some kind of trouble?'

'I don't want to talk about it. It's all a bit raw.' When he raised an eyebrow, she felt her face warm even more. 'No, nothing of *that* sort. It's just that I've had quite a few upheavals these last days. Nothing to do with Jack – in fact, he helped me, b-but—'

She felt her eyes sting.

'Come on, love. You can tell your old dad.' He gave her

an encouraging smile. 'And explain how this Jack comes into it.'

Her heart contracted. 'You're not that old,' she managed a weak smile in return.

And then a wave of helplessness threatened to sweep her off her feet. She felt dizzy. Maybe it was just the smoke from her father's pipe. Without warning, she put her head in her hands and sobbed.

She felt his hand on her shoulder, and knew he was trying in his way to comfort her.

'Shall I go and fetch your mother?'

Madeleine's head shot up.

'No, don't. She always criticises everything I do. I can't take it, Dad.'

'Oh, dear. I think you're in some sort of delayed shock. I wish you'd tell me what happened when you were out in Germany. I'm not an ogre, you know. I will listen.' He handed her his handkerchief.

She mopped her eyes and hearing the concern in his voice said:

'I witnessed some pretty horrible things and saw how it's affecting everyone, especially Jewish people. Worse, the children. It's made me determined to do something to help.'

'I reckon completing your language degree would get you closer to the war when it comes. There's bound to be a huge demand for fluent German speakers and likely not enough to meet that need. But employers are always impressed with the piece of paper showing your qualifications. It will put you in front of everyone else.'

She was beginning to see that her father's suggestion made sense.

'Well, if you think it really would make a difference, I'll go back and do the final year.'

'That's my girl.'

Two days later Madeleine found herself for the second time in an interview at her old college facing Mr Graham, the principal, who was leaning back in his leather chair looking at her, a sanctimonious expression on his face.

'So you want to come back to us, hmm? I'm not sure about that.'

'I made a mistake a year ago,' Madeleine said. 'I've grown up a bit since I've lived in Germany. There's going to be a war sooner or later and I want to be as well prepared as possible to help. And I think my German could help.'

'I doubt very much you'll need it in that capacity,' he said. 'Thank God our Prime Minister is determined to avoid war. That's what the Munich Agreement is all about.' He looked at her. 'They've all signed. Chamberlain, that French chap, Daladier, Mussolini and Hitler. They don't want a war any more than we do.' He paused, his piercing eyes fixed on her. 'You've just come from Munich so you should know better than anyone.'

'The German *people* don't want a war,' Madeleine conceded, 'but the Nazis *do*.'

He shook his head. She could see he was not going to be persuaded. So how would she persuade him to allow her back in the school?

'Anyway, I'd be grateful if you'd give me a second chance,' Madeleine said, pushing down her irritation with this ignorant man.

He drummed his fingers on the desk, his mouth pulled

tight. After a while he got up from his chair and strolled over to the window, his hands linked behind his back.

'I thought long and hard about your letter and decided to allow you to finish your degree. But if there's any trouble *what-so-ever* –' he swung round and shot her a steely look '– you'll be out. And I won't be listening to any excuses.'

She swallowed the retort that had sprung onto her lips.

'I won't let you down.'

'See that you don't.' She waited while he went back to his desk and lit his pipe. He took his time to get it going before he continued. 'You can sign in at Reception. The autumn term has already started so you'll have to work hard to catch up. We'll send you an invoice which needs to be paid in full before you start.' He blew a stream of smoke above her head. 'We'll expect to see you at half-past eight tomorrow morning. Let us hope you'll stick the full year this time.'

The next day as Madeleine looked round the classroom, there was no one she recognised. Of course, there wouldn't be, she told herself crossly – they'd all finished their three years and been given their certificate and had probably got teaching jobs by now. Which *she* should have done. But when she heard the others moaning about their boyfriends and worrying about what they were going to wear at the next dance, with little mention of what was threatening to explode on the other side of the English Channel, Madeleine was glad she hadn't followed suit. At least she wasn't ignorant about what was happening over there. She'd 'saved' two children. It sounded dramatic, but that's how the twins' parents would see it. She'd met Gwen with whom she'd keep in touch . . . and she'd met Jack.

To her disappointment, the German she'd learnt in Bavaria was mostly a hindrance. She didn't pronounce the words in the right way – 'Auf hoch Deutsch, bitte,' Frau Heil snapped several times a day, throwing her arms up in exasperation. She hadn't studied any literature which put her at a disadvantage when Frau Heil announced the first test result. She'd come bottom but one in class. But in her oral tests she shone with only one girl beating her, who had a German mother.

*Just put your head down for once, Maddie, and get on with it.*

She soon fell into a routine. Evenings were usually taken up with homework but once a week she spoke to the twins on the telephone. Then after a fortnight she went to the Whites to see how everyone was coping. Although the twins looked well they were puzzled that their parents hadn't joined them by now and couldn't understand why they hadn't even had a letter.

'When are they coming to fetch us?' Lotte kept asking, to which she could only give vague answers.

Madeleine bit her lip. She couldn't tell them her fears and worry them unnecessarily when they might well receive a letter from home soon. But weeks had gone by. The good thing was that they'd seemed to have settled in well and Lotte in particular enjoyed playing with her three girl cousins, the older two having taken her under their wing. Erich only joined in if he could be in charge, Lotte said, but that only worked when she was playing with Eva, the youngest cousin. And the two of them together often didn't allow him a look-in. *Poor Erich*, Madeleine thought. He was a good boy and had always kept an eye out for his sister. But at least now they'd started school Erich was sure to make friends of his own. Ruth said their teacher told her they'd settled in well and their written and spoken English was improving considerably.

Although she'd written twice to Herr and Frau Weinberg she'd never heard back from them. And when Fran wrote to tell her she'd had a piece of wonderful news that the Gestapo had allowed Freddie to come home, *although he knows they're watching him closely*, Fran had written, *I'm afraid we have to expect the worst for the Weinbergs as I've heard nothing either.*

Madeleine shivered at the enormity of Fran's words. Supposing it *was* the worst. How would she break the news to the twins? She felt her stomach knot. And it was the twins' ninth birthday this month, 26th November. Even if the Weinbergs were not able to travel to England, she prayed they would manage to send a birthday card in time.

At any rate, she would risk the wrath of Mr Graham and take a day off from college to see the twins on their birthday.

Madeleine could hear Lotte's excited shouts before Ruth even had the front door open.

'It's lovely to see you, dear. Come on in. I'll make a pot of tea.'

'Look what Auntie Ruth 's made for us,' Lotte squealed as she rushed into the kitchen. 'A chocolate birthday cake.'

'That's wonderful, love,' Madeleine said. Goodness, where was the child's German accent? It had all but disappeared. She smiled. Lotte would have poured every effort into speaking like the English children.

Erich came through the door and formally held out his hand. She shook it, and then unexpectedly he flung himself into her arms.

'We have not had a letter from Mutti.' His eyes were bright with tears. 'Have you, Maddie?'

She shook her head.

'Not yet, love. But I expect they're busy sorting and packing. It's a big job.'

Oh, was she saying the wrong thing? Getting their hopes up. Erich threw her an old-fashioned look but didn't say anything. Thankfully, Lotte was too absorbed in her new jigsaw puzzle.

It had been a wrench to say goodbye to the twins. She prayed they'd hear from their parents by the time she saw them at Christmas.

But Christmas came and went and still there was no news from Munich.

But there was a letter from Jack. It was dated 21st December 1938.

*Dear Madeleine,*

*I hope this reaches you in time to wish you a Merry Christmas and a Happy New Year, although I'm not optimistic about what the next year will bring. I'm sorry not to have written before but my job has kept me very busy.*

*I wanted to check how you were and also, of course, the twins. What have you decided to do now you're back in England? Or is that too personal to ask?*

*I'll cut this short but I'd love to hear from you.*

*Yours,*

*Jack*

Madeleine frowned. What did he mean about being 'too personal to ask' about what she was doing now? Then it struck her. Of course! He was hinting that she might be making preparations for her wedding day! Oh, it was too bad. There was no possible way she could tell him about Frau Weinberg's engagement ring – well, not in a letter anyway, even though Jack had assured her that any letter would never be opened by anyone but himself.

She'd write back and tell him her decision to finish her degree and describe her last visit to the twins with no mention of anything personal, even though she longed more than anything to let him know the truth about the non-existent fiancé.

138

# Chapter Thirteen

*Richmond*
*1939*

Winter gave way to spring, which seemed to offer fresh
hope to people's spirits even though Chamberlain
announced to the German government that if they invaded
Poland, then France and Britain would go to their aid. It
was an ultimatum of the most serious kind but whether it
was enough to frighten Hitler off any invasion plans,
Madeleine doubted, by the little she'd gleaned about the
dictator when she'd lived in Germany. And so, it seemed,
did the government doubt, as a few weeks later they
introduced the Military Training Act for all British men
aged twenty and twenty-one who were 'fit and able' to take
six months' military training. It looked to Madeleine very
much as if Britain was gearing up for war.

The weeks at the college were flying by. She might have
had one more year to go, but she was way ahead of the
class in the oral tests, thanks to having recently lived in
Germany. It had bolstered her confidence but all the time
she felt she was playing a waiting game. As though the
whole world was on the edge of something momentous,

something terrible they were rolling inexorably towards, and there was nothing anyone could do about it.

She'd heard nothing more from Jack after her reply to his letter at the end of last year and had learnt to swallow her disappointment when the postman left her the occasional letter from her brothers, more regularly from Gwen, and the odd note from the twins. Maybe thinking she and Jack had something special was on her side only, she forced herself to conclude. Well, why should he write? He probably thought she was already married by now. Should she write to him again? Telling him how she was getting on with her German? Shrugging, she decided against it. What would be the point? She had nothing interesting to tell him.

Then when Madeleine had almost given up hope and was about to leave for college, she heard the postman drop something through the letter box. Rushing to the front door she stooped to pick up an airmail letter from the mat. She glanced at the typed address with the British Embassy postmark dated 16 March 1939; it was now 2nd April. Her heart leapt. Jack! She shouldn't stop now or she'd be late for class. Too bad. She ran upstairs to her room and tore open the envelope, quite forgetting to use the paperknife.

*My dear Madeleine,*

*Take no notice if you don't hear from me very often because I never know what my movements will be from one day to the other. This time I was called away unexpectedly for a few weeks but I'm back in Berlin now.*

*I think you're wise to finish your degree course as it will hold you in very good stead for anything that turns up. Did you do anything about the Foreign Office? I'm just thinking out loud – have you thought about joining up? If so, I think the WAAFs would suit you to a tee.*

*Let me know how the twins are doing. Did you ever hear from their parents? If not, you may have to be prepared for the worst, I'm sorry to say. The news is not good here. I try to keep occupied in a positive way when I'm not working by reading German literature and listening to music. Funny how Mozart was born an Austrian, the same as the Führer. Difficult to reconcile, isn't it?*

*I often think about writing to you but there's so little to tell you in these strange circumstances. But then if things were normal we would never have met! Have you ever thought of that? I'll leave that question with you and sign off.*

*Yours,*

*Jack*


Madeleine read the letter so swiftly she felt she wasn't taking it in.

Slow up, she told herself. There was a difference in Jack's tone and wording in this latest letter. *My dear Madeleine.* And that last paragraph. It was more personal. And an intriguing ending, as though inviting her to have a good think about what it meant to her that they had met. She shook herself. As usual she was reading far too much into an ordinary friendly letter. But it wasn't ordinary; it wasn't Jack just being friendly – she was sure of it. And what was all that about being away unexpectedly? Had he come to London? If so, it would have been nice if he'd looked her up. Maybe met for a drink.

Not for the first time her mind flashed back to that kiss.

She could feel the pressure of his lips on hers. The hint of tobacco. His mouth warm and firm . . . and that strange sense of unfulfilled longing. She'd sensed it, too, and kissed him back with the same intensity. Her cheeks flushed with the memory – now so strong, he seemed to be within touching distance. She felt her body quiver.

And then she remembered how he'd put her away from him. The shock she'd felt when she was no longer in his arms. The way he'd apologised for kissing her.

'You're engaged to someone else,' he'd said.

It all came back to the same thing. It was too late for her to ever let him know the truth.

# *Chapter Fourteen*

Jack shut his office door, which he mostly kept open to invite anyone in who might wish to speak to him, or was simply passing. He longed for a few minutes' peace from phone calls and letters that had needed his urgent and focused attention since he'd returned from his monthly meeting with the Polish cryptographers in Warsaw. The letter from Madeleine was burning a hole in his pocket and he was grateful to see that his colleague was not at his desk, neither was his jacket on the back of his chair. Jack blew out a sigh of relief. It seemed he might have a bit of privacy for the time being. Not that Norman Sudgeon, the commercial attaché, was difficult at all. On the contrary, Sudgeon was an easy-going bloke to rub along with when he wasn't attending some business event or other, although when in the office he had a terrible habit of repeatedly clearing his throat, setting Jack's teeth on edge. But at least Sudgeon didn't question his schedule or delve into his personal life.

Things were reaching a crisis point. Only a week ago

Ribbentrop met Mussolini's son-in-law, Count Ciano, in Italy, the two of them agreeing to sign a military alliance of the Rome–Berlin Axis. Thank heavens Great Britain had made it formally known they were ready to assist Poland if Hitler attacked them. It had put the British into a stronger position of trust and decency, and the Poles were willing to share their knowledge on their astounding success with cracking the Enigma cipher machine keys in traffic they were picking up.

Jack sighed. It was becoming more difficult by the week to play-act that he was merely a cultural diplomat; he had enough new intelligence now for the Government Code and Cypher School to warrant another trip to London. To Whitehall, precisely, although he'd been told by his superior that they'd bought another place in the country – some Victorian pile only fifty miles from London – and would shortly be moving. Jack was interested in seeing the set-up after they'd moved, which was planned for August. He needed to touch base with them within days, not weeks. The only thing now would be to clear it with the ambassador, Sir Nevile Henderson – a decent enough bloke though a bit too obsessed with fashion for his liking. Ambassador Henderson always endeavoured to look the perfect English gentleman in his Savoy suits and that daily fresh carnation pinned to his lapel, appearing not in the least worried if the German government sniggered behind his back.

Jack gave a wry smile. It wasn't his cup of tea at all but perhaps it wouldn't hurt to smarten himself up a bit – something he hadn't bothered quite so much about in these last years – that is, until he'd set eyes on Maddie Hamilton, as he called her in his head.

But all he wanted to do this minute was read her letter.

With a tingle of anticipation, he sat at his desk and lit a cigarette, then slit open the envelope with the now familiar handwriting that had been delivered by the office boy more than two hours ago. He wouldn't admit his heart was beating a little faster as he wondered what it might contain. It always felt like a red-letter day when he heard from Madeleine, which was not often enough for his liking. He just couldn't get her out of his mind. Those alluring eyes – a luminous green – he'd never seen such a colour. Her hair streaked with gold. He let his mind drift, imagining himself taking out those combs, letting her hair fall loose to her shoulders. That figure . . . Damn shame she was already engaged to someone else. Lucky bugger to get someone so stunning who was not only intelligent but brimming with courage – the way she'd got those twins to safety, knowing she could be endangering her own life. And then there was that kiss. The way she'd responded. He would never forget it as long as he lived. He felt the hairs stand up on the back of his neck just reliving it. Damn it all, why couldn't he have met her first? He took a swallow of the tea Joan had left him, now lukewarm, and read:

*Dear Jack,*

*Thank you for your last letter. The time has flown by and I'll be taking exams in a month's time. I fervently hope I'll pass them, particularly in German, which I imagine would be more useful when one sees what's happening over there. You would know this more than anyone. As soon as I get the results – we're told no later than the beginning of September – then I thought that would be the time to apply to the Foreign Office for any suitable vacancy. Do you have any advice on this?*

145

Yes, he did. He'd come to that later. Pulling in a deep drag of his cigarette, he read on, blowing the smoke out, causing the two sheets of paper to flutter:

*The twins are doing exceptionally well at school but we have still heard nothing from their parents. I dread to think what might have happened to them. It's difficult to know what to say to the children. Lotte in particular is taking it hard. I think Erich feels just as bad but puts on a brave face. It's heartbreaking but their aunt and uncle are kindness itself. I'm so relieved I could bring them with me rather than have them do that journey on their own on the Kindertransport that I keep reading about. But I'm happy more Jewish children are managing to get out of Germany, even though some of them will be scared to death – poor little mites. But every child we save seems to me a miracle.*

Jack briefly shut his eyes, thinking of his own child. Would it have been a boy or a girl? Either way it wouldn't have mattered. He'd been as thrilled as Kathy when she'd told him she was going to have a baby. But now he would never know. All he could see, filling his head, was the shocking image of Kathy, blood pouring from her head, her skin transparent . . . the doctor's dreadful two words – *I'm sorry*. Jack swallowed hard. It was three years ago now but it was still raw.

Thank God those twins had arrived safely in England. He read on:

*As for news, I imagine you are witnessing much more than we do here at home but we are definitely preparing*

146

*for the worst. The signs are everywhere – sandbags, posters encouraging men and women to join up, bomb shelters springing up like mushrooms in gardens lately – yet people are carrying on with their lives. I suppose there's not much else we can do.*

*I'd better close as I have exams looming and need to revise.*

*As you said to me, look after yourself.*
*Madeleine*

Frowning, he read the letter again. Why was there never any mention of the fiancé? Or any wedding plans. It was puzzling. Maybe she thought with the impending war, now was not the time. But when the war *did* start – and the way things were going it would be within weeks rather than months – it would almost certainly last for several years. It seemed to him a long time to be engaged. Well, it was none of his business.

He stubbed out his cigarette with more ferocity than the action warranted. He just didn't want to lose contact with her, that was all. Telling himself he just needed to know she was safe and well after her difficult time in Germany, he tried to swallow but his mouth had gone dry. He stood and took his jacket from the back of the chair.

*Too many cigarettes, old chap. What you need is some air . . . and a gallon of coffee.*

# Chapter Fifteen

'This morning, the British Ambassador in Berlin handed the German government a final note, stating that unless we heard from them by eleven o'clock that they were prepared at once to withdraw their troops from Poland, a state of war would exist between us. I have to tell you now that no such undertaking has been received and that consequently, this country is at war with Germany.'

Even though the grave announcement was no real surprise, Madeleine felt shock waves pounding through her body. It was unbelievable that it was really happening – what everyone had dreaded. Her brothers. A knot of anxiety took hold of her. What would happen to them?

'Dear God, here we go again.' Walter Hamilton blew out his cheeks. 'Poor old Chamberlain sounds on his knees with exhaustion.' Turning to his wife sitting in her armchair gazing at the empty fireplace, he added, 'I don't like to say "I told you so", my dear.'

Henrietta Hamilton didn't stir, even when the National Anthem began and her husband and daughter automatically jumped to their feet lustily singing 'God save our gracious King', but stared stonily ahead.

'Mother, are you all right?'

It was as though her mother hadn't heard. Or had decided to ignore her. Madeleine glanced at her father who shook his head at her, warning her not to delve further.

'I'll go and make some tea,' Madeleine said.

Out in the kitchen, Jack sprang to her mind. Had he already left Berlin? If not, he'd definitely be on his way back within days, maybe hours, now that the two countries were finally at war. Even the Nazis wouldn't arrest diplomats, would they? A frisson of anticipation swept through her. Could it mean they might meet again? His kiss – had it been just a mild flirtation of the moment? She'd turned the question over in her mind so many times. It had seemed so much more than that but she hadn't been kissed properly by anyone since Andrew, so how could she judge it with any accuracy? She sighed, wondering how long the world would be in turmoil before it returned to normal – whatever that was.

She picked up the tea tray and was just bringing it into the drawing room when the most terrible whining scream shrilled through the air, causing the hairs to stand up at the back of her neck.

'What on earth—?' she began, her heart giving sickening leaps.

'It's the air-raid siren,' her father said, 'but Jerry couldn't have got here this quickly. It'll be a practice one, don't worry.' He paused. 'But I'll go outside and have a look, just to make sure.'

Madeleine followed her father out of the front door. His head was thrown back as he scanned the clouds.

'Can't see any sign of any action,' he said as she came and stood by his side.

'I'm joining up, Dad,' she said quietly.

He swung round to look at her. 'What service?'

'The WAAFs.'

'Not the Army, like your old dad?' He struck a match and attempted to light his pipe in the breeze.

She shook her head. 'No, the Air Force appealed more.'

'I thought you were going to apply to the Foreign Office.'

She shrugged. 'I don't want to waste time and then be told they don't have anything for me. But now there really is going to be a war, I'm sure I won't have any difficulty in being recruited.'

'Hmm. I can't see you enjoying all that marching and saluting.' Her father studied her. 'This wouldn't have anything to do with this Jack you met in Germany who helped you in some mysterious way, would it?'

Madeleine felt her face flush at the sound of his name.

'He did mention it as a possibility when he last wrote,' she said reluctantly.

'So he keeps up with you?'

'Occasionally.'

'Well, good for you. It's probably sensible. And I'm sure they'll make use of your languages when you tell them.' He cleared his throat. 'But I don't envy you telling your mother.'

'I'm going in right now to tell her.'

'Yes. Best get it over with.'

She left him making little popping noises to get his pipe going.

Her mother was sitting in the same position, her cup of tea still full.

'Mother? You've let your tea go cold.'

Henrietta shook her head. 'It doesn't matter, does it?' Her tone was flat. 'Nothing matters now except my boys.'

'Mother, I understand. I know you're worried what this will mean for them.'

'Not just them!' Her mother's deep blue eyes flashed as she looked up at her daughter. 'For every mother. It's the most dreadful news. We've only gone twenty years since the last one. Oh, to think I believed Chamberlain's "peace in our time". Silly old fool.' She caught her breath, keeping her gaze fixed on Madeleine. 'But when you secure a sensible teaching post you'll be able to stay home because it will be a reserved occupation.'

*Now, Maddie.*

'Mother, I have to do my bit for the country. All my friends are going to join up and I'm going as well.'

There was a sharp hiss of breath.

'This was your plan all along, wasn't it?' Henrietta said sharply. When Madeleine didn't answer she carried on, 'You've failed me once before, Madeleine – don't do it to me again.'

*Will Mother ever let me forget it?*

She turned her attention to her father who had followed her in.

'Dad . . . can you please talk to Mother. She won't even try to understand—'

'Madeleine's right, my dear,' he interrupted. 'I remember saying the same thing to my own parents in the last one.'

'You were a man,' Henrietta said. 'We're talking about our daughter.'

'I was a boy,' Walter reminded his wife. 'Eighteen, to be precise. We lads thought it would be a bit of a lark –

151

girlfriends telling us we were heroes – that sort of nonsense. But we were soon brought down to earth when we saw our living conditions and the full horror struck us when our mates were blown to pieces.' He took out a handkerchief and wiped his eyes. 'Those of us left could never work out the reason why the war had erupted into a world war, but this time Hitler's a huge threat to our democracy . . . to the world. He's a maniac. And Madeleine's seen some of that first hand. We have to stop him. And if Madeleine wants to help, that's her decision. The good thing is that women won't be sent to the front – unless they're nurses.' He smiled at his daughter, then turned back to Henrietta. 'So I will support her every step of the way.'

The next day Madeleine sat in the drawing room, filling in the forms she'd picked up in the library to join the Women's Auxiliary Air Force, when the doorbell rang. She jumped up and opened the door to a young lad, smartly dressed in his navy-blue uniform, his pill-box hat cheekily angled, and his bicycle propped against the wall.

'Hello, miss,' he said, giving her an admiring grin. 'Are you Miss Hamilton?'

She nodded, bracing herself.

'Telegram for you,' he said, thrusting a brown envelope in her hand. 'Sign here, miss.'

She scrawled her signature on the lined form underneath several other names. Her heart beat hard. Telegrams had a reputation of bringing bad news. A sickening thought occurred to her. Was it something to do with the twins? She gulped and fled indoors, then remembered something, snatched a sixpence from her purse and opened the front door again, pressing it into the boy's open palm.

'Very kind of you, miss.' And with that, he ran his bicycle up the drive, jumped on it and sent her a cheery wave.

With dread in the pit of her stomach, she sat in her father's armchair and tore open the envelope.

Miss M Hamilton please report for duty at Station X in Buckinghamshire on 5 September stop Your postal address is Box 111 c/o The Foreign Office stop Travel warrant to follow.

*Dear God. The Foreign Office! Where Jack suggested I might apply for a job. Could he have had anything to do with this?*

She stared at the words again. The date – she was supposed to report the day after tomorrow! Was it a hoax? After all, war had only just been declared and now she had just one day's notice to pack her things and leave home for who knows how long. Her mother would certainly have something to say about it. She'd be furious and come up with all kinds of reasons why her daughter shouldn't – *mustn't* – be allowed to go. Madeleine took in a jagged breath. It was impossible. But now the war had started perhaps this kind of thing was to be expected if the government was trying to recruit people as quickly as possible.

Should she accept it? But the way it was worded, it didn't look like she had any choice. The sudden realisation swept over her that this was her chance, her opportunity to do something interesting, to make her own contribution, small though it may be, to fighting Hitler. Even though it would mean yet another row with her mother.

The travel warrant for her one-way train fare came in

the midday post with strict instructions not to breathe a word to anyone – even her close family. Security was paramount. If anyone questioned her she was to say that she was a clerk in the war office, but the anonymous writer had given no hint as to what her work would actually be. When she arrived at Bletchley station she was to call this number from the phone box just outside and would be given directions as to how to get to Station X. She was to arrive no later than 10 a.m.

How badly she wanted to discuss it with her father. He'd be so interested. But she couldn't even give him a hint. All she could say was what the letter had commanded her to say – that she was going to work as a clerk in the war office. But she was sure her father would immediately gather it was something more out of the ordinary than that. He was a shrewd man. After all, he'd served in the Great War.

A shiver of excitement ran across her shoulders. It seemed certain now where her destiny lay, even though she had not the slightest idea where Station X was or what it could possibly stand for.

# *Chapter Sixteen*

*Berlin*
*3rd September 1939*

'Sylvester, stop the clock!'

The hands of the clock in the British Embassy's meeting room showed two minutes after eleven. Jack stayed the pendulum with his hand. There was a sharp intake of breath from one of the younger secretaries as the timepiece ticked its last tock. Jack went back to his standing position on the sidelines where he could watch everyone's reactions, then glanced towards the Ambassador who had issued the order.

Sir Nevile Henderson looked grey, as though any remnants of energy had now evaporated. Gone was the fresh carnation he wore in his lapel every day; the moustache drooped over tired lips, and under his eyes were deep bags. His hands held on to the edge of the table in front of him as though he was worried he might keel over at any moment. It wasn't surprising, Jack thought. That morning at nine o'clock the Ambassador had gone to the German Foreign Ministry to deliver a message to Hitler from the Prime Minister but had ended up having to hand it to Schmidt,

Hitler's interpreter. It stated that unless the German government withdrew its troops from Poland or began the process by eleven o'clock that morning, a state of war would exist between Britain and Germany.

'There has been no reply to our ultimatum.' He briefly closed his eyes, then continued: 'I deeply regret that all my efforts did not bring about peace, although I ask you to bear no grudge against the German people.' He paused. 'I must tell you all that we are now at war with Germany.' Failure oozed from every pore of the Ambassador's tired face as he spoke those words. 'And now I'm afraid I have something more to add.' Fingering the spot on his jacket where his carnation was usually pinned, he cleared his throat. 'When the Germans invaded Poland on Friday, I was made to understand that if we declared war on Germany, I would be obliged to leave a number of staff behind until every German diplomat around the British Empire has returned home. I'm afraid that means thirty-seven of you.' He cast his eyes around the room, allowing his gaze to alight on some of the senior officers. 'Being forewarned, I've made a list and anyone on it will remain here at the Embassy until such time.'

'As hostages.' Jack's raised voice was coated with exasperation. Several colleagues turned to stare at him.

'You could call it that, Sylvester.' Sir Nevile cleared his throat. 'To carry on –' he sent an unblinking gaze around the room, large enough to seat the two hundred or so diplomats '– I will now read out the names from the list.' He paused. 'You'll note I've kept to single officers as far as possible.' He cleared his throat again and Jack realised the man was not only worn out but also nervous. There was a deathly hush.

'Harold Blunt, William Carter, Colin Clark, Irene Davis . . .'

Sir Nevile's voice droned on until the last part of the alphabet. Jack was counting. Already thirty-six and he hadn't been called. Only one more to go and there were several other single officers like Taylor, Vant and White to choose from.

'And finally, James Sylvester.'

Jack startled. Damn and blast. The last thing he wanted when he had such vital work to do for the Foreign Office. If only he'd been able to have a conversation with Sir Nevile beforehand. But he'd been told even the Prime Minister wasn't aware of this new set-up in Buckinghamshire, it was so hush-hush. He forced himself to listen to the Ambassador's next words.

'Anything that could be of the merest interest to the Nazis – machinery, paperwork, files, etcetera, must be destroyed. The Embassy is to be closed down but those of you staying behind will all live under this roof until it's time for you to be released. And that means twenty-four hours a day, *every* day. Take your pick of the various fold-up beds and bunks. Obviously, the women will live in separate quarters. When you need to buy food you will be escorted by armed guards who will be permanently placed outside the building. The canteen staff, albeit dwindled, will prepare your meals as usual.' He paused. 'There's no need for me to say that you will all behave impeccably. I don't want anything to come to my ears that can be construed as hostile in any way to what was once our host country. We will show those Nazis how people behave in a civilised society.' He glared at the crowd, as though daring them to be anything other than high-minded ladies and gentlemen.

\* \* \*

157

The following morning at half-past eleven, Jack and the other remaining staff crowded outside to say goodbye to the Ambassador and the other diplomats. Several German soldiers hung around, fingering their rifles as though warning against any trouble.

'Good luck to all of you,' Sir Nevile said, turning to the group for the last time. 'I'm only sorry to leave some of you behind. We gave it our best shot, trying to show the German people the British have more in common with them than with issues we disagree on.' His forehead creased. 'Just a shame we weren't successful.'

That afternoon Jack sat in the office he'd shared with Sudgeon for the last two years. The only one he was sharing with now was Dexter, once a forlorn-looking mutt he'd noticed sniffing round the rubbish bins at the rear of the block of flats where he lived. The dog had kept up a steady trot behind him, despite having lost one of his hind legs, when Jack was on his way to the Embassy one morning. Since then the dog had barely left his side and was now in his basket snoring contentedly.

Jack put his feet on the desk and blew out his cheeks. Dexter would have to be put into quarantine in Britain for several months – that is, if the Nazis allowed the dog to go with him. Well, he'd bloody smuggle him out if he had to though how, he had no idea. He lit a cigarette and inhaled deeply, thinking of Sudgeon and the others. Lucky buggers going home. It was plain Sir Nevile had tried his very best to mediate for peace right up to the final moment but at the last meeting he'd had with Hitler only days ago, the Führer had been in no mood to listen or discuss it. His war machine was standing by, ready for action, and he was obviously itching to press the button.

It was too depressing for words. Jack stretched his arms above his head and yawned. What was the time? He glanced at his watch. Only four. Pity it was too early for a drink. Tea would have to do. He'd ring Nancy, his favourite secretary and ask if she'd organise it.

He picked up the receiver, then changed his mind. He needed to speak to someone – *anyone* – urgently in SIS. Let them know the situation.

'Operator, put me through to—'

The line suddenly went dead. He tapped the connection button vigorously but there was nothing. In an instant he realised what had happened. The buggers had cut the bloody wires. He slammed the receiver down. The next couple of months – because that was the minimum time it would take those diplomats in far-flung countries like Australia and New Zealand to return, even if there were ships and planes immediately available – were going to be frustrating, to say the least. He went to the window and looked out to see two armed German police officers hobnobbing below.

*We're only a step away from imprisonment. Correction. Right here is now our prison.*

All very well for those who were at this very minute on a sealed train making its way back to England just when he'd thought he was going home and there'd be a good chance of seeing Maddie again. Finding out if she was any closer to being married than when they'd last met. But his hopes had fallen around his feet yesterday morning. Thirty-seven to stay behind. And he was bloody one of them.

Jack blew out an irritable stream of smoke. What else did the Nazis have tucked up their sleeves as punishment? His thoughts wandered to Sir Nevile. Poor bloke. It hadn't been for the want of trying that their Ambassador had failed miserably in his mission to coordinate Britain and Germany in negotiating for peace. But then, Jack admitted, his own official role in bringing British culture to the Germans had had little chance to do any good. Hitler was in total control of what music could and couldn't be played, ordering certain books to be burnt that he considered a bad influence on the German people, and curtailing any pleasures that he saw as a threat to the purity of the Aryan race. And Jack's contact at the Culture Ministry had been the most obnoxious and uncultured bigot he had ever come across. He inhaled deeply on his cigarette. At least that was one bloody Nazi he'd never have to set eyes on again. Or have to keep up the pretence. He could concentrate on intelligence gathering. But how prepared the SIS was for war, he dreaded to think.

Jack's eye caught sight of the glass paperweight his wife, Kathy, had given him on their last wedding anniversary together, and the small, framed snapshot of her holding their black and white cat, Billie. He stared at the photograph. She looked so happy then, her fair hair blowing back in the breeze. But that was before the accident . . . He closed his eyes, heart thudding as it always did when he thought about that lorry suddenly looming out of nowhere.

In the years since Kathy died he hadn't felt close to another woman. Yes, he'd dated a few – probably taken things too far occasionally – and he'd even had the odd supper with one of the secretaries at the Embassy who he knew had a soft spot for him. But no one had given his life any meaning – until Maddie.

He looked round the room, taking in all the details as though for the first time when he'd arrived in May '37, a

160

month after Sir Nevile. Even then, Hitler was giving orders to persecute the Jews. And things were going to get a lot worse for the German people, but so would they for the British. He dreaded to think how it would all end and what the two countries would look like afterwards. He only knew that Britain must win. There was no other possible outcome.

He grimaced. He'd just have to bide his time until all the German diplomats were safely back in their country, but he could hardly wait.

Neither could he wait to be in the same country as Maddie and be free to contact her. Had she found a position in the Foreign Office? Something really interesting to keep that sharp mind of hers well oiled. At least he'd contacted one of his pals at Whitehall about her which might have put the wheels in motion. But how long would he be imprisoned here? He only hoped by the time he managed to get back to Britain she wouldn't have completely forgotten him.

As for him, if he never set eyes on her again, he would never forget that kiss. Or her response. It had simply knocked him off his feet.

# PART THREE

# Chapter Seventeen

*5th September 1939*

'Can you tell me which platform for Bletchley?' Madeleine said, as she rushed up to one of the guards at Euston station.

'Platform 10, love. You want the train that goes to Birmingham New Street. But it's been delayed.'

'For how long?'

'We've not been told. Hopefully, not much longer. But check the platform – sometimes they change it and don't give you a lot of time to get there.'

Damn! It was her own fault for not leaving enough time but it hadn't been easy to get away this morning, and a bad night's sleep hadn't helped.

Her mother had been sitting up in bed when Madeleine had gone into her parents' bedroom to say goodbye.

'I now have three children to worry about,' she'd grumbled as Madeleine kissed her cheek. 'Why you couldn't have settled into a good teaching position now you have your exam results, I'll never know—'

Madeleine had taken a few minutes to revel in the distinction she'd gained, but now she needed to concentrate

165

on this new opportunity, cloaked in mystery, which appealed to her sense of adventure.

'Mother, I don't think you understand. This is an order from the Foreign Office. I can't just say I'm not interested. I'd have to have a very good reason.'

'Well, you have. You—'

'Mother, please say goodbye and wish me good luck.'

Her mother's expression changed to one of resignation. 'Goodbye, then, Madeleine.'

'I'll write and let you know I'm there.'

Her mother nodded and sank down into the bed, closing her eyes. 'Tell your father not to disturb me when he comes back – I'm going to have a lie-in.'

*Like you do most days, Mother.* But she bit her tongue so as not to make any retort.

'Take good care of yourself,' her father said as he'd driven her to the Underground. 'I wish I could come with you. It'll be most interesting to know what work they give you, but I imagine you won't be able to disclose it even to me.' He turned his head to her as he pulled up outside the station entrance. 'Make sure you tell them you're proficient at Morse Code. I'm quite sure that will tie in nicely with your German.'

'I will, Dad, though I wouldn't say I was *proficient* in Morse.'

He smiled. She noticed the lines round his eyes had deepened.

'You know the rudiments and that's the main thing. Practice will make speed.' He paused. 'Don't be too hard on your mother, Maddie. She means well.' He suddenly reached in the back of the motorcar. 'Oh, that reminds me. She asked me to give you this.' He put a hard-edged

166

packet wrapped in brown paper, with an envelope tucked into the string, into her hands. 'I expect it's for your birthday.'

She knew exactly what it was.

'Please thank Mother for me.'

He nodded. 'I'll see you on your train.'

'No, don't, Dad. I'll be fine. I'd rather say goodbye to you right here.'

He gave her a brief hug.

'Good luck, my dear. Do your old dad proud.'

The last image she had was of him standing by his motor-car waving his white handkerchief.

Now, she hurried along platform 10, heaving with young men in a variety of army, navy and air force uniforms, along with girlfriends, wives and mothers tearfully waving them off. She gulped.

*Dear God. We really are at war.*

She blew out her cheeks, calculating her time in hand would be quickly eaten up. It was twenty to nine. If a train didn't come in very soon she'd be late. She could do with a cup of tea but daren't risk it. Instead, she sat on a bench with her suitcase resting against her leg. In the end it was another half an hour before she heard the announcement.

'The train now standing on platform 12 – that's platform 12 – to Birmingham New Street is ready for boarding.'

Grabbing her case, Madeleine rushed with all the others to platform 12, and miraculously found a seat in a compartment squashed between two soldiers, one of whom sprang up to lift her case onto the rack above. Thanking him, she sat down with a thump on the seat, which felt as though it had lost its springs. The three standing soldiers were smoking, one sending smoke rings across the compartment. It was not going to be a very comfortable journey, Madeleine thought as she opened her mother's package, which would be her mother's latest novel. She pulled off the brown paper and grimaced. She was right. *The Enchanted Summer* by Henrietta Hamilton. She gave an inward sigh to think her mother considered it an appropriate twenty-second birthday present which hadn't cost her anything. Inside, her mother had written: *To my darling daughter, love from Mother.*

Not for the first time did she wonder how her mother could write such tender love stories that tens of thousands of her readers adored yet didn't seem to think any of that love should be spent on her youngest child. Madeleine shrugged. Her mother was never going to change from her adoration of her sons.

Grimly, she opened the book to Chapter One and began to read. Five minutes later she joined the other passengers by thankfully drifting asleep.

'Bletchley – this is Bletchley!'

Madeleine jerked awake and peered out of the window but there was no usual platform sign to confirm the announcement. Then she remembered that many signs had been taken down even before the war started as a way of confusing the Germans if they invaded. Thank goodness she was a light sleeper or she might have missed it. Jumping up, she hauled down her suitcase, shrugged on her jacket, adjusted her hat and opened the sliding door into the corridor. Outside, the guard opened the door and she stumbled out. He blew his whistle and the train pulled away.

It was quarter to eleven and she had no idea how far this Station X was. She was already three-quarters of an hour late.

Madeleine glanced round the platform. It didn't look as though anyone else had alighted. She picked up her case and walked through the exit and there was the phone box on the other side of the road.

Setting her case on the ground outside, she opened the stiff kiosk door, the smell of stale cigarettes and male body sweat from yesterday's unusually hot weather greeting her. She wrinkled her nose as she fumbled for the letter telling her the number to dial. When a male voice at the other end answered she pushed some penny pieces through the slot.

'Good morning. I'm Madeleine Hamilton and I've been told to report to Station X.'

'We expected you before ten. It's now nearly eleven and you're still not here.'

'I know. I'm sorry but the train was delayed and—'

'Never mind.' The brusque tone became even more impatient. 'At least you've arrived. It's only a short walk.' He proceeded to give her directions.

It sounded more than a short walk carrying her case which was becoming heavy. But she'd just have to grin and bear it. They were at war. Young men would be having a much worse time when the fighting really started.

She picked up her case and began walking along the main road. *Then turn right,* the voice had said, *and you'll come to a country lane.* So far so good. Here was the country lane. She hadn't walked far down it when she noticed a long chain-link fence with rolls of barbed wire attached to it. Her heart beat a little faster. This was obviously some

169

kind of security boundary. She must be getting close to the mysterious Station X. Ah, here was the pair of iron gates he mentioned, and the sentry. She put down her case, rubbing the top of her arm, which was beginning to ache.

An armed guard – a short stocky man – stepped out of the sentry box.

'Morning, miss. May I see your pass?'

'Um, I don't have one.'

'Are you new?'

'Yes. I have a letter telling me to report here. Will that do?' She handed it to him.

He glanced at it and nodded. 'Right you are. Go along the drive to the main house – the Mansion as it's known – and they'll register you.'

She thanked him and picked up the case again. She'd be pleased when she could finally sit down and have a cup of tea and a bite to eat.

Passing a gate on her right as she crunched up the gravel drive, Madeleine's first sight of the Mansion, looking smaller than its nickname suggested, took her by surprise. Built of red brick, the turrets, gables and green metal roof at the very left were an odd addition to what must once have been a private Victorian home. But to Madeleine's eye it didn't look worthy of housing anything of importance as she'd been led to believe. And yet there was something about it . . . And what were all those wooden outbuildings used for? She gave an inward shrug. She guessed she'd find out soon enough.

The heavy entrance door opened as she got within twenty feet and two men, perhaps in their mid-twenties, casually dressed in open-necked shirts, stepped out, deep in conversation.

'Could you tell me if I'm in the right place to register?'

They looked up. The taller one raised his eyebrows and gave her an admiring look.

'Yes, just go through there into the library – second door on your left. Mrs Jones will see to you.' He glanced down. 'Let me help you with that case.' He turned to his friend. 'I'll catch you later, Bailey.'

Madeleine followed him into a panelled room with an intricately plastered ceiling and a Regency-styled window overlooking the front garden. Shelves heaved with what looked like reference books. Two workmen were setting up desks and typewriters under the instruction of a woman in her forties.

'Mrs Jones doesn't seem to be around,' the tall man said, still holding her case. 'Have you any paperwork so maybe someone else can help?'

Should she hand it over? The tight security was making her nervous. Suppose he gleaned something he shouldn't. She hesitated, noticing how very attractive he was.

'Name's Charles Longden, by the way,' he said. 'And you are—?' He raised an enquiring eyebrow.

'Madeleine Hamilton.'

'Delighted to meet you.' He paused. 'Have you come far?'

'The other side of London. I'm supposed to be seeing someone by ten o'clock and the person on the end of the phone when I arrived in Bletchley already told me I was late. So I need to find him. But I don't know who I'm looking for.'

'Mrs Jones will know.' He regarded her with more than casual interest, then looked towards the door. 'Ah, speak of the devil – here she is.'

A motherly-looking woman, her salt-and-pepper hair pulled back from her pleasant features, smiled as her eyes alighted on Madeleine.

'Madeleine Hamilton?'

'That's me. So sorry I'm late. The train—'

'Don't worry. It happens all the time these days. I just need your papers.' She walked over to her desk.

Feeling embarrassed that Charles Longden was standing behind her, Madeleine opened her handbag and took out the letter. Mrs Jones glanced at it, then looked in her ruled book.

'Here you are, my dear.' She handed Madeleine a small card with her name on it and pushed the book towards her. 'Just sign that I've given you your pass.'

Madeleine quickly signed, then tucked the card into her bag.

'Let's see where you'll be billeted.' Mrs Jones riffled through some index cards and pulled one out. She caught Charles Longden's eye. 'Miss Hamilton won't be needing your assistance, Mr Longden.'

'Oh, right.' He nodded to Madeleine and disappeared.

She turned her attention back to Mrs Jones.

'We like to keep it private where we send our recruits but I believe you're in the grounds rather than billeted in the town.'

That sounded convenient. Madeleine waited.

'Let me see.' Mrs Jones pushed her glasses back onto the bridge of her nose as she peered at a card. 'Ah, you're down for one of the hostels for girls in Wilton Avenue – not quite in the grounds but only a two-minute walk. You turn left outside the gate – you'll need to show your pass each time you go out and come in – and it's the first

172

building you come to – a large Victorian red-brick house. You can't miss it. But first Major Stanley will want to speak to you. You're rather late, my dear, so he went to the tearoom for a cuppa. It's in Hut 2. You should find him there. He's the person who'll be interviewing you.'

'Thank you, Mrs Jones.'

Mrs Jones bent her head back to the papers on her desk so Madeleine stood and left.

Blast! She hadn't asked Mrs Jones where Hut 2 was. But standing outside was Charles Longden who gave her a beaming smile.

'Can you tell me where Hut 2 is?' Madeleine asked.

'I certainly can. That's where the tearoom's housed. Come with me.'

His eyes caught hers and she glanced away. She didn't need any of that nonsense . . . though he was *very* attractive.

'Who're you looking for?'

Again, she hesitated. But surely people knew one another who worked here.

'It's a Major Stanley.'

'Oh, old Buggerlugs Stanley,' he chuckled. 'We call him that because his ears stick out like jug handles and he can be a pain in the backside. He's not convinced women are up to it in this place and can be quite rude. Don't take any notice of him. You have to give him as good as you get – in the politest way, of course.'

A curl of anger wound itself in her chest. It must have been him on the other end of the phone when she'd first arrived.

'Right then,' Charles said, 'let's find the old sod.' He turned to her. 'Excuse my French but you'll probably come across the odd swear word or two working here, especially

173

amongst the chaps.' He gave a rueful grin. 'This must all seem very strange to you, to say the least, but most of us haven't been here that long – me included – and don't know if we're coming or going half the time, so you're not alone.'

Was that supposed to make her feel better after he'd told her what an ogre Major Stanley was? Madeleine stiffened her back and pulled herself up another inch as they walked over to Hut 2.

As soon as Charles Longden opened the door, streams of smoke drifted towards them. There were a couple of dozen or so people chatting and drinking tea.

'I see him,' he said, taking her elbow and guiding her over to a table where two men were seated. He addressed a heavy-set balding man in army uniform. 'Major Stanley, I believe you're to see Miss Hamilton so here she is.'

'About time.' He drained his cup and gave Madeleine a curt nod, then stood. 'You'd better come with us, Miss Hamilton.'

'Thank you very much for your help, Mr Longden,' Madeleine said pointedly as she turned to speak to him.

'Oh, do call me Charles,' he answered, offering her a sympathetic grin as he opened the door for them. 'Well, I'll leave you to it.'

Madeleine followed the other two men into a nearby hut and along the narrow corridor until they came to the last door on the right.

The other man, who was a civilian, gestured her through, giving her a brief smile.

'Have a seat,' Major Stanley said.

She sat down nervously, facing the two men behind a table.

'Now, then, Miss Hamilton, before we go any further you will sign the Official Secrets Act.' He passed a large document over to her.

She glanced at it.

'Could you please explain what I'll be signing for . . . sir? I don't have any idea what work I'll be doing . . .' she trailed off.

'You will know more when you've signed the document,' he snapped. 'Security is extremely tight here. Under no account will you disclose anything of your work to anyone, not even family or friends . . . or boyfriend.' His eyes pierced hers. 'Do you have a boyfriend?'

*Jack.* She shook her head.

'Just as well,' the Army officer continued. 'A slip of the tongue on the pillow could cost lives.'

A bubble of irritation rose in her throat. Did he take her for some loose woman? Then a vision of Mr Graham dangled in front of her, not bothering to disguise his contempt when he informed her she'd been caught with a boy in her bed. She gritted her teeth, desperate to keep calm so as not to allow the tell-tale flush.

As though the major had read her mind he shot her a stern look. 'If you do any of the things I've warned you against, the consequences will be severe and will merit extreme punishment. That could mean long-term imprisonment. And if you give any information *on purpose* that could be of vital use to our enemy, you will be committing *treason.*' He paused to let the terrifying word sink in. 'For that, you would receive the death penalty. And I'm not sure these days if that's by hanging or being shot by a firing squad!'

Madeleine startled. What on earth had she got herself

into? Surely he was exaggerating. But when she glanced at him he didn't move a muscle on his face. Nor did the man by his side, who so far hadn't said a word. Forcing herself to stay calm, she took the yellow-looking paper, though the slight tremor of her hand caused Major Stanley to raise his bushy grey eyebrows. How badly she wanted to skim it, get the damn thing signed and find out about her work. But this was not the right time to show any impatience, with his eyes firmly fixed on her. She gulped, and taking a deep breath, began to read.

With all the dire warnings and in her nervousness she couldn't take in what she was reading. There was a whole list of DO NOTs in capital letters which she tried to digest but failed. *DO NOT talk at mealtimes. DO NOT talk when travelling. DO NOT talk in your billet . . . And if anyone asks what work you do, you say you are a clerk or a shorthand typist doing war work.*

She pretended to read the whole declaration carefully but the words swam. All she could do was assume that other people who worked here had risked their lives by signing the same document and she would have to do the same. There was no alternative.

Even her writing didn't look like hers, she thought, glancing at the shaky form of her signature as she handed it back. Major Stanley stared at it, stared at her, then turned to his colleague.

'Ask Miss Hamilton where she learnt her German and for how long,' he said. 'And find out what she was doing.'

The younger man cleared his throat.

'*Wo haben Sie Deutsch gelernt?*' His German accent was good.

'*In München,*' Madeleine answered.

'Wie lange her?'

'Dieses Jahr. Ich habe zwei Kindern Englisch beigebracht.'

He asked a few more questions and then put his head near the Army major's and said a few words under his breath about her teaching children in a family. They both regarded her intensely.

'Thomson, here, says your German is quite fluent.' He pushed his glasses up on the bridge of his nose.

Madeleine waited.

'Have you anything to add that might be useful?'

How could she add something when she had no idea in the world what she'd be doing. And then she remembered the last remark her father had made.

'Um, I do know Morse Code.'

She stifled a nervous giggle as she saw in her mind's eye both pairs of ears prick up.

'Really?' Major Stanley regarded her, a gleam in his eye. 'When did you last use it?'

'Um, a few years ago.'

'Well, you would have lost any speed . . . but useful, nevertheless.' He paused and looked at Thompson who inclined his head. 'We'd better put you on a refresher course.'

That didn't sound terribly exciting but she mustn't show by even a flicker that she was disappointed to learn that's all she'd be doing.

'We have it on the best authority that you've come from a good background and can keep a secret,' the Army officer went on. 'You've come highly recommended,' he added as though almost reluctant to pass on such a compliment.

*It had to be Jack. There was no one else who would have got in touch with them through the Foreign Office and put*

177

her name forward. *And crucially, the only one who was in a position to recommend her.*

A warmth stole round her heart. Jack obviously thought she was capable of doing an important job. And she was. She couldn't wait to start.

'You'll be in a training programme for the next nineteen weeks,' Major Stanley broke into her thoughts as Thompson made a note. 'But first of all, have you registered?'

'Yes, I did it as soon as I arrived . . . and I have my pass,' she added.

'Good. Don't lose it or you'll be fined.'

*Something else to remember.*

She hesitated. 'When do I start the training?'

'Tomorrow morning – eight a.m. sharp.' He glanced at the file. 'You'll be doing your training in Hut 3. It's along the corridor and take the last door on the right marked, as one would expect, "Training".' He paused and to her horror she heard her stomach rumbling. For the first time the hint of a smile lifted the corners of his lips. 'I'd get something to eat now if I were you.' He nodded for her dismissal.

But no, the most pressing thing on her mind now was to find the hostel in Wilton Avenue where she was destined to lay her head.

# Chapter Eighteen

Following Mrs Jones's directions, Madeleine found the hostel easily, thankful it had been only a short distance to carry her suitcase. Three women came out at the same time as she was opening the door. They threw her curious looks.

'Hello, there,' a girl of medium height with merry eyes and dark curly hair said. 'Are you new?'

'Yes. I've just registered.'

'You carry on,' the girl said to her two colleagues. 'I'll show . . .' She looked at Madeleine.

'Madeleine Hamilton.'

The girl raised a pencilled eyebrow. 'We're all on first name terms here. Do you like it shortened?'

'As long as it's not Mads, I don't mind.'

'Well, Maddie, come with me and I'll show you where you'll be sleeping.' She paused. 'I'm Josie, by the way, and that's Olive –' she pointed to a tall, solidly built girl '– and that's Sally.'

Sally sported round rimless glasses and with her tawny hair pulled back from her face, and a slightly beaky nose, reminded Madeleine of a wise owl. But all the girls' expressions were welcoming and that was the main thing.

'We'll be in the canteen,' Olive said over her shoulder as she and Sally disappeared.

Madeleine followed Josie up a flight of stairs, then along a dark chilly passage. She wondered how many bedrooms there were as Josie passed by two doors.

Josie opened a door to her left and stood aside for Madeleine to enter.

*Oh, no.* She counted twelve bunk beds. *Twelve.* Six on each side. It would be worse than boarding school. She remembered once sharing a room with a friend when they'd gone on their first independent holiday to St Ives in Cornwall, and the girl's heavy breathing and mumbling had kept her awake all night. And if anyone snored she wouldn't sleep a wink.

*Stop that! You've been completely spoilt all your life. This is the real world.*

But she couldn't help seeing her mother's horrified expression.

'Yours is the last but one in the far corner.' Josie gestured to the left. 'There's a bedside cabinet with a light – nowhere near good enough to read by, I'm sorry to say. You'll just have to find some space in the nearest cupboard which serves as a wardrobe. At the moment it only has Cora's things – she's in the last bed. It's a case of bunging your things in where you can.'

'Where's *your* bed, Josie?' Madeleine asked, trying to disguise her deep disappointment in not having her own room.

'Right by the door. I'm afraid the beds are pretty awful. They don't even have a proper mattress. It's a palliasse.'

'What!'

Josie pulled the one blanket aside to show her a large woven bag with bits of straw poking through.

Madeleine recoiled in horror. 'And is this the only sheet?' She fingered the rough twill material under the blanket.

"Fraid so. And just one flat pillow, which thankfully has a proper pillowcase. Apart from that, there's not a shred of comfort here, plus I'd better warn you –' she paused and looked directly at Madeleine as though to weigh up whether the newcomer would be able to take what she was about to say '– we do get an occasional visitor such as a mouse . . . or worse.'

Madeleine gulped. She could handle a mouse, but a rat? And not a nice tame little white rat like Erich had tried to frighten her with. And with all that straw there'd likely be cockroaches. She shuddered. Best not probe for any details.

'We all complain but apparently there's no alternative at the moment.' Josie sighed. 'And you have to book for the bathroom just down the corridor.' She caught Madeleine's expression. 'It's surprising what you get used to.'

Madeleine's mouth tightened. *It'll be like sleeping in a barn.*

'I'm a sort of prefect,' Josie continued. 'But not too much of an ogre, I hope.' She grinned, her hazel eyes lighting up at the very idea. 'We were just off to the canteen – it's in the dining room at the Mansion.' She glanced at Madeleine. 'You could probably do with something yourself if you've come far.'

'I nearly got a cup of tea earlier but I was whisked away—' She stopped suddenly, horrified that she'd been about to say before she'd been taken for an interview. The major's words about being shot pounded in her head.

'Don't worry. We've all been through various interviews which we've never discussed in any detail with one another

181

because of signing the Official Secrets Act. We know absolutely nothing about one another's work here and wouldn't dream of asking. And that's how we keep it – under the pain of death.'

Madeleine gave her a sharp look. Was that a mocking tone? But no. Josie's animated expression was serious now. Madeleine hadn't realised she'd been holding her breath as she breathed out her relief that she wouldn't be questioned any further.

'I'll leave you to it then,' Josie said. 'Don't be long – we'll hold you a place.'

It didn't take long for Madeleine to unpack. There was little space in the cupboard the woman called Cora seemed to have commandeered. She pushed Cora's coat hangers tighter together and managed to hang most of her things by placing two or three items on each of the four hangers. There was a small bedside light on the table but the interior of the building was already dim even in the middle of the day. The room felt airless even though there were three windows. She looked around at the three washbasins for twelve girls, with only one bathroom. And not even a proper mattress on the bed. That was more shocking than anything.

Suddenly, Madeleine felt completely at a loss. Everything was so different from how she'd imagined. But the country was at war. Rumours were that it would turn into a world war. Something too frightful to contemplate. She needed to stop moaning and get on with it.

She piled her books in the cupboard underneath the bedside table, and laid her mother's latest novel on the top, giving a wan smile when she thought of her mother's expression at the sight of the palliasse, then propped up a photograph in a silver frame of Raymond and Gordon, grinning at her in their smart uniforms.

*Dear God, please keep them safe when it all starts.*

She left her toiletries in her suitcase and picked up her bag.

The moment she stepped through the heavy oak entrance door and into the porch she gave an inward smile. She didn't need to ask where the dining room was located; she could follow her nose from the rich aroma of onions and gravy.

When she'd first set foot in the Mansion with Charles Longden she'd barely been aware of the interior of the building. Now, she took in the large, panelled hall with its deeply moulded ceiling, and on the right at the rear an elegant curving staircase. It had too many riotous architectural features for her taste, yet somehow it was charming. Madeleine walked on through a row of marble arches into another room where a huge marble fireplace took up the whole of one end. Tilting her head upwards she took in the predominantly red and green stained-glass ceiling. It was quite lovely but she couldn't explore any further. She needed to placate her rumbling stomach.

The dining room, another graceful room with oak-panelled walls, deep cornice and imposing marble fireplace, was humming with thirty or so mostly men and a handful of women. Some of the people were in uniform but most appeared to be civilians like herself.

Her three new friends were not alone. Two young men sat at a table for six.

'Maddie, just go to the counter and choose,' Josie called out, 'then bring your tray over.'

'Mince or cauliflower cheese, love?' A thin woman

wearing an apron big enough to wrap round her twice raised her brows for Madeleine's answer.

She chose the cauliflower cheese. The woman plonked a baked potato on the plate.

'Help yourself to the bread-and-butter pudding and custard, love,' she said, her attention already taken with another hungry staff member.

As Madeleine walked towards the table the two men half rose, then sat down again once she'd settled.

'Maddie, this is Tom Blackmore –' Josie gestured to the man with the spectacles '– and Daniel Strong.'

Madeleine noticed Josie put her hand on Daniel Strong's. Mmm. Looked as though there was something going on between those two.

'Very pleased to meet you,' Tom said, his rather plain features lit by eyes that were warm and candid behind his glasses. A genuine smile hovered over his lips as he gave her a firm handshake.

'Strong by name and strong by nature.' Daniel Strong's grin was broad. Pulling his hand abruptly away from Josie's, he thrust it across the table to almost crush the bones in Madeleine's hand. Was he trying to prove to her that he lived up to his name? Inwardly, she groaned. He was just the sort of man she despised. So what on earth did Josie see in him?

She wondered how many times he'd made that feeble joke to a woman, but she gave a slight smile of acknowledgement as she took a mouthful of cauliflower cheese. They were both friendly-looking men – in fact, Daniel was more than friendly-looking with fair wavy hair brushed back from his forehead showing flirty blue eyes.

'I don't believe we've seen you around before, have we?'

184

'No, I've only just arrived.'

'Well then, welcome to Bletchley Park,' he said. 'Or just the Park, or BP.' He gave her an appreciative look.

'So where's Station X?'

'It's the codename we use to anyone not actually working here but part of the set-up – who we liaise with. The dispatch riders, for instance.'

'Oh, I see.'

A frisson of anticipation rushed through her. But she didn't see at all. Was she going to be cracking enemy codes? If so, how important would they be? Would – could the war rest on her findings? She shook herself. She was getting carried away.

'I expect you feel as though you've been set down in an alien country,' Daniel went on.

'A bit,' she admitted, 'but I'm sure I'll get used to it . . . just as soon as I begin the training.'

Sally sitting opposite gave the merest nod of her head towards a large poster on the dining-room wall. Madeleine twisted her neck round to see a glamorous blonde, her curls piled high on her head, her lips the brightest red, her dress showing every detail of every curve, leaning languorously back in an easy armchair, surrounded by three admiring men. The caption in large black letters read:

### *Keep mum*
#### *she's not so dumb!*

And in red capital letters underneath:

**CARELESS TALK COSTS LIVES**

Madeleine felt her cheeks flush. They mustn't think she was already being careless.

'Don't worry, Madeleine,' Tom said. 'We're all still training in one way or another. That's no secret. We just aren't allowed to discuss what the training is, that's all.' He looked at Josie. 'Isn't that right, Josephine?'

'What?' Josie had a faraway look on her face. She seemed to drag her eye away from Daniel as she turned to Tom. 'Oh, yes, that's right.'

Madeleine pretended to concentrate on her meal. It was the safest way. As if taking her cue, the two men both lit cigarettes and began talking to one another about cricket until Josie brought her back into their conversation.

'What will you do this afternoon while we three are having to work?' Olive asked.

'I'm not sure. Can you suggest anything?'

'Why don't you go to the ballroom and have a read. Just relax. You'll be working flat out once you start. Then what say we all meet at the café for tea at four o'clock. And this evening, since we're on the same shift, we could maybe go to the flicks.'

'What – do they have a cinema here?' Madeleine said, surprised.

'They do sometimes show a film, but I thought we might go and see the latest Cary Grant in the town. The one about the pet leopard.'

'*Bringing up Baby*,' Sally, usually quiet, put in.

'That's the one – with Katharine Hepburn,' Olive said. 'They're both great.'

'But Cary Grant,' Josie said, almost drooling. 'That cleft in his chin. He's simply divine.'

Madeleine noticed Josie glance at Daniel to see if he'd

186

heard, but he was still talking to Tom. She wondered if the relationship – if that's what they had – was a little one-sided. She hoped Josie wouldn't get hurt. She liked her and the other two girls already.

Madeleine decided after all to go for a walk along the lanes to try to get her bearings. Leaves had already begun to turn. Sniffing the air, she could almost smell autumn arriving although it had not yet turned to cold and damp. This was her favourite time of the year. She passed several fields as she meandered along the lanes, and decided to follow the signpost pointing to Fenny Stratford, only two and a half miles away. A five-mile walk would do her the world of good, she decided. Clear her head.

She found Fenny Stratford to be not the village she'd imagined but a small market town with some lovely Tudor buildings. After wandering along the High Street, peeping in the windows, she glanced at her watch. Hmm. She'd already been gone well over an hour. By the time she got back it would be coming up to four – almost time to meet the girls in the café.

'I'll get teas,' Josie said. 'Anyone fancy something to eat?'

'Maybe a Kit-Kat if there's one,' Sally said.

'Madeleine?'

'I'll come with you to help.'

'You sit right there. I'll get this.'

Josie was back in under five minutes. Madeleine leapt up from the table to take the tray.

'Only one Kit-Kat left and a Fry's Cream,' Josie said.

'It's fine. We'll share,' Olive said.

It was as though she'd found a ready-made group of

friends, Madeleine thought happily as the four of them chatted. But not friends you could talk to about *everything*, she reminded herself. She needed to be on her guard with whatever work she was given as far as others were concerned.

Josie placed a mug in front of the four places, then split a Kit-Kat in two. She did the same with the Fry's Chocolate Cream.

'Take your pick,' she said.

'Do you speak any languages, Maddie?' Olive enquired.

'Yes, I just finished my degree course in Modern Languages,' Madeleine said, taking a strip of Kit-Kat.

'Oh, congratulations – if you passed, that is,' Josie chuckled.

'Yes, I did. In fact I just got the results this morning . . . with distinction.' She couldn't help the note of pride in her voice. Then she remembered the comment her mother made when she'd given her the news.

'Not before time,' had been the dry response.

Now in the Park's café, Sally raised her cup and clinked it with Madeleine's.

'Congratulations, Maddie. If there's one thing we all seem to have in common here, it's another language.' She looked at Madeleine directly. 'So what's yours?'

'German mostly and French as the second one.'

'Ah, it'll be German that will be most useful to them, I imagine,' Josie put in.

Madeleine shifted in her chair. Had she said too much? No, she hadn't said any more than she might have said to anyone, Official Secrets Act or not.

'Do you have siblings, Maddie?' Olive said.

'Two older brothers – both joined up even before war was declared.'

'Any boyfriend?' Josie asked.

Madeleine felt her cheeks warm, though why, she couldn't say, except that Jack's face flashed in front of her. She pictured his grin as he dared her to answer. The three women were looking at her expectantly, but she'd only been in their company for a very short time to speak of such personal things.

'Um, not exactly.'

'Then there *is* someone!' Josie pounced. 'There'd have to be with your looks and those amazing green eyes.' She bent closer. 'They hardly look real.'

'Both mine.' Madeleine chuckled. 'But you wouldn't have noticed them when I was a child and had to wear horrible metal-framed glasses.' She paused. 'And no, there's no one special.'

'Stop it, Josie.' Sally threw Madeleine a sympathetic look. 'Maddie's only known us five minutes and here we are throwing personal questions at her.' She glanced at her watch. 'Come on, we have to go or we'll be late.'

The four of them scraped back their chairs as one.

'Thank you, Josie, very much for the tea and Kit-Kat,' Madeleine said. 'It was much appreciated. And my turn next time.' She gave a grin. 'I might even stretch to one choc bar each if they've come in by then.'

'We'll keep you to it,' Olive chuckled.

In the end Josie had gone to the cinema on her own as Madeleine had felt too jaded to go with her. She couldn't blame the journey as it hadn't been a long one. And although she must have walked several miles this afternoon, she'd needed that exercise and fresh air. She could only put her tiredness down to trying to absorb so much

189

information at the Park in a short time while being conscious that she mustn't ask certain questions beyond what was specifically relevant to her. Everywhere she looked there were posters on the walls warning you not to blab. In the dining room she'd noticed several. One was the back view of an enormous man with square shoulders, a placard pinned on him saying: *Be like Dad – keep Mum!*

She couldn't help a wry smile when she thought of what her mother would say to that.

Until it was time to get ready for bed, Madeleine spent the evening in the ballroom where there were several armchairs scattered around as a welcoming refuge from the day. She glanced round, not recognising anyone. Taking off her shoes, she curled her legs under her and opened her mother's novel, still with its bookmark at Chapter One. It was the first time she'd really relaxed all day, wondering what tomorrow would bring. She began to read until finally her eyelids drooped.

# Chapter Nineteen

Last night had been every bit as bad as she'd feared, Madeleine thought, as she left the hostel the following morning to head for Hut 3 where she was to do her Morse Code training. But at least the girls were friendly, and that was the main thing. They'd introduced themselves to her and chatted together until ten-thirty, but then, as though it was an unwritten rule, everyone had settled down. And apart from one girl snoring gently several bunk beds away from hers, all was quiet. Madeleine had tried to read by the dim bedside light but it had been impossible, as Josie had warned her. And when she'd given up and put the light off, it seemed every piece of straw was sticking to her arms, her back, her head.

After what had felt like a sleepless night, she'd got dressed, noticing several beds hadn't been occupied. Josie explained that the missing girls were on the two late shifts.

'And although the four to midnight is quite hard, it's not nearly so bad as the graveyard shift,' Josie said, screwing her face up in a most unladylike fashion. 'That one's midnight to eight and it's a killer.'

'Do most people who work here do shifts?' Madeleine asked, dreading the graveyard one.

'Mostly, except some of the boffins,' Josie replied. 'They sometimes work two or even three shifts together.'

'Goodness. They must be exhausted when they finally pack up.'

Wouldn't she love to know what they were doing to be so carried away for all those extra hours? But she knew she mustn't ask. And even if she did, Josie wouldn't have known the answer.

'Does the shift you're given change?'

'Oh, yes, and too often. Just as you get used to one, the week's up and you're doing another one. Your stomach will take a beating, so be warned. Luckily, this is Sally's and my week for the daytime shift, but Olive has to start at midnight. That's why she was able to join us for tea. But you sort of get used to it.'

'I see my neighbour didn't come in,' Madeleine said.

'Who, Cora? No, she's on the graveyard this week.' She paused. 'Just as well you're on different shifts.'

'Any reason?' Madeleine felt slightly uncomfortable with Josie's change of tone.

'She's not the easiest person,' Josie said. 'She's been spoilt rotten all her life and doesn't understand the word "share".'

Madeleine chuckled. 'I got that from the wardrobe space. She only left me a few inches.'

Now, as she pushed open Hut 3's door, she wished she'd already met Cora. Got it over with. Then she shook herself. The girl couldn't be that bad.

It was the first time Madeleine had been in Hut 3, which appeared to be much bigger than Hut 2 but felt just as airless. She hurried along the corridor, dimly lit by dangling light bulbs, barely aware of the drab brown paintwork below the dado rail, and the lighter yellow-brown above. People were

192

spilling out of doors – probably just finished their shift, she thought, as she found the door marked 'Training'.

Inside, two long tables were placed on a red-painted concrete floor, and at each setting was a notepad, pencil and Morse key. Stale smoke invaded Madeleine's nostrils and the only window still had the blackout blind down. Heavens, it was stuffy. By the time the twenty or so took their places, she saw only one other young woman, who looked round at all the men, rolled her eyes, then sent Madeleine a brief smile.

Madeleine nodded and smiled back at the girl, then sat down next to a lad who didn't look more than seventeen or eighteen.

'Good morning. I'm Madeleine – Maddie for short.'

'I'm Bobby.'

'Have you ever used one of these?' she asked, picking up the Morse key.

'No.'

If he'd been about to add anything, he was interrupted by a tall, bony man with rimless glasses who entered the room, quickly glanced round, then shut the door behind him. Madeleine watched as he walked with an awkward gait over to a desk set on the side between the two tables – a spot where he could presumably keep a sharp eye on them all.

'Right,' the man said, still standing. 'You all appear to be here. I'll just go through the register to make sure.'

When he was satisfied and a few of the trainees began talking to one another, he rapped his ruler on the desk.

'Anyone here learnt Morse Code?'

Madeleine raised her hand. No one else's arm moved. Oh, no. She should have kept quiet.

'Good.' He gave her a hard stare. 'If I don't turn up, then you can take over.' His lips didn't twitch so she had no idea if it was his dry sense of humour or if he was deadly serious. There were a few muted chuckles. 'I'm Leonard Watts and I'll be your tutor for the next nineteen weeks. Here you will learn the Morse Code alphabet. It may seem daunting at first, but you will keep learning every day in your time off until it becomes second nature. You won't have time to improve your speed only in these sessions. You must build it up at any opportunity whenever you're off-duty so you become useful to us as quickly as possible.' He looked round and caught Madeleine's eye. 'What is your speed, Miss, um . . .'

'Hamilton.' Madeleine hesitated. 'I'm afraid I'm rather rusty.' If only she'd taken more notice of Dad, who had heavily hinted that her Morse Code might come in useful. 'I used to do eight to ten words a minute . . . but it was a while ago,' she added hastily when she saw his heavy frown.

'Is that receiving or transmitting?'

'Um, receiving.'

His smile was more a smirk. 'You'll be doing triple that before you leave here. And don't think it will come easily just because you've dabbled in it before.' He looked round at the class. 'You won't ever be transmitting in your work, only receiving, but you need to know the procedure thoroughly. You will all have a unique way of transmitting – commonly known as one's "fist" – which only a receiver at the other end would begin to recognise after they got to know your call sign. It doesn't take much imagination to realise how useful that might be in your future work.'

*When the enemy is transmitting.*

Madeleine was sure that's what Leonard Watts was

194

implying. She could sense Bobby getting more and more nervous. Well, they'd all have to get on with it. And at least she had a head start.

'You will all examine your Morse key,' he went on. 'These are for trainees as they show the alphabet and the symbol by the side of each letter. When you've mastered the alphabet, I'll be replacing them with the grown-up ones that are blank.'

There were a few sniggers.

'Right, then, we can make a start.'

'My machine doesn't have any letters or marks on it,' Bobby whispered, showing it to her. 'Has yours?'

She nodded and slid hers over, then took his. He sent her a grateful smile.

'Take a good look,' Leonard Watts said. 'You will see the alphabet with its corresponding dots and dashes. These will make up letters and then words, depending upon the way they're grouped. But I don't want you to think of them as dots and dashes but as rhythms. You'll find it's much easier if you can sense the rhythms from the start. They're all around you – the Park's cockerel crowing, horses clip-clopping, the chug of a train – they'll all be sending messages to you.'

Madeleine felt a rise of impatience as he droned on. Why had they put her on a training programme when she was more than halfway there already? She didn't have to learn all this. Just practise every day for speed. This was such a waste.

'Please put your headphones on, everybody.'

Madeleine set hers on her head and immediately felt the pinch of metal. She tried to adjust them, but nothing helped. She supposed she'd been used to wearing her father's and his head would be bigger than hers. But she wouldn't complain. Heaving a sigh, she heard in her head the dits and dahs of the Morse alphabet. And at that moment she was determined to be the most speedy and the most accurate one in the class.

'How did you get on, Bobby?' she asked him after more than two solid hours of intense concentration.

'I can't remember even one of the letters,' he said with a forlorn expression.

'You will. It's just so new. You'll soon get the hang of it.'

As she put her notes together Leonard Watts said:

'Do not remove any notes from the room. Put your name on the exercise book and I'll collect them. They will go into a locked cupboard.'

Madeleine took in a sharp breath. She'd been going to take her notes back to the hostel. That would have been a real slip-up. She'd have to be very careful in every aspect of her new life at Bletchley Park.

Coming out of the stuffy hut, she decided to walk into town before practising her Morse. She needed fresh air. But first she had to finish her unpacking.

As she entered the room a figure at the far end turned. Madeleine didn't recognise her. It must be someone on one of the other shifts she hadn't yet met. She sent her a smile as she walked towards her bunk.

'Oh, you must be the new recruit,' the woman said, looking her up and down and, judging by her expression, seeming none too pleased with what she saw.

She was a striking-looking woman, Madeleine thought, taking in the woman's ebony hair partly pulled back from her face, and heavy eyebrows over large dark eyes. Maybe

Spanish or Italian? The naturally coloured lips weren't smiling. What made her look so unusual was that she wore trousers.

'Hello. Yes, I'm Madeleine. You must be Cora.'

'That's right.' The woman kept her eyes fixed on Madeleine. 'Are they your things in the wardrobe?'

'Yes, the little space that was left,' Madeleine answered, trying to curb any sarcasm. 'How many of us share it?'

'There was supposed to be three of us but someone hasn't turned up. So it seems like it's you and me.'

*Start as you mean to go on, Maddie. Let her know you're not going to put up with her nonsense.*

'Well, you've taken at least two-thirds,' she said firmly. 'So if you don't mind, I'd appreciate your giving me a little more room for the rest of my things which I've had to leave creased up in my case. And a couple of extra hangers, if you wouldn't mind.'

'Well, I *do* mind,' came the unexpected reply. 'I've left you plenty of space—'

'Let's not argue,' Madeleine cut in. 'I'll just show you so you can see what I mean.'

'Sorry, I'm late. You'll have to sort it out yourself.'

With that, Cora spun on her heel and slammed the door shut behind her.

Right. Sort it out she would. Madeleine opened the door of the wardrobe and removed four hangers, then doubled up Cora's clothes and swung them over to the left as tightly as she could. Even then, she had nowhere near half the space but it was better. She shook out the last contents of her case and put her remaining clothes on the four empty hangers. At least the creases might now have a chance to come out. Just her luck that Cora was so selfish. She

197

slammed shut the wardrobe door. She needed that walk into town.

Josie had warned her you could get your daily bits and pieces there but if you wanted a decent frock or pair of shoes, well, she always went to London, making sure it coincided with an exhibition she wanted to see or the theatre.

'I daren't buy anything in the way of clothes,' Madeleine gave a rueful smile. 'Cora would go spare if I grabbed another coat hanger.'

'She's a selfish so-and-so,' Josie said. 'It's like treading on eggshells sometimes around her. None of us know each other very well yet as we're almost as new as you, but she seems to have a chip on her shoulder for some reason. She hasn't made friends with anyone.' She pulled a face. 'It's as though we don't measure up to her.'

'Hmm. Wonder what her problem is,' Madeleine said.

'Olive says she's jealous of anyone who's prettier or has a boyfriend – obviously something missing in her own life.'

'I'm not surprised, if that's the way she treats them,' was Madeleine's comment.

It was a pleasant walk along the lanes that finally led to Bletchley itself. The sun was shining now and then in a grey-blue sky with thankfully no sign of the dreaded Luftwaffe. A bicycle sped past her dangerously close, the owner furiously ringing his bell as she pressed herself into the hedge. But instead of simply hearing the bell, Madeleine's brain translated it into Morse for 'Bloody idiot'. She couldn't help grinning. Leonard Watts was absolutely right. Morse Code was poised to take over in exactly the way he'd predicted.

The town of Bletchley didn't seem to have much going for it, Madeleine thought. In fact, it was a bit of a dump, and there was an odd smell about it – maybe from the brickworks. The only saving grace of the wide High Street was a row of trees at one side of the road. She glanced through the windows of a couple of cafés that appeared to be bustling, but wasn't tempted to go in.

There was a small department store that had an uninspiring window showing a mannequin sporting a woman's dull two-piece costume complete with handbag, hat, shoes and gloves, partnered by a male mannequin in a charcoal-grey, pin-striped, double-breasted suit topped by a trilby and carrying an umbrella. There were a few pieces of bedlinen and a hint of other household items you could presumably buy inside. Josie was right. There was nothing she could see to entice her in.

But at least there was a cinema. Madeleine gazed up at the building calling itself 'The Studio Cinema' displaying Gary Cooper's latest film. Mmm. She might try it one evening. But for now she needed to get back to Bletchley Park as she'd told herself she'd practise Morse for an extra two hours every day.

# Chapter Twenty

'Do you fancy seeing a play this evening, Maddie?' Josie said the following day when she and Madeleine bumped into one another, going and coming from the hut housing the lavatories.

Madeleine's heart soared.

'Oh, yes. But I've not noticed a theatre in the town though it was good to see two cinemas.'

'We do a makeshift theatre right here at the Park,' Josie said with a grin. 'Anyone who can act – or imagine they can—' She broke off with a giggle. 'Well, they can go along and volunteer.' She studied Madeleine's face, now flushed with excitement. 'Why – are you a budding actress?'

'Well, I've had various parts at school.'

'They'd welcome you with open arms,' Josie said. 'They're always looking for people to take on the main roles but when we're really working hard, especially on the midnight and graveyard shifts, it's sometimes difficult to find time to learn a big part – though I do sometimes do a maid when the play calls for one – she never has much to say but I like to give her a bit of character – make her saucy.'

Madeleine chuckled. She could just see Josie doing it.

But she wouldn't tell her new friend she'd never had any difficulty learning lines, even with all the homework she'd had to plough through every school night. It would sound too much like bragging.

'You need to talk to Cecil Bell if you're interested in taking part in future plays. He set up the Dramatic Club so he's usually the producer.'

'I might do that.' Madeleine endeavoured to keep her tone casual as a thrill of excitement rushed through her. Oh, to think she might have a chance to perform while she was here. What heaven! 'What are they putting on tonight?'

'*The Thirty-Nine Steps*.' Josie grinned. 'It's only supposed to have four players, but they've got at least ten so it should be a hoot.'

'Where do they show it?'

'In the ballroom,' Josie said. 'We'll meet at seven in the bar.'

Madeleine wondered how 'dressy' people would be that evening. She didn't want to overdo it but felt she ought to appear as though she'd made an effort. In the end she chose her mid-calf bottle-green dress with short puffed sleeves and narrow belt emphasising her waist. She wouldn't bother with any jewellery as the cream outsized bow at the neck was more than enough decoration, so her mother would say. Though she'd add, 'Goodness knows why you're not wearing a proper evening gown to attend the theatre.'

As soon as Madeleine stepped into the ballroom, where three rows of chairs were laid out in theatre style, she spotted Josie. To her relief, Josie was dressed just as casually in a plain navy skirt and pink blouse. But one girl stood out above all the rest. And that was Cora! Gone were the masculine trousers, the sensible shoes, the severe hairstyle. In their place was a striking brunette, her hair tumbling around her shoulders, and wearing a bright-pink dress with a plunging V-neck displaying several inches of cleavage, and high-heeled gold sandals. Her make-up was flawless, her lips a hungry crimson. The transformation was complete and Madeleine had to admit the woman looked stunning.

At that precise moment Cora caught her eye and smirked as though to say: 'You didn't think I could scrub up so well, did you?'

Considering they were amateurs, the quality of the acting was excellent. Madeleine chuckled along with the rest of the audience at one actor who played the part of the three main women, all the while itching to be one of the cast herself, even though she hadn't spotted another actress. Someone – maybe this Cecil Bell – had turned a thrilling spy story into a satire. It made her determined to speak to him if he was around afterwards to see whether she might be suitable for any further productions.

'There will now be a fifteen-minute interval,' one of the actors announced.

'Let's get a drink.' Josie took her arm as they walked towards a long trestle table covered in a white sheet. 'Oh, there's Cecil.' She gestured to a chubby blond man of medium height, his back to them, talking to two other women. 'Go and have a word. Tell him you're an actress.'

'Not quite,' Madeleine said ruefully. 'But when he's free I'll see what he says about my joining them for the next production.'

But just as she was only a few feet away and the two women had left, Cora stepped right between her and Cecil Bell, then gave the producer a dazzling smile.

'Cecil,' she cooed. 'It's a triumph.'

'Wait 'til you see the second part,' he said, grinning at her appreciatively.

'If it's as good as the first . . .' she trailed off, her lips in a seductive pout.

Madeleine drifted away. She wasn't going to let Cora think she'd wanted to speak to Cecil Bell. But she couldn't help feeling a little miffed.

Admonishing herself for being so ridiculous, she walked across to the bar, but Josie was no longer there. Well, she'd buy herself a drink and then . . . well, what?

She was just putting the change in her purse when a voice behind her said:

'I understand you'd like to talk to me about joining the BP Dramatic Club.'

She turned to look into the smiling eyes of Cecil Bell. He wasn't in the least good-looking but there was something about him – with his thick fair hair curled around his boyish face, he reminded her of a cherub in a Renaissance painting. A pair of bright blue eyes were now regarding her with what seemed like intense interest.

'Why don't we go to that table and have a chat. I'm Cecil, by the way.'

'So I gathered.'

He grinned, and taking her drink guided her through the crowd. She'd hardly sat down when he plunged straight in.

'You're new, aren't you? Right, tell me about any experience you have.'

'Well, I've played Titania in *Midsummer Night's Dream* and Viola in *Twelfth Night* and Nora in *A Doll's House*.'

Cecil raised his eyebrows. 'Professionally?'

'No, at school. But we had a proper theatre and a very good drama teacher.'

'So you can play straight or comedy?'

'Yes.'

'Hmm.' He stroked his smoothly shaven chin. 'Any preferences?'

'If it's a good play, I don't mind.'

'What about contemporary plays?'

'I haven't had much chance. School was always classical stuff.' She glanced at him. 'My parents wouldn't allow me to go to drama school which is what I desperately wanted.'

How was it she was able to come right out and tell Cecil when with everyone else she clammed up? She supposed it was because he was in the theatre world, he'd probably understand better than most how disappointed she'd been.

'A pity. I think you would've done well . . . *very* well, in fact.' Cecil gave her a sympathetic glance. 'So what did you do instead to find yourself here?'

'I studied modern languages.'

'Was that French and German?'

'Yes, but I liked learning German better.' She wouldn't mention she'd recently spent nine months in Munich.

'Ah.' He nodded. 'Now we're at war they'll certainly use you here for your German. Have you been told yet what you'll be doing?'

She straightened her back. Cecil was charming in his casual and friendly approach, but she must be on her guard.

'I'm on a training course at the moment, but of course I'm not allowed to discuss it.'

'No, of course not. Official Secrets Act and all that.' He kept his gaze on her. 'They'll work you hard, whatever you do, and the shifts have a nasty tendency of taking the stuffing out of you, but you'll find the entertainment we put on at BP is what keeps us sane – well, some of us.' He laughed as though he included himself.

Madeleine smiled politely.

A bell rang and he jumped to his feet like a jack-in-the-box.

'Sorry, um – I didn't catch your name.'

'Madeleine Hamilton.'

'Nice. Well, got to fly. Second Act. Be in touch.' He patted her hand.

Madeleine returned to her seat. What an unusual man. He rather had his head in the clouds but she couldn't help smiling. She didn't care how hard they worked her if she could be in a play, however small a part. To be part of the fun at rehearsals. To hear the applause after a successful night. To be part of a theatre family – her spine tingled at the thought.

'I saw you with him,' Josie whispered as the play started again. 'Did it go all right?'

'Tell you later.'

Madeleine didn't have a chance to talk to Josie until they were back in the dormitory. Cora was at the sink applying cream to her face. *To wipe off that inch of make-up*, Madeleine thought, knowing she was being catty. The woman turned round as she walked in.

'Oh, there you are, Maddie, though I think I will call you Mads.' She smirked. 'It suits you better.' She waited, seemingly for a reaction.

Madeleine gritted her teeth at the 'Mads' but refused to rise to the bait.

'How did you like the play?' Cora pressed.

'It was very good.' She looked straight at the woman. 'What about you?'

'It was okay.' Cora tore a piece of cotton wool from a roll and wiped it over her face. She tossed it in the wastepaper basket and pulled off another piece. 'But I'm down to play Amanda in *Private Lives* that we're putting on next month for Christmas, and that really *is* a decent play.' She gave Madeleine a pitying look. 'I hear you're a budding actress. Shame you won't be able to play one of the other leads as Patsy Taylor is playing Sibyl. But you wouldn't have had time to learn a big part like that anyway in such a short time.' She curled her lip. 'Never mind. Better luck next time.'

'Thank you, Cor. I'll cross my fingers.'

Cora glared at her. 'The name's *Cora*, actually.'

'The name's *Madeleine*, actually,' Madeleine said, perfectly mimicking Cora's inflection.

Knowing she was being completely childish, but satisfied nonetheless, Madeleine sauntered over to Josie who was sitting on her bed, the sheet against her mouth, stifling her giggles. Sally on the other side looked worried.

'I can't believe how rude Cora was,' Sally said under her breath. 'She seems to have taken a dislike to you.'

'*Cor* blimey, methinks she smells competition,' Josie said in a voice loud enough to carry.

Cora swung round, her eyes like daggers. She opened her mouth but must have thought better of it and closed it again, turning her back on the three women.

*Just my luck that not only does Cora grab most of the*

*wardrobe space but is an actress as well and is starring in my favourite Noël Coward play.*

Madeleine sighed. There was always one, and maybe it was best to know who it was now rather than later. The devil you know . . . and all that.

# Chapter Twenty-One

Madeleine's birthday, 9th September, had come and gone and the month was fast coming to the end. It hadn't mattered. She'd opened the card from her parents, and there was one each from Raymond and Gordon. She was glad to hear from them, and relieved that her brothers sounded their usual breezy selves, but her family seemed a million miles away from her completely different world here at the Park, as everyone called it.

'Would you stay behind after class today, Miss Hamilton?' Leonard Watts said one Saturday when she'd reached twenty words a minute for her Morse Code speed.

Her heart gave a little flip of excitement. Finally, he was going to move her to another section where she'd put her skills to good use. She'd done everything he'd set and she was well ahead of anyone in the class, although one of the young men, Michael, was fast catching up.

'You've done well,' Leonard Watts said, when everyone had left the room. 'We have a new lot of trainees to teach this coming Monday and I'm putting you down to run it. You'll be in the next room at the later time of four until six.'

She should be flattered but to her it felt like more of the

same instead of the challenge of learning something new. So how were they eventually planning to use her skill? She ventured a question.

'Thank you for your faith in me.' She paused. 'And of course I will do it. But am I to teach Morse for the rest of my time here? I did hope to use it for something important and—'

'Learning Morse is extremely important,' he cut in, impatience coating his words. 'Don't ever think otherwise.'

'Yes, but surely it's not enough being able to do it if it's not actually applied.'

'I can assure you, Miss Hamilton, it *will* be applied. But not yet. In the meantime, do you need to know what you will be using your skill for in order to teach Morse?'

'Well, no, but—'

'If you don't need to know in order to do your job, then don't ask.'

She'd been duly put in her place.

'Any questions pertaining to your new position?'

'How long will I be teaching?'

'About a month. It's only for the initial training. Once they get to a speed of fifteen or thereabouts, someone else will take over and you can come back to this class, who by then will have caught up with you.' He looked at her directly. 'Any other questions?'

'I don't think so.'

'Good.' He shuffled his papers together. 'I'll be here if you need me for anything. In the meantime, keep practising. You need to be a top-notch operator for the next phase.'

*At least that sounded more hopeful.*

Madeleine joined another table for lunch in the Mansion's dining room but after the two women introduced themselves, she left them to their conversation. She was supposed to practise her Morse Code this afternoon, but she wasn't in the mood. Needing a few items from the chemist she decided to walk into town. A change of scenery and fresh air would clear her head.

Back at the Park, she stopped by the Post Room to see if there just might be a letter for her. It had been more than three weeks since she'd arrived.

'Nothing for you, I'm afraid.'

Disappointed, she turned to go.

'Just a moment, miss. There's a note for you.' The clerk handed her a folded and stapled piece of paper.

Curious, she opened it there and then to read:

*Madeleine, please come to an audition at 1.15 p.m. tomorrow. I'll be in Hut 1, 4th door on left marked Auditions. No need to rehearse anything. C.B.*

*It looks as though it's quite a professional group if the volunteers have to be auditioned,* Madeleine thought, with a pleased smile. Tomorrow couldn't come quickly enough.

At ten past one Madeleine followed Cecil Bell's instructions and knocked on his door. A cheery voice called out:

'Enter.'

The room was scattered with various costumes and props, and a piano pushed between two clothes racks looking part of the muddle.

Cecil was checking items of clothing and hats and shoes from what appeared to be the 1920s and glanced up with a vague expression.

210

'It's Madeleine for my audition,' she said.

'What? Oh, yes, of course.' He went over to his desk, which was piled high with papers and photographs and books. He took up a sheaf which had been clipped together and handed it to her. 'We'll do an extract from *Private Lives*.' He glanced at her. 'It's our next production. I'll play the part of Elyot, you'll do Sibyl and we're on the balcony. Take it from the top.'

Madeleine glanced at the extract. It was the famous kissing scene at the beginning of the play. Wondering why he'd chosen that particular piece she felt a prick of apprehension. He nodded for her to start. She drew in a breath.

'It's heavenly. Look at the light of that yacht reflected in the water. Oh, dear, I'm so happy,' she began.

She continued reading the play for a couple more minutes, giving Sibyl's tone the need for constant reassurance until he put up the palm of his hand.

'You seem very familiar with Sibyl's character,' he said, his expression bland.

*What is he thinking? Am I any good or not?* She took a breath.

'I once played Amanda so I suppose I got to know her that way, though I've always wanted to give Sibyl a smack when she keeps probing into Elyot's marriage to his ex-wife and whom does he love more.'

'Well, you portrayed her perfectly.' He fixed his gaze on her. 'Shame it has a full cast. I can just see you as Amanda. We're showing it at the beginning of November.' He stroked his chin. 'Can you dance?'

'A little.'

'Sing?'

'Yes, soprano.'

'Let's try you out.' He sat at the piano and shuffled through some music sheets. 'Are you familiar with *Anything Goes*?'

She nodded. 'I know some of the songs.'

'"De-Lovely"?'

'Yes.'

'Right. You're Hope Harcourt. So give it a whirl.' He played a few notes.

She took in a breath. 'The night is young, the sky is clear . . .' She sang the first words a little wobbly, then began to gain confidence as Cecil's playing became more strident. 'It's delightful, it's delicious, it's de-lover-ly . . .'

She moved her body in time to the music and twirled round on the last note, then laughed a little self-consciously as Cecil raised his head from the piano. He was beaming.

'Gorgeous voice. Could do with a bit of training but not overly. You're a natural. We're putting it on early in the New Year –' he looked Madeleine up and down, his blue eyes missing nothing '– so be sure you put your name down for it – but not for Hope – for Reno Sweeney, the nightclub singer. I think that's more you.'

She left the room in high spirits. Things were definitely looking up.

Teaching Morse Code to the new class presented few problems but Madeleine was itching to be challenged more. The only thing that broke the daily routine was to see if there were any letters for her. At every opportunity she walked over to the Mansion to check the post but she had been disappointed until today. To her delight the postboy handed her the first letter from home and one from Gwen.

Glancing at her father's familiar but almost illegible writing on the envelope immediately perked up her spirits.

*4th October 1939*

*My dear Madeleine,*

*I hope this letter gets to you via this PO Box address. All very mysterious!*

*We're all okay but it's very quiet without you. We did have brief visits from Gordon and Raymond who both look well though they didn't go into detail about their jobs – quite rightly. But so long as they're flying planes they're happy. Everyone's calling it the Bore War – a play on both the Boer War and boredom, I suppose, but I'm sure we won't be bored for much longer and I'm not looking forward to it. Your mother is becoming increasingly nervous about you because you're not allowed to tell us where you are. I try to explain it's obviously secret war work, but she says that shouldn't stop you from telling your mother! Thank heavens she's started writing another novel. At least it keeps her occupied for several hours a day.*

*I'm building my own Anderson shelter. You can buy it in kit form for £7 but they're very small. It gives me something to do and makes your mother feel better that I'm doing something practical against the Luftwaffe that could save our lives, she says. Well, who knows. She may be right!*

*Well, Maddie, I hope you've been given something interesting to do that requires your languages. Drop us a line when you can. We haven't heard from you since you told us you'd settled in but I expect they're keeping you very busy.*

*Love from your old Dad*

Madeleine smiled. He often called himself that even though he wasn't yet fifty and she liked it when he sometimes called her 'Maddie', much to her mother's annoyance. It was good to learn that Gordon and Raymond were well and happy.

She opened Gwen's letter.

*Dear Maddie,*

*Thanks for your note saying how to contact you. Can't believe you're not allowed to tell anyone which town you're in. I must keep reminding myself there's a war on and we can't blab everything anymore. But isn't it awful?*

*I decided to join up and chose the ATS. Mum and Dad are worried but told me how proud they were when they saw me in uniform for the first time. I know it's not so glam as the WAAFs or the WRNS but I don't mind. I've just passed my driving test so I'll either be driving an ambulance or some colonel or other if I'm lucky. If so, I'll let you know if he's tall dark and handsome!*

Madeleine briefly squeezed her eyes shut. *Tall, dark and handsome. Like Jack.* She almost saw his name floating in front of her. But there'd been no word from him. She shouldn't keep hoping she'd hear. But he must be back by now. The Nazis wouldn't have allowed him to stay a minute longer in Germany since Britain had declared war on them. She would have to assume he hadn't wanted to keep in contact. Maybe there was another woman involved. Her stomach clenched at the possibility. She knew so little about him and nothing of his background. She *must* stop thinking about him. She did when she was in class. But any time she had off, her mind would wander. His hands. His voice.

The way he smiled at her. And that never-to-be-forgotten kiss.

Her body trembled and she made herself come back to earth and finish reading Gwen's letter, then tucked it back in the envelope to answer later.

Leonard Watts stuck to his word and by the end of a month he told her the others were now up to speed and she could return to her class. The only trainee who was no longer there was Bobby. Obviously, he hadn't cut the mustard. But at least Sandra, the one other female, raised her head and smiled.

'Right.' Leonard cleared his throat. 'Now this is where the fun begins.'

To look at his expression, Madeleine couldn't see the vestige of any fun. But his words had made her sit up straighter and she couldn't stop a frisson of anticipation.

'You will not automatically be picked as not everyone has the aptitude for what you are about to learn – which is to become a wireless telegraphy operator – that is, Morse traffic or by teleprinter. But if you pass your training examination, and demonstrate a fluency in German, you will be rewarded by knowing you are doing an extremely important job – more on that later if you pass.' His eyes narrowed as he glanced, one by one, at every participant. 'In order to pass the Morse Code part of the exam, you need to receive at least twenty-two words a minute and copy it down accurately. Any wrong letter could have an unfortunate consequence.'

Madeleine set her jaw. She would make damned sure she had the right aptitude necessary for whatever the Park held in store for her.

'The Morse you've already learnt will be your immediate language, and you will be learning about radio waves, the physics of atmospheres and ionospheres, etcetera.' He tapped his pen on the desk. 'Are there any questions?'

Feeling ignorant but desperate to keep abreast with everything the tutor said, Madeleine put her hand up.

'Can you please tell me what an ionosphere is?'

'Anyone care to explain to Miss Hamilton?'

One of the men raised his hand.

'It's where the Earth's atmosphere meets space.'

'That's right. It forms a boundary between the Earth's atmosphere – where we humans and animals live and breathe – and the vacuum of space.' The tutor paused. 'We'll be going into more detail as the course continues.'

Madeleine drew in a deep breath. It sounded as though the course was going to be highly technical rather than practical as she'd imagined. She wasn't sure she'd be up to it after all. Then she reprimanded herself. Surely she was as bright as most, if not all of them, and if not, she'd study night and day if that's what it took to learn whatever was needed to pass the exam. It was imperative to grab the chance to do her bit in the war against that rotten stinking Hitler.

# Chapter Twenty-Two

Not only did Madeleine need to keep up her Morse Code receiving speed to at least twenty-two words a minute and to transmit at more than ten words a minute, she was working solely in German, but to her relief it soon became almost as automatic as in English. On top of that, Leonard Watts gave two long lectures every day about wireless telegraphy and meteorological conditions.

Sometimes she thought her brain would burst with everything she tried to take in. The only saving grace was that while the lectures were going on, she didn't have to do the night or the graveyard shifts. Even *they* must have realised it would be almost impossible to learn completely new technology at three o'clock in the morning, Madeleine thought grimly.

On her one day off a week she usually went to one of the two cinemas in Bletchley, sometimes on her own and sometimes with Olive or Sally or Josie. They were still her favourite dorm mates, as she called them, although the other girls were friendly enough – all except Cora, who rarely spoke to anyone when the others chatted about their personal lives just before getting ready for bed.

\* \* \*

'Don't forget they're playing *Private Lives* this Friday and Saturday,' Josie said when they were having a walk one afternoon.

'I'm really looking forward to it.' Madeleine smiled. 'Shall we go Friday?'

'Yes. I'll get tickets and ask Sally if she wants to come with us. Olive's on nights so she won't be able to.' She paused. 'I expect you miss acting.' Madeleine nodded. 'Did you put your name down for *Anything Goes*?'

'Yes, I did, Cecil got me to sing. It was more like an audition and apparently, I passed.'

'I hope you'll be the night club singer,' Josie said with a chuckle. 'I can just see you as . . . what's her name – the one the chaps love.'

'Reno Sweeney,' Madeleine laughed. 'Well, of course I'd love it but . . . He mentioned that part but he may choose someone entirely different. I just hope it's not Cora. But even if it is, I'm looking forward to rehearsals in a fortnight's time.'

There was a sudden screech from the corner the two of them had just walked round.

'Look out! Car coming!'

She and Josie pressed into a hedge to let a red sports car pass and Madeleine just caught sight of the fair-haired driver as he roared by, tooting his horn and waving. It was Daniel Strong – with a female passenger, a scarf around her head, and leaning closely towards him. Madeleine gave a surreptitious glance at Josie who was looking after the retreating car with an expression of pure desolation.

'Well, that's it, then,' Josie said, her voice coated with misery. 'He's got someone else. And did you see who it was?'

'Not really. He was driving so fast – and she had on a headscarf.'

'Her name's Patsy Taylor. She's playing Sibyl in the play tonight.'

Josie blew her nose and they continued their walk.

'What did you think when you met Daniel that time in the dining room?'

'I thought the two of you had something going.' Madeleine patted her friend's arm. 'So what happened? But don't tell me if you don't want to,' she added quickly.

'I went out with him a few times,' Josie muttered. She looked up at Madeleine, her eyes wet with tears. 'I thought he liked me. Even more than that. He said he loved me once but I knew that was only to try to get me into bed with him. I wouldn't and he hasn't asked me out since.'

*How wise Josie had been*, Madeleine thought. *If only I'd had the willpower.*

'He's not worth it if he can't see how gorgeous you are,' she said.

Josie gave a watery smile. 'Thanks, Maddie. But it doesn't make me feel any better.'

Madeleine hummed a tune as she fastened her stockings to her suspender belt, checked the seams were straight, then slipped on a simple turquoise-blue evening dress with boat neck and short pleated sleeves matching the pleated skirt. She clipped on a pair of opal earrings her parents had given her on her eighteenth birthday and checked her hair and make-up. She was ready and looking forward to seeing Cora playing Amanda, the divorced woman, in *Private Lives*, the character Madeleine herself had played in Richmond's local amateur dramatic society. As it was, Cora was nowhere in sight – she'd obviously dressed and applied her make-up early while she had the mirror above the dorm sink to herself.

'Ready, everyone?' Josie said. 'Let's go so we can get a decent seat.'

The wind whipped Madeleine's hair and chilled the back of her neck in the jacket she'd flung on to go the short distance with Josie and Sally to the Mansion. Her hair was going to look a mess and there was no mirror in the ballroom – as far as she knew – to tidy it. Oh, well. She wasn't going to be in any limelight so it didn't matter.

All the front seats had already filled, so the girls found three together on the second row. They chatted with one another until some of the lights were switched off and the first couple came onto the stage. By her side she felt Josie stiffen. This would be Patsy, the girl snuggling up to Daniel in his sports car, playing Sibyl. She gave Josie's hand a squeeze and her friend lightly pressed Madeleine's hand in return. Goodness, Elyot was none other than Charles Longden, the chap she'd met that first day she'd arrived at the Park and not seen since. Now a smiling Cora waltzed in on the arm of a man several inches shorter playing Victor. Madeleine sat a little straighter in her chair. This was going to be a most interesting evening.

The play had hardly started when Patsy stumbled on her next line, then repeated it, as though to assure herself she'd remembered it. But after Charles had finished his next piece, the girl just stared up at him. The prompt from the sidelines spoke the line audibly but still she didn't pick it up. Madeleine watched, full of sympathy for her, as Charles mouthed his 'wife' the words. But she seemed rooted.

Without warning, Patsy gave a moan and dropped to the floor. Madeleine was startled. That wasn't in the play. Had they altered it for some sort of dramatic effect? But no, Charles was cradling her head in his arms. A woman rushed to the girl's side saying she was a nurse and took over.

'What's going on?' Josie said, her voice blending with all the other murmurings, as she addressed Madeleine.

'I've no idea.'

The doctor turned to the audience.

'Patsy's fainted. I'm sure she'll be fine but she needs to go to the sick room.'

The doctor and Charles led her off the set and people started to get to their feet. At that moment a familiar figure strode onto the stage.

'Good evening, ladies and gentlemen. Most of you know me – Cecil Bell, the producer. This is most unfortunate and we do wish poor Patsy well. She's in the right hands. But we must abide by the old adage – the show must go on.' His jerked his head to the left and right of the audience, then frowned and placed his spectacles on his nose and gazed round again. He cleared his throat. 'Thank you for your patience, everyone. I believe we can resolve this . . . but only if Miss Hamilton is in the audience.'

Madeleine's heart almost stopped. Surely he didn't think she could just stand up and take Sibyl's part without having learnt it.

But Cecil had spotted her. 'Ah, there you are, Madeleine. If you could just come this way and help us get the play moving again. And if everyone would regain their seats.'

'Go on, Maddie,' Josie said. 'You can do it.'

With warmth flooding her cheeks, Madeleine walked over to the stage to the enthusiastic clapping of the audience. Charles Longden, who had returned to his position, grinned as she stood next to him on the terrace.

'Well, well, this is a treat,' he said under his breath. 'Do you know the part?'

'Not exactly. I might have to ad-lib.'

Thank goodness Charles couldn't hear her heart pounding in her ears.

'That's fine by me. I'll give you all the help you need. Just take a few deep breaths and you'll be great.' He paused. 'Right, now where were we? Oh, yes, Sibyl is about to tell me how happy she is.'

Madeleine shut her eyes for a few seconds, a rush of adrenaline coursing through her body, then opened them. It was now Sibyl who was smiling at him.

'Isn't this heavenly? The first day of our honeymoon. I don't think I've ever been so happy.' She gazed up at him. 'Are you as happy as I am?'

Charles, now Elyot, answered. 'Of course. Tremendously happy.'

She puckered her forehead. 'Kiss me to prove it.'

His lips lightly touched her cheek, near the corner of her mouth.

'That wasn't terribly enthusiastic,' Sibyl reprimanded. 'You must kiss me again – three times because I'm very superstitious.'

He pulled her to him and twice kissed the air close enough for her to feel his breath on her cheek. The last one. Before she knew it, his lips touched hers. They were warm and inviting and for a split second she was tempted to respond. But he wasn't Jack and she deftly turned her face away. Life was complicated enough without a flirtation with Charles.

'I'd like to kiss you properly one day,' he whispered in her ear as though it were part of his acting, 'if you'll let me.'

222

She looked up at him. There was no doubt he was good-looking and charming with it, and it would be easy to encourage him. Half the girls at the Park must already be in love with him. She must be careful in future not to give him the least encouragement.

To her relief, the rest of the play to the interval went without any major hitch.

'May I buy you a drink?' Charles said when the clapping had died down.

'I'm meeting the girls,' Madeleine said. Oh, dear, that sounded rather cutting. After all, he'd been a real sport when she'd stepped in, unrehearsed. 'But do join us.'

'No, you be with your friends. I'll see you in fifteen minutes.'

'You were marvellous, Maddie,' Sally said admiringly when they were at the bar sipping an orange squash in the interval.

'I'll drink to that,' Josie said. 'You looked as though you're really enjoying yourself.'

'I loved it,' Madeleine said. 'When I'm performing I always think it's where I truly belong – on the stage.' She looked at her friends and couldn't help laughing. 'It sounds so pretentious, doesn't it, but it's true.'

'After we win this damned war you should definitely become a professional actress,' Josie said.

'Charles was certainly being attentive,' Sally said. 'I bet he couldn't believe his luck when he realised he was going to be playing opposite you as Sibyl who demanded all those kisses.' She chuckled.

It was nice to see the serious Sally enjoying the joke, Madeleine thought.

'He's just an old flirt,' she said, chuckling.

The bell rang and Cecil called out: 'Would you please take your places.'

'I'd better go,' Madeleine said, quickly downing her drink.

At the end of Act 3, when the players were taking their curtain call without the aid of an existing curtain, Cecil stepped up and spoke.

'Ladies and gentlemen, I hope your evening wasn't spoilt by Patsy's unfortunate plight. I'm told she's fine but needs to rest. I'm afraid she's not going to be able to act in tomorrow's performance, but if Madeleine is happy to do a repeat—'

There was a burst of clapping and one or two cheers.

Cecil waited until it died down.

'As I was saying, but of course we must ask Madeleine if she's happy to oblige.'

Madeleine, her hand grasped on one side by Brian playing Victor, with Charles pressing her other, answered him:

'I'd be honoured. I know I fluffed some of the lines, but maybe you can give me a copy of the script, Mr Bell, and I'll try and swot up so I'm a bit more polished tomorrow night and don't get Sibyl's lines muddled with Amanda's lines as I did a few times tonight.'

Laughter broke out but, scanning the audience, Madeleine knew it was all in good fun.

'I don't know how you pulled it off with no rehearsals,' Sally said as the three of them walked back to their hut. 'It was so good – however did you remember that part when you'd never played it before and not even had one rehearsal?'

'I'd played Amanda before. That's why I spoke her lines

224

by mistake a couple of times. You hear everyone else's lines so many times you just absorb them.'

'Well, you were the best, Maddie. You sounded so completely natural.'

'Charles sometimes had to mutter my next line when he saw my blank expression,' Madeleine laughed. 'But I must say, I thoroughly enjoyed myself.'

'And Sally and I enjoyed *Cora's* expression when she heard you'd be on again tomorrow evening,' Josie giggled. 'The way she flirted with Charles was something to behold.'

'Well, they realise they should never have got divorced,' Madeleine said, though why she was sticking up for Cora, she had no idea. 'That was the story.'

'If truth be told, he didn't make an overt play for Cora at all, like I expected,' Sally said.

'That's because he has his eye on our Sibyl,' was Josie's gleeful reply.

In her bunk that night, Madeleine lay awake thinking. Was Josie right? Did Charles have more than an interest in her? If so, she was going to have to decide how to handle him tomorrow night. What if he became more amorous? She lay there, her mind teeming, reluctant to put into words that the only person she ever wanted to kiss her was Jack. And he had obviously lost all interest.

She sighed and turned over in bed, coming face to face with Cora who was sound asleep with her mouth open, quietly and rhythmically snoring. She couldn't help a smile spreading across her face. All that glamour and the woman snored.

# Chapter Twenty-Three

Every break between Morse Code practice and lectures, Madeleine managed to go over her part and by the end of the day felt more confident that she could carry it through without getting muddled with Amanda's lines. She would give Sibyl's part everything she'd got to persuade Cecil to allow her to play Reno Sweeney.

After she'd eaten a light supper with Olive, who'd managed to swap her shift so she could watch tonight's performance, Madeleine felt the familiar fluttering in her stomach. She looked at her watch for the umpteenth time as she swallowed another piece of the cheese and tomato on toast. A crumb got stuck in her throat and she started to cough. Olive handed her a glass of water.

'Are you nervous?'

'A bit,' Madeleine said. 'It's worse when I'm about to go on. My mind goes blank and I think I'll never remember the first line even.'

'You'll be fine from what I hear from Sally and Josie,' Olive said, patting her hand. 'Come on, girl. You need to get changed and do some calming breathing.'

* * *

When Madeleine stepped into the ballroom, a few people having a drink at the bar gave her an enthusiastic clap. Cecil Bell put his drink down and walked over to her.

'Delighted to put you through the torture again, Madeleine.' He gave her shoulder a light squeeze. 'Thanks for being such a sport.'

'I hope I can live up to it,' she murmured.

'If you're as good as last night, you have nothing to worry about.'

'Oh, dear. That's already making me nervous.'

'Nothing to it.' He put his hand on her arm. 'Why don't you have a drink. Calm your nerves.'

'Oh, no,' Madeleine said quickly. 'That would tip me right over the edge.'

He smiled and looked round as Charles Longden tapped him on the shoulder, at the same time sending Madeleine a warm smile.

*As though there's something going on between us.*

Her thoughts flew to that last kiss he'd given her. It was a kiss, if she'd allowed it, that threatened to go beyond acting. She hoped she'd be able to handle him better this time. It would be fatal to give him any hint that she was being more than simply the actress playing Sibyl.

'Can I get either of you a drink?' Charles said.

'Still got one, old chap,' Cecil answered. 'And Madeleine refuses to have one. Says it will have an effect on her memory.'

'Very sensible.' Charles turned to Madeleine. 'You look quite the part for a simpering second wife,' he said admiringly.

'Less of the simpering,' Madeleine said more abruptly than she'd meant. 'I'm not going to have her totally pathetic or Elyot wouldn't have married her in the first place.'

'Mmm. Perhaps you're right.' He kept his gaze on her.

'I'll leave you both to it, then,' Cecil said.

Charles glanced at his watch, then smiled down at her.

'It's time to leave the room so we're ready to make our appearance on the so-called terrace in ten minutes' time.'

In one of the smaller rooms at the back of the ballroom that had to serve as a dressing room, Madeleine noticed Brian was having trouble doing up his cufflinks. She was about to ask if she could help him when Cora breezed in, summed up the situation, and rushed over.

'Allow me,' she said, throwing a triumphant grin at Madeleine as though knowing she'd beaten her to it.

'Everyone ready to go on?' Cecil stepped into the room and when the four agreed, he clapped his hands. 'Off you go.'

Madeleine had seen a couple of posters in the dining room and Hut 2's teashop advertising the play a week ago but was amazed now to see double the number of people since last night as the four of them stepped onto the stage, Charles's arm firmly round her waist. They waited for the polite clapping to subside and then she and Charles stood together as Cora, playing Amanda, spoke the first line. She was good, Madeleine had to admit, after she listened to Amanda's frustration with her new husband, Victor.

Breathing out her tension and waiting for her cue, Madeleine glanced over to the audience just as a tall, dark-haired man carrying a raincoat hurried in. She blinked. Dear God. Was it . . .? Oh, if only it wasn't so dark out there. If she could just see the man's face properly, she'd laugh at herself for imagining things. It was just wishful thinking. She peered out again. No. She wasn't hallucinating. It was a real person. But he did remind her . . . She swallowed hard, ready to turn back to Charles who was speaking his lines.

But the man had seen her. She could almost hear his sharp intake of breath. He held her gaze. The play was forgotten. It was as though they were the only two people in the room. She couldn't drag her eyes away. This time there was no mistake. He gave a tiny, almost imperceptible nod as though to confirm it was definitely him before he found a seat in the aisle and sat down. And then he smiled at her. That wonderful smile that lit up her insides.

Trying to ignore her heartbeat thumping in her chest, Madeleine's mind flew in every direction. How could he be here at the Park? He was a diplomat at the British Embassy the last time she'd seen him. He must have changed jobs. He—

'Madeleine, ask me for a kiss,' Charles said without moving his lips.

Madeleine jumped.

*Dear God, where are we in the script?*

She couldn't speak. It was as though her lips were stapled together. Oh, no, what was her line?

'Prove you love me,' Charles ad-libbed in a clear tone, then bent his head and planted his lips firmly onto her mouth.

She couldn't move her head one inch. He'd trapped her. Her head felt like cotton wool. And then her brain swung into action and she said with what sounded to her ears a hysterical giggle:

'Kiss me three times because I'm superstitious.'

As he lowered his head again, she said through gritted teeth:

'We're acting – remember?'

All she could see was his smile as his lips lightly touched hers.

*Thank goodness.*

Then the second one – the same. She realised she was holding her breath and breathed out. It was going to be all right. He might be a flirt, but he was a gentleman. Only one more to go. Without warning his mouth came down hard on hers, forcing her lips apart. She felt his tongue slide in. *Dear God.* Hardly realising what she was doing she nipped it with her teeth, then threw her head back, laughing, as though it was part of the script and she was simply teasing her new husband.

'You didn't have to do that,' he hissed.

'Are you glad you married me?' She was hardly able to arrange her mouth into Sibyl's sweet loving smile, she was so angry.

Furious with Charles and conscious of Jack in the audience watching them, it took all Madeleine's willpower to slip back into Sibyl's character. Occasionally, she muffed a line though by and large she managed to rescue it so no one would notice. Charles, on the other hand, was word perfect.

The blood still warming her cheeks, she was relieved when the play finally ended and she took her bow with the other three, Charles gripping her hand. But all she could think of was Jack and finding out what had happened to him. If he knew she was at the Park. If he'd even instigated it. She had so many questions to ask him but they needed somewhere where they could speak in private.

Her eyes scanned the audience as people were beginning to leave their seats and spotted Jack's tall figure making for the bar. At that moment he turned and caught her gaze.

The smile had disappeared. Even from the distance, his mouth looked grim. But perhaps it was her overwrought imagination at work again.

He was asking the barman for a beer as she approached. As if he knew she was there, he swung round. No, she hadn't imagined it. Gold flecks in his normally warm brown eyes sparked with anger. But what could have changed since that smile when he'd first come into the ballroom?

'Hello, Madeleine. I must congratulate you on your performance tonight.'

She'd never heard him sound so cool. She forced herself to look steadily at him, desperate to ask why he hadn't written to the address she'd given him – not one word since war was declared. But pride forbade it. She didn't know what she'd been expecting to see in those brown eyes, but she hadn't bargained for that hard glint. It was as though he were annoyed with *her* instead of the other way round. He'd been back in England all these weeks and hadn't attempted to get in touch with her. And now he was here in person, standing so close to her and yet so far away. She felt bereft of words.

'Would you like something to drink . . . a glass of wine perhaps?' he said, still in that strange, over-polite manner.

She felt all her pent-up emotion draining away. If they were going to quarrel . . .

'No, thanks. It's getting late.'

His eyes locked with hers. It was as though he could tell what she was thinking. Abruptly she focused on some of the others who were having a drink at the bar and noticed Charles talking to an animated Cora. Jack followed Madeleine's gaze, and she noticed his jaw harden before he turned back to her.

231

'We need to talk,' he said finally.

'Not now,' she said. 'I'm rather tired.' At least that was true.

'You sure?'

'Yes.'

He nodded. 'All right. I understand. All that incredibly convincing acting –' he slightly emphasised the last word '– must have really taken it out of you.'

She gave him a sharp look. What was *that* supposed to mean?

'But I do need to speak to you and—'

'Jack, I'm sorry, I have to go.'

'As you wish.' His tone was distinctly cool.

The intensity of his gaze didn't change. Then his mouth tightened and he simply shrugged.

It took every ounce of Madeleine's will to walk away, certain he was staring after her.

Only Sally and Rita were in the dormitory. The two girls were chatting quietly while Madeleine prepared for bed. When she'd slipped under the covers they were still talking but she was glad. Their murmurings were comforting. She didn't want to be alone with her thoughts after Jack had been so distant – annoyed even. If circumstances hadn't brought them together – no thanks to any effort on *his* part, she reminded herself – then no doubt he wouldn't have bothered to keep in touch. She wasn't being unfair, she told herself – she should have heard from him weeks ago. But she couldn't forget that hard glint in his eye after the play when he'd said they needed to talk. Well, if that was his mood, she had nothing to say to him. She gulped, but refused to let the tears start. And yet she could have sworn there'd been a connection between them when he'd caught her eye before he'd sat down to watch the play and he'd smiled as though to let her know he was happy to see her. Well, she'd been wrong.

*But he has a decent side to him,* her inner voice said. *Look how kind he was when he risked his position to arrange the twins' fake British passports. He didn't have to do it. His job was to look after British people, not Germans.*

*I've already thanked him,* she argued with the voice. And that was in the past. No, she was glad she'd refused to stay and listen to him. He had nothing to say that would interest her anymore.

She turned over in bed, then put her hand under the pillow and drew it towards her face to muffle an unexpected sob. She mustn't cry – she just mustn't. Not in front of the stream of girls who were now coming through the door, chattering away and sounding happy. She startled when she heard her name:

'Wasn't Maddie good? Fancy being able to take over at a moment's notice.'

It was Olive. Then came Cora's cool tones.

'I suppose she was bearable if you overlook the beginning when she didn't seem to know which way was up or even what play she was in. She was obviously a bag of nerves. Brian and I couldn't believe it. From where I stood I could see Charles getting most frustrated wondering when the devil she was ever going to say anything. I could lip-read him telling her her next line on several occasions. Personally, I don't think she cuts the mustard.'

'Shhh, Cora. Don't say such things. You'll wake her up.'

It was too much. Madeleine shot up in bed and glared at the woman.

233

'I've had precious little time to rehearse, unlike some people I know.' She stared at Cora so there was no mistaking who the barb was directed at.

There was a sudden silence. The other girls, who were in various stages of undress or removing their make-up, paused.

'My, my, we are touchy,' Cora said. 'Sorry if I spoke a few home truths, but I won't take back my words – in my opinion, you'll never make it as a professional actress.'

'Let's get something straight, Cora,' Madeleine snapped. 'I'm not here to become a professional actress. In case you've forgotten, there's a war on. I'm here to do my bit for my country. But if I ever need to hear your opinion on my acting, I'll let you know.' She doubled over the one thin pillow. 'Right now, I'm going to get some kip. Goodnight.'

There was a nervous giggle as Madeleine curled under the bedcover but soon any murmuring died down. All was quiet except the crackle of dying embers in the wood-burning stove. But try as she would, she couldn't drift off. Not when this evening she'd seen Jack hurry into the ballroom – their eyes meeting – that lingering gaze when she'd forgotten where she was. Her eyes stung with tears as she finally admitted to herself that at that very moment she'd done the most unwise thing in the world. However angry she was now, she'd gone and fallen head over heels in love with him.

No wonder she'd forgotten her bloody lines!

# Chapter Twenty-Four

The first thought on Madeleine's mind the moment she awoke from a fitful sleep was that she loved Jack. The revelation left her breathless. But she must never let him know. Not a hint. Though heaven knows why she was worrying. There wouldn't be any opportunity for them to meet as she didn't even know what hut he worked in – that is, if he was working here at all. Perhaps he was just a visitor. She'd already worked out there were many different departments at BP even though she had no idea what went on behind the closed doors. But a cultural attaché at the Park? It didn't make sense.

How long had he been here? It can't have been that long as she would have noticed the tall figure in the dining room or in Hut 2 having a break, or even bumped into him in the town. At least now if she spotted him she could easily avoid him.

Even though it was Sunday, her one day off, she felt restless. Normally, she loved being up early before anyone else stirred, wanting to pack in as much as she could into the day, but this morning her legs felt wooden. She sat on the edge of her makeshift bed, her breath appearing in misty clouds in front of her. Bending over, she tried to massage some life into her calves, then wiggled her toes, seeing but not feeling the movement. The cold permeated her very bones.

She stumbled from the bed and over to the sink, catching sight of herself in the mottled mirror. Oh, dear. Her eyes looked strained and her hair needed washing. She'd do it this evening when she was allowed her weekly slot in the massive marble bathroom in the Mansion. For now she needed to have a quick wash and get dressed before she turned into a snowman. Then breakfast.

It felt a fraction warmer outside than it did inside the hostel, Madeleine decided, as she hurried along the paths to the Mansion. An enticing smell of bacon met her as she entered the dining room, the door already ajar to welcome the early risers.

'Good morning, Madeleine.'

There was Jack sitting over by the Regency-modelled window.

Just to hear his voice saying her name made her catch her breath. He looked so dammed attractive, his dark head turned towards her, his eyes meeting hers across the elegant room.

There was only one other person – an older woman sitting in the corner on the far side of the room. Thank heavens she was immersed in her book.

*Don't react. Be normal.*

But no admonishing could stop her heart beating hard and fast.

'Do join me.' He half rose, folding his newspaper and putting it to one side.

*You have to, Maddie. You'd look ridiculous if you ignored him. Go on over.*

She bit her lip. 'I'd better get something to eat first.'

It would give her time to calm down. All she could think of was that he was the one who was churning her insides. She walked over to the counter where one of the cooks was bringing a plate of fried eggs.

'May I have one of those?' Madeleine said. 'And a tomato.'

'Anything else, dear?' the woman asked.

'No, thank you.' Somehow she couldn't tackle bacon after all.

She put a piece of toast on the plate and poured herself a cup of tea. She took her tray and set it down on Jack's table as he pulled a chair out for her.

'I thought you'd like to face the window,' he said.

Madeleine gave him a surreptitious look. The hard glint had gone from his eyes. She couldn't read his expression at all. She noticed he'd finished his breakfast.

'I'm glad we have this chance to talk before anyone else comes in.' He caught her eye. 'Why don't you eat before it gets cold and give me a chance to explain why you haven't heard from me for the last two months.'

'If you must.' She tried to make her tone casual as she picked up her knife and fork.

'I was imprisoned in the Embassy the day after Britain declared war.'

Her forkful of egg stopped in mid-air.

*A likely story.* She stared at him.

'I know it sounds bizarre but it's true. Quite a few of us were left behind on purpose, more or less as hostages, because we had orders to wait until every German diplomat was back from the whole of the British Empire.'

'Had they never heard of aeroplanes?' Madeleine could hardly contain her sarcasm.

237

He threw her a look. 'They need planes for troops, not for bringing back a bunch of diplomats. They had to return by ship . . . and places like Australia and New Zealand take the best part of eight weeks . . . often longer nowadays.

'The day the Ambassador and most of the other diplomats went home, the Germans cut our external telephone wires,' he continued. 'They said all contact between us and England was now broken. We couldn't write a letter . . . we couldn't even go out and get a packet of cigarettes without an escort from two armed soldiers. It was pretty grim. And all I could think of was how you'd feel not hearing a word. Thinking I'd forgotten you. But believe me, I hadn't.' He allowed a moment to pass before adding, 'I just hoped you hadn't forgotten *me*.'

She didn't know how to respond. It sounded genuine. Of course it was. She stabbed a piece of her tomato.

'Why aren't you wearing your engagement ring?'

She gave a start. Jack was staring at her left hand. He looked up at her with raised eyebrow. Oh, she could kick herself. Of *course* he was bound to notice but she hadn't prepared any reason. Now it was too late to explain about bringing Frau Weinberg's precious jewellery to England. He'd want to know why she hadn't trusted him before.

'It didn't work out,' she said feebly.

He gazed at her, then lightly touched the finger the ring had once occupied. Just that tiny, unexpected physical connection between them sent a tingle of shock waves through her.

'I couldn't be more glad.' He smiled for the first time.

She forced herself to carry on eating, but her throat was tight and after a few moments she looked directly at him.

'Can I ask you something?'

'Anything. You know that.'

'Why did you act so strangely after the play finished? You looked positively angry.'

'Did I?' He frowned.

'Yes, you did. That's why I didn't want to stay and talk.'

'Oh, that. It doesn't matter – it's not important.'

'Yes it is,' she persisted. 'I want to know why you suddenly changed.'

'If you must know, I thought you were still engaged to some chap – probably a decent enough bloke – and there you were in front of my eyes, looking for all the world as though you were kissing someone you loved.' He leant back in his chair waiting for her response. 'And that "someone" couldn't possibly have been your fiancé,' he added when she didn't speak.

'So you thought I was being unfaithful to him?'

'Yes, that's about it.'

'Well, I wasn't.' She met his eyes. 'Have you never heard of acting?'

'That's my point. It didn't look like acting to me.'

He was uncannily close to the truth.

'It might not have been on *his* side,' she admitted, 'but it definitely was on *mine*.'

'Ah, now we're getting somewhere.' Jack lit a cigarette.

'What's that supposed to mean?'

Jack inhaled. 'Sounds to me as though this co-actor has already been "making out" with you, as the Americans say, if you've come to that conclusion.'

'I'm not interested in what the Americans say,' Madeleine flashed, her voice rising.

Jack blew out a stream of smoke to one side, glanced at

his watch, then stubbed the hardly touched cigarette in the ashtray. He stood up and looked down at her.

'I'd best be going then. I have a shift about to start and I don't want to be late on my first day. Maybe we can continue this interesting subject later.'

Before she could answer he bent to kiss her cheek and was gone.

The woman in the corner threw her a sympathetic look as she, too, left the room.

Her cheeks burning, wondering how much she'd heard, Madeleine pushed her unfinished breakfast to one side. It was cold anyway.

Feeling at a loss but resolute that Jack wasn't going to set her mood for the day, she decided to call in at the Post Room as she'd had no time yesterday when she'd been caught up with the play. To her delight, the postboy handed her a letter from the twins. It was only their second one, even though she wrote to them every week. But as they'd had so many major changes to come to terms with, apart from school lessons being in a foreign language, she wasn't surprised.

*Dear Maddie,*

*Lotte and ~~me~~ I have not a letter from Mutti and Papa. Aunt Ruth and Uncle Joseph have also not had one. Please can you find if they are well and when they will come to England. Tell them we miss them very much.*

Madeleine's eyes filled with tears. Their world had drastically changed like so many other children's. She could no longer comfort herself with 'no news is good news' when after all this time there was a strong possibility that they'd either been sent to a concentration camp – or worse.

She swallowed hard. She mustn't let her mind dwell on the 'worse'. Until there was definite news there was always hope. She read on.

> *Lotte is good at arithmetic. She will learn the piano. I am good at the violin and I like drawing. When we have a test in English we are not last in class like the beginning.*
>
> *When will you come to see us? Aunt Ruth says it is secret. But Lotte and I can keep secrets. Lotte wants to write now. Love from Erich.*

> *Dear Maddie,*
>
> *Auntie Ruth and Uncle Joseph are kind but we miss Mutti and Papa and you. Erich gets cross with our cousins but I like them and Ellie is my best friend. I play with Eva but she is a bit young. Erich has a friend at school called Robert and they do everything together. I am to learn the piano.*
>
> *I will end now because I can hear Auntie Ruth call us for supper.*
>
> *Please visit soon.*
>
> *Love from Lotte XXXX*

Madeleine read their letters again. They didn't sound quite so frantic or homesick as they used to be and were near perfect in their English, but their messages told her they were still homesick and worried about their parents – as she was. How proud Herr and Frau Weinberg would be to know their children were getting on so well at school and that Lotte had started to learn the piano. She prayed the twins would be able to tell them in person one day.

# Chapter Twenty-Five

*November 1939*

It was the start of Madeleine's ninth week. It was also the exam day when she'd be doing a Morse Code speed test, seeing how competent she was in taking down messages in German, and an oral exam to see how fluent she was in the language.

Feeling a little nervous knowing her next duty at the Park rested on speed and accuracy, she put on her headphones and picked up her pencil. Hardly aware of the time passing, she was startled when Leonard called for the class to stop.

Silently she thanked her father as she removed her headphones. He'd definitely given her a head start.

'If you've finished, Miss Hamilton,' Leonard said, 'please go next door where you'll be given your German oral test.'

Madeleine's stomach tightened as she knocked on the door and was told to enter. Behind the desk sat a woman in WAAF uniform, an officer, who regarded her with not the slightest hint of a smile.

'*Setzen Sie sich, bitte.*'

Madeleine sat in the chair opposite as directed.

'We will now conduct the entire conversation *auf Deutsch*,' she said.

The woman, who never introduced herself, flung question after question to Madeleine, who served them back as deftly as though she were playing a game of tennis. After ten minutes the woman said:

'I note you have a degree in German yet your use of the language is somewhat colloquial,' she said, continuing in German. 'Why would that be?'

'I lived in Munich for the best part of last year teaching English to two German children.'

The woman raised an eyebrow. 'Hmm. Bavaria. That would explain the strangled accent.'

*Damn. Is that going to scupper my chances?* But Madeleine didn't want to put that idea into the woman's head.

'We did study literature as well,' she said.

The woman nodded.

'*Danke*, Miss Hamilton. '*Das ist alles*.' She rose to her feet. '*Wir werden Sie später sprechen*.'

'*Vielen Dank*,' Madeleine murmured as she turned to leave.

Phew! She was glad that was over, even though the woman had said at the end they would be speaking later. Ten more weeks of training to go which she calculated would take her into the middle of January. It would be 1940. A new decade. What would it bring? According to articles she'd read in the newspapers, this war was going to last several years. Madeleine sighed. She was one of the lucky ones – working and living in a part of the country that was probably as safe as anyone could be from the Luftwaffe eye. And at least the lectures grabbed her attention. At the end of each one, providing she could understand it, she told herself she was that bit nearer to becoming a wireless telegraphist. She and her colleagues would then be sent to one of the huts which presumably had a special department for their work. Then she would really feel she had something definite to contribute.

It was still frustrating not to be told more detail of the work she'd be doing and this train of thought led her to Jack. What work was he earmarked to do? Even though she'd had it drummed into her not to even ask anyone which hut they worked in, she longed to know about Jack. Maybe she could accidentally keep an eye out to see where he went if he divulged his shift. Surely that wouldn't break any rules. And was this a permanent transfer? If so, where did that leave her? They hadn't exactly quarrelled but they'd parted on not the best of terms the day before yesterday at breakfast, which was the last time she'd had sight of him. The last thing she wanted was for him to guess that she loved him and put him in an awkward position, as he still thought she had an ex-fiancé whom she'd probably ditched when she'd met Charles. As if the war wasn't enough to complicate lives, she thought with a sigh.

'Do you fancy going for a coffee?' Sandra, one of the few other female trainees, asked when Madeleine was just thinking it was time for a break.

It was the first time there'd been any contact between them besides a nod and a greeting. She ran a tongue over her lips. She needed water more than anything. But she smiled at Sandra.

'Good idea. I'd love one.'

As soon as they entered Hut 2, the first person Madeleine set eyes on was Jack sitting on his own, waving them to join him. Oh, not again! It was the last thing she wanted to do with Sandra present. This time he was smiling. Was that an act for Sandra's benefit?

'That bloke seems to know you,' Sandra said, looking at her curiously.

'Only vaguely.' She made her voice non-committal.

'Did you meet him here?' Sandra pressed.

Madeleine hesitated. How to answer. She certainly wasn't about to go into any personal details.

'I've chatted with him a couple of times.'

'Oh, do I smell romance?' Sandra winked.

'No, you don't,' Madeleine snapped.

'Hmm. I wonder.' Sandra threw her a searching look, then grinned. 'Come on, then, let's go and keep him company and find out a bit more about him.'

Irritation mounting in her throat at Sandra's nosiness, Madeleine reluctantly followed her to Jack's table.

'Sandra, this is Jack Syl—' She broke off when she saw his frown. Damn. He might not want his whole name bandied about. 'We'll stick to Christian names,' she added with a nervous laugh. 'I've met so many new people, it's hard enough to remember *those*.'

'How do you do?' Sandra put out her hand and Jack briefly shook it, then stood.

'May I get you ladies a drink?'

'Coffee, please,' Sandra said.

'Madeleine?' Jack looked directly at her.

'Oh, um, there's no need . . . well, just a glass of water, thank you.'

'I could do with another coffee so I'll get three.'

He was barely out of earshot when Sandra, her eyes following him, said:

245

'Mmm. Nice arse.'

'*Sandra!*'

Sandra chortled. 'You're blushing, Maddie. Have you led such a sheltered life?' She put her elbows on the table and sent Madeleine an intense stare. 'He seems to like you more than just a casual acquaintance.'

'Don't read something into something that doesn't exist, Sandra,' Madeleine said firmly, not wanting to pursue this line of conversation. 'Have you any brothers and sisters at home?'

'No, I'm an only, thank God.'

'What work did you do before coming here?'

'Oh, I worked in a posh store.' She tossed her head. 'Accessories . . . hats and belts and things.'

'Sounds interesting.'

Sandra wrinkled her nose. 'S'all right. Helped with the bills.' She paused. 'How are you getting on with the lectures?'

'They're quite interesting.'

'That radar one this morning. What did you make of it?'

Madeleine hesitated, hearing the sound of people chatting. Jack was heading towards them carrying a tray.

'Sandra, I don't think we should be talking about our work.'

'We're not exactly giving away any secrets to anybody.'

'I know, but we've signed the Official Secrets Act and we're not supposed to be discussing anything at all we do here.'

'I can't see the harm in asking that.' Sandra gave an impatient exhale of breath. 'Oh, lovely, here's our coffee.'

Jack set the tray down and put steaming mugs in front of them and a plate of biscuits.

'Very kind of you,' Sandra said as she helped herself to a biscuit.

'You ladies seemed to be in deep conversation,' he remarked.

'I was just asking Maddie what she thought of our lec—'

Madeleine nudged Sandra's foot in warning.

'We were talking about our jobs before we came here,' Madeleine said.

Jack caught her eye. His held a warning. 'Well, so long as you don't discuss your work. They really mean business when you've signed the Official Secrets Act.'

'Duly told off,' Sandra muttered.

'It's better to be safe than sorry,' Jack returned. 'We need to be aware of what we're saying at all times.'

He made polite conversation, then swallowed his coffee in a few gulps and took his jacket from the back of his chair.

'I should get back to work.' He buttoned his jacket. 'Nice to meet you, Sandra.' He turned to Madeleine, his eyes lingering on hers. 'I hope to catch up with you soon.'

Without waiting for any reply he left.

'Catch up?' Sandra said. 'Mmm. Sounds like you got along famously over that breakfast.' Sandra's baby-blue eyes regarded her from under curly eyelashes. 'You realise he's crazy about you.'

'Stop that nonsense.' Madeleine glanced at the wall clock. 'Come on, it's time to go.'

It was only after she scraped back her chair to leave that she noticed someone sitting at a nearby adjacent table. Cora was gazing at her with eyes like steel. It was obvious she'd heard every word of Sandra's ringing tones. Madeleine had been so conscious of Jack she hadn't noticed the woman walk in.

# Chapter Twenty-Six

Madeleine switched off her wireless set. Nine more weeks to go. She was becoming dah-dit crazy. Every time she ventured outside for a walk, the sound of raindrops splashing down in the puddles and the mocking wind whisking up the already fallen leaves and whirling them into the air – even her own footsteps – caused her to translate the rhythms into Morse Code. She gave a deep sigh. If only Leonard would give them some practical work to do. She couldn't remember even half what she was trying to cram into her brain and they were due to have a signals test in a week.

Today the weather was filthy. She couldn't face it. If only there was a swimming pool in the town so she could exercise her legs and arms. She'd been getting cramp lately in bed and could only think it was sitting around so much. Well, rehearsals were soon to start on *Anything Goes*, so at least there'd be some dancing if she only made it into the chorus, though she'd learnt the part of the night club singer just in case. It would be a very different part for her that she felt would stretch her acting abilities. She was seeing Cecil this evening to confirm her part as he'd not heard her sing Reno Sweeney's songs. She'd go to the ballroom and read the lyrics one more time so she was word perfect. And on the way she'd see if there was any post.

'One for you, miss,' the postboy said.

She glanced at the envelope. Ruth. Lovely. Ruth wrote nice long newsy letters. She'd read it first and then look at the songs.

In the ballroom she settled herself in one of the leather chairs, threw off her shoes and tucked her feet under her bottom, then opened Ruth's letter. It was dated 12th November 1939.

*My dear Madeleine,*

*I hope you have settled into your new job.*

*I know you're not allowed to have telephone calls where you are or where you live, so this is the reason why I'm writing to you. You must prepare yourself for what I'm going to tell you. Fran and Freddie are back in England. They were lucky that Fran was not interned. Even more lucky that Freddie has a brother in Basel who sponsored him so they were able to get to England via Switzerland – a long journey and they're worn out. They arrived late last night and rang me first thing this morning.*

But that's wonderful news. So what did Ruth mean by preparing herself? Madeleine frowned and read on.

*You must brace yourself for a terrible shock. Fran told me the Weinbergs were taken away the same week you left with the twins. We fear they've been sent to a concentration camp. They were given no warning and no reason. Fran never heard anything more from the kind neighbour who had informed her that Jews are disappearing at an alarming rate, and we never set eyes on them again. We're told these places are merely labour camps though we've heard through the grapevine that at best the internees are malnourished and overworked, and some of them are just children. But worse, there are unspeakable rumours that some of them are being tortured! This could be the reason why these people never come home. They haven't survived.*

Madeleine swallowed. Then again. Her mouth tasted stale. Nausea filled her stomach at the thought of the Weinbergs being tortured. And all the other Jewish families. Bile came up in her throat. Dear God, she was going to be sick. She flung the letter down on the table and rushed to the cloakroom, not taking time to bolt the door. She knelt over the pan and vomited. Then again, until she had nothing more left. Sweating with the exertion, she slowly rose to her feet, dizzy now as she hung on to the sink for a few moments to get her balance before she felt capable of washing her hands. Her mouth tasted stale and bitter. She positioned it under the tap, rinsing and spitting out, over and over until she swallowed a few mouthfuls of the blessed water. It was then that she began to shake. Her whole body trembled. The walls of the tiny room felt they were closing in on her. It was dark. Choking back the tears, she reached for her handbag. Where the hell was it? In her confusion she tried to think. Then she remembered. Oh, no, she'd left her handbag in the ballroom. Not only that – Ruth's letter was open for anyone to see. How stupid of her.

Wiping her eyes with the back of her hand, she half ran along the hall and opened the ballroom door. It was much more crowded now. Where had she been sitting? Ah, it was that black leather armchair near the fireplace because her raincoat was where she'd folded it over the back. She rushed over to where Cora was occupying the chair opposite, her head bent, reading. To Madeleine's relief her handbag was exactly where she'd left it by the side of the chair. But the letter where she'd flung it on the table had vanished. It took only one glance to see that Cora was reading Ruth's letter.

'What the hell do you think you're doing?' Madeleine's voice trembled with fury.

Cora looked up, unblinking. 'Oh, it's you. Is this yours then?' She nonchalantly held out Ruth's letter.

Madeleine snatched it from her hand.

'Now, Maddie, don't get in a paddy.' Cora gave a slow smile.

'Perhaps you'd care to explain why you were reading my private letter.'

'What do you take me for?' Cora's eyes widened with innocence. 'I didn't *read* it. I just wondered who it belonged to, that's all, so I could give it back.' She stared at Madeleine. 'It was left open for all the world to see, so you should thank me for rescuing it before any prying eyes got hold of it.'

'And your idea of *rescuing* –'. Madeleine deliberately emphasised the word, pausing to look Cora face on '– was to actually *read* a letter addressed to me personally? You couldn't have just looked at the envelope?'

'Like I said – I just glanced at the salutation,' she smirked. 'Why should I want to read it?'

Madeleine swallowed. It was her own fault. And she knew without any doubt that it was Cora with the prying

251

eyes. And Cora had read the letter from beginning to end – which is more than *she'd* been able to do. She put the letter in her handbag, the tears welling up again as she thought of dear Frau and Herr Weinberg in one of those horrifying camps. Were they at this moment starving? Being tortured. Oh, it didn't bear thinking about. But she had to think. She had to find Jack. He was the only person she could talk to about Ruth's letter. Advise her what to do and say to the twins. But she didn't know which hut he worked in, where he lived, or what shift he was on. And because everything was so secretive here, she couldn't even ask anyone his whereabouts.

'Maddie?'

It irritated her the way Cora used her diminutive name. It was reserved only for friends and her father and brothers. But this wasn't the time to make such a comment.

Madeleine gazed at her, trying hard to find something nice about the woman's manner. But all she saw was that mocking smile.

'I'm most grateful to you for . . . as you call it, *rescuing* my private correspondence,' Madeleine said in as cool a voice as she could muster.

She turned on her heel and marched across the floor, her heels clicking angrily with every step, shoving her arms through the sleeves of her raincoat as she stepped out of the entrance door into the porch and straight into the arms of Charles.

'Hey, where are you off to in such a hurry?'

'I'm sorry, I've got to go. I have to—'

He gazed down at her. 'Just a moment, Maddie. You sound upset. What's up?'

'N-nothing. Nothing at all.'

'Let's just go inside a minute. It's filthy out here and you'll get soaked.' He guided her back into the porch, then studied her under the weak light. 'You sure you're all right?'

'Yes.' Oh, she just wanted to get away. To see Jack. To speak to him. Oh, please . . .

'Cecil asked if I'd seen you. He's waiting to confirm your part in *Anything Goes*.'

'Tell him I've changed my mind. I don't want to be in it after all.'

Charles frowned. 'I guess that's a woman's prerogative to change her mind, but I wish you'd reconsider. You know I'm playing the ship's captain, but if you've made up your mind, you'd better go and tell him yourself.'

'All right.' She hesitated. 'Charles, how many people work at the Park, do you think?'

He raised an eyebrow. 'Why do you want to know?'

'Just curiosity.'

'Hmm. I'd say about five hundred and increasing daily.' He looked at her intently. 'Does that answer your question?'

'Yes . . . and thank you.'

'Before you go, let me ask *you* a question, Madeleine.' He fixed his eyes on her. 'Who exactly are you looking for in these five hundred people?'

Her stomach jolted. How on earth had he guessed that's what she was doing?

'It wouldn't be that chap I saw you with at the bar that Saturday night after we finished *Private Lives*, would it?' When she didn't answer, he said, 'Because if it is, I would steer clear of him if I were you.'

Madeleine felt herself bristle.

'First of all, I'm *not* you and second, what's he supposed to have done that I have to *steer clear* of him?'

Charles narrowed his eyes. 'Ah, so it *is* him. I did wonder when I saw the two of you.' His voice trailed off leaving her in no doubt as to what he was referring to. 'You looked like you knew each other – quite well, I should say, by the sound of that argument.'

'I don't know what you're talking about. But if you want to cast aspersions on someone's character, you need to back it up. And as he's not here to defend himself, you should at least give me an explanation.'

Charles shook his head. 'Sorry, Madeleine, but I'm not getting into that. I'm just giving you some friendly advice, that's all.'

His tone sounded quite the opposite to 'friendly'. He certainly wasn't being his usual charming and helpful self. She couldn't hold back her retort.

'I'm not interested in your friendly advice, and if you can't tell me why you said what you did, then you should keep your opinions to yourself in future.' With that, she strode off.

*First Cora and then Charles. Well, blast them to Timbuktu. Just let me find Jack.*

She looked everywhere she could think of where she was allowed to go without arousing suspicion but there was no sign of him. If only there was someone she could confide in. Someone who knew him and could throw some light as to where he might be.

It was only then that she remembered she still hadn't finished Ruth's letter. She sighed. There was so little privacy at the Park and it was too cold to sit outside. She'd try the library.

The clattering of typewriters met her ears when she opened the library door. It was such a contrast to the library

254

she was used to at home, but at least the women were busy at their desks and wouldn't bother her. Mrs Jones smiled as Madeleine entered.

'Would it be all right if I sat here a few minutes to read a letter which is rather important?'

'Yes, of course, my dear. Go and sit at that empty desk.' She glanced at the clock. 'No one will claim it for half an hour.'

Madeleine sat on the hard upright chair and took out Ruth's letter. She read:

*Because all contact was cut between us since the war started, Fran couldn't let us know until now. I haven't said anything to Lotte and Erich yet, even though they keep asking when Mutti and Papa are coming to England. I can't keep fobbing them off but I'm hoping you can help me explain the situation and what they should and shouldn't be told. You're a familiar figure from their home and their parents and they trust you. I know it's their birthday but this would be a natural time for you to see them. Could you possibly plan for that?*

Madeleine tucked the sheets of paper carefully back into the envelope, her mouth tightening with determination. She would go and see the twins on their birthday, or as near to it as she possibly could. And somehow gather the courage to stand by Ruth to talk to them about what had happened to Mutti and Papa.

In bed that night she tossed one way and then the other, thinking of Erich and Lotte and what on earth she was going to say to them. Her mood at the lowest ebb, she

255

grabbed hold of her one thin pillow and punched it into as high a mound as the feathers would allow, then breathed slowly and deeply, willing herself to fall asleep. When at last she did, she dreamt that the twins were screaming and crying and nothing she could say would comfort them. Finally, she woke up in the early hours to discover her pillow was wet with tears.

# Chapter Twenty-Seven

'You've definitely made up your mind, then,' Cecil said the following morning when Madeleine plucked up the courage to face him and apologise for forgetting her appointment. 'Because I think there's more to it than simply that you haven't got time to do rehearsals while you're concentrating on your training here. We're *all* endeavouring to do that but some light relief can stop some of the most vulnerable from having a nervous breakdown. You haven't had to tackle the shifts yet but it's a shock to the body, and your sleep patterns will go up the creek. Entertainment is the one thing that helps to relax people – physically and mentally.'

'Cecil, I—'

'Let me finish,' he interrupted. 'You told me yourself how you feel at home when you're on the stage performing. The way you filled in, not even having played the part of Sibyl, was quite remarkable. It tells me you have a superb memory. Put together with being able to act and your looks . . . well, I would go so far as to say that when this bloody war is over you wouldn't have any trouble becoming a professional actress. Of course, it will take some hard work as nothing comes easy when it's worth it.'

They were words Madeleine had dreamt of hearing – and for the first time from someone in the know. A producer who had spotted her potential. How different from her mother who hadn't encouraged her in the least. In fact, she'd gone so far as to make it impossible for her to pursue her dream by refusing to pay the drama school fees to learn something so 'frivolous', as she called it. And here she was telling Cecil she didn't have time to do the rehearsals and every other wonderful part that went together to put on a show. How pathetic.

'You go and think about it,' Cecil said. 'I definitely want you for the nightclub singer in *Anything Goes* but if you're set on giving it up, I'll have to think of someone else.' He gave her a sharp look. 'Do you trust me, Madeleine?'

She startled. 'Y-yes. Of course.'

'Enough to tell me what's *really* on your mind? Your eyes are all red and puffy. Looks to me as though you've been sobbing yourself silly. What's the matter, Maddie?'

'I can't tell you.' Tears of frustration welled up.

'Yes, you can. You can tell me. I'm like a hairdresser. People tell me things they wouldn't anyone else and I'll go to my grave carrying their secrets.' He grinned. 'Just don't put me there before my time.'

Maybe he was the very person who could locate Jack. A producer made it his business to make contacts. He might even remember Jack at the bar. She gave him a wan smile.

'Cecil, I'm trying to find someone. It's really urgent.'

Cecil raised a blond eyebrow. 'You've met someone already? Is it your co-star, Charlie-boy?'

'No, it's not Charles,' she said quickly. 'His name is—' She stopped. Was he 'Jack' here at the Park, or was he

258

James Mark? He'd already stopped her from using his surname.

'He's known as Jack,' she said, 'but it's a nickname.'

'Surname?'

'I can't remember.'

'Hmm. Not sure I believe that, but perhaps he doesn't want it spread about.' He tapped his fingers on the desk. 'What's he look like?'

'Well, he's tall, very dark hair and—'

'Handsome, obviously . . . or at least *you* think so,' he added mischievously.

Her cheeks warmed. 'Well, yes, I suppose he is.'

'Anything unusual about his appearance?'

She thought for a second. It was going to sound ridiculous but she'd say it anyway. 'His eyebrows practically meet in the middle.'

Cecil put his head back and roared with laughter.

'You've obviously studied him hard.'

Was he making fun of her?

'Sorry, Maddie, I couldn't resist. I know exactly who this Jack is. I had a drink with him and a couple of others after the play. He'd only just arrived that evening and told me he'd seen one of our posters advertising *Private Lives*. Didn't I see you talking to him after the curtain bow?'

'Yes. But it was all a bit fraught. But I need to speak to him urgently – in private.'

'You're in love with him.' He said it as a statement. She opened her mouth, but he stopped her with the palm of his hand. 'Don't deny it, Maddie – it's as plain as the nose on your face.'

She felt the heat rise on her neck. Dear God, everyone seemed to know before *she* did. *But maybe it's the perfect way to justify why I need to speak to him so urgently*, she thought. It will put him off any other clandestine reason.

'Is he in love with *you*?'

'I think so. But we've had a falling-out. I owe him an apology.' She bit her lip. The 'falling-out' was true at least.

'Well, who am I to stand in the way of true love?' he chuckled. 'What are your movements this morning?'

'I'm working until four o'clock, then I'll be free.'

Cecil nodded. 'All right. You can use this room. I'll be here to see you in and then you're on your own.' He looked at her. 'That all right with you?'

'Yes. Thank you so much. But what about if you can't find him?'

'I'll find him – don't you worry. And I'll keep Mum –' he jerked his head towards the opposite wall '– just like that poster and –' he paused '– I'll keep Reno's part open for you.'

At five past four Madeleine knocked on Cecil's door. She could hear men's voices. Her heart beat fast. One of them was Jack's. Oh, thank goodness. She knocked softly and Cecil opened the door.

'Come in, come in, dear,' he said. 'I've got Jack for you.'

Jack closed the gap between them in three easy strides.

'Hello, Madeleine.' He put his arms out as though to embrace her, then quickly withdrew them.

This man was her love. His dear face. Just to be near him . . . and then she remembered how curt she'd been with him on the last two occasions, both times in the Park's dining room.

'H-hello.' Her voice sounded thin and hesitant to her ears.

260

'I'll leave you to it.' Cecil went out of the door, shutting it quietly behind him.

'Come and sit down.' Jack drew out a chair for her and sat a few feet away. 'You look tired out. Cecil said you had something urgent to tell me, so I'm listening.'

'Jack, I'm sorry I was rather rude to you after the play. I was in a bit of a state and it was the shock—'

'Of seeing me?' Before she could answer he said, 'I've forgotten it already. And anyway, I was just as bad getting jealous of Longden of all people.' He gave a rueful smile. 'Now tell me what's on your mind.'

It was best to plunge straight in. Get it over with. See if he was willing to help her in any way.

'Read this.' She handed him Ruth's letter.

He read it without once breaking off and glancing at her. After some minutes he folded the letter and handed it back, then took a packet of cigarettes from his pocket.

'The terrible thing is, I'm not surprised. The Nazis are carting Jews off right, left and centre, whether or not they suspect them of doing anything against the regime. They simply regard Jews as sub-human and are doing their level best to eliminate them, poor devils.' He lit a cigarette, inhaling deeply. 'I'm afraid these people are either literally worked to death, starved on purpose, or if we are to believe some of the rumours – which I'm afraid I do – depending upon who they are and what information the Nazis want to extract from them, they don't stop at torture.' He looked at her. 'I imagine you were pretty shaken up to read this.'

She swallowed hard. 'I was. I still am. I just don't know what to do. But I feel I must go just as soon as I can. The trouble is, I don't have a day off until next Sunday. And when I get there I have no idea what to say.'

261

There was a long moment between them. Jack's eyes never left her face. Madeleine didn't realise she was holding her breath until he said:

'Would it help if I came with you, Madeleine?'

Madeleine gave a start. 'I didn't expect that,' she said, truthfully. 'I just thought you would be the right person to ask advice, as you did at least meet the twins and get to know them a little on the train.'

'Well, what do you think?'

She breathed out her relief.

'I'd like that very much.'

'Good. I'll drive you there.'

'But won't that use up most of your petrol ration?'

'No. Maybe half the month's allowance but there's nothing I'd rather do than be with you when you face the twins.' He paused. 'When *we* talk to the twins.'

A warm glow settled inside her despite the reason behind his decision.

'We'll meet outside the Park gates, just round the corner first thing at half-past six so no one sees us leave together. Look for a dark-green Austin. The morning shift won't have started and it will give us a good early start.' He looked at her. 'Can you manage without breakfast?' When she nodded, he said, 'We can stop for a cup of tea on the way. Is that okay with you?'

'Yes, that's fine.'

She fingered the empty spot where Frau Weinberg's ring had been. 'I know we need to keep this to ourselves, Jack. I haven't told anyone about bringing the twins to England and as far as I'm concerned, it can stay that way. The only reason I confided in you was that you were the one person who knew.'

262

'I hope that wasn't the *only* reason.' He stubbed out his cigarette with some force before it was finished.

*What did he mean by that?*

'What about Cecil?' Jack said, when she didn't reply. 'Can we rely on him to keep his mouth shut?'

'Yes, we can.'

'How can you be so sure?'

'Because I said it was urgent I speak to you and he said he wouldn't say anything about it.'

'Wasn't he curious as to what all this secrecy is about? If I know people in his world, they love a bit of gossip.'

'Yes,' she admitted, 'he was curious. But he thought he knew the answer. He said . . . he said I was . . . well, it doesn't matter.' She willed her heart to keep steady. 'I just know he won't say anything,' she finished lamely.

Jack frowned. 'All right, if you say so.' He stood. 'I don't think there's anything more we can do today, but maybe you can write to tell the aunt and uncle we'll be coming to see the twins on Sunday as you're not working. It will give them something to look forward to.'

Madeleine bit her lip. 'Saturday is their birthday and I've not been anywhere near any shops to get them anything.'

'Don't worry, Maddie. We'll think of something.'

He'd used her diminutive name – just like he used to. She primed herself to look at him directly, causing a tiny quiver as he gazed back at her. Was there an unspoken question in those warm brown eyes?

'Thank you, Jack,' was all she managed to say.

## Chapter Twenty-Eight

The six days until Sunday dragged. Madeleine thought it was never coming round, but at least she'd managed to slip into Bletchley town and buy the twins birthday presents – a mathematical geometry set for Erich and a book of English folk songs for Lotte.

Madeleine's days were filled with the usual Morse Code practice and the two, now sometimes three, lectures. The only bright spot was that Leonard Watts promised they would be starting some practical work the following week.

On Saturday night she set the alarm on her travel clock for six in the morning, burying it under her pillow so as not to wake any of the girls who liked to lie in as long as possible. But even so, she couldn't trust it and woke every two hours thinking it must be time to get up, her mind teeming with how she was going to face the twins. How much to tell them. She'd have Ruth. But this was different. Ruth had never had to tell her daughters something so shocking, so cruel – something that defied any human being's understanding. *Any except the bloody Nazis*, she thought, sick at heart as she turned over once again.

She'd just drifted off for the third time when she heard the muffled sound of her travel clock. Quickly, she switched it off. Her heart beat hard in her chest as though the twins were actually in front of her, open-mouthed with shock at what she'd just told them about Mutti and Papa.

*Stop this. Jack will be with me, lending his support.*

The idea calmed her. She scrambled out of her warm bunk and shivered. The dormitory was freezing at this time of the morning. The stove had gone out hours ago. She listened but there was no sign of anyone else stirring. She'd had her bath the night before so now she had a quick wash at the sink in ice-cold water, splashed her face and reached for the warm winter dress she'd already taken from the wardrobe – not wishing to disturb Cora, who would inevitably have a moan.

It was dark in the room and she didn't dare put a light on. Silently, she brushed her teeth and put a comb through her hair. She couldn't put it up as she usually did when she was working because it was too dark to see what she was doing in the mirror. She could only hope she looked presentable and not like someone who had just crawled out of bed. Giving a rueful smile, she eased her coat off the rack. If she did look that bad, Jack would just have to put up with it.

Her watch showed nearly twenty-five past as she shut the main entrance door behind her. She walked briskly to the gate, wishing she'd remembered her scarf as the cold wind whipped into the space where her coat collar met her neck. She showed her pass to a sleepy guard who waved her through, then turned the corner to find a dark-green motorcar parked close to the kerb. Her pulse raced at the thought she would soon be sitting close to him, completely private. She looked about her, but there was no one else around except a paper boy on his bicycle who flew round the corner ringing his bell. Jack emerged from his motor and opened the passenger door.

'*Madame*,' he said, sweeping his arm into the interior. 'Your carriage awaits.'

'Thank you, kind sir,' she responded, smiling.

He saw that she was settled, then slammed the door shut. Madeleine sank into the leather seat, her anxieties lessening a fraction. Once Jack was in his seat he reached over the back and brought out a grey blanket.

'Allow me.'

He opened the blanket onto her lap, then wrapped it round her legs. Every movement of his hands sent a thrill through her body as he patted the blanket into position. Was he spending more time than necessary tucking it around her? Or was it just her overwrought imagination? When he appeared satisfied, he switched on the engine, leaving her cocooned in a snug nest.

'There's no heat in here,' he explained, 'and I don't want you to get cold.' Throwing her an apologetic smile, he said, 'The heater was working perfectly yesterday. I just hope it doesn't need a new one as anything to do with car parts is hard to come by these days.'

'I'm fine, honestly, with this blanket.'

*Not that I need it while I'm sitting next to you*, she felt like saying, hoping he didn't spot her sudden grin in the dark interior.

'I can assure you you'll be glad of it.'

When they were on the main road towards London, he said:

'How have you been?'

'Not too bad. But I keep thinking about how the twins are going to react.'

266

He eyed the road again. 'Don't overthink. It won't help.'

'But how do I begin to tell them what's happened to their parents? And there are bound to be questions. How will I answer them?'

'We'll talk to the aunt and uncle first. You said they have three daughters. They might have some advice.'

'Oh, Jack, I haven't told you. They anglicised their name to White shortly after they came here. Isn't that an extraordinary coincidence?'

'Good news,' Jack said. 'Keeps everything nice and simple.'

He didn't seem particularly surprised. Maybe it hadn't been a coincidence after all. If not, surely he wouldn't have come across that sort of information in the British Embassy at Berlin as a cultural attaché. So was his job something more than it appeared on his business card? She stole a look but his profile seemed to be set in concentration on the road ahead.

They rode along in comfortable silence until Madeleine said:

'How long will it take us?'

'Roughly two hours – unless we stop for a coffee.'

'No, I think we ought to keep going.'

She rested her head on the back of the seat thinking she'd be quite happy if the Whites lived in Scotland.

'Madeleine.'

Jack's voice broke into her dream and she jerked awake.

'I'm sorry I startled you but we're almost there. I just need your help with directions.'

No. She'd wanted to be awake every moment. To be able to revel in his company.

'I can't believe I slept through the whole journey,' she said, flushing with embarrassment and thoroughly cross with herself. 'It must be the awful night I had. I kept worrying that I'd oversleep so I didn't get much.'

Keeping his eyes on the road ahead, he smiled.

'I'm glad you felt relaxed enough to fall asleep. You looked so lovely – as though you hadn't a care in the world.' He slowed down at a junction. 'I'm not sure where I go.'

She blinked as she tried to pull herself round. 'Oh, I recognise the canal . . . and the Brentford Lock. We're not far now.'

Thankful she had something to do to take her mind off the fact that he must have been glancing at her when she'd been asleep, she sat up straight and directed him to the Whites' front door, hoping they weren't too early.

To Madeleine's surprise it was Joseph who let them in. His face was drawn and hollow-looking. Poor man. He'd tried so hard to persuade his brother and sister-in-law and the twins to come to England, offering to sponsor them. And now it seemed as though it was far too late. If they were already in a camp there was little hope they would ever be free – unless the war suddenly ended, and by all accounts there was no chance of that. She bit her lip.

'I'm so glad to see you,' Joseph said, giving her a warm hug and kissing her cheek. He looked at Jack with mild curiosity.

'Jack Sylvester.' Jack thrust out his hand. 'I work at the same place as Madeleine and offered to drive her down.'

Joseph didn't blink. 'Come in, both of you. Ruth's laid up with a sprained ankle so I'll pop the kettle on. Madeleine, take Jack into the sitting room.'

Ruth was in her favourite chair by the fireside, her leg

propped on a cushion on the pouffe. She tried to haul herself up when Madeleine rushed over to kiss her.

'Don't get up, Ruth. You don't want to make your ankle worse.'

'Stupid thing to happen. I caught my foot under the edge of the rug and couldn't shake it free. It's less painful now, and thankfully I can walk though I'm a bit slow.' She paused. 'Let me look at you, my dear. It's been quite a while since we saw you. The twins are so excited. They've all gone off to school but the twins will be home for lunch. Now tell me who you've brought with you?'

'We work together,' Madeleine said. 'Jack Sylvester. He offered to drive me here.'

'Good to meet you, Mrs White.' Jack shook her hand.

'Thank you for bringing Madeleine, Mr Sylvester.' Ruth looked up, giving him a warm smile but there was an alertness behind her kind brown eyes. 'You said you'd be early so I've laid the dining-room table for breakfast. So shall we go in?' She shifted to the edge of her chair.

'May I escort you?' Madeleine was amused to hear Jack say as he extended his hand. Ruth took it, letting him support her as she led them to the adjoining room.

'Sit where you like,' she said. 'We're not formal here.'

Minutes later Joseph wheeled in the tea trolley and the glorious smell of buttered toast wafted into the room. He set a large brown teapot and jug of milk on the table.

'I can recommend Ruth's marmalade,' he said, glancing at his wife with a loving smile. 'I hope I've done everything to your satisfaction – not being used to the role of cook –' he added '– so have I passed?'

'If you've made a decent pot of tea,' his wife said with a chuckle, 'though there's talk that rationing will start early

269

next year on many of our staples and we may have to cut down, though if that happens to tea, I think there'll be a riot.' She smiled at Madeleine. 'Sit down, my dear, and eat before we talk.'

After Madeleine and Jack had finished several rounds of toast with Ruth's delicious marmalade, taking care just to scrape it on, Ruth said:

'I wanted you to come and help me break this terrible news to the twins, Madeleine, because I honestly don't know what to say to them. How much to tell them. And you know them better than we do.'

'I don't suppose you've heard any further news, Mrs White?' Jack said.

Ruth shook her head. 'No, nothing. That's three months ago and the children are becoming more and more upset.'

'I'm wondering if I can have a word with them,' Jack said. 'Sometimes an outsider is better at giving bad news than a close family member.' He looked at the Whites across the table. 'Strangely enough, I have actually met the twins. I happened to be on the same train from Munich to Berlin, and the four of us had a meal or two together.'

Madeleine noticed he never mentioned he was the one who had got the twins their British passports. That was fine. So long as she knew what she could and couldn't say.

Ruth's eyes widened. 'So you two had already met and now you work together in this secret place?'

'Not together,' Madeleine put in hurriedly. 'But we are at the same place and sometimes bump into each other.'

Ruth gazed at her with a slight smile, then apparently putting two and two together, sent a knowing look to her husband who responded with a nod.

*Is it so obvious that I love this man?*

270

As though Jack knew what she was thinking, he smiled at her. She quickly looked away. She could have crowned him when she saw Ruth's smile change to a beam of approval.

'Auntie Ruth, Uncle Joseph, is Maddie here?'

The twins rushed into the house calling out her name. Before Maddie could get up from her chair they'd burst into the sitting room and rushed over to her.

'Maddie, we thought you would never come.' Lotte threw her arms round Madeleine's neck and left a wet kiss on her cheek. 'It was our birthday yesterday.'

'I know. And I have something for you – but later.'

Erich stuck his hand out.

'Good afternoon, Maddie,' he said, shaking her hand firmly. Then he flung his arms around her. 'We miss you every day.' Then he realised what he'd said because he immediately turned to his aunt. 'Although we love Auntie Ruth and Uncle Joseph.'

'I'm glad to hear that, my dears,' Ruth said, chuckling.

The twins suddenly caught sight of Jack.

'Mr New Year,' they screamed in delight. 'What are *you* doing here?'

'I drove Maddie down from where we both work,' Jack said, giving them a formal handshake.

'Oh.' The twins eyed him.

'Are you really a spy?' Erich said.

Jack laughed. 'Not quite.'

'Your lunch is ready, you two,' Ruth said. 'Sit down and have it, and then we need to talk to you.'

Erich shot her a look but didn't say anything.

When the twins had wolfed down their sandwiches,

Joseph said to Jack, 'I think it's better just for the two of you to talk to the twins or it will seem overpowering with all of us.'

'You may be right,' Jack said.

'Then take the twins to my study. We're here if you need us.'

The twins chatted and Lotte hopped and skipped into the study.

'Sit down, children,' Madeleine said, just as she had done many times before. 'I'm afraid we have something serious to tell you both.'

'But we want—'

'Shhhh, Lotte. We must allow Maddie to tell us something.' Erich looked straight at her. 'Is it about Mutti and Papa?'

Madeleine gave a start. How on earth had he worked that one out?

'Your mother and father love you very much,' she began. 'But they were worried about you. That's why they asked me if I'd take you to your other aunt and uncle in Berlin.'

'They're not our real aunt and uncle,' Lotte piped.

'I know, darling,' Madeleine said. 'But they want the best for you. So when those men took Uncle Freddie away, Aunt Fran asked me to take you to England where you'd be safe.'

'From the Nazis?' Erich looked at her, his eyes fierce. 'Because we're Jews?'

She jolted at his correct analysis. The twins were growing up.

'Yes, love.'

'Why do they hate us so much, Maddie?' Lotte asked, her voice trembling and tears shining in her eyes.

'B-because . . .' Madeleine cleared her throat. How terrible to have to explain to a child about those ignorant pigs. She began again. 'Because they don't know any better. Maybe they didn't come from a loving family like you to show them that cruelty to other people, just because they look different, or believe in a different religion, is very wrong.' She drew in a breath. 'Can you both be very brave?' she said.

They nodded, staring at her.

'I'm afraid, my loves, the Nazis took your mother and father away early one morning without any warning, so they didn't have any time to say goodbye to anyone.'

'Where did they take Mutti and Papa?' Erich's voice was choked. 'Was it prison?'

She hesitated. This was it. She bit her lip, conscious that Erich and Lotte were dead silent, staring at her with the same dark eyes. 'It's a kind of prison but Mutti and Papa will be with other Jewish people so they won't be alone.'

'Where is the place?' Erich asked.

'We don't know exactly. We'll try to find out, but I'm afraid they won't be able to send you any letters for the time being.'

'Is that why we haven't had a letter from them?' Lotte demanded.

'Yes, ever since the war started no one in Germany is allowed to write to anyone in England.'

Erich twisted his neck from Jack to Madeleine. She suddenly caught a glimpse of the man he would become. His expression was as though he were weighing them up – whom to trust to get to the truth.

'They made a mistake with Uncle Freddie,' Erich's voice rose, 'and they let him out of prison.'

273

'Because he isn't Jewish,' Jack broke in quietly. 'And now he and Aunt Fran are both safe in England so eventually you'll be able to go and visit them.'

'Will Mutti and Papa come to England and be safe?' Lotte said in a small voice.

'They'll probably have to stay where they are until the end of the war.'

'When will it end?'

'We don't know,' Jack said. 'No one does. But it might be quite a long time.'

'Will the horrible men kill Mutti and Papa?' Lotte said, starting to cry.

'No, of course not,' Madeleine said. 'You mustn't worry.'

'Papa will look after Mutti,' Erich said, putting his arm round his sister, 'and I will take care of you, Lotte.' He looked up at Madeleine. 'We are not babies. If something extra bad happens to Mutti and Papa, do you promise to tell us the truth?'

Madeleine bit her lip hard to stop herself bursting into tears.

'I promise,' she said. 'Now, about that birthday of yours – tell me all about it.'

For the first half-hour, she and Jack were practically silent as they were driving back to the Park, Madeleine wrapped in her thoughts. When Jack suddenly spoke, she jumped.

'The cruel thing is that the twins' parents might have perished weeks ago,' he said sombrely.

Madeleine had thought the same thing but couldn't bear to voice it. If she did, it might be true.

'I know, but we've told them as much as it's possible to take in for the moment. As much as *I* can take in. And we don't know anything for sure ourselves yet, so there's always hope.'

She shifted a little in her seat to ease one of her legs that was threatening to stiffen into cramp. It was already getting dark and hadn't stopped raining. The windscreen wipers had a hypnotic effect, making her feel light-headed, her mind dazed. But not enough to block out the afternoon trying to comfort Lotte. Erich was just as bewildered but had tried to put a brave face on. That wicked Hitler and the men with whom he surrounded himself. If only someone would bump him off. She wondered if anyone had actually tried.

'Penny for your thoughts,' Jack said.

'Oh, I was wondering if anyone had tried to assassinate bloody Hitler.' She sneaked a look at him. 'And don't tell me off for swearing. He has blood on his hands. That's enough for me to call him "bloody".'

'I'm not going to tell you off. I use far worse when I'm on my own. And I imagine there are people at this very moment who are plotting how to get rid of him.' He paused. 'Changing the subject, I don't think I've ever told you about Dexter.'

'No, who's he?'

'He's the dog we had as our mascot in Berlin. He was a stray and followed me when I used to walk to the Embassy. He wasn't in good condition but I got him put right and he became *my* dog – hated to let me out of his sight.'

'What happened to him?'

'I brought him with me to England but of course he had to go straight into quarantine. I've not been to see him because I knew he'd be heartbroken when I left him again. But he'll be out at the end of February. It's hard for me to have him when I never know where I'm going to be sent, so I suddenly thought he might bring a bit of comfort to the twins. He'd definitely help take their mind off what might be happening to their parents as he's quite a character.' He gave her a quick glance. 'Do you think it's a good idea?'

'I think it's a marvellous idea. Mind you, we'd have to ask Ruth and Joseph if they would have him before the twins set eyes on him because it wouldn't be fair otherwise.'

'I thought we could just take him with us soon after he comes out and introduce him as my dog and see what everyone thinks. He's not any beauty to look at, and he's lost one of his back legs, but that doesn't stop him and he works his way into your heart very quickly.'

'Oh, poor little dog. But in a way that sounds even better. The twins will be more protective towards him, being maimed. And if Ruth and Joseph take to him, do you mean we could leave him there?'

'Exactly. But if they can't deal with him, we'll just take him back with us. But frankly, I can't see them doing that if the twins ask if he can stay.'

'I agree.' Madeleine's smile was wide. 'Do you know, Jack, it's not a good idea – it's brilliant.'

'I hoped you'd say that.'

They were silent for a while. What a wonderful man he was. Fancy thinking about the twins and how he could help. He was probably attached to the dog himself. Her heart overflowed with love for him. She couldn't stop looking at him. Giving him little glances as often as she could without his noticing. She loved watching his hands on the steering wheel, the way he spread his fingers wide as he changed gear, the way his hair wouldn't lie flat at the front . . .

'You're looking at me,' Jack chuckled as he kept his eyes on the road. 'Don't deny it.'

She couldn't help laughing. 'You looked at me when I was asleep.'

'That's true. So we're even,' he said, glancing at her, still grinning. Then he said, 'Can I ask you something personal?'

Even before she answered, she knew what he was about to say.

'You mentioned it didn't work out between you and your fiancé. But I had the strongest feeling you weren't telling me the truth. Or not the whole truth at any rate. Do you feel comfortable enough with me to tell me? Or am I probing where I shouldn't?' He changed gear as they approached a set of traffic lights that were about to turn red. 'Before you say a word, do you trust me?'

She could answer that without any reservation.

'Yes, I do.'

'But I'm right, aren't I? There's something more to this fiancé you're holding back.' He stopped at the red light and turned to her, waiting.

'Well?'

She realised it was important that he knew the truth – if only to show him how much she trusted him.

'I never had a fiancé,' she began. 'The ring was Frau Weinberg's engagement ring. She gave it to me to take to Fran along with a few other pieces of jewellery I hid in my bag. You know the rest of the story, so I ended up taking not only the twins but the jewellery to England. I've now passed it on to Ruth to help pay for their education and their board and lodgings, which was what it was meant for.'

'Why on earth didn't you tell me this before?'

'Because I thought you might think it was a likely story. That maybe I'd even stolen the jewels.'

'You? Steal? Never!'

'I didn't know you enough at the beginning to explain. And when I realised you would believe me it was too late. It was easier to let you think I'd broken it off.'

'The trouble is –' Jack kept his eyes on her '– you didn't mention that you'd been the one to break it off – you just said it hadn't worked out. And I've been torturing myself that he broke it off with you and you were still in love with him.'

'Oh, no, Jack, I . . .'

'Yes?'

She swallowed hard. She couldn't be the one to say it first even though she was sure he felt the same.

'What do you want to say to me? Is it something important?'

'Yes,' she muttered.

'Then say it!'

There was a loud hooting from several vehicles behind them.

'The lights are green,' Madeleine said.

'You see what you've done to me.' Jack put his foot on the accelerator. 'You can tell me as we go along. I don't want to wait any longer.'

How could she say what was in her heart when Jack was driving and she wouldn't even see his reaction? He'd think her forward. She'd be throwing herself at him. And anyway, shouldn't he be the first to say it?

Jack turned his head a fraction. 'Well, Maddie, come out and say what you have to say.' He turned back to the road. 'You should know by now you can tell me anything,' he added quietly.

Her heart pounded in her ears. She took in a jerky breath. *Go on, Maddie, tell him, for God's sake.*

'I love you!'

Jack drove on in silence. His profile was as fixed as one of Madame Tussaud's statues.

Dear God, she'd misunderstood him completely. He just liked her as a friend. He must be thinking she was going to propose to him next. Oh, why had she blurted it out in a motorcar of all places. If only the seat would swallow her up. Her face felt on fire with humiliation and misery that he didn't feel the same. Another judgement she'd made that was wrong. Why would she never learn? But she couldn't take the words back. She loved him and that was the end of it. Worst of all, she knew she would never stop loving him.

Jack slowed down and turned off the main road, then stopped. He turned to her, an unfathomable expression in his eyes.

'Why are we stopping?'

'Because you've just said the most wonderful thing that I've been wanting to hear from those luscious lips since the first moment I met you on the train. And I wanted to tell you I love you, too. With all my heart. And I wanted to kiss you. I've wanted to so many times but let the opportunity go. Except that one time when we were at Fran's. The way you responded, I had such hopes that you felt the same way.' He ran the tip of his finger down the edge of her cheek. 'This isn't an ideal place to choose – but I'm not ever going to let another opportunity pass by.'

Before she could grasp all he'd said, all that it meant from now on, he took her in his arms and kissed her. This time she snaked her arms around his neck, pulling him closer. It was even more magical than the first time.

\* \* \*

It was as though a fire had been lit inside her. Madeleine grinned to herself at such twaddle in the dark interior of Jack's motorcar. This is how it felt to love and be loved in return. And by the way he gave her hand a loving squeeze whenever they had to stop, she was sure he felt the same.

'And when we had that lunch together on the train I never doubted it was *you* I wanted to spend the rest of my life with. But I'd been beaten at the post by the non-existent fiancé whose eyes I would gladly have torn out if I'd met him.'

She laughed. 'Poor chap – if he *had* existed.'

They laughed. She'd never felt so happy. But all too soon they were within a couple of miles of Bletchley.

'I think we need to decide how we're going to play it once we're back at the Park,' Jack said. 'I've signed the Official Secrets Act the same as you, but I'm obviously in a very different role from when I was at the Embassy in Berlin, and I wouldn't want anyone at the Park or anywhere else to find out about that.'

'They won't from me.'

'I know. I've been thinking. So long as we don't let anyone know we knew each other in Germany it's perfectly feasible that we've met at BP for the first time and have fallen in love – at first sight.' He glanced at her as he manoeuvred his way through one of the villages. 'That bit's certainly true, isn't it, my darling?'

It was the first time he'd used an endearment. She hugged it to herself.

'It's crazy but it's definitely true,' she laughed.

'A question for you,' Jack said. 'When I asked what reason you gave Cecil about needing to find me urgently, what reason did you give?'

She was glad the darkness wouldn't show him she was blushing.

'I pretended we'd had a row and I needed to apologise.'

'Anyone can row so that wasn't nearly a good enough excuse,' he chuckled.

'It was,' Madeleine retorted, 'because he'd already accused me of being in love with you – and I let him go on thinking that. It made it sound more urgent that we should kiss and make up,' she added a little self-consciously.

Jack turned his head towards her for a second.

'Ah, *now* I'm getting the full picture. So you've already told everyone at the Park you're in love with me?'

'Not quite *everyone*,' she said, mischief in her tone. 'I don't think the ladies dishing out the meals in the dining room know yet, but I'll make sure I tell them tomorrow.'

'Oh, I'm sure they already know. News travels very fast at the Park.'

Madeleine laughed. Then she remembered something. She shifted a little closer to him.

'Can I now ask *you* a question?'

'Fire away.'

'Did you put my name forward to the Foreign Office and that's how I came to be at Bletchley Park?'

There was a pause. Then Jack said, 'What do *you* think?'

'I think you did – and it must have been even before the war started.'

'Of course it was me. I thought if you'd get a job there, there'd be a good chance I'd see you again.'

She couldn't help a little smile of self-satisfaction.

'One other question,' she said.

'Go on.'

'I think you found out Ruth and Joseph changed their

name to "White". It was too much of a coincidence for you to come up with the same surname on the twins' passports.' She stole a glance but Jack's eyes were on the road ahead. 'That's what I think, anyway.'

'Then go on thinking it.'

'But you haven't answered my question.'

'I'm not going to. Not that I don't want to, but I can't, darling. The less you know about those passports, the better.'

She had to be content with that.

Jack pulled up just before they were at the Park's gates.

'One more thing I have to do . . .' he murmured, taking her in his arms.

'What's that?'

His answer was drowned in his warm lips on hers.

It felt good not to have to worry about whether anyone saw them together, Madeleine thought, as they walked into the Mansion.

'Why don't we get something to eat in the dining room,' Jack suggested. 'And you can let the dinner ladies know how passionately in love you are with me.'

'Good idea. It will save me having to do it tomorrow.'

It was like a private joke they shared.

As they entered the dining room someone was just on his way out. Charles.

'Hello, Maddie.' His eyes hardened as he looked over the top of her head to Jack. 'Oh, what do you know? It's Sylvester. Sorry I've not had a chance to welcome you into the fold, old chap, but I see Maddie has already done that for me –' he gazed at her '– haven't you, dear heart?'

Madeleine's jaw clenched. 'Dear heart' indeed. Charles

282

was being deliberately provocative. But would Jack read something into it?

Jack gave the semblance of a smile. 'Don't give it another thought . . . *old boy.*' He turned to Madeleine. 'Can you grab that table by the window . . . *darling?*'

They were like two schoolboys. Madeleine smothered a giggle at the sight of Charles's dazed expression. Then he appeared to collect himself as he stared at them.

'Well, well – it didn't take you two long to get cosy – unless, of course, you already knew one another,' he added, his eyes narrowing.

'Look, we need to get something to eat.' With that Jack strode up to the counter.

'Seems you didn't take my advice,' Charles said stiffly.

'There was nothing to advise me against.' Madeleine hesitated. Yes, she'd have to say it. 'Charles, can I ask you a favour?'

'Anything.'

'Please don't call me "dear heart" again, or anything equally ridiculous. That's all.' She spun on her heel and made for one of the vacant tables.

'It's about all they had left,' Jack said as he set down two plates of macaroni cheese, 'but I thought they were a safe bet.'

'Mmm. It's not bad,' Madeleine said as she finished the first mouthful. She looked up. 'So you and Charles know one another.'

'Only slightly.'

'But not here.'

'No.'

'So where *did* you meet him?'

'Oh, at the Foreign Office some time ago. I never really

283

liked the bloke. Bit of a cocky devil. ' Jack concentrated on his macaroni cheese for a few moments, then said, 'Now I have a question to ask *you*.' He looked pointedly at her. 'What's all this "dear heart" nonsense?'

'I've told him never to call me that again.' Madeleine put her fork down. 'When we were in that play, I could tell he wanted to take things further than the script. I've never given him any encouragement but I realise now he's jealous of you and used the term on purpose to get under your skin.'

'Well, he hasn't succeeded though I did wonder when I saw him kissing you on the stage . . . And if we weren't in a public place I would kiss you again – just to remind you of *my* kiss.'

'As if I need reminding.' Madeleine smiled. 'Because whatever happens in this war, I'll never forget your kiss as long as I live.'

'Sounds a bit final.'

'It's not meant to be. But we don't really know what's going to happen, do we?' She turned her eyes on Jack. 'Hitler's unpredictable. He could bomb us at any time or even—'

'Invade us,' Jack finished.

Madeleine's stomach turned over at the thought.

'Do you think he will?'

'He warned us he's going to, but there's no telling at this point whether he's bluffing or not. I just hope to God if he does, we're ready for it.'

# Chapter Twenty-Nine

A fortnight slipped by and December at Bletchley Park was beginning to look quite festive for the season, Madeleine thought, as she and Josie stood back to admire their work decorating the Christmas tree. It now stood draped in tinsel and coloured baubles in the Mansion's entrance hall.

'The angel is slipping a bit,' Josie chuckled, tilting her head, 'even though I've tightened her bow at the back, but maybe no one will notice.' She screwed up her face. 'Oh, I've just seen a bit near the top that needs filling . . . just up there.' She pointed.

'I'll do it.' Madeleine pulled the ladder into position again.

'There's a silver star left and another candle,' Josie said. 'I'll hand them up.'

Madeleine stepped up the three rungs to the little platform and tied on the star and clipped the candle onto one of the small branches. With a cursory glance she decided that one more trinket further to the right would complete the gap. Keeping one hand on the side of the ladder, she twisted round and looked down at Josie.

'Anything more left in the box, Josie?'

'One of those red apples.'

285

'That'll do.'

Josie put the bauble in Madeleine's dangling hand.

Madeleine turned back to the tree, stretching to hook the loop over a branch. It was at that moment her foot slipped and she felt herself overbalance. She tried to grab hold of something . . . anything . . . the thin trunk of the tree . . .

'Maddie, watch out!' Josie shouted.

Madeleine felt she was in slow motion as she toppled and fell in a heap on her side. A burst of pain shot up her arm and into her shoulder.

Josie flew over.

'Oh, Maddie, are you all right?'

'I don't know. My left shoulder's killing me.'

With Josie's help she struggled to a sitting position, then noticed her friend stiffen and her face flush as Daniel Strong entered the hall.

'What an earth's happened?'

'Oh, Dan, you've come at just the right time,' Josie said. 'Maddie's fallen off the ladder.'

'So I see.' He bent down. 'Here, Maddie, take my arm.'

She reached up with her good hand and he hauled her up.

'You okay?'

'My shoulder . . .'

'Come and sit on this chair. Right. Let me see if you can raise your arm. Just go slowly.'

She tried, but the pain was excruciating even before she got to shoulder height.

'Let it down gently,' Daniel said. 'I reckon you've wrenched the muscle. I think you'd better go and see Nurse.' He glanced at Josie. 'Can you take her to the sick room, Jo?'

'Yes, of course.' She turned to Daniel. 'See you at the concert this evening, Dan.'

He hesitated before answering. 'I'm not sure I can make it after all, Jo.' He patted her arm. 'I'm sure Maddie would go with you,' he added, flashing a smile at Madeleine.

'But you—'

'Sorry, Josie, must go.' He vanished.

'He was the one who asked *me*.' Josie voice was bitter as she led Madeleine outside into the freezing-cold air and over to Hut 1. 'I'm getting tired of his excuses.'

Madeleine glanced at her. In spite of Josie's flippancy, her eyes shone with tears. It was obvious Daniel didn't harbour the same feelings as Josie had for him.

The temperature in Hut 1 was no warmer than it was outside. Madeleine shivered as they walked to the end of the corridor where Josie tapped on a door marked Sick Room. Without pausing, she opened it to reveal a small ward of six beds, two occupied by sleeping patients. It smelt strongly of disinfectant but at least there was a stove putting out some heat. A plump woman in a nurse's uniform, the apron stretched to its limit over her bosom, was sitting at a desk filling out some notes. She looked up as Josie said:

'Oh, Nurse Bull, my friend has just had an accident.'

The woman frowned. 'What happened?'

Madeleine told her briefly.

'Come here.' She took Madeleine's arm and raised it.

'Aghhhhhh!'

'Hmm. You'd better take your blouse off and let me examine it.'

Madeleine took her good arm from her sleeve but it was impossible to remove the other.

'Let me do it.' Nurse Bull pressed her fingers around

the area. 'It's already quite swollen. You've definitely sprained your shoulder.'

*Tell me something I don't know.* Madeleine bit her lip hard to stop herself from calling out.

'Take these aspirins.' Nurse Bull dropped two white tablets into Madeleine's hand, then turned to Josie, 'And fetch some ice from the dining room.' When Josie had disappeared, she told Madeleine, 'You're going to have to wear your arm in a sling to support it for at least a week.'

Madeleine groaned. Oh, no. It was all she needed with work.

Josie was soon back, holding out a bag of ice to Nurse Bull, who wrapped some cubes in a cloth and told Madeleine to hold it there for fifteen minutes, indicating that Josie should go.

'I'll meet you in the teashop, Maddie,' Josie said as she left.

'Are you right-handed?' Nurse Bull asked Madeleine.

'Yes.'

'Good. Whatever work you do usually involves some writing so you'll still be able to be of some use to us.' Her mouth pursed in disapproval.

*As though I had the accident on purpose to get out of work,* Madeleine thought crossly.

'Move your shoulder as often as you can without causing any extra pain,' Nurse Bull said as she tied on the sling. 'And when you're sitting or resting, then you must support it. The sling will remind you. After forty-eight hours exercise it regularly. It's the best way to get it back to normal.'

'How long will that take?'

'Maybe a fortnight.'

'In time for Christmas?' Madeleine gave Nurse Bull a hopeful smile.

The nurse's lips drew into a thin line. 'Christmas is like any other day of the week as far as I'm concerned. I'll be here looking after people who do stupid things the same as usual.'

With relief, Madeleine rose from the chair and thanked her, thinking how the woman's name perfectly suited her. But Nurse Bull obviously knew her job and already the throbbing in her shoulder had begun to subside. But the first thing she wanted to do was meet Josie in Hut 2. From what she had observed of her friend, Josie was feeling pretty miserable. Maybe this evening's concert would cheer her up.

'I'm not in the mood,' Josie said, when Madeleine caught up with her in the tearoom, sitting on her own, looking forlorn. 'You go. You'll enjoy it. It's a quartet and I think they're playing Mozart. I'll go and have a game of table tennis. Get rid of some of my anger. There's usually someone around who'll partner me . . . though that's usually Daniel.' She turned from the table and wiped her eyes with a handkerchief.

'Josie,' Madeleine said gently, 'is he worth your getting so upset?'

'I don't suppose so,' Josie said. 'But I love the idiot.' She glanced towards the door. 'I believe this one's yours,' she said with a watery smile as Jack approached. 'I'll leave you both to it. Just hope you have better luck with him than I've had with Daniel.'

Madeleine's heart flipped as Jack strode over to their table, then nodded to Josie as she departed. She had seen him a few times in the distance, and once when she spotted him going into Hut 1 where presumably he worked, but they hadn't had a chance to speak in private since coming back from Ealing.

'Madeleine! I've been looking for you everywhere. They said you'd had an accident.' His eyes dropped to her sling. 'Did you break your arm?'

'No. Just wrenched my shoulder.' She told him briefly what had happened. 'But thank goodness it's my left one so I can still do Morse Code.' She clapped her hand over her mouth, her eyes wide. Dear God, she wasn't supposed to use that word – or any other words to do with work – outside the lecture room.

'Don't worry,' he said under his breath, his hand briefly closing over hers. 'No one heard that. But we can't talk here and it's bitter cold outside.' He frowned. 'Have you had tea?'

'No, I've only just come in.'

He glanced at his watch.

'Hmm. Nearly five. The pubs will be open soon. Let's get away from the Park for a while and have a drink. Then maybe a spot of supper.'

Ten minutes later she was in Jack's motorcar and he'd tucked the blanket round her.

'Sorry it's so cold in here,' he said. 'I'm still waiting for the part for the heater but hopefully the engine will help to warm it up.'

'Where is this pub?'

'In Stony Stratford.'

Stony Stratford was a charming ancient town and the Old George Inn was a medieval pub nestled in a line of similar-aged buildings and shops. Jack opened the door to a buzz of noise and an atmosphere heavy with smoke from the roaring log fire and nearly everyone, mostly men, smoking. Madeleine immediately felt her throat tickle.

'What would you like, Maddie? A sherry?'

A glass of water would be more like it, but she nodded. 'Thanks, that would be nice.'

She stood back while Jack went up to the counter.

'A medium sherry and a beer, please.' He turned to her. 'Maddie, I need to talk to you and we never have a chance at the Park. And in here –' he waved his arm at the crowd of men, laughing and clinking glasses '– you can't hear yourself think, let alone talk. I'm going to ask if we can go somewhere a bit more private if that's all right with you.'

She nodded. It would be a relief to get out of this smoke-filled atmosphere. Jack turned back to the barman.

'Is there a meeting room unoccupied that my fiancée and I could have for half an hour?'

'Certainly, sir. Up one flight and first door on the right.'

'Thank the Lord to be out of that racket,' Jack said when he opened the door to a dark room with slanting polished oak floor and Tudor windows, sparsely furnished. 'I didn't realise it was going to be that bad downstairs but this will do.' He turned to her, his eyes twinkling. 'I hope you didn't think I wanted to have my wicked way with you when I asked the barman for somewhere more private?'

'I can't imagine you choosing this place for such an event, if that's what you had in mind,' she teased.

He took her glass and placed it with his on the modern rectangular table in the middle of the room. 'Actually, there's nothing I'd like more than anything in the world, but I wouldn't – unless I had your full consent, of course.' He grinned. Then his smile faded.

'Madeleine,' he said softly.

Instinctively, she walked straight into his arms.

'I don't want to jolt your bad arm,' he said, pulling her, gently, more closely towards him.

'You won't hurt it,' she whispered, not sure why she was whispering. 'I just want you to kiss me. I—'

But whatever she was going to say was lost as his mouth met hers.

'Oh, Maddie, I've longed to do this so many times,' he said when he finally stepped back to gaze at her. 'It's driven me crazy that there's no privacy at the Park. I just see you in the distance – your lovely face, and I want to ravish you.'

He kissed her again, this time with a passion that left her barely able to stand.

'I wish we could make love,' he said thickly. 'I want you so much.'

This time she kissed *him*. 'I want you, too,' she whispered against his lips. 'But not here.'

'No, definitely not here. And not in that coat,' he chuckled. 'When it happens it must be special.' He pulled away and gazed at her. A loud cheer from below echoed through the floorboards. 'Do you know, I don't want the beer after all. And this room's gloomy as hell. Let's go and get something to eat.'

'I thought you wanted to talk to me about something in private.'

'It can wait.' He took her good arm. 'Come on.'

She left the full glass of sherry on the table and followed him down the stairs.

Outside, Madeleine pointed to a restaurant sign a few shops away.

'Okay, that looks fine. I just want to grab something from the car so why don't you get in the warm and wait for me.'

Madeleine breathed a sigh of relief as soon as she stepped into the interior of the restaurant, so different from the pub. It was nearly full but with none of the clattering and banging they'd just left. After enquiring, the waitress found her a table for two in the No Smoking area and she gratefully sat down at a white-clothed table decorated with sprigs of holly and a lighted candle. The waitress took her coat and hat.

'I'll be back with the menu in a jiffy,' she said.

Madeleine looked around her, smiling at the sight of a Christmas tree propped up in the corner, festooned with every imaginable coloured bauble, its pot wrapped in red crêpe paper and tied with a bow. She was just reading the menu, trying to decide what she might choose, when Jack arrived carrying a parcel about the size of a book wrapped in brown paper. He hurried over and put the parcel in the middle of the table, then removed his coat and hung it on the nearby coat rack with his hat.

'Right,' he said, taking the seat opposite. 'Have you seen anything you fancy?'

'Only you,' she quipped.

'Naughty girl,' he chuckled as he picked up one of the menus. 'What do you think?'

'The casserole looks nice.'

'Let's both have it and a glass of red wine. Better not have any more than that as I'm driving – but you can, darling.'

'One is enough.'

She eyed the parcel. He glanced at it.

'Yes, it's for you. It's Christmas in a few days but I won't

293

be here. That's what I wanted to tell you. I'm being sent away – but only temporarily,' he added quickly, 'so I wanted you to have it now.'

She blinked, then looked directly at him. 'Where are they sending you?'

'They haven't even told *me* yet.'

'But will it be in this country . . . or abroad?'

He shook his head. 'I don't even know that, my love, and even if I did, I couldn't tell you or anyone.' He reached across the table and took her hand in his. 'You know how that sort of thing is always hush-hush at the Park.'

'Can't you tell me at least how long you'll be gone?'

He hesitated as though he was finding it difficult to tell her. 'They're saying anything from three to six months.'

'Oh, no. Not now we . . .' She couldn't finish. Tears sprang to her eyes.

'Darling, it could be worse. I might have been sent away for the rest of the war and who knows how many years that could drag on.'

She gazed at him. His dear face that she loved. She must stifle her own selfish feelings. Maybe it would only be the three months.

Jack picked up the parcel. 'Aren't you going to open it?' His brown eyes twinkled.

'You're supposed to keep presents until Christmas Day.'

'I want you to open it now – but it's not a real present. I'll explain when you open it.'

She'd just undone the string when the waitress came to take their order. When he'd vanished she opened the brown paper and stared. Nestling in white tissue paper was a scarlet writing case. She picked it up and held it to her nose, breathing in the warm, unmistakeable smell of the

294

leather, then set it on the table and ran her fingers over it. There were some slight indentations and a sign of wear, especially around the fastener.

'Oh, I love it, Jack. It's beautiful.'

'I'm sorry it isn't new – it was my mother's.'

She saw him swallow hard. '*Was*,' he'd said.

'I never knew her. She died giving birth to me.'

'Oh, Jack, I'm so sorry.' She paused. 'Did your father take care of you?' Once again she realised how little she knew about him.

'No. My aunt – his sister – told me he couldn't cope and started drinking. He didn't last long. So I never knew him either.'

'How awful for you. When the twins began calling you that silly name you said you'd have to have a word with those who named you, so I just assumed—' She looked at him. 'What happened to you?'

'My aunt took me in.'

'That was kind of her. Did she have her own children?'

'No, she'd never been married and it must have been a shock to her to have to bring up her brother's child. She was strict but I'm sure did her best though I didn't appreciate it at the time. I just remember she never gave me a hug or really much sign of any affection.' He gave a wry smile. 'It was a bit grim, but I survived.'

'Oh, Jack, I'm so sorry.'

'Don't be. It's all of twenty-six years ago. But Dad gave my mother the writing case when he went to fight in the First World War. I found several of their love letters still inside.' His eyes glistened. 'My aunt, who'd kept the case to give me when I was old enough, said my mother told her it was the most precious thing she owned.'

'I can understand that.' Madeleine blinked back the threatening tears. 'She must have loved it –' she looked directly at him '– but you should keep it. It's a special link to your mother.'

'No, my darling. I want you to have it.'

'If you're sure . . .'

'I'm very sure.'

'Then I'll love it too, even more, knowing it was your mother's.'

He pressed her hand. 'Look inside.'

She opened the small leather strap and laid the two sides flat to expose a new Basildon Bond cream writing tablet with matching envelopes and a pen in a bright-red case. She removed it from its leather pocket and unscrewed the top. The nib was a shiny silver but there were a few scratches on the case. Jack's mother had used this pen. She swallowed.

'The sheet of tuppenny-ha'penny stamps is new.' Jack grinned, pointing to another pocket, 'so you'll have no excuse for not writing.'

'No, I won't. And thank you for entrusting me with it.' She leant over and briefly kissed his lips just as the waiter approached with their two plates and set them down.

'Be careful – they're very hot.'

When he'd disappeared, Madeleine said, 'Can I ask you something?' He nodded. 'Your work at the Park. I know you can't tell me what you do, but it seems so different from when I first met you in Berlin and you were a cultural attaché – though I don't really know what that means exactly.'

Jack cleared his throat. 'You're supposed to learn the culture of the country you're now in and introduce the British culture to them.' He looked at her. 'I had a dual-purpose role at the British Embassy which I can't go into, but the other bit is what I'm involved in now.'

*Oh. That explained his sometimes secretive manner. Could Erich actually be right? Was he a spy?*

Her scalp prickled at the thought. She shook herself. Her imagination was running away with her. She longed to know more but his mouth had tightened as though physically buttoning his lip before he was tempted to say more than he should.

'Did you know when you finally left Berlin that you'd be coming to Bletchley Park?' When he hesitated, Madeleine added quickly, 'Don't tell me if you're not allowed to.'

'Well, I can't see that would hurt,' Jack replied. 'I knew about this set-up because I had contacts in the GCCS – the Government Code and Cypher School. They bought Station X last year, about the time you and I first met – solely to break German and Italian codes.'

'And now these mysterious people are sending you away?'

'Only for this one assignment. I hope then they'll let me come back to the Park and stay . . . especially now you're here,' he added softly.

'When do you go?'

'Tomorrow. That's why I was frantic, trying to find you.'

Her eyes flew wide. 'Tomorrow! Oh, no. I haven't got *your* Christmas present yet.'

'I don't expect anything. Bletchley isn't exactly a shopper's paradise.'

She gave a deep sigh. 'I wish you weren't going. It's not fair.'

'War isn't fair. But we have to get on with it.' He covered her hand with his. 'Our love is the most important thing in the world to us, and you mean the world to me, but as far as the world is concerned, it's nothing more important than that cruet sitting there –' he jerked his head towards the salt and pepper pots '– and that's the brutal truth. For many of us there are partings and meetings. Some people will sadly have partings and no more meetings. And so it will continue until this madness ends.' He leant across the table and swept a strand of hair away from her face, making her skin tingle under his fingertips. 'Madeleine, you are the dearest person in my life. I want you to know that whatever happens I'll always come back to you.'

She swallowed hard. What did he mean by that? But she couldn't bring herself to ask.

'You sound as though you're going away forever.'

'I'm not, but whatever happens to us, that's what I want you to remember.' He pressed her hand. 'Will you?'

'All right.' She suddenly had a thought. 'Will you get a day off?'

'I don't know.'

She bit her lower lip. 'We're not allowed to receive phone calls at the Park. So you can't telephone me and I probably won't be able to telephone *you*.'

'Ever heard of letters?' he said, smiling as he picked up the writing case and turned it towards her. 'We'll write to one another.' He took her good arm and turning her hand very gently, kissed the palm, all the while gazing at her. He was so close she could almost see her own reflection in his eyes. 'There's so much I want to tell you – but now isn't the right time, darling. So let's enjoy our supper. It's still quite early and I heard there's a concert on this evening at BP.'

* * *

298

Back at Bletchley Park in the ballroom, Jack sat on her right side holding her hand. The lights were always dimmed because of the blackout, but for the first time Madeleine was grateful for the dark as she tried to sort out her anxieties that he was going away tomorrow and she didn't even know if he'd still be in England. But every second she was aware of his closeness. She could smell the musky scent of him, hear the sigh of his breathing, feel the pressure of his thigh against hers. What would he be like as a lover? *Her* lover. A quiver of desire raced through her.

As though he knew what she was thinking he looked at her and smiled, giving her hand a little squeeze, then winding his fingers through hers. How well he understood her when they'd only spent such a short time together. How lucky she was to have his love. She must stop thinking only of herself. There were the twins to write to and see as often as she could. There were her brothers. Her parents. And there were her final weeks of training to be a wireless telegraphist.

In the background the four musicians were tuning their instruments – two violins, a viola and a cello. After a minute they became silent. The cellist gave an almost imperceptible nod, and the string quartet began the first notes. She didn't recognise the piece by Mozart but the musicians played beautifully and she was amazed at such a high standard. It would have been the perfect ending to the evening if Jack hadn't suddenly announced he was being sent away. After half an hour, when it was time for the interval, he guided her over to the makeshift bar.

'You didn't touch your sherry earlier on,' he said.

'I know.'

'Would you like one now?'

'No, thanks. But a juice would be nice.'

When he'd put a glass of apple juice in her hand, someone sauntered over. Cecil.

'How are you both enjoying the concert?'

'It's lovely,' Madeleine said. 'And you?'

'Balm for the soul, dear.' He looked at Jack, then back at Madeleine. 'I've put you down for *Anything Goes* whether you like it or not. No, don't argue,' he said when Madeleine opened her mouth.

'All right, Cecil, I won't argue. But just to confirm, am I playing Reno Sweeney?'

'Yes, dear, so you'd better start learning her songs,' he said as he loped away.

After the concert was over and Jack had helped her on with her coat, he said:

'Why don't we have a walk round the lake. It'll be our last time together for a while.'

Momentarily, she closed her eyes to blink back the tears. It wasn't just a while, it was going to be months.

*There's a war on, in case you've forgotten*, her inner voice admonished. *Stop behaving like a spoilt brat.*

Outside, he took her gloved hand. 'Goodness, the lake's frozen over.'

'It's not the only thing that's frozen,' she said, her words causing her breath to condense in little puffs of smoke.

'Oh, sorry, darling. It's just that we never have anywhere for private conversation.'

The icy air cut through her coat and her hat wasn't keeping her ears warm. It was only nine o'clock but Madeleine already felt tired. After a few minutes she stopped and turned to him.

'How long do you think the war will last?'

'I hate to tell you, but as far as Britain is concerned, it hasn't even started yet. The Yanks are calling it the Phoney War. It'll only be taken seriously by the public when Hitler pulls the plug. And you won't know when until the first bomb drops on us. Look at poor old Finland, just invaded by that bastard. Their lives are now turned upside down. We could be next. But at the moment Hitler still thinks he can convince us to work with him.' He gave a mirthless chuckle. 'He has another think coming. But even if it never happens we're going to be in for a rough time from the Luftwaffe. We don't have nearly the number of aircraft the Germans have, so I only hope our boys are ready for them.'

Gordon and Raymond's faces loomed in her vision. Dear God . . . She shuddered.

'It's horrible to think about.' She looked at him. His dear face. 'Can I see you off tomorrow?'

He shook his head. 'Best not. We'll be leaving before breakfast so we should say our goodbyes now.'

She clung to him, hating herself for suddenly feeling so desperate. She was being ridiculous. He'd be back in the spring – or latest, the summer.

'What address do I write to?'

'It'll be a box number like we have at BP for secrecy.' He stopped and turned her around to face him. 'I'll leave the number in an envelope in the Post Room so you'll get it when you collect your letters.'

'You won't forget?'

'No, my darling, I won't forget.' He looked at her and grinned. 'But *you* nearly forgot this.'

He opened his coat and pulled out his mother's writing case, then put it into her hand.

# Chapter Thirty

*December 1939*

'Madeleine, I'd like you to come with me to meet someone,' Leonard Watts said one morning after he'd finished the first lecture and the others had left the room.

*What was this all about?*

Outside, he took her over to the Mansion, through the entrance and into what must have once been the drawing room. It was now transformed into an office with maybe twenty people, mostly men, some sitting at desks scribbling on notepads, two or three reading files and frowning with concentration, and a man and woman in what looked like deep discussion. A bear of a man with dark hair, bushy eyebrows framing the top of black-rimmed round spectacles, sat at a desk looking blankly into the distance.

'That's Josh Cooper,' Leonard said. 'A very important man and head of the Air Section. Very nice chap. Joshua really but we all call him Josh.' He walked up to the desk but Mr Cooper didn't move.

'Josh, I've brought a young lady to see you.'

Still no sign that the gentleman in question had even heard.

'Miss Hamilton's top-notch at Morse Code,' Leonard went on, 'and is well advanced in learning WT. Oh, and she speaks very good German.' He glanced at Josh. 'I'll leave you to have a chat then.'

At that, the man jumped up, knocking his chair over, and stuck out a hefty hand, practically crushing Madeleine's good hand. He took no notice of her sling, seeming to take it quite for granted.

'How long have you been here . . . at the Park?'

'About four months.'

'Hmm.' He peered at her through the thick spectacles. 'A year here is as good as a university degree.'

'Oh, I already have that – with a distinction,' Madeleine blurted, then worried that she'd sounded like she was boasting.

'Oh.' He whipped off his glasses and looked at her with interest. 'What did you read?'

'Modern languages, but I concentrated on German.'

To her relief he beamed.

'Excellent choice!' He picked up a sheet of paper and put it into her hand. 'So you'll be able to transcribe this without any difficulty.'

Madeleine gestured to a chair. 'May I sit down?'

'What? Oh, yes, certainly.' He waved her to an empty desk. 'There's paper and pen.'

Madeleine scanned the text. It seemed to be mainly about weather conditions. She took up the pen and wrote as closely as she could the English equivalent, realising it was the kind of information pilots needed. There were a few technical terms that she didn't understand but hoped that would be taken into consideration. It was only a couple of paragraphs and she swiftly finished it, read it through, checked with the original German and was satisfied she'd accurately translated it. She handed it back.

Josh Cooper scrutinised it, impatiently flicking back a lock of hair, then looked at her and nodded.

'Good. You'll soon learn all the jargon.' He paused for several seconds. 'Jerry won't win this war, you know.'

'No one at the Park thinks we'll lose,' Madeleine agreed.

'But to do that we've got to make sure we crack the Luftwaffe codes.'

A shiver of excitement played across her shoulders.

'Let me show you something so you understand the kind of thing we're looking for.' He pulled open a drawer and took out a large brown envelope, then shook the contents on his already overflowing desk. 'This is what one of our Spitfire boys managed to get hold of after he shot down a German bomber about to attack our ships in the Firth of Forth.' He glanced round at Madeleine. 'You can tell a lot from what Jerry keeps in his pockets.'

Madeleine peered at the untidy pile of bits and pieces.

'See this.' Josh passed over a leaflet. 'What does that tell you?'

She quickly scanned it.

'It's an opera – *The Magic Flute* – showing in Rotterdam on 29th October.' She looked up. 'I don't understand.'

'It tells you the pilot was in Rotterdam that night. And the silly fool should have destroyed the evidence.' He paused. 'So where do you think he flew from?'

Madeleine shook her head. 'I don't know. It could be anywhere. I suppose he was on leave and having a night out.'

He gave her an encouraging nod.

'Good guess. But not correct. It's typical when Germans

304

have leave they go home.' He took the paper from her hand and glanced at it again. 'No, he was on a weekend pass or out for the evening.'

*What was he getting at?*

'That means his station was in the vicinity of Rotterdam on the night of the 29th of October . . . and look at these cigarettes.' He handed Madeleine a beaten-up packet. 'They're not German – they're Dutch. So in all likelihood our German pilot flew from an airfield near the border.' Josh gave a triumphant grin. 'He was shot down on the 31st and here at the Park we've found out what units operated from that area on that particular night.' He peered at her through his thick spectacles.

'So do we now know the exact airfield he flew from?' Madeleine asked tentatively.

'We do,' he said.

Tantalisingly, Josh chose not to enlighten her. Instead, he removed his spectacles and regarded her.

'You've been highly recommended by Watts. So I'd like you to work here with me.'

'What would I be doing?'

'We don't have enough really good German linguists,' he said. 'Hundreds of messages are pouring in from the Y station every day. The German pilots talk one to the other in the air and from air to ground to keep in touch with their station and it's imperative we keep up with them.' He shot her a penetrating look. 'Any questions?'

'What are these Y stations?'

'Where we get our messages from. They're scattered around the country. Those recruited listen to the pilots' coded messages and send them to us to transcribe. Your job would be to check the messages for any security blunders that we can use, filling in any gaps to make sense of it – any *scrap* of information could prove crucial.' That look again. 'So, Miss Hamilton, are you game?'

This was unexpected and she didn't know how to answer. An opportunity to work with someone who was obviously a brilliant academic seemed too good to miss. But what about the work she'd been trained to do? All that Morse Code and getting up her speed. And all she'd be doing was transcribing messages from German to English. But you wouldn't turn down anything from a man of this calibre, she told herself.

'I would like that very much,' she said, 'though I'm worried I'll lose my Morse speed.'

'Don't worry about that.'

She hesitated, then said, 'When would you like me to start?'

'Right away.'

*Was he joking*? No, he was looking at her quite seriously.

'Anything wrong?'

She shook herself.

'No, not at all.'

'Have your lunch and then start this afternoon,' he said, opening a file, then frowning. He turned over a page.

Quietly, she said goodbye but he didn't look up, already immersed in his document.

'Everything all right?' Leonard Watts said, turning round from the blackboard where he was chalking a diagram. It was between lectures and he was there alone.

'It was all a bit sudden but Mr Cooper wants me to work with him and start this afternoon.'

'Good. I hoped he'd say that once he set eyes on you.

He's got a small team and they're top-notch. You'll soon settle in.' He paused. 'If you were in the forces it would be a promotion. Cooper's one of life's geniuses. You can learn a lot from him.'

'He's already given me a demonstration on how to find out information from the enemy,' Madeleine blurted, then worried that she should have been more discreet. But Leonard gave a wry smile.

'His brain works in a completely different way from the rest of us – same as the other boffins here – so I think you'll be challenged with this new position.' He glanced at her. 'You deserve it, Madeleine. You're well ahead of the others and you have the right tenacious attitude to dig further – just what we want when it comes to understanding the enemy. And you'll be using your German every day.'

Warmth spread through her body at his words.

'Thanks for putting my name forward, Mr Watts,' she said. 'I'm really grateful.'

'Call me Leonard,' he said gruffly. 'Now, be off with you.'

Working with Josh Cooper was an eye-opener. He sometimes sat for an hour without saying a word, his cup of tea going cold, apparently just thinking as he gazed out of the window. Then he would rush outside and for reasons unknown to anyone, throw his cup into the lake. Then he'd come back to his desk and scribble notes and make diagrams, not always sharing it with the two men who worked closely with him. To her surprise, one of the men was Tom Blackmore, Daniel Strong's friend. And what a nice, unassuming chap he was, Madeleine thought. That's who Josie should go for. Maybe she could get the two of them together. She grinned at the idea.

The other man, Sir Percy Baker, was older and quieter but kept everyone, including Josh Cooper, focused on the job. They seemed to be more involved in actual codebreaking. How she wished they would train her to do the same. But she found quite quickly that at German she was streets ahead of Percy (as he'd said to call him) and had a better colloquial mastery of the language than Tom – apparently useful when the pilots were signalling to one another and sometimes bróke into informal chatter – so perhaps she was a valuable member of the team. It was a good feeling to know she was doing her small but practical bit for the war effort.

# Chapter Thirty-One

Madeleine noticed more people were arriving daily at the Park and several new huts were being erected at top speed. Best of all, she'd heard a rumour that BP staff who were in the hostels would be billeted to private homes and inns in nearby villages and towns. Well, that move couldn't come quickly enough, especially if she was given her own room with surely a normal mattress, not to mention privacy and peace – and to be out of earshot of Cora's barbs and moans. Oh, what heaven.

Not only were the new huts taking shape and being fitted out, but Madeleine noticed several male members of staff, some of whom she recognised, digging in the Park's grounds. When she asked if they were building another hut they told her it was going to be a large air-raid shelter. From that moment the war seemed closer. She pictured herself being underneath the ground with a bombing raid going on overhead and her blood ran cold. But if it saved lives . . .

Christmas was upon her before she realised. She'd bought Christmas cards and sent them to her parents and brothers and one for Jack that she signed with all her love, though she hadn't heard anything back. She tried not to worry. The war made everything unpredictable.

'Right,' Percy said, looking at his watch. 'It's bloomin' Christmas Day. Most folk are home with their families so why don't we knock off and get a breath of air before lunch which is any minute.' He glanced over to where Josh was deep in one of the files. 'Coming, Josh?'

'You go,' Josh answered without looking up. 'I'll be along.'

'He won't, you know,' Tom said, shutting the door behind him. 'This is what he does. He gets caught up with a problem and can't leave it until it's solved – even if it means missing a meal. He doesn't even notice he's missed it – nothing changes just because it's Christmas Day.'

Bundled up in coats and hats and scarves, Madeleine, with Percy and Tom, stepped outside to face the icy wind. They were just pressing forward to the area round the back of the Mansion where three cottages stood when Tom suddenly stopped and yanked Madeleine to one side. 'Look out. A crazy dispatch rider is just about to mow us down.'

The rider, clad in a bright tan-coloured coat and cap, came to an abrupt halt and untied a large canvas bag from the back of the seat, then casually removed the cap to disclose a halo of platinum-blonde curls falling to her shoulders.

'Nice,' Percy said, grinning.

Madeleine noticed Tom was silent.

'What about you, Tom?' Percy said. 'You haven't got a girlfriend. Go and ask her for a date.'

'There's only one girl for me,' he muttered, then said, 'Come on, let's go in. I can smell Christmas dinner out here.'

As they entered the dining room, an aroma of roasted chicken and sage stuffing wafted into Madeleine's nostrils. Mmm. She was more hungry than she'd realised. The room heaved with all the extra people but the dining-room staff had accommodated them by putting tables together in long lines, masking the joins with red-checked tablecloths, though they hardly noticed, being covered in dishes. Percy spotted four vacant seats and Madeleine put her bag on the fourth just in case her boss turned up. People wearing paper hats passed round bottles of white and red wine or poured it for their neighbours. A paper chain had fallen from the plastered ceiling and was hovering over a tureen of roast potatoes, and American big band tunes emanated from a gramophone which stood in the corner. It all felt very festive. The only thing missing was Jack.

Madeleine caught sight of Josie, Sally and Olive sitting together on the opposite table. Olive and Sally waved but Josie just gave a wan smile. Where was her usual bubbling energy? And then she saw that Daniel was sitting on her other side but half turned towards a pretty blonde. He obviously hadn't been giving Josie much attention, she thought crossly. At the same moment she noticed Tom looking longingly across at Josie, who had no idea. There wasn't any need for matchmaking, Madeleine thought. Her heart contracted. It was as plain as anything. Tom was in love with Josie and the poor bloke, a quieter personality altogether, though far more genuine, in her opinion, didn't stand a chance.

After the plum pudding and brandy sauce, both delicious, and a second glass of wine, Madeleine felt quite mellow. She glanced across the table. Daniel was still sitting there, his head thrown back, laughing at something the blonde

311

had said. But where was Josie? Maybe she'd just popped to the Ladies'. She'd go and see. But the cloakroom was empty. Madeleine sighed. What should she do? Her head felt a little woozy and she wasn't absolutely certain she was walking in a straight line. She shouldn't have swallowed that second glass so quickly but it had tasted so good. Well, she wouldn't rest until she found her friend and knew she was all right.

But Josie didn't appear to be anywhere in the Mansion. So where was she? She'd try the teashop in Hut 2 but it was closed. She walked through the gates and to the hostel. No, Josie wasn't there either. After that she couldn't think where else. Maybe she'd simply gone for a walk to clear her head. Actually, that wasn't a bad idea. Madeleine decided she'd fetch her coat and walk towards the town. Perhaps she'd bump into her. But the only sign of life on the road was a tired-looking horse slowly pulling a rag-and-bone cart. Its owner, an old man with a patched coat, raised his cap to call 'Merry Christmas', then pulled it well down over his forehead, and prodded the weary animal to get a move on.

She walked up Bletchley High Street and down the other side. All the shops were closed and there were only a few people about walking dogs. The wind felt icy on her face. This wasn't such a good idea after all and there was no sign of her friend. She hurried towards the Park gates and gave the guard her identification. Shivering, she went back to the Mansion but everyone had left. Only the dining-room staff were there clearing up.

'You haven't seen my friend Josie, have you?' Madeleine asked. 'She's a bit shorter than me with dark curly hair.'

'That description fits plenty of girls,' one of the older

312

serving women said. 'But I think I know who you mean. She's usually with you and two others.'

'Yes, that's right. Have you seen her?'

'She asked me for a glass of water. She didn't look well. I got someone to take her to the sick room.'

Drat! Hut 1, where the sick bay was set up. The only place she'd not looked in.

'Maddie! What are you doing here?' Josie was having a cup of tea and for once there was a nurse on duty other than Nurse Bull. This one was petite with a sunny smile, her cap a little askew. 'Thanks, Nurse Poulter,' she said as the nurse took Josie's cup.

'Looking for you,' Madeleine said, going over. 'What happened?'

'Oh, nothing.' She looked up with tear-stained eyes. 'I'm tired, I expect.'

'Hmm. Looks to me like you've been crying. And there's only one person who would upset you – and that's Daniel Strong.'

'I don't want to talk about him,' Josie said. 'As far as I'm concerned, it's over.'

'Are you sure?' Madeleine studied her friend. 'I hope so because he's not worth it, Josie. I saw him with that blonde.'

'She's new here,' Josie said bitterly. 'He's already captivated. Well, she can have him.' She looked directly at Madeleine. 'You know his friend, Tom. The one you met with Dan in the dining room on your first day?'

Madeleine nodded. It was on the tip of her tongue to say she now worked with him.

'Yes, I remember him. He seemed like a nice chap.'

'I think he likes me.'

*I damn well know he does.*

'Has he asked you out?'

'Not yet. He thinks I'm in love with Dan. But I'm going to give him a little encouragement. It might show me whether Dan's jealous or relieved.'

'Tom's too nice to use in that way,' Madeleine said with feeling.

Josie's head shot up. 'But you've hardly spoken to him. So how are you so sure?' She frowned. 'Are you hiding something from me?'

'Not exactly.'

'What's that mean?'

'Well, let's just say I've come across him several times and he seems like a really decent person. And also extremely intelligent.'

Josie's eyes widened. 'Don't tell me anything more so neither of us gets into trouble.' She paused. 'But thanks for that . . . and for coming to find me . . . you're a darling.' She got to her feet and gave Madeleine a hug. 'Have you heard from that man of yours?'

'Not yet. Not even a Christmas card or anything. I'm beginning to get a bit worried.'

'Well, don't . . . because he's crazy about you. Have you been to the Post Room today to see if there's anything?'

'No, we were busy working this morning. But come to think of it, I saw a dispatch rider earlier but didn't think anything of it because it's Christmas Day.'

'Well, at home postmen deliver on Christmas Day, but they go home afterwards instead of doing the usual midday delivery and the afternoon one, so I'd check if I were you – they might well have brought you a love letter from Mr

Gorgeous . . . and if he has,' Josie added with a mischievous twinkle, 'I want to know every detail!'

'Two for you, miss,' the girl in the Post Room said, handing them to her.

'Thank you.' Madeleine glanced down. One from her brother, Raymond. The second one . . . her heart beat hard. Josie had guessed correctly. It was from Jack. Oh, Christmas Day was a wonderful day! She'd read her letters in the library. There was always the clatter of typewriters but no one would take any notice of her if she picked a quiet corner.

One of the typists glanced up, nodded, then went back to her machine. Madeleine slid into the leather armchair and tore open the envelope. Raymond's would wait. Jack's wouldn't.

It was dated 18th December 1939.

*My darling Maddie,*

*Well, my love, Christmas is not far off. I hope this will reach you in time. If not, you'll know I was thinking of you on the day.*

*I'm sorry not to have had a chance to write before now but it was a prolonged and difficult journey fraught with delays and it's been non-stop since I arrived. All I'm allowed to tell you is that I'm overseas.*

*They've put me in charge of a new set-up and I'm pleased to say it's extremely interesting. I certainly need something to take my mind off you. And at least the weather is much warmer here.*

So he's gone abroad, she thought with a sinking heart. And if the climate is so different it must be quite a long way away. That meant less communication and absolutely no way of ever meeting until he came back to England. She'd been counting on an occasional day off when they could be together. Chewing her lip, she read on.

*I've been thinking a lot about the twins lately. They're such brave kids. Let's go and see them as soon as possible after I return. Don't forget we're taking Dexter to meet them. In the meantime, I'm sure you'll be going whenever you can so please write me a newsy letter and let me know how they're getting on.*

*I'm already counting the days, my darling, until I'm back and I've only just got here! I just want to look at your beautiful face. Hold you in my arms and taste one of your magic kisses that make me float on air.*

*Oh, my darling, to sweep you under the mistletoe and kiss those lips. I'll just have to be content with paper kisses. (Can you guess why there are seven?)*

*I love you. I always will.*
*Jack*
*xxxxxxx*

Madeleine put her lips to his name.

*Yes, Jack, I don't have to guess. To remind me that you love me every day of the week.*

She read the letter again, more slowly this time. His expression 'much warmer here'. Could it be Malta? Or somewhere in the Middle East? Cairo, perhaps? It was so frustrating not to be able to ask and have the answers to the simplest questions.

She turned her attention to the other letter from her brother and was soon immersed in Raymond's chatty style,

316

wanting to know how she was and if she liked her job. It told her nothing about his own or Gordon's job. But then presumably they'd all signed the Official Secrets Act as well. She heaved a sigh.

*Oh, I know you can't give me details,* Raymond had written, *but I hope you've made friends by now, and maybe even met someone who's captured your interest.*

*That's exactly it,* she thought. *Jack has captured my interest. And my heart.*

# Chapter Thirty-Two

*May 1940*

Madeleine had been working for Josh Cooper for nearly six months, transcribing mostly aviation messages until it became almost automatic. Josh had explained that the German pilots had no time to communicate in complex codes as they needed to focus all their attention on the job in hand. But just like the British, Josh told her, they used a number of simple cover words. He'd given her a list when she'd first started: where the RAF used the word 'angels' for 'altitude', the German equivalent was '*Kirchturm*' meaning 'church tower'. After only a matter of days she'd memorised dozens of these terms as the German pilots talked to one another in the air and kept in touch with their station on the ground.

It was all fascinating but she wondered what it would be like to actually take down the messages from the pilots as they occurred. A thrill of excitement rushed through her at the thought.

On her way out from the dining room at the Mansion, she picked up one of the newspapers from the rack in the entrance porch. The news had been dreadful lately. Last month Germany had invaded Norway and Denmark and a few days ago it was France. That was the worst shock of all. Who would be next? Hitler was getting closer, Madeleine thought with a shudder. The only good thing was that Chamberlain had resigned and Winston Churchill was now the Prime Minister, and the general feeling was that the old bulldog was more than a match for that Austrian megalomaniac.

She'd only received a dozen or so loving letters from Jack to her twice-weekly ones, but that was to be expected if he'd been sent to the Middle East – still her guess as there was no way of knowing. She'd carefully tucked away his letters, often mentioning the twins, in her precious scarlet writing case, her heart warming that he was still thinking of Erich and Lotte. She'd only managed to see them twice since she'd gone with Jack to break that terrible news. On both occasions they'd been thrilled to see her but they were much more subdued. She wondered when she and Jack would have the chance to take Dexter to be their loving companion.

And then this morning she received a letter from Jack that made her heart sing.

*All going well I'll be back on 18th May*, he'd written. *I can't wait to see you, darling.*

*Neither can I*, she thought happily. Only three more days and she'd see his smiling face. Feel his arms wrapped tightly around her. Oh, the next few days would drag but she'd work her socks off to pass the time.

The following morning Josh Cooper stopped by her desk as he often did first thing to give her the workload for the day. But this time he sat down with a serious expression.

'I'm afraid I don't have good news for you.'

Her heart stopped. *Dear God . . .*

'Only bad so far as *I'm* concerned,' he said hurriedly. She drew in a deep breath of relief. 'I've been asked to send you away.'

*Oh, no.*

'But I *like* it here working with you. I feel I'm being of use and part of the team.'

'You are. That's the trouble.' He lit his pipe, taking his time to get it going.

She thought she would scream if he didn't soon explain. He puffed on his pipe and stared at her through his thick lenses.

'Your work is top-notch and your knowledge of German is exceptional. Because of that you're going to be more valuable in another station. You leave early tomorrow morning.'

*No. No he can't. Not when Jack will soon be here. Not after waiting all these months and then miss him by three days. That wouldn't be fair at all.*

*But there's a war on,* her inner voice admonished her. *Nothing's fair. You just have to get on with it.*

Tears pricked at the back of her eyes. Maybe it wouldn't be too far away. Her mouth felt dry. She licked her lips.

'Where are they sending me?'

'Somewhere on the south-east coast,' he said. 'I can't say exactly, but here's your new box number for the post.' He handed her a slip of paper. 'As usual, it's all very hush-hush. You'll be given sealed instructions when you board the train for London. Read them discreetly and don't discuss the contents with *anyone*. Remember you're still under the Official Secrets Act.' He gave her a wan smile.

320

'I'm going to miss you, Madeleine. But I'm afraid you've proved yourself too good.'

Her insides crumpled. She drew in a deep breath.

'So, Mr Cooper, what's on the agenda today?'

The rest of the day flew by. It was no use even thinking of sending a letter to Jack. He'd never get it in time. All she could do was leave a message for him in the Post Room with her new PO Box number.

She needed to find Cecil and say goodbye. Taking a chance she knocked on the door of his special room in Hut 1. He opened the door immediately.

'I'd put you down for *Pygmalion*,' he said gloomily, when she explained she was off in the morning. 'The starring role.'

It had always been her dream to play the part of Eliza Doolittle. She swallowed.

'Don't tell me anything else or I'll be even more fed up.' She patted his arm. 'I won't forget how kind you were to me, Cecil, and how the rehearsals and the show of *Anything Goes*—'

'My best Reno,' Cecil interrupted with a woeful expression.

'Thank you.' Madeleine smiled. 'It certainly helped take my mind off—' She broke off, embarrassed.

'Jack who'd been transferred,' he finished. 'And now *you're* going.'

'And he's due back straight after I've gone.'

He pulled a face. 'Oh, that's too bad. Here. Come and give old Cecil a kiss.'

She gave him a hug and kissed his cheek.

'I don't think we've seen the last of you,' he said, wiping his eye. 'I hope not, anyway.'

'So do I,' Madeleine said fervently.

It was time to pack her things. She definitely wouldn't be upset to leave her straw mattress, but she would miss Josie, Sally and Olive.

The only occupant in the dormitory, Lilian, heard her come in and shot up in bed.

'Wasser time?'

With the blackout curtains it was difficult for Madeleine to see the hands of her watch. She peered at the face.

'Just gone nine,' she said finally.

'Morning or night?'

Madeleine smiled sympathetically. With all the shift changes and effects of the blackout curtains, it was sometimes difficult to keep track of time.

'Night. The others will be back soon to get ready for bed.'

Lilian sighed. 'I supposed I'd better rouse myself and get something to eat. I'm on the graveyard shift.'

She looked across at Madeleine. 'It's bloody awful.' And with that, she lay down again and turned over.

So much for rousing herself, Madeleine thought with a rueful smile. She must be tired out.

She crept around her bed, mindful not to disturb the girl. She opened the wardrobe and removed her clothes, deciding what she would wear in the morning. She carefully laid all the other clothes in the bottom of her suitcase, tucking her toiletries and shoes around the edges and putting her books on top. Then she took her precious writing case from her locker, rewrapped it in its tissue paper, and placed it on the top.

Thank goodness she'd trimmed things down a lot when she'd packed to come to Bletchley. Even so, she had to stick her foot on the case while she snapped it shut. All she'd have in the morning to throw in were her pyjamas and toilet bag. She'd lock it just before she finally left tomorrow morning. As for now, she'd go and see if her three friends were around to have a cup of cocoa with.

At seven o'clock the following morning Larry Burton, the Park's driver, took Madeleine to Bletchley railway station. As he helped her from the car he handed her a sealed envelope with only her name marked on the outside.

'Not to be opened until you board the train,' he said, then added, 'I wish you good luck.' He touched his cap and disappeared.

The platform was eerily empty. The stale smell from cigarette butts the night before made her wrinkle her nose. Josh had given her a railway ticket to London, but after that she had no idea where she was heading. After a few minutes' wait she saw black smoke swirling in the distance followed by the rumbling of an oncoming train. No sooner had it ground to a halt than a guard took her suitcase, opened the nearest door and set the case inside. Madeleine sprinted up the two steep steps, the guard slammed the door and blew his whistle and the train pulled out of Bletchley station.

She gave a last quick look out of the grimy window. Would she ever see Bletchley Park again? Would she ever see Jack again? She blinked back the tears. She must keep faith or she would dissolve into self-pity. These two thoughts stuck with her for several minutes until she remembered the sealed envelope. With trepidation she tore it open and unfolded the sheet of paper inside.

She glanced at the address. All it stated was 'The Foreign Office'.

Dear Miss Hamilton,

Enclosed is a railway warrant from Euston where you change trains to London Bridge. There you will take the train to Hastings on the south coast of Sussex. You will alight at Hastings and will be met by a woman who will approach you and say, 'Are you going far?' You will answer, 'Too far to walk, I'm told.' She will give you a lift to your billet to leave your case before you report to your CO.

No signature. Just stamped 'The Foreign Office'.

Madeleine folded the letter and tucked it back into the envelope, not knowing whether to feel irritated at the childish tone or thrilled that she might be part of some top-secret spy mission.

She couldn't help thinking this was yet another step forward on this strange path she'd found herself taking ever since the war began.

# PART FOUR

PART FOUR

# Chapter Thirty-Three

*May 1940*

As soon as Madeleine stepped onto the platform at Hastings station along with several other people who had alighted, a slim woman, maybe in her late twenties, in WAAF officer uniform, approached her.

'Are you going far?' she said.

'Too far to walk, I'm told,' Madeleine answered, feeling a little self-conscious and at the same time wondering how the woman knew who she was from the other passengers.

The woman gave a slight smile. 'Ah, then you must be Miss Hamilton. Follow me. I have the motor outside.'

Without saying another word she marched to the exit, Madeleine following, where the woman had parked in a bay right outside the station. She took Madeleine's suitcase and put it in the boot, ushered her into the passenger seat and with barely a glance for traffic, swung the motor onto the road.

'By the way, I'm Penelope Waterfield, Deputy Company Commander. Bit of a mouthful, I know, so call me Penny. We're not too formal here. You'll see me around quite a bit. I'm in overall charge of the personnel – any work problems beyond the usual routine stuff, personal issues, etcetera, just come and see me. I'm one of the operators but apparently I'm known as Auntie Penny, problem solver. We're only a very small unit but we're a friendly bunch.' She turned sharply to Madeleine. 'How's your German?'

'Fairly fluent,' Madeleine gasped, clutching the edges of her seat as the tyres squealed when rounding a corner.

The woman nodded as though pleased and turned back to the road.

'Morse Code speed?'

'I was over twenty, though I haven't used it for the past six months.'

'You'll only need it at certain times – when you're intercepting messages from one station to another – or ground to ground, as we call it.' She drove a little further, then said, 'Wireless telegraphy?'

'That's pretty much what I've been doing lately.'

Penny chatted as she pushed her foot hard on the accelerator, with Madeleine hardly taking in the stunning views of the South Downs because she was so aware of the woman's erratic driving.

'The motor's been sitting in the sun while we were parked outside the station so wind the window down if it's too stuffy.'

Madeleine took her advice and immediately felt the benefit of a light breeze.

'We're stationed in quite a remote spot above Fairlight village, which as you might imagine is on the coast.' She changed gear as they rounded a corner, the tyres squealing in protest. 'But first I'll take you to your billet which is quite comfortable. There are several other girls and a couple of blokes doing the same job as well as the CO billeted there.'

Madeleine gave an inward sigh of relief that she'd have some company.

'Mind you, we all do shift work round the clock so they'll be in and out, as you will be.' She crunched the gears as she finally slowed down to take a particularly sharp bend. 'You'll answer to Flight Lieutenant Douglas Siegle.'

'Are there other civilians?' Madeleine said.

'No, you're the only one, though they rarely wear uniforms because we're so isolated.' She pulled a face as though she didn't approve of taking *quite* such a casual attitude where uniforms were concerned. 'We're screaming out for more linguists at our station so we're having to look outside the RAF and the WAAFs. We enquired at Station X. That's how we found you.' She paused. 'Oh, and by the way, we call ours a Y station.'

So she was going to be working at one of the listening stations Mr Cooper had mentioned on her first day with him . . . she'd be listening in on the enemy itself when they were actually speaking! A frisson of excitement rushed through Madeleine as a few pieces in a large incomplete jigsaw fitted together. Penny would likely have no idea that Station X was really called Bletchley Park or where it was located, and probably neither would the people in the Fairlight station have any inkling with whom they were liaising. She imagined that would go for Flight Lieutenant Douglas Siegle as well. It was essential she must always be on her guard about where she'd come from. She sighed when it sank in that she'd be the only civilian. That might not be quite so easy working with everyone else who was in the forces. Then she pulled herself up.

*For goodness' sake, woman, there's a war on. Who cares if you're the only civilian. I'm sure they don't. We're all working for the same outcome.*

Fifteen minutes later they passed the Fairlight village sign and pulled up outside a large Edwardian house with a swinging board stating 'The Cove' and underneath in red letters: **Full**.

Hopefully they'd included her in their announcement. Madeleine gave a wry smile.

Once inside the gloomy interior, Penny rang the bell on the reception desk. A woman of around sixty with swollen ankles shuffled forward.

'Morning, Mrs Knight. I've brought your latest guest, Miss Hamilton.'

'The last one, I hope,' the woman replied with a sniff. 'We don't have no more rooms available so it's no use bringin' any more people.'

'Yes, we are aware,' Penny said briskly.

'You'd best sign the register.' Mrs Knight slid a large notebook towards Madeleine. A young girl in white cap and apron appeared from one of the doorways. 'Ah, Ena, show Miss Hamilton to her room.'

Mrs Knight's accent had suddenly become upper class. Madeleine hid a smile. Ena bobbed her head.

'Just drop your case inside and you can unpack later,' Penny said.

Madeleine followed the maid up a narrow winding oak staircase, their shoes clattering on the uncarpeted steps. Several narrow rag rugs, end to end, were placed the length of a long landing. Ena unlocked the second door on the right and allowed Madeleine to go before her. Even though the window was open, the room smelt faintly of cigarette

330

smoke from the previous occupant but at first glance it appeared quite clean and serviceable. But there was something important she needed to check. Pulling back the bed covers, she ran her hands over the bottom sheet, and wonder of wonders, not a stick of straw – just a normal mattress. She grinned and set her case down.

'The lav's down the far end of the passage,' Ena told her.

'Is there a bathroom nearby?' Madeleine held her breath, waiting for the answer.

'Oh, yes. It's next door to the lav. But you can't have one just when you please. The rota's pinned on the door but your name's not down yet. You'd best check with Mrs Knight what *your* night is.' She giggled at her own joke. 'Would there be anything else, miss?'

Madeleine managed to stop herself from making any comment though she was determined not to be restricted to just one bath a week. The main thing was that the bedroom was clean and neat. And she'd be in heaven with a room to herself.

'Thank you, Ena,' she said as she closed the door behind her and the maid handed her a key.

'Everything okay?' Penny asked when they were back in the motorcar.

'Yes, thank you.' Madeleine hesitated. 'Are you billeted here as well?'

'Oh, no. You wouldn't catch me. It's all vegetarian and I like my meat too much. I go to my parents in Hastings after my shift.' She turned to Madeleine for a second. 'But I hear the food they serve at The Cove is excellent.'

*Well, that's something new for me to try*, Madeleine thought. And if that was all, then this posting might turn out really well. For the first time since Josh had given her the news she felt her spirits rise.

The road wound upwards and now the English Channel was in full view, sparkling below in the summer sunshine. If you didn't count returning to England on the boat train, Madeleine thought, it was the first time she'd been to the coast since she was a child and her parents had taken her and her brothers to Brighton for the day. She and her brothers had loved it even though they pretended to be too sophisticated for buckets and spades. They'd taken her swimming instead, keeping her safe as they positioned themselves on either side of her. She briefly closed her eyes, not sure if it was to enjoy that childhood memory or to block out the very steep incline with Miss Penelope Waterfield at the wheel.

A final push and the motor, its engine grunting and spluttering, reached a flat piece of ground.

'Right, this is the closest we can get.' Penny turned off the ignition. 'That's our unit.' She pointed to what looked like an outsized caravan perched on the edge of the sandstone cliff. 'It's what's called a signals office tender.'

Madeleine gulped. 'Is that where we all work?'

'Yes.'

'It looks rather precarious.' She wouldn't say she wasn't keen on heights and this 'caravan' looked as though it might topple over the cliff at any moment.

'It is, rather,' Penny said soberly. 'Some chap who was setting this site up actually fell to his death.'

'Oh, no, how dreadful.'

'So we take sensible precautions. Never go out in the dark – or even the dusk – without a torch. Keep in twos whenever possible and stick to the paths.'

Although the officer's warning was loud and clear, Madeleine couldn't stop the thrill that she was about to be much more closely involved in fighting the enemy than ever she'd been at BP.

'Who's in that tent?' Madeleine asked, fearful that Penny was planning to put her in it, on her own.

'That's for the guard. He is actually armed. Officially, he's there to spot any suspicious planes and keep an eye out for curious locals.' She looked at Madeleine. 'Very few people, even in the RAF, know we're here, let alone members of the public. But his *real* job is to protect us weak, vulnerable women from all the predatory men who work here and might try to make passes at us – or worse.'

*Really? Or was the woman kidding?*

'I mean it,' Penny said when Madeleine didn't answer. 'There are only a handful of men and they're all perfect gentleman, but the powers that be truly think they need to look after we women as if we're fragile flowers. As if we can't deal with any straying hand ourselves.' She opened the car door, then turned round. 'I for one would give them a good kick up the bollocks if they tried anything with me.'

They caught one another's eye and burst into a peal of laughter. It altered the atmosphere entirely – no longer were they a military officer and a lowly civilian, Madeleine thought, but two young women who shared a sense of humour.

'Right,' Penny said, still chuckling, as they walked towards the caravan, 'I'll introduce you to everyone. Are you Madeleine or is it shortened?'

'I'm happy to be Maddie but not Mad . . . even if I am,' she added with a rueful smile.

'A serious word of warning.' Penny's answering smile faded. 'As I said, you must stick very carefully to the paths. Don't wander off because there are landmines scattered all over the place. We'll need them if and when the time comes when Hitler manages to invade us, because he'll go for the south-east coast as the main target. And that'll be us.' She glanced at Madeleine. 'Don't look so worried. He hasn't succeeded yet. So until that happens, follow me until you get the hang of it.'

Heart beating loud in her eardrums, in case she forgot to keep to the path, or fell off it, Madeleine placed her foot practically in the identical position Penny had just stepped from. She was thankful when she spotted a middle-aged man, dressed in RAF uniform complete with cap, standing in the doorway watching their approach. He was smoking a cigarette.

'Here's Miss Hamilton – Madeleine – safe and sound,' Penelope said.

'Good. We desperately need another pair of hands.'

He flicked the cigarette butt away and it was only then that she realised the jacket sleeve of his left arm was hanging loose. She wondered how he'd lost it.

'Actually your pair of hands plus a spare one for me would be jolly useful,' he said with a rueful smile while shaking her hand. 'Flight Lieutenant Douglas Siegle – known as "Siggie". Never sure if that's just a corruption of my name or if it's to remind me I smoke too many cigarettes.' He studied her. 'If you don't smoke, then don't start . . . that's my advice and I won't charge you for it.' His face broke into a grin.

'That's kind of you.' Madeleine couldn't help grinning back.

'I suppose I should let you get settled in, seeing as you've only just arrived.'

'Oh, no,' she interjected. 'I've left my luggage in the guest house so I'm more than happy to get a feel of it.' She looked about her. 'It does feel strange out here in the country with all this space when I've been rather hemmed in these last few months.'

'You've come from Station X,' he said as a statement. She nodded. 'I don't know the place – where it is or what it does – though I've got a pretty good idea. Only thing important to me is that I'm told they do a fine job. But this is where it all starts – it's like working on the front line but we desperately need more space to accommodate more personnel. You'll see when we go round how tight it all is. Anyway, come on in.'

As soon as she stepped into the tender, Madeleine was aware of movement beneath her feet. Every nerve ending quivered as she glanced through the open windows. It really did seem close to the edge. Forcing herself to breathe steadily to maintain her equilibrium, she looked about her. A few personnel were at their desks, three with earphones placed on their heads, completely absorbed as they wrote furiously on notepads. She pulled her stomach in tightly. If anyone suspected her dread of heights, she'd be sent home immediately as being perfectly unsuitable. She'd get used to it, she was sure. Well, she'd bloody well have to.

'Our aim is to take down all the messages the Luftwaffe send either with high- or low-grade cyphers or by radio telephony – that is, voice traffic,' Siggie was saying. 'I believe you've been transcribing these kinds of messages at Station X.'

'Yes, I have.'

335

'Good. But now you'll be monitoring messages transmitted from the pilots between themselves or between the pilot and his contact on the ground. Or sometimes intercepting one station to another on the ground. Sometimes we can work out what's going on even before dear Mr Hitler has received the message. Can you imagine his face all red with rage if he knew?' he chuckled. 'The main thing is that you keep a meticulous account of every message in the logbook.' He paused. 'You'll be told more detail when you're actually on the job.' He looked at her. 'Any questions so far?'

'What about the shifts?'

'Right. We have four shifts of six hours each to cover the whole day and night. You may have been used to longer hours at Station X but you'll find this work extremely intensive and the messages we're trying to record are often distorted because of poor signals. That alone can be stressful – *and* it's getting busier by the day, so you'll feel as though you've done a double shift at least. Sometimes that's exactly what you might be called on to do. But . . . and it's a big "but" –' he gave her a lopsided smile '– it's damned interesting. I think you'll enjoy it.'

He took a cigarette from a silver case, put it between his lips and lit it, then snapped his lighter shut. Madeleine couldn't help noticing how deft he was with the movements using only one hand.

'You start tomorrow morning at eight,' he continued. 'Carry on until two. Do that for a week, then take the next shift from two p.m. until eight p.m. . . . and so on. Some shifts are much busier than others but even on a quiet night you can sometimes pick up a crucial message.' He inhaled, then blew out the smoke to one side of his lips.

'There's no running water in here so we have it brought up in bottles, but there's one thing we do have – an electric kettle.' He jerked his head towards a table laden with mugs, an enormous teapot and a smart-looking kettle with Bakelite handle. 'Wouldn't be without it.' He grinned. 'Well, Madeleine, have you any more questions?'

'I'm sure things will occur to me when I'm actually here working,' she said. 'But while I'm here, could I just stay and watch so I get a feel of the work?'

'Yes, of course. Come over and sit by me.'

He set an upright chair to his left and Madeleine sat down. The first thing she noticed was his receiver.

'Oh, my father has a Hallicrafter receiver,' she said, with a ridiculous feeling of delight. It seemed to bring him closer to her. He'd be so interested in all this but she doubted she would ever be allowed to tell him.

'Ah, he must be a ham radio chap,' Siggie said. He gave her a penetrating look. 'Do you know his call sign?'

She blinked. 'Yes. It's "2BV".'

'I was a ham before I came here,' Siggie said. 'I might even know him. I'll have to look him up in the logbook. I've got it here somewhere.'

She could almost see his brain sieving the information, picturing all the contacts in his logbook. Maybe remembering her father's call sign.

He glanced at her and his mouth twitched. 'Hmm. Very interesting.'

# Chapter Thirty-Four

Madeleine's brain was spinning an hour later when she came out of the tender, and she hadn't had to do anything except watch. How on earth was she going to cope tomorrow when she'd be plunged into a six-hour shift? She hadn't had a chance to say hello to any of the operators, except to smile and say, 'See you tomorrow' when she was leaving to a red-haired man who was passing his headphones to another operator. With barely a pause, the girl pulled them onto her blonde curls and took down the very next message.

Penny was waiting a little way away, sitting on a bench smoking. She looked up when she spotted Madeleine walking towards her.

'Right, if you're ready, I'll run you back.'

Penny filled her in a little on the daily routine as she drove the few minutes to the guest house, then pulled up.

'Please don't get out, Penny. You've been so kind and thank you for all your help.' Madeleine hesitated. 'Do I catch a bus tomorrow?'

'No bus stops near enough and if they did we wouldn't use them. It's too secret to allow anyone a whiff of what we might be doing. But don't worry. One of us will take you in at ten to eight sharp. If the worst comes to the

338

worst, then you'll have to walk – but it's quite a stretch as you'll have noticed in the motor.'

Ena opened the front door and Madeleine breathed in the welcome smell of a savoury supper. She hadn't realised how tired she was. It had been a long day with the broken-up journey that had taken nearly six hours altogether, then having a taste of what was in store for her. In her wildest dreams she'd never imagined being in such a remote place in such primitive conditions. No wonder she was exhausted.

'Supper's at quarter-past six, miss,' Ena said. 'Madam don't like it if yer late when she takes trouble to keep it hot.'

'Thanks, Ena, I'll remember that.'

Madeleine could hear female voices from one of the ground-floor rooms but first things first. She'd go and unpack, freshen up for supper and write to Jack to let him know that she'd arrived safely.

Upstairs, she unlocked her door and stepped inside. It wasn't a bad size, she thought, and best of all, it was hers. And there on the right beyond the sink was her own wardrobe. No more sharing with Cora. Quickly, she unpacked, using the long drawer under the wardrobe for items that could stay flat, and putting her underwear into a small set of drawers by her bed. A desk and hardback chair stood on the opposite side – a perfect spot to sit and write her letters. She set her writing case on the desk and glanced at her watch. Oh, dear. Twenty-past six. She was already late.

Splashing a handful of water on her face, she dragged a comb through her hair, not stopping to pin it up, and dabbed on some lipstick. Feeling a little more respectable, she ran down the stairs, nearly bumping into Mrs Knight passing by on her way to the reception desk.

'Everyone's in the dining room . . . first door on your left,' she told Madeleine with more than a hint of disapproval that she wasn't already at the table. 'I've laid you a place.'

'Thank you very much.'

The buzz of chatter and laughter stopped as Madeleine opened the door. Four pairs of eyes turned to her from a long refectory table. The same girl and red-haired young man she'd seen in the tender, a woman with gleaming dark hair pulled back in a chignon, and an older man with a dark moustache. The two men immediately leapt to their feet.

'Oh, please sit down,' Madeleine said, feeling a little self-conscious. 'I'm Madeleine Hamilton – Maddie for short.'

Were the two unfamiliar faces also working at the Y station? She mustn't take it for granted and say the wrong thing. There could easily be an RAF station nearby that had nothing to do with Fairlight.

'Do come and sit down.' The red-haired man pulled out a chair next to him.

'Thank you.'

'Alan Goodman –' he stuck out his hand and she took it briefly '– and this is Howard Moore. Any of the guests you meet here will be at Fairlight on various shifts, so no need to worry about what you say when us lot are on our own – but just to remind you, don't speak about anything to do with work in front of the staff. Because they don't interact much, people tend to forget they're there.'

'Oh, no, I wouldn't dream of it.'

'Sorry we didn't get a chance to introduce ourselves

340

when Siggie brought you in,' the curly-haired girl said. 'Sometimes it goes mad in there. Anyway, I'm Kelly – and that's Elaine.'

The striking brunette opposite smiled at her.

'Pleased to meet you all,' Madeleine said, her eyes flicking over the small group.

'Have you come far?' Kelly asked.

'Not massively.' Madeleine's voice was casual. 'But I had to change trains with long waits in between. But it was all right – I had my book.'

Howard Moore edged a casserole dish towards her. 'It's "help yourself" here, Madeleine.'

She lifted the lid to the enticing smell of fried onions and gravy, while the group resumed their chat. The meal was delicious. From what she could tell, everyone was enjoying the baked vegetable dish with kidney beans. She tucked in, chatting when anyone spoke to her. After the apple crumble and custard – the best she'd ever tasted – she decided she'd hit the jackpot as far as food was concerned – vegetarian or not.

She watched as people helped themselves to tea or cocoa.

'Are we allowed to take a drink up to our rooms?' Madeleine asked Kelly.

'Mmm. Not sure. There are quite a lot of rules here. Mind you, I've only been here a fortnight myself, though it seems like home now.' Kelly smiled, but to Madeleine it was a little grim.

'I'll chance it,' Madeleine said. 'I could do with an early night.'

'Don't blame you,' Elaine put in. 'You'll feel a new woman tomorrow.'

No one stopped her as Madeleine took her mug of tea

341

upstairs. It wasn't even eight. Plenty of time to write to Jack and have a read before switching off the light.

The evening air felt cool on her bare arms. She pulled the sash window down leaving just a small gap at the bottom, then she sat at her desk, looking forward to telling Jack as much as she was allowed about her latest venture.

She put the writing case to her nose, inhaling the leather as she often did. What a thoughtful man Jack was to entrust her with his mother's most precious item. He couldn't have given her anything nicer, and she loved how he said it would remind her to write to him. It was a pity they wouldn't see one another very easily but at least in a few days' time they'd both be in the same country, and surely their days off would clash occasionally. She must try to keep positive. For now, she'd send her letter to the usual Bletchley Park PO Box number. Even though he'd be disappointed she wasn't there, at least he'd have a loving letter to read on his return.

She removed the cap from the red fountain pen.

*My darling Jack,*

*I was thrilled to receive your last letter telling me you'd soon be home. But you're going to be so fed up to learn that I was told that same day I was being sent away with no notice! I arrived this afternoon. I'm still in England but quite far from BP so unless we manage to get two days off at the same time, I don't suppose we'll have a chance to meet regularly. But as you've so often told me – we're at war and mustn't expect things to run the same.*

*I can't describe how much I miss you. I'm in a remote area of the countryside and close to the sea, working with only a few others. The air smells wonderful and the seagulls have been squabbling and vying for food this afternoon. I know you love the countryside so I feel close to you just writing this. The twins would love it. Maybe we could bring them here one day when this is all over. I hope they're doing well at school as I haven't heard from them for more than a month. Not heard lately from Ruth either. I must write to her and find out how they are.*

She put her pen down. What she longed to do was open her heart. But it was so difficult to write. If he were here she'd fling her arms around him, kiss his lips and tell him never to stop kissing her back . . . She picked up her pen again.

> *I want to feel you, touch you, gaze at you and love you. What a miracle that you feel exactly the same. And then I want to talk and talk and listen to you talk and talk. I'd better stop this nonsense. But just know that I love you and always will, my darling, and can't wait to see you.*
>
> *I love you,*
>
> *Madeleine XXXXXXX (one for every day of the week!)*

She drew an envelope out of its pocket and was about to close the writing case when she noticed something was poking out beyond the neat stack of envelopes which all fitted edge to edge perfectly. She pulled out a piece of paper folded in four. She didn't remember seeing that before or putting it in. Maybe it was a letter she'd had from the twins that she'd tucked in there. She unfolded it and scanned the short note in hand-written capitals. She blinked, trying to clear her blurred vision. What on earth . . .?

YOU ARE BEING HOODWINKED BY JACK SYLVESTER. IF YOU DON'T BELIEVE ME ASK YOURSELF IF HE'S TOLD YOU ABOUT HIS WIFE! I KNOW BECAUSE HE LEFT ME WHEN HE MET THE WOMAN HE MARRIED. AND HE WILL LEAVE YOU TOO. ALSO HE IS NOT ALL HE PURPORTS TO BE IN HIS WORK. A FRIEND.

A wife? Jack was *married*? It wasn't possible. Someone was having a joke at her expense. She shook her head in puzzlement. Who could have slipped the note into her writing case without her knowing? And more importantly, why?

And anyway if that were true she'd know about it. He would have told her. No, this looked like a message from someone crossed in love. Someone at the Park was jealous when she noticed the two of them and put two and two correctly together. But the woman who wrote this implied that she once knew him – had in fact been going out with him. So that must have been way before she'd first set eyes on Jack on the train for Berlin.

She read the note out loud, slowly. It didn't make sense. She tried to get a hold of herself. *Let's see. Jack met this woman and after a time he couldn't stand her jealous nature so he broke it off with her. Then he met another woman and fell in love with her. And married her.* Her pulse quickened. She forced herself to think further. *Then his job took him to Berlin and that's when he met me. The war came and he forgot he had a wife and began to fall in love with me.* Madeleine snatched a breath. *He'd given his love to three women in the space of . . . what? A year? Maybe two years?* No, that didn't make sense. He was definitely not the sort of person to 'forget' he had a wife and not tell her. Not the way he'd given her his undying love before he'd been sent away. No, this was the pen of a jealous woman. But who?

She looked again at the last sentence: 'Jack is not all he purports to be in his work'. What did *that* mean? Was the writer saying he appeared to be disloyal to his country? Was she implying he was some sort of spy?

How ridiculous! Look how he helped me when that guard started to get suspicious on the train. If he hadn't intervened it could have turned into a nasty situation for me and the twins. And then getting the children's fake passports, risking his career if he'd been found out. She shook her head. No, he was a thoroughly decent person and that's why she loved him.

She bit her lip.

But maybe there *was* something in it. People always said about rumours that there was no smoke without fire. Could Jack possibly be hiding something about his work? She remembered how cagey he'd been in the restaurant when she'd asked him about his job.

She shook herself. Of course he was cagey – he'd signed the Official Secrets Act.

Oh, if only he were standing in front of her, she'd make him tell her the truth. She'd watch his face, see the expression in his eyes. She'd know damned well if he was lying. She'd just assumed he was single. And he'd been so gentlemanly when he thought she was engaged to someone else . . . except for that kiss, she reminded herself, her cheeks flushing.

*Be sensible, Maddie. Someone out there wants to cause trouble. It's just a pack of lies.*

The heavy capital letters of the note stared up at her, warning her.

Bile rose in her throat. She stumbled over to the sink and spat it out, then collapsed on her bed, the note still clutched in her hand.

Dear God, if it *were* true, he was making a fool of her. What the blazes did he think he was doing? Was this just to get her into bed? She recalled how he'd often grumbled that they had no time alone because of her dormitory and his lodgings run by a landlady who constantly reminded him there were strict rules that no women were allowed. Was that all he wanted her for? Sex? She swallowed the threatening tears.

*Oh, how could I have been so stupid – so naïve – as to believe him.*

His face dangled in front of her, his warm brown eyes, once so full of love, now mocking her. She put her arms around her stomach as though to protect it but the blow had already knocked her back. Angry tears poured down her cheeks.

*He never told me about his wife because he thought he'd lose me. Well, too late, Jack. You've lost me already. And all this time I've been in love with a married man. A married man who might be deceiving his own country, let alone me!*

Furious with herself and sickened with Jack, she leapt from the bed and snatched up the letter she'd written to him. Without even a cursory glance at the loving words, she tore it into little pieces, tossing the scraps into the wastepaper basket, feeling she had just torn out her own heart.

346

# Chapter Thirty-Five

Madeleine awoke in a daze from the persistent ringing of her alarm clock. She didn't recognise anything in the room. Where on earth was she? Why did Cora's face bob in front of her? She rubbed her hand across her forehead to brush the image away and still the throbbing in her head. A fog of unhappiness almost overwhelmed her when she remembered Jack was not all she had believed him to be. His idea of love was not the same as hers. She blinked to try to clear her mind. All the sleep she'd had was only in the last couple of hours. Now it was time to get washed and dressed, she wanted to pull the blanket under her chin and curl up underneath like a child to allow the numbness of last night to take over. But she couldn't. It was her first day and she needed to be alert.

'Alert.' Her voice was bitter as she spoke aloud. 'My clock is more alert than I am.'

*Who* had written that note? She ran her thoughts over all the women who had seen her and Jack together. There was Sandra. Madeleine didn't know her very well but she hadn't warmed towards her the way she did Josie and Sally and Olive. And it definitely wasn't one of those girls. The only other possibility was Cora. Could it be her? Was she the 'friend' who'd sent the message warning her about Jack? Cora knew she and Jack were in love – or *had* been, she told herself bitterly – because the girls in the dormitory had teased her on several occasions, Josie once even saying, 'Has he asked you to marry him yet, Maddie?' Thinking about it now, she realised that Cora had never joined in with the other giggling women. Just the opposite, Madeleine mused, remembering Cora's mouth downturned as she lay on top of her bed with a book ignoring everyone who mentioned boyfriends. Was *she* the one Jack had dated, then he'd met someone else, broke it off, and married the other woman? And now he professed to be in love with *her*.

Madeleine brooded for a few more minutes, visualising the scene when she would confront Jack. But she couldn't bear to even imagine it. Angry with herself for being such a fool, she flung back the covers and pushed her feet into her slippers. It was a quarter to seven. Her eyes stung with tiredness from so little sleep – she'd checked her alarm clock hour by hour throughout the night. Tears threatened again. Where was that hateful note? Had she torn it up with the letter to Jack? It wasn't on the desk. She needed to read it again. Maybe it had become exaggerated in her mind. Maybe it didn't even exist. But she knew it did, and she knew every word it contained. Even if she set light to it she would never be able to erase the contents. And he would never be able to convince her that his wife had simply slipped his mind.

She looked in the wastepaper basket, but all that was in there was her letter to Jack – the letter she'd poured her love out to him – and now the letter was in shreds – just like her heart. She looked on her desk again, her bedside table, on the floor . . . what had she done with it? She gave a juddering sigh. She'd go downstairs and get a cup of tea. Maybe that would clear her head.

Alan Goodman was sitting alone at the breakfast table, finishing his scrambled eggs.

'Morning, Madeleine. Did you sleep well?'

'Not really . . . but I expect it was being in a strange bed,' she added hurriedly.

'Hmm.' He looked at her.

Had he noticed her red eyes, puffy with crying? If he had, he didn't comment.

'The others have already eaten and I'm the lucky one taking you in this morning.' He grinned. 'But no need to rush. We've plenty of time. The tea's still hot though maybe a bit stewed.' He glanced at her. 'May I pour you a cup?'

'Yes, please.'

She couldn't face an egg, or even porridge. Instead, she took a cold piece of toast from the toast rack and spread some butter and a scraping of marmalade onto it, conscious that her hand was shaking. This couldn't be allowed to carry on. They'd send her home if they thought she had the least problem concentrating. Josh Cooper might well have vouched for her; she couldn't let him down. He was such a marvellous man and had such faith in her. Oh, if only she'd never found that note. But it wouldn't have mattered. It existed. Someone – Cora? – had been determined to warn her about Jack but couldn't or wouldn't tell her face to face. Did she dislike her that much or was she actually being kind?

With every bite she felt it stick in her throat before she could swallow. In the end she gave up and simply drank her tea.

'Is there another one in the pot?'

'Yes. Allow me.' Alan poured her a second cup and smiled. 'A word of advice. You won't remember everything or anywhere near until you've had at least a week with us. So don't beat yourself up if you feel overwhelmed. Take it all calmly until you get to grips with the different procedures. We'll do what we can to help today but I have to warn you – it's a madhouse sometimes. The messages are coming through thick and fast now and the main thing is to keep on top of them. But it doesn't happen overnight, no matter how much training one's had. It's gruelling mental work for six hours on the trot but hidden amongst the dross there's sometimes a gem that could have a bearing on the outcome of the war.'

When she didn't comment, he gave her a direct look. 'And excuse me for saying, Madeleine, but you look as though you've had a lousy night which won't be the best start for you so don't push yourself today. No one expects it – not even Siggie.'

She had to bite her lip hard to stop herself from bursting into tears at his concern.

'Thanks, Alan.' She dabbed her mouth with her napkin. 'I'll try to remember your advice.' She glanced at her watch. 'I'd better go and finish getting ready. The last thing I want is to be late.'

Back upstairs she cleaned her teeth, noticing her eyes were still swollen. She applied a bright lipstick, more to boost her confidence than to look attractive, then wished she hadn't. It looked like a bleeding wound in her white face. She tried to wipe it off but only succeeded in smudging it, making it look worse. Damn it all! Pulling her hair back, she rammed a comb in each side. It would have to do. Then in the mirror she saw the unmade bed. With a sigh she quickly pulled up the covers and puffed up the pillow. A small piece of paper fluttered onto the floor. She bent and picked it up. That blasted note. Words that had the power to change her future. Already had. She swallowed hard as she thrust it into her handbag, then, slamming the door behind her, hurried downstairs where Alan was waiting by a shabby black motorcar. It looked exactly like her brothers' old Ford the two of them had shared when they lived at home. But inside she quickly saw Alan didn't give it the loving attention Gordon and Raymond had with theirs. It reeked of stale smoke. But she mustn't be ungracious. He was doing her a favour by giving her a lift to work.

'Right,' he said. 'Off we go.'

Despite the state of his vehicle, he was a much smoother driver than Penelope and within minutes they reached the top of the cliff and the tender.

'We're a few minutes early but we'll go in and take over the graveyard shift,' Alan said. 'I'll show you how it's done. It's quite an art.'

Siggie was already at his work station, immaculately dressed, although Madeleine couldn't help her eyes flicking to the empty sleeve of his jacket. But you'd never notice in the way he managed everything, she thought. And there didn't seem to be any bitterness on his part. She wondered exactly what had happened and how it must have felt at the beginning to lose a limb. He looked up and smiled.

'Morning, both,' he said. 'Madeleine, grab that chair and just watch again for an hour or two and then have a go if you feel comfortable about it.'

How kind everyone was. It seemed almost worse in comparison to the turmoil inside her. She set her jaw. She would *not* carry out the work required with anything less than a hundred percent concentration. Using every inch of her willpower, she shoved aside all thought of Jack as she stood behind Alan, watching him practically snatch the headphones from the girl sitting there, who jumped up, yawning heavily. Immediately, he plonked in her seat and began where the girl had left off taking down the messages in the logbook.

The logbook was laid out exactly the same as she was used to: time of message, radio frequency and call sign with a space for the translation underneath. The only difference was the urgency, Madeleine thought, as she sat next to Alan, her heart racing at the smooth changeover. A quiver shot through her. This was real. If Alan was right, it was possible to take a message down today that could have an impact on the way the war was going.

'Right, Madeleine, you have a go.' Alan handed her the earphones. 'You'll find many of the messages are spoken in ordinary German because the Krauts are obviously in a hurry when they're flying fighter planes. Main thing is, you're looking for a call sign.'

In her hurry to get the headphones on, she put them round the wrong way. Exasperated, she had to allow Alan to help her. Meanwhile, she could hear all sorts of distorted German coming through the speaker. After a wasted minute she was sitting at the desk, headphones on correctly, and pencil poised. Nothing – only a crackling noise of blurred words. She twiddled the knobs, trying to find a clearer signal. To her delight she clearly heard a word she recognised: '*Kommen*' from the verb 'to come', and then a reply from a different voice. Just before the first one took up the conversation, the second pilot repeated the word

'*Kommen*'. From the context, she deduced that the pilots were sending messages to one another and saying 'Over' at the end when they listened for the other pilot's reply. She strained to listen for his answer, but many of the words blurred. She could only write down fragments, automatically translating them into English, frustrated that she hadn't managed to record the whole message.

*Damn! That one might have been important.*

But there was no time to apologise to Alan or explain the poor signal because more messages were coming through. Out of the corner of her eye she noticed Alan was already working from another desk. She just had to get on with it.

But after two hours, the lack of sleep began to take its toll. She wished she could hold up her eyelids with toothpicks. Her writing was becoming untidy and if she continued at this rate it would soon be illegible. She licked her dry lips, then felt a shadow over her. She dared to take her eyes off the logbook for a second to see Penelope.

'Coffee, Madeleine?'

She could have hugged her.

'Oh, yes, thank you.'

'Sugar?'

'No, just milk, please.'

Two minutes later Penny called, 'It's ready. Come and have it outside.'

Madeleine removed her headphones, stretched her arms above her head, then rose to her feet. Thankfully, it had gone quiet in the last ten minutes.

'We're not allowed to eat or drink at our work station,' Penny said, handing her the mug, 'though most of us have the odd piece of chocolate if there's anything going.'

Madeleine stepped outside, glad to take a few steadying breaths of air, if only briefly. Gratefully, she took a deep swallow of the coffee, almost burning the roof of her mouth. Not caring, she took a few more sips. Oh, it was so good. It tasted like real coffee, not the awful chicory-flavoured Camp coffee that the Park frequently served. Already she was feeling better. But when she returned to her workplace, the signal had almost vanished and she spent several minutes searching for the right band before she found a message she could partly decipher, although it seemed to be only friendly chit-chat between one pilot and another, unless that was in code too. She remembered her training under Josh Cooper about the pilots using completely different words for some of their actions and locations. But there was nothing at the moment she recognised. It was all very confusing and she wasn't confident she was any use at all. *Probably more of a hindrance*, she thought grimly, now thoroughly fed up with herself.

At noon Penelope brought in a basket of cheese and ham sandwiches and some apples. Siggie stood from his desk and rapped with a teaspoon on his empty coffee mug.

'Will the early lunch stop now,' he said. 'You have precisely twenty-five minutes. Then the second lunch will go.' He nodded at Madeleine. 'You'll go on this early one, Maddie.'

Madeleine quickly rose to her feet and stepped out of the way of a young man who immediately took her seat. Her back was aching, hunched as she'd been for the last four hours, not even daring to leave her seat for the primitive toilet outside, and her neck was stiff as though set in plaster of Paris.

Her bad night was really catching up on her now. She

would have given anything to have a nap. But that was completely out of the question. Maybe when she'd had some food she'd be more alert. She mustn't waste another minute. Fresh air was what she needed . . . and paying a quick visit to the lavatory.

It was a chemical toilet and she had to wait behind Megan – a well-built Scottish girl who always had a smile.

'I'll only be a wee while,' the girl assured her, then chuckled. 'That was an unintended joke.'

As good as her word, Megan appeared two minutes later. 'All yours,' she said.

Madeleine was in and out fast, splashing some water from a large can over her hands. Oh, if only she could sleep. But instead, she must rush back to eat her sandwich.

The afternoon was a repeat of the morning though it felt to Madeleine harder and harder to find a station. She was allowing too many messages to slip by. She half raised her hand for Siggie's help. He immediately came over.

'You're looking for a call sign which will be attached to a group,' he said. 'And until we know which frequency and call sign each group – or *Geschwader* – uses, the messages aren't terribly helpful.'

'How do I find the right station?'

Siggie hesitated. 'It's not easy when you're not experienced. It can take a few days to get used to it. I'll have a look myself and when I find a German transmission I'll call it out to you. Then you write down the message.'

She gave an inward sigh of relief. That would help enormously. She set her jaw, determined she wouldn't take as many as a few days to get to grips with the procedure. She looked round at her colleagues. Everyone had their headphones on. She might venture a question without being overheard.

'What happens to the messages we translate in our logbooks every day?' she said, hoping she wouldn't get reprimanded for asking questions she didn't need to know the answer as far as her job was concerned – something that had been constantly drummed into her at Bletchley Park. But Siggie didn't baulk.

'They're immediately sent on to Station X – where you've just come from – to be decoded if it's not all in plain German,' he added, his eyes twinkling. 'Obviously, if anything of significant importance and urgency turns up which will be of tactical use, they will pass it straight on to our air force or navy.' He paused. 'The only reason I'm telling you this much is because you worked there.' He paused once more. 'Well, if you're ready, let's crack on.'

Within two minutes Siggie called out, 'Righto, Madeleine, I've found a transmission so take down the message.'

To Madeleine's immense satisfaction, she wrote down the message, translating it into English as she went, about a reconnaissance aircraft sending a weather report on the English Channel.

But that evening when she was alone in her room at the guest house Madeleine felt a very different person. The anonymous note about Jack instantly came flooding back with all its evil connotations. There was no doubt now in her mind that Cora had sent it. Only Cora would have had the opportunity to slip the note into the writing case because they were in adjacent beds in the hostel. The woman was always ready to throw some barbed comment at her and she'd never understood why. Yet the note had been signed: A FRIEND. The last thing Cora had ever been. Well, that at least must be a bluff. No real friend would tell her the truth in such a cruel way.

# Chapter Thirty-Six

*June 1940*

The next morning Madeleine was first downstairs for breakfast. She picked up the morning paper that had been pushed through the letter box. The huge letters of the headlines in the *Daily Express* shouted out triumphantly to her.

**Through an inferno of bombs and shells the B.E.F. is crossing the Channel from Dunkirk – in history's strangest armada**

## TENS OF THOUSANDS
## SAFELY HOME ALREADY
*Many more coming by day and night*
*SHIPS OF ALL SIZES DARE THE*
*GERMAN GUNS*

She quickly skimmed the columns, which described the troops as being tired, dirty, hungry but coming back unbeatable. How they'd been surrounded on both sides by the Germans who thought they'd got them in a bottleneck.

But the Navy with their destroyers along with hundreds of little boats of all sizes, including fishing boats, lifeboats and paddle steamers, were bravely making their way backwards and forwards across the Channel picking up the soldiers in what the government had named Operation Dynamo. A tear trickled down her cheek. Then another. To think of those hundreds of valiant rescuers fighting the stormy crossings.

She wiped her eyes and folded the paper neatly, putting it on the hall table, her head full of images of the men who might not survive. Thank the Lord that such a rescue was going on. She'd read there were more than 350,000 men, mostly British but also French soldiers. Please God, let all of them return safely. But she was forced to face the stark truth that it wasn't possible. There were bound to be many losses – and for the RAF, who were involved as well. And what about Gordon and Raymond in the Royal Navy's Fleet Air Arm? It was extremely likely they would have been called in to help the evacuation. Her stomach turned as she pictured her brothers in their aircraft trying to throw off the Luftwaffe in order to allow the ships to make it across the Channel in safety. But there was nothing she could do except to whisper for them to keep safe.

Back at work, Operation Dynamo was on everyone's lips. There'd been brief radio broadcasts about the rescue started a few days before, but at the same time the Nazis had stated only *they* were in control of Dunkirk.

'Bloody marvellous organisation without a lot of notice,' were Siggie's words when the small daytime team took over from the graveyard shift. 'And the usual propaganda from Jerry. But now we have to get our own heads down and do *our* bit.'

* * *

Three hours passed. It must surely be time for a break. Madeleine glanced at her watch, then caught sight of a dispatch rider roaring up the cliff top. A man this time. He set the motorbike against a wire fence, untied the leather bag which was perched behind the saddle, and swung it on his arm. Siggie got up and opened the door.

'Anyone here by the name of Miss Madeleine Hamilton?' the young man said.

She jumped at the sound of her name.

'Yes, she's new,' Siggie answered. 'What else have you got for the rest of us poor blighters?'

The young man grinned and handed Siggie a pile of envelopes tied with string, picked up some outgoing post in the tray by the door and was gone.

'Two for you, Maddie,' Siggie said, handing them to her.

Madeleine glanced at them. One from Gwen and one from . . . Jack. It felt quite thick. She swallowed hard. She should throw it straight into the bin. But she knew she would read it just in case he begged her forgiveness for not mentioning anything about being married. She was being stupid. How would he know she'd found out? He couldn't possibly. But still she needed to know the tone of this letter.

Her opportunity came in her twenty-five-minute lunch break. She sat on her favourite bench overlooking the English Channel and opened the letter.

*30th May 1940*

*My darling Maddie,*

*I got back to BP late this evening and to my utter disappointment was told you'd been transferred only two days ago! Can you believe such rotten luck? But let me tell you, they must think highly of you at BP to transfer you* like this. They do an incredibly important job on which BP totally relies. I know many of these stations are right off the beaten track so I hope it's not too remote. That is, if they haven't sent you to one of them overseas. Hopefully, not, so maybe there's a chance we can meet in London. I will let you know when I next have a couple of days off and if you can do the same, then not all is lost. We could go and visit the twins and take Dexter like we planned. It's probably a while since you've seen them and I'm sure they must miss you. Have you heard anything about their parents through Ruth at all?

Talking about missing you – I miss you terribly. And have missed you all the time I was overseas. Can you imagine me counting the days, and then missing you by just two? Totally unfair, but war is unfair so there's no point in grumbling when you think of those poor devils in France, frozen cold and soaked through, waiting to be rescued. I hear our little ships are doing a fantastic job. I expect you're keeping up with all the news.

I do hope you have by now settled into your new job and hope you're working in a friendly team.

I wish I had a photograph of you. But I don't really need one. When I shut my eyes I can see your lovely face in front of me, and I want to gather you into my arms and never stop kissing you. I hope you feel the same as I do!

All seems to be well here. Cecil asked to be remembered to you. He said he wants to produce Pygmalion next but there's no one who can play Eliza Doolittle now you've gone. In fact, he's thinking of shelving it because he says it's a difficult role for an amateur (sorry, darling, I don't mean to sound rude) and it takes someone special like you, he said, to pull it off.

*Have they told you how long this posting is? I sincerely hope not until the end of the war as that could be years away, especially as we've still not seen any bombing. But it'll come – there's no doubt about it. Let's just hope it won't be a full-blown invasion as Hitler never tires of warning us.*

*Well, my love, I'm going to finish this and hope there'll be a letter waiting for me when I go to the Post Room after breakfast. I just wanted to get this written straightaway to feel near you.*

*Please write a.s.a.p. from wherever you are.*

*Your lonely Jack*

*XXXXXXX*

*P.S. Have just collected your letter with your new PO Box address, thank goodness.*

Madeleine took in a jagged breath as she came to the end of Jack's letter. If she hadn't known any different, she would have thought he was the dearest, kindest, most loving man she'd ever met. How thoughtful he was to mention the twins and how their lives had been turned upside down. And offering to spend some of his two-day pass visiting them. But he wasn't kind and thoughtful. He'd held back the bitter truth that he was married. She swallowed hard. Why hadn't she ever asked him if he'd ever been engaged even, let alone married? But it hadn't seemed necessary, any more than she'd felt the need to tell him about Andrew.

Her eyes flicked to his last line: *Your lonely Jack.* She grimaced. Lonely, when he had *a wife.* If his poor wife found out what he'd been up to, the woman would be a laughing stock with everyone saying she couldn't hold on to her husband. How dare Jack treat them all with such disdain.

361

*You do realise you haven't actually allowed him to defend himself,* her inner voice suddenly barged in.

'He has nothing to say that I want to hear,' she answered out loud, her voice coated with anger. 'I don't wish to hear his excuses.'

*He's innocent unless he's proven guilty,* her inner voice persisted.

'I have the proof – in that bloody note.'

*That's not proof.*

She refused to allow this conversation with herself to continue. It wasn't doing any good. All it did was upset her even more. She just wanted to forget she ever knew Jack bloody Sylvester. Even his name was false. He was really James Mark, or so his British Embassy card had stated. Unless that was the false one. It seemed everything about him was a sham and she'd fallen for it. Heat, like fire, coursed through her body. She read the note again, but every word sounded false. He'd been unfaithful to his wife – and it didn't matter that she and Jack had never slept together – it would still count as disloyal to his innocent wife as if they had.

In her humiliation she was about to screw up his letter – but something made her stop. Instead, she folded it and slipped it into the writing case he'd given her for that very reason. Now the beautiful red-leather case mocked her.

*But that's the point.* Her inner voice refused to let it go. *He gave you his mother's writing case. It was obviously very precious to him. He didn't give it to his wife, he gave it to you. Now why would he do that? Could it be that there's some sort of explanation – even though you don't know it yet?*

She shook the possibility out of her head.

Another thing – he seemed to know quite a lot about

362

what she was doing. And she'd never got to the bottom of how a diplomat – a cultural attaché – in the British Embassy to Berlin could end up at Bletchley Park. Was this something to do with Cora, or whoever it was, saying Jack was not all he purported to be in his working life either? The questions tumbled around in her head and needed answering. But for now, she had to get back to work. She still had plenty of questions to ask Siggie regarding her work and they were far more important.

'The German air force have grids – in code, of course,' Siggie was explaining when Madeleine had asked if she could have a few moments with him in his cramped office. 'They use them to locate their own positions and also where the ground forces they plan to attack are located, or if they need to carry out reconnaissance duties. It's our mission to crack those codes.' Siggie looked at Madeleine. 'Are you any good at crossword puzzles?'

'I used to do them sometimes when I was at college,' she said. 'I wouldn't say I was expert but I did usually manage to complete them in the end.'

He looked thoughtful. 'I'll get you to work with Elaine for an hour today. She's pretty good at them but more importantly, she's experienced in the way the Germans put their information into code when they're using the grids. Also, she'll give you a list of some of the German words they use for code words.'

'I learnt some of them already at Station X.'

'You'll pick up more as you get used to the traffic you're listening to, and of course their different accents, which are not always easy to understand – especially Bavarian. That's a nightmare.'

363

Madeleine smiled. 'Actually, that's the easiest one for me to pick up, having lived in Munich for nine months or so.'

Siggie regarded her with renewed interest. 'Really? What were you doing?'

She quickly explained and he nodded.

'Understanding the Bavarian accent is a real bonus for us – and having lived there, you'll probably know some of their slang when the pilots talk to each other.' He lit yet another cigarette. 'You'll find the whole listening process easier as you get to know the pilots individually and get used to the expressions they use.' Siggie looked at her disbelieving face as he inhaled. 'It sounds astonishing but it's true.'

She blinked. *Easier as you get to know the German pilots individually.* Dear God, what were the implications of that? They're humans like everyone else and more than likely most of them don't want to kill their fellow British pilots, even though they're the enemy, any more than our boys want to send them hurtling to *their* deaths. But it's a case of them or us.

Tears pricked her eyes at the image she had of two aeroplanes battling it out. As could happen any day now over the English skies when Hitler decided to press the button and attempt the invasion. She swallowed hard at the image. But she mustn't show Siggie any emotion. Tears could play no part. Her male colleagues would soon lose any respect for her. She had an important job to do – and do it to the best of her ability.

'You'll find that many of the messages are from reconnaissance aircraft,' Elaine said as she handed Madeleine the list Siggie had mentioned.

'Oh, yes, I've had quite a few of those reporting on the weather conditions,' Madeleine said, 'though I'm hoping I might listen in to something a bit more exciting.'

Elaine raised an eyebrow. 'They don't report on just the weather. But even the weather can provide vital information for us on enemy plans – whether they're going ahead or not on a raid. And they're often informing one another of our convoys – their positions and how strong they are – as they steam up the Channel. That's crucial information for the Germans so they know where to attack us and crucial for us in turn that we're prepared for those attacks. We're desperate to get as much food and fuel and military equipment through safely.' She paused. 'But that's not all. The German messages provide *us* with valuable information on their military detachments and where they're located so *we* can go in for the kill. And sometimes we're right in at the beginning and hear of their intention. So we can often disrupt their plans before they've even got started.'

In spite of herself, Madeleine shuddered. Jack was right. This was real front-line stuff. She mustn't form an opinion on any of the messages she was taking down. They were *all* of the utmost importance.

# *Chapter Thirty-Seven*

Even though the Prime Minister firmly stated that wars weren't won by evacuations, Dunkirk was still looked upon as a significant British victory despite it being a withdrawal. Not surprising, Madeleine thought, when 338,000 Allied troops had been rescued – the main body being the cream of the British Army, Winston Churchill had called them. On the last day of the evacuation, 4th June, the BBC announced that the Prime Minister was to give one of his speeches that evening at nine o'clock.

Madeleine and Kelly finished their shift at eight and Penelope offered to drive them back to the gloomy guest house before going home to Hastings. At the stroke of nine, Winston Churchill's unmistakeable deliberate voice, with its endearing speech impediment, came through the speakers. He talked of the ever-threatening invasion and how Britain would always defend their island.

'. . . we shall not flag or fail. We shall go on to the end. We shall fight in France, we shall fight on the seas and oceans, we shall fight with growing confidence and growing strength in the air, we shall defend our island, whatever the cost may be. We shall fight on the beaches, we shall fight on the landing grounds, we shall fight in the fields

366

and in the streets, we shall fight in the hills; we shall *never* surrender.'

Hairs rose on the back of her neck as Madeleine listened to Winston Churchill's rousing words that she was sure he believed in with his whole heart. There was no question about it in her mind – however long it took, Britain would win the war.

The following week Madeleine was on the most hated shift, from two in the morning until eight. She didn't even bother to stifle her yawn as she glanced over to Kelly at the adjacent desk, the only other person in the tender, whose brow was furrowed as she concentrated on taking down the current message. Madeleine rolled back her shoulders. Surely it was time for a break.

'Shall we have a cuppa, Kelly?' she said, loud enough for her colleague to hear.

Kelly stuck her thumb up, still scribbling furiously.

As Madeleine was filling the electric kettle, Kelly took her earphones off.

'There's usually not a lot of traffic this time of the night – or should I say morning,' she said, turning to Madeleine, 'but I wanted to get that one down – it was "our" pilot again.'

'The one who constantly threatens to bomb us?' said Madeleine.

'Yes, him. Let's hope he never gets the chance. But you can't help liking him. He's so saucy the way he says it in English and imitates a bomb exploding.' Kelly looked serious. 'The trouble is, when they're that young they think they're invincible.'

'That's true. And boys are worse if I go by my brothers and their escapades.'

She had a sudden image of her brothers trying to outdo one another on who could dive off the highest rock when the family went on their usual summer holiday in Cornwall. Gordon slipped as he was about to take his fifth leap and ended up in hospital having stitches put in his forehead.

She shuddered as she heard Kelly say:

'Isn't it weird that he knows we're listening to him and we can't talk back? Tell him what an idiot he and his friends are, believing Hitler's madness.'

'Yes, if only we could. But he doesn't have any choice but to follow Hitler's evil instructions. They've all sworn allegiance to him and would probably be shot if they tried to do otherwise.' She shuddered. 'Have you had much traffic this last couple of hours?'

'Not really. But wait another hour and it'll go barmy. We call it "the Milk Train". Kelly's smile was rueful. 'That's really busy right up until we finish the shift.' She took the mug of tea Madeleine handed to her. 'Are you ready for it?'

'As ready as I'll ever be,' Madeleine said, this time covering her mouth as she yawned.

'Have you done shift work before?'

'Hardly ever, unless I was stepping in for someone because I was doing telegraphy training, so the lectures and practical work were mostly through the day.'

'Where did you train?'

Madeleine's mind raced. She doubted anyone knew about the Park.

'Buckinghamshire.' She'd keep it brief.

Kelly's face lit up. 'Oh, I come from Chesham. Was it anywhere near there?'

'I'm not sure,' Madeleine said truthfully. 'We didn't get a lot of time off to explore our surroundings.'

Thankfully, Kelly heard a crackling on her receiver and picked up her earphones again. Madeleine took her mug to her work station, knowing it was against the rules, but she didn't dare leave her post any longer. She wished she had a few squares of chocolate she could munch on – or anything to keep her awake as she twiddled the knobs. But the constant crackling wouldn't allow her to pick up anything that was clear enough to take down. Her mind roved. She hadn't dealt with any of her personal issues. Work was very intense and she was mentally exhausted by the time she'd had supper and maybe a chat with someone at the guest house before retiring to bed with a book. But now the traffic was so quiet she couldn't help thinking about Jack's latest letter. She'd received it that afternoon and it had caught her by surprise.

*5th June 1940*

*My dearest Maddie,*

*I have a dreadful feeling something is wrong. Maybe I'm rushing to the wrong conclusion but I was so sure I'd have heard from you by now telling me you've settled in. If only I had a telephone number. If you're billeted somewhere where they have a phone, could you send it to me. It's all so frustrating. I just pray you haven't had some kind of accident or are sick and I don't know it.*

*If you are well and able to answer this straightaway, whatever has held you back from writing to me, please, darling, do so. I'm going quietly crazy here. Whatever you have to tell me, I'd rather know than this strange silence. And if it's just that you've been too busy and tired from work I will understand if it's only a couple of lines.*

*Never forget that I love you. I have done right from*

*the start. Right from when I entered your compartment on the Berlin train. And I will always love you, no matter what. And when we are together next we have much to catch up on.*

*I wish you could see the Park. The magnolia tree is in full bloom. It's absolutely stunning. Just as you are, my love.*

*That's all. I'll keep looking for a letter from you.*

*Ever yours,*

*Jack*

*XXXXXXX*

Now in the quiet of the tender with only Kelly, who had lit a cigarette and was staring out of the window, she wondered how Jack had come to the conclusion in less than a week that something wasn't right between them. Tears pricked her eyes as she thought what might have been. She was going to have to answer it or she wouldn't put it past him to do something foolish and attempt to see her. He'd already guessed she was in a Y station. He might even find out she was near Hastings. If so, it wouldn't take much for him to find Fairlight. She'd better write back after a few hours' sleep. Her head would be clearer then.

Nine o'clock that morning, after she'd eaten breakfast, Madeleine went upstairs to her room. She didn't bother to take her clothes off, but instead lay on the top of the bed and puffed up the pillow. But no matter how she tried, sleep wouldn't come. An hour passed. She could have wept with frustration. Maybe if she just got that damned letter written and sent off she'd feel better. Languidly, she walked over to her desk and pulled out the notepaper from the writing case. She'd just write. Not think about it. If she did, she'd never finish it let alone post it.

6th June 1940

Dear Jack,

I received both your letters. But just before the first one I had another from someone telling me you were married. I don't think you can imagine how I felt – still do, to have my trust in you completely shattered. There is no point in saying any more, except that I do not wish you to ever contact me again. I'm only thankful I no longer work at the park where I would be forced to see you and be reminded of your deceit.

Madeleine

Terrible words which she could hardly read, the letters were so blurred through the haze in front of her eyes. She blinked to focus them but instead she felt the tears pouring down her cheeks. It was the worst thing she had ever done in her life. Mechanically, she folded the sheet of paper in half and put it into an envelope. Would Cora ever know how successfully she'd turned Madeleine's world upside down?

Madeleine had been sure Jack would answer her letter, begging to carry on seeing her, so she wasn't surprised when a few days later the dispatch rider left a pile of correspondence for the team and there were two – one from Josie and one from Jack. She almost tossed Jack's straight in the bin, but curiosity made her open it to see how he'd reacted now she'd found him out. She read:

*Darling Maddie,*

*I am now desperate with worry that you haven't written. Something terrible must have happened unless it's 'out of sight out of mind' and I don't believe this is so. If only I could see you, make sure you are not ill or injured in any way. But if you were, I'm sure I would have heard. I did speak to your friend Josie, and she said she would write and jog your memory that you haven't written!*

*I can't believe the very worst – that you have stopped loving me. Please, please tell me you haven't. Please write as soon as you read this. Put me out of my misery as only you can do.*

*Whatever has happened, I have never stopped loving you. I want you to believe that.*

*Jack*

*XXXXXX*

He must not have received her letter. But she'd posted it several days ago. Letters practically always arrived the following day, even if they came in the second or third post. It must have gone astray. Confused, she couldn't think what to do. If only she could telephone him, but even if she was allowed to make a call from the guest house, he wouldn't be allowed to take it at the Park. Automatically, she folded the letter and put it into the writing case with the others.

She'd send a telegram. He'd definitely receive that. On second thoughts, there was only so much you could put in a telegram. She could hardly say she knew about his wife and ask him to leave her alone, when the post office operator might pass on such gossip.

She needed to think. If only she could talk it over with

a friend. But she didn't know anyone at Fairlight well enough to have that kind of conversation. Penny had mentioned she dealt with personal matters that could affect one's work but she couldn't bear to confide in her about Jack's deceit. And what could Penny do anyway? She was stuck – well and truly. The only thing she could do was throw everything into her work. Block him out of her mind and out of her heart. She didn't need some man to find fulfilment. Work was fulfilling enough. Her immediate concern was to do her bit. And after the war ended . . . well, she couldn't think that far ahead.

Her mind slipped this way and that until she felt a wave of fury towards Jack that he should have treated her so shoddily and she hadn't noticed anything amiss. Hot tears fell silently down her cheeks. Irritably, she brushed them away, feeling more alone than she had ever felt in her life. Her eyes fell on Josie's letter. She wasn't in the mood to read all the comings and goings at the Park. It wasn't part of her life anymore. But maybe it would cheer her up to listen to Josie's happy chatter. She opened the envelope. The letter was dated the 8th, just like Jack's. Briefly, she closed her eyes and sighed, then opened them to read:

*Dear Maddie,*

*It's just not the same here without you and I really miss you. So do Sally and Olive. But not half as much as your Jack. He goes around with the most miserable expression as though all the life has been vacuumed out of him. At first I thought it was because he'd missed you by a couple of days and he won't see you around as he must have expected. But it doesn't seem to be that simple. I did bump into him yesterday and said hello to him. It took him a few moments* to recollect who I was. Then he gave a sort of twisted smile and asked if I'd heard from you. I said I had, soon after you arrived at wherever you are, and I'd be writing back today, which is what I'm doing.

He said could I ask you to please write to him. He hasn't heard a word from you and is anxious that something awful has happened. I must say I was surprised you hadn't been in touch with him as I know how you are both so mad about one another. Is there something wrong, Maddie? If so, do you want to tell me about it? I think we've become friends but will understand if it's private or too painful.

Cora is still being her usual unpleasant self. I don't know what's up with her – she's so bitter and twisted. I'm beginning to wonder if she hasn't had a bad experience with a man in the past and has never got over it.

Madeleine stiffened. There it was in black and white. Without realising it, Josie had just summed up Cora's behaviour. It matched the anonymous note exactly. The woman's bitter experience was falling in love with Jack, then being thrown over for another woman whom he ended up marrying. To cap it all, Cora had been forced to witness the man she obviously still had feelings for when she saw him at the Park fall in love with yet another woman – *me*, Madeleine thought grimly – right under her nose. She suddenly remembered Josie telling her on her first day what Olive's opinion was of their prickly room-mate – that the woman was jealous of anyone prettier, especially if they had a boyfriend. Her mouth felt dry as her eyes dropped to her friend's letter again though she could hardly bear to read on.

*The usual three of us – R, O and I – went to the pictures in town last night. We saw Gone With the Wind. You'd have loved it. If it comes on near you, do go and see it. I played rounders after lunch this afternoon with some of the chaps – Daniel nowhere in sight, but Tom was. In fact, he wants to take me to see GWTW. I didn't tell him I'd already been, haha, but I can easily see it again, even though it's very long. And it might prove rather interesting sitting with Tom on the back row in the dark. (We've not kissed yet, but I'm determined it will happen soon!)*

*Well, Maddie, that's all for now. Please get a letter off to your Jack a.s.a.p.*

*The girls send their love as do I.*

*Josie XX*

Madeleine bit her lip hard at the 'your Jack'. He wasn't her Jack any longer. But deep within her heart, despite the bitter hurt, she knew she would never feel the same towards any man as she did for him. If she were honest, she still loved him deeply and knew she always would.

## Chapter Thirty-Eight

If she hadn't been so engrossed in her work, Madeleine thought she would have gone crazy. Day after day she expected another letter from Jack saying he'd just received hers, delayed in the post, and could explain why he'd never told her he was married – though it was impossible he could ever do that, she thought grimly.

And then, when she'd given up, Siggie handed her an envelope with Jack's writing.

It was just after eight and she'd finished the dreaded two in the morning until eight shift. The dispatch rider, another young girl who took off her helmet and tossed her hair, then slapped the post on Siggie's desk, was early. Her pulse racing, Madeleine took it outside, moving away from the tender and finding the seat overlooking the Channel where she sat quietly watching the sea. There was a mist hovering on the horizon but she could tell it was going to be another beautiful day by the way the sun was warming her face, even this early.

She appreciated the scene, knowing she was lucky to be here when others were having such a dreadful time, but her mind was filled with Jack and what excuse he was about to give. Slowly, she opened the envelope and removed the

sheet of paper. It was dated 12th June. Her heart jumped
when she read the greeting:

*My darling,*

*By the time you read this I will be away again. It was
all out of the blue with no notice. We are already en route
and unfortunately it's somewhere where I can't send (or
receive) any correspondence. The only thing I can say this
time is that I'm still in GB. I'm sorry to be so mysterious
but I don't have much say in these events – it's the usual
hush-hush. I hope there'll be a pile of letters from you
waiting for me as I've still heard nothing and am still
wondering why. But perhaps it's the post in these strange
times. That's what I'm going to keep thinking anyway so
send anything to the Park as I hope not to be away too
long.*

*In haste, darling. Train is waiting. I'll let you know
when I'm back.*

*From the one who loves you.*

*Jack*

*XXXXXXX*

*P.S. If anything bad happened to you I think I would
have heard. So I'm blaming everything on the post. I can't
bear it to be anything else.*

Madeleine closed her eyes, her hand over her chest to
calm her racing heart. He still didn't know she'd found out
about his wife. But he could be going somewhere dangerous
for all she knew. If something happened to him . . . Oh,
please don't let it. Maybe there was some kind of
explanation. She opened her eyes to the sea that seemed
to have become a little more blue. She gave an inward

377

groan. Perhaps it was wrong of her to immediately believe someone who hadn't even signed their name.

But what did it mean about Jack not being all he said he was? Could Cora possibly know something more about him? Or was the woman guessing to put even more doubt in her mind? Might it be possible he was using the diplomatic title as a cover-up for *legitimate* secret war work which might disclose important or even crucial information for the British – not be some spy for the Nazis, as the note-writer had implied?

She sighed. Even if it were true, he wouldn't be able to mention it.

But it *would* mean she'd jumped to the wrong conclusions. Even so, it was difficult to reconcile the fact that he was married. But then, maybe he and his wife were separated – not just by the war, but living separate lives, even in separate houses. Taking the idea further, she supposed they could even be divorced. If so, would that make it all right that he hadn't told her? Her mind somersaulted to the evening in the restaurant when he'd given her his mother's writing case. What had he said? *There's so much I want to tell you – but now isn't the right time.* Could it be that his failed marriage was what he was alluding to? And he hadn't wanted to spoil the moment? And now there would be no contact between them for however long he was gone. But wasn't that precisely what she'd told him in that letter which he didn't appear to have received? Oh, it was all so confusing.

'Charles de Gaulle is going to make a speech this evening,' Siggie announced when Maddie and the small group met for the eight 'til two in the morning shift, 'so I've brought a wireless in.' He lit one of his interminable cigarettes. 'He only arrived in London yesterday, so it's going to be important for the French to listen to . . . and us.'

An hour later the newsreader's clear, clipped voice came over the air.

'Good evening. This is BBC London, nine o'clock on Tuesday, 18th June. Here is Brigadier General Charles de Gaulle speaking to you from British Broadcasting House.'

How grateful Madeleine was that her knowledge of French allowed her to follow the speech reasonably well. When it came to the part that France had surrendered to the Germans, she looked over at Siggie, whose cigarette was frozen midway to his lips. The General appealed to his people to resist the Germans every step of the way, saying France was not alone – she had Great Britain and the British Empire as her loyal allies. 'The flame of resistance must not be extinguished,' Madeline translated in her head, 'and *will* not be extinguished.'

There was a silence when Charles de Gaulle had finished his speech.

'Do you all know enough French to understand what he said?' Siggie finally asked.

There were murmurings of 'yes'.

'Well, de Gaulle might say that France is not alone now, but I bet Churchill won't see it like that,' Alan said, turning in his chair. 'He'll be devastated to think that *Britain* is now on its own to continue the fight.'

The hot weather seemed to increase daily as July took hold, with Fairlight beginning to see some action in the skies as well as a huge increase in messages between pilots and the ground.

'You see that plane up there, Maddie.' Alan squinted as

he pointed to a small plane quite high up when she was having no more than ten minutes for a lunch break. 'It's a Henschel – a good little observation plane. I reckon Jerry's planning an attack sooner rather than later.'

'Do you mean the invasion?'

'I think we're closer to being invaded at this moment than at any other time since the war started. Hitler's not going to give up just because we got our troops back to Blighty.' Alan paused to light his pipe. 'Maybe not a full invasion at the moment, *if* we're lucky, as it will give us more time to prepare. But certainly we'll get some air action soon. Göring will be doing some nosing at our south-eastern ports to see what kind of defences we've put up and if there are any locations where they don't spot any. That's what that reconnaissance plane will be doing. The worrying thing is that if we can see him, then ten to one he can see us and will report it to his superior. So *I* need to report this. The other worrying thing is that they have superior aircraft like the Messerschmitt – *and* many more of them.'

'The odds seem to be stacked against us,' Maddie said, with a worried frown.

'Perhaps not when we take other aspects into consideration.' Alan inhaled deeply. 'We have our radar to tell us where they are. It can pick up enemy aircraft nearly a hundred miles away.' If it wasn't so frightening it would be fascinating, Madeleine thought, as she quickly finished the egg and cress sandwich and went back inside where she sat at her work station and adjusted her headphones. After twiddling the knobs for a minute, she found a German station and had her pencil ready to take down any messages.

\* \* \*

Madeleine stared open-eyed as she reread the latest message in her logbook. Had she correctly translated it? Because if so, it was clear that the Luftwaffe reconnaissance aircraft was masquerading as the Red Cross! The next message confirmed it. She left her seat and showed her logbook to Siggie.

'Hmm. Very interesting.' Siggie lit one of his many cigarettes of the day and blew the smoke out thoughtfully. 'This has to be reported immediately to the Air Ministry. I hope they come down heavily on this as it's breaking international agreement. Göring needs to be warned that the Allies will not honour their so-called Red Cross planes and they'll be dealt with exactly the same as we do with any other enemy planes – shot down. They must think we're a load of nitwits to be taken in.' He looked up at her. 'Well done, Maddie, for bringing it to my attention.'

She went back to her seat, pleased that something she'd spotted in her translation might be of some real importance and tuned in to the next message. After some heavy crackling, a voice spoke in English, startling her.

'Hello, English chap . . . or is it English *girl*?' His heavy mocking British accent was more comical than grating. 'It is Fritz here. I know you are listening. I am listening also. Any minute I can drop a bomb on you. Would you like that?' He made a banging noise and chuckled.

It was their cheeky German pilot. He sounded no more than a youth who was playing a game. But war wasn't a game. She was relieved when the following messages were unrecognisable. Somehow it was worse, she decided, when you heard the voice of someone speaking directly to you and giving a name, even though 'Fritz' was bound to be a made-up one.

'Be prepared that when we inform Number 11 Fighter Group he's in action, they'll go after him,' Siggie said when Madeleine mentioned Fritz's latest jibes. He stubbed his cigarette out and looked directly at her, his eyes hardening. 'And I'm afraid the consequences won't be very pleasant. But that's war. Him and his lot or our boys.'

She only hoped she wouldn't be on the same shift when the time came to do the deadly deed.

Swallowing her sandwich later that morning, Madeleine couldn't stop thinking about the young German pilot with his silly nonsense who might be shot down in flames. She closed her eyes. But the same could happen to Raymond or Gordon . . . or, God forbid, both. If only she could picture where they were and what exactly they were doing. Everything was so damned secretive. Then she scolded herself. Of course it was. If people started blabbing everything, who knows where that would lead. They'd be finished before they'd hardly begun. She must be overwrought from that raid. How immature she'd been to think it would be more interesting and exciting to be 'on the front line'. The reality was so different. An image of the Mansion loomed in her mind. The drawing room where she'd worked for Josh Cooper. She wondered if he'd found a replacement, and swallowed, remembering how inspiring he had been. Such an innovative man – a genius really – and dear Percy and kind Tom Blackmore, who made up his small team. Idly, she wondered if Josie had made any progress on going all out to ensnare poor, unsuspecting Tom, who would be upset to be used as a pawn.

It was at that moment the dispatch rider roared up the hill. He handed her a few envelopes tied with string and was on his motorbike within seconds.

To Madeleine's surprise and delight there was a letter for her on the very top – from Josie.

*Dear Maddie,*

*I have to tell you my news! Tom asked me to marry him! And I said yes, please! Can you believe it. Gone With the Wind was the most romantic film ever, and we did kiss in the back row. That was when I first started to fall for him. You were right. He's an absolute poppet. Neither of us can stop grinning. You'd think we were the first couple ever to fall in love – but that's what it feels like. We're not going to announce anything at the moment so we're not officially engaged but that's fine. We both have our work to get on with to help shorten this damned war. But I wanted you to be the first to know, Maddie.*

*I hope you've heard from Jack by now. I can't forget his face – how miserable he was because he hadn't heard from you. You mentioned in your last letter that you'd heard something about Jack you didn't like. I can't imagine what. I only know that if something's gone wrong between you – a misunderstanding or whatever – then swallow your pride and be the first one to write and tell him you're upset. I bet he'd soon put your mind at rest. You know, Maddie, there's nothing more precious than loving someone other than one's self – and I should know!*

*Life goes on here. Cecil put on a play – I forget the name. It was well attended but then anything here we put on always is because there's no alternative! We're lucky that we have such good amateurs. A new chap by the grand name of Brinley Newton-John has joined Cecil's players and had the leading role – he was fantastic!*

*I suppose I'd better end. Playing rounders again. We don't*

*have any posts but just go by certain trees. Someone will
shout 'Get to that beech' and everyone dissolves in giggles.
It's a scream. Anyway, write soon. I do enjoy your letters
though wish I could picture where you are and what you're
doing. I'd love to ask you if it's anything at all to do with
BP.*

*sally and Olive send their love and I send mine.*
*Josie XX*

Even though there was a lot to think about in Josie's
letter, Madeleine couldn't help smiling. Her friend was
incorrigible. How she missed her. But it was doubtful she'd
ever set eyes on her again until the war ended. Whenever
that was.

She read the letter again, frowning at the part where
Josie urged her to ask what had happened between her and
Jack. She *had* told him. She couldn't have spelt it out any
clearer. But it seemed he'd never received it. And somehow
she couldn't bring herself to write it all over again.

# Chapter Thirty-Nine

On 10th July, the Prime Minister gave a broadcast in solemn tones that now the Battle of France was over, this was the Battle of Britain, a battle for survival. Several times a day, Madeleine could see the sky thick with Spitfires and Hurricanes roaring towards the Continent to meet the Luftwaffe head on, then coming back hours later. And sometimes it seemed there were fewer planes returning. Every time this happened her stomach churned. Last night she'd cried herself to sleep.

It hadn't taken long for Madeleine to distinguish the different sound the Luftwaffe made from the British planes. Theirs were twin-engine heavy fighters, Siggie had told her, but nowhere near as nippy as the Spits. She heard the German ones long before they appeared, mostly at the same time of day, around two in the afternoon. Heart in her mouth, she'd listen and pray their own boys would all come home safely.

The following afternoon, as she was eating the usual sandwich outside the tender, Madeleine heard the roar of a motorbike. It would be one of the dispatch riders. He was late today. When close enough, the figure dismounted, silently handed her the usual bundle of post and roared off. She quickly riffled through it and came to the familiar writing of her mother. She hoped there might be one from Gordon as well in the pile. It had been weeks now since he'd written. Thinking of him, Madeleine tilted her head upwards. Where were her brothers at this moment? She daren't think too deeply. Heaving a sigh, she began another gruelling six-hour shift in the confines of the tender. Her mother's letter would have to wait until their tea break.

Dear Madeleine,

You haven't written lately so I have nothing to answer.

Well, the real war has finally started and I expect you know more about it in your job than we do. I do know I'm very worried about Raymond and Gordon. Dad says they could easily be in combat over the Mediterranean and that taking off and landing from the carrier of a ship is one of the most dangerous things a pilot can do. I'm worried sick but your father appears quite sanguine about it. He says they're more than capable and he wished he were one of them!

My new romance is now with the publisher – I expect you've forgotten the title as I'm not even sure if you still read my books but they are now what keeps food on the table – but to remind you, it's Forever Yours. Strange, but I feel quite bereft now it's out of my hands. I miss it, especially the divine hero! And for once I can't think of a single idea for the next one so I only hope this is temporary and after a good night's sleep I'll be back to normal.

You said in your last letter that you liked the job so I hope that continues. You don't mention the people there or if you've made any friends. Have you told any of those women that your mother is an author? I bet they'd love to

*know they were hobnobbing with the daughter of such a
famous mother! Haha.*

*I hope to hear from you soon, though I know your letter
will give me no idea about the work you are doing.*

*Love from Mother*

*P.S. Now the novel is in the hands of the publisher I
need a break. I don't wish to go in the school holidays as
it will be crowded so we'll be away from the beginning of
September for a week, though it shouldn't affect you as you
never speak of coming to see us. We'll be home on the 12th.*

Madeleine rolled her eyes. Her mother hadn't even
mentioned where they were going. In fact, right from the
very first sentence almost everything about her mother's
letter jarred. She was far more interested in the characters
she created in her novels than in her own daughter. As for
Dad, he didn't get much of a look-in, so no wonder he
buried himself in his shack most days.

Back at her desk, Madeleine recognised the call sign of
the cheeky German pilot. He'd spoken to her on several
more occasions and she almost looked forward to his latest
nonsense. But this time she immediately realised it was
very different. He was trying to ward off his attackers. The
noise was deafening through her headphones. Out of the
corner of her eye she could tell Kelly and Alan, rigid in
their seats, were tuned in to the same frequency. And then
it happened. Number 11 Fighter Group got him.

'Bail out! For heaven's sake, bail out!' Madeleine shouted
the words at him until her throat constricted. And then
she realised she wasn't the one screaming. The screams
were spilling from her headphones. Her blood ran cold.
Unconsciously, she held her breath.

'*Liebe Gott, liebe Gott.*' His voice was now a heartrending sob. '*Mutti, Mutti, hilf mir*' . . . a split second's pause . . . '*der Schweinekerl Führer*' . . . then no more.

Tears pouring down her cheeks, Madeleine, her eyes glued to the reception range, followed his descent . . . until he fell from sight.

Kelly, her face white, swung round in her chair.

'Oh, Maddie, wasn't that horrible? His poor mother. She'll be broken-hearted when they inform her.'

Alan removed his headphones and stood, stretching his neck.

'It was either him or us,' he said. 'That's how we have to look at it.'

Madeleine's heartbeat echoed in her eardrums. She couldn't catch her breath. It was as though she'd taken part in his murder. She couldn't think of him as German. As the enemy. Thoughts raced through her head. He was young and brave, just like their own boys. He was right to call Hitler a swine. There was no other word for that monster. She tried to speak, to answer Kelly and Alan, but a stream of bile rushed into her throat. She flew outside and was violently sick.

Madeleine began to feel the strain of being with such a small group of people, so unlike the busy Park where there had been hundreds, with more turning up every day. More than ever, she relished any letters from home, pouncing on any news about her brothers. Josie was the only person from the Park who kept in regular contact with her. She wouldn't allow herself to think it was Jack she was missing so terribly. What was he doing at this very minute? Was he thinking of her? She felt in some kind of twilight zone, not being able to erase him from her mind, but knowing she must dismiss all thoughts of a future with him. She exhaled a sigh of misery.

*Oh, Jack. Why didn't you come clean and tell me you were married? Maybe it isn't a happy marriage. If so, maybe we could have worked something out.*

She began to miss all the different characters and the social events at the Park. She and the team here were much busier these days, often doing two lots of six-hour shifts, sometimes broken up, in a twenty-four-hour day, so it didn't leave much time to have a proper sleep and have normal mealtimes, let alone explore something of the area. The station was so remote that going anywhere depended upon having a car, so when Alan suggested taking a run in his old jalopy, as he called it, she jumped at it.

'We'll go straight after we finish tomorrow morning at eight o'clock,' he said. 'Just a pity we can't have an early morning swim but it's off-limits.'

'Oh, I'd have loved that,' Madeleine said. 'Every time I have a few minutes to look at the view, I wish I could just run down to the shore and cool off in the water – especially in this hot weather.'

On the dot of eight when Elaine took over her shift, Madeleine grabbed her handbag and stepped outside, blinking. Her eyes took time to adjust before she saw Alan waving her over to where he'd parked. He cranked the engine, then climbed into the driving seat, gave her a brief look and grinned.

'Sometimes I see the tender in my dreams,' he said. 'It's becoming claustrophobic, not to mention how stuffy it's getting.'

They chatted about nothing in particular as the motor wove its way down the hill.

'I thought we'd go to Hastings,' Alan said. 'It's not too far and it's quite a nice old town.' He paused. 'Have you ever looked round it?'

'No, I'd never been to East Sussex until this job.'

Alan smoothly found his way through the town, parking as close as he could to the promenade.

'We'll leave the car here but first, shall we go and have a look at the castle? Time we've done that we'll be ready for a coffee.'

'Good idea.' Madeleine smiled.

They had just begun their walk up Castle Hill Road when an aeroplane appeared out of nowhere. Alan looked up. His face drained as he spun round to her.

'Bloody hell, it's Jerry!' he said, grabbing hold of her and pulling her into the nearest doorway, a café. Seconds later there was a terrific explosion. People rushed into the flimsy shelters of open porches of nearby houses and shops, mothers dragging their screaming children, as a second explosion, even louder this time, shook the very buildings where they were taking them.

Madeleine's heart thumped.

'Oh, Alan, do you think the invasion has started?'

'I don't think so. There was only one plane as far as I could tell. But I suppose it could be the start of an air battle, though I'm surprised they've picked Hastings as I would have thought Dover was a much more likely target.' He paused. 'I'm going to risk it and have a look. You stay there.'

But even though she was trembling with fear, Madeleine had to see for herself. She stepped from the overhang of the café where a few other men, their hands shading their eyes, were looking upwards.

'You should have stayed where you were, Maddie,' Alan said as she joined him. 'I can't see any more planes but you never know how high they might be or how far behind this one—' He broke off. 'Bloody hell, it's coming back or it's another one!'

Alan grabbed hold of her and pushed her back into the café doorway, shielding her with his body while it felt the world was exploding around them – one bomb after the other. Dear God, how many more? After what seemed forever, there was a silence.

Alan touched her arm, his expression full of concern. 'You okay, Maddie?'

'I-I think so,' she answered, her voice thin and faltering.

His eyes raked the sky. 'It seems to be a solitary plane jettisoning his bombs before he returns to France. I've already counted nine explosions—' He stopped. 'Oh, Lord, here comes another. We need to get out of here – back to the car.'

Madeleine jerked her head skywards. To her horror she saw a bomb spiralling towards them. He grabbed her hand and they flew down the road towards the promenade as the thunderous boom felt it would burst her eardrums. Gasping and panting, she was terrified the plane had them in sight and would drop another bomb right on top of them. She told herself not to be so ridiculous – what would be the point of a German pilot blasting sightseers– but the relief when she saw the old motorcar still standing faithfully where they'd left it overwhelmed her, and she choked back the tears.

'I think we should go back to Fairlight and report what

we've seen,' Alan said, as he started the engine, 'because they would have heard the explosions, but we can give a more accurate report.' He turned to her. 'What do you say?'

For a few moments Madeleine couldn't utter a word. Knives were cutting her chest as she tried to catch her breath. Gasping, she could only shake her head.

'I think . . .' She dragged in a breath and tried again. 'I think it's a g-good idea.'

Alan patted her hand and steered the car away from the town.

'Why didn't the air-raid siren go off?' she managed.

'I suppose there was no warning whatsoever of any raid. One solitary plane is usually on a reconnaissance mission and doesn't pose a threat. But one thing's strange. Did you notice we didn't see any signs of damage? I reckon the bombs must have fallen just outside the town.'

A few minutes later Alan parked the motorcar in a flat space below the tender.

'I'm relieved to see you back,' Howard said, rising from the seat he'd taken over from Siggie for the next shift as Madeleine and Alan entered the tender. 'We were getting concerned when we heard the explosions sounding like they were coming from Hastings because we knew that's where you'd gone.'

'We were in the middle of it,' Alan said, quickly outlining what had happened.

'Hmm. This needs to be reported to the Air Ministry immediately.' Howard turned to his telephone. 'I'll get onto it right away. You two disappear. You could have been injured – or worse. We'll see you back later.'

Outside, Alan said, 'Shall I drop you off at our digs?'

Madeleine hesitated. It was another cloudless day. But she needed to think. To work out what had happened. Her reaction.

'Thanks, Alan, but I think I'll walk. I need some fresh air.'

'Righto – if you're sure.'

Alan was a dear. But for the time being she needed to be alone.

As she carefully made her way to the guest house, keeping to the paths, Madeleine hardly took in the beauty of the countryside, her mind was so busy with thoughts of what she'd just witnessed. She'd never forget the date – 26th July – when she and Alan could have been killed. Desperately hoping no one had, she wished now she'd persuaded him to take her back into Hastings town centre in case anyone needed help. She felt guilty, as though she and Alan had sped away from danger when others might be caught in it. Is this how she was going to react when the Luftwaffe really got serious?

# *Chapter Forty*

Next morning the local paper was full of the raid in Hastings. Those round the dining-room table at The Cove were unusually subdued.

'It was too close for comfort,' Kelly said with a shudder. 'I still feel quite shaken even though it wasn't overhead like it was for you and Alan.' She sprinkled some salt and pepper into her boiled egg. 'I just hope nobody was killed or badly injured but there's probably no way to find out.'

To Madeleine's surprise, Alan said, 'I can give you an update because I drove back to Hastings to see what the damage was. One of the shopkeepers told me nearly all the bombs exploded on the central cricket ground, so thank God for that as no one was there. It could have been so much worse. There weren't even any injuries but it did give everybody a fright.'

'Do you think we should expect the invasion soon?' Elaine said.

Alan shook his head. 'Only that monster knows when he's going to press the button, although some of the messages coming through lately are giving carefully veiled hints. I tried to get to the beach to see if anything was happening down there but couldn't get beyond the coils

394

of barbed wire right the way along the sea front and warning notices about unexploded mines. It was all very grim-looking but at least we're taking it seriously now. I just hope we're prepared for the worst.' He glanced at Madeleine. 'Are you okay, Maddie?'

'Yes, I'm all right.' She drained her tea and forced a smile.

'You sure?' Alan was looking concerned. 'It was rather a shock yesterday, to say the least.'

'I'm just a bit tired, that's all.'

'Have an early night,' Siggie advised. 'Probably what we all need.' He looked round the table and glanced up at Madeleine who was about to go. 'And while I'm about it, you've all noticed the huge increase in the messages.' They nodded. 'I have to tell you that I can't let anyone off for any leave at all, even though you all deserve it. Most I can do is a day, and that with the greatest reluctance. So it really is important that you rest between shifts.' He sat back in his chair, lighting a cigarette.

Madeleine excused herself and went up to her room. She'd been going to ask if it was possible to have a couple of days off and stay at the Whites' so she could see the twins but getting there and back in a day with time to spend with them would be cutting it fine. Trains were running reasonably at the moment although delays and diversions weren't unknown since the war began. Also, it wasn't always easy to get a ticket on trains in and out of London when they were often full of uniformed men and women. She sighed. For the time being she would have to keep in contact with the twins by letter. A little thought crept into her head that she couldn't do that with Jack, even if she wanted to.

* * *

The heat of July only worsened in August. Madeleine would gaze longingly at the Channel, wishing she could just wade in to cool off. Often a dogfight took place right overhead and the staff on duty would rush from the tender to see which plane would cop it. Madeleine mostly remained at her station, not wanting to witness the horror either way. When it was a German one she'd hear her colleagues cheering, but when it was a Spitfire or a Hurricane they'd have tears in their eyes when they sombrely came through the tender door.

August gave way to September. The might of the Luftwaffe hadn't diminished. There was much talk about whether Fighter Command could hold out against them, let alone send them packing. She was beginning to feel the tension from the messages now that fighting was in full force. She knew she was doing an important job to let the Spitfire and Hurricane pilots know where the German activity was about to take place so they were ready for the next battle, but it was beginning to tear her nerves. No one had had any time off. The messages were coming thick and fast, one overlapping the other. Sleep was snatched whenever she could grab a couple of hours. But no one complained, and she certainly wasn't going to.

The trouble was, there was nothing to break up the day or evening. She did accompany Penelope to Hastings once but was on edge the whole time from the raid she'd witnessed with Alan that first time. And Fairlight, pretty little village though it was, had little to offer in its limited variety of shops.

But almost more than anything, the worst of her listlessness was down to the fact that her joy of loving Jack had been so short-lived and now there'd be no future with him.

*Don't be so pathetic*, she told herself sternly. *Your personal life must take second place.*

The most important thing was to do her level best to help bring this war to an end.

Madeleine stood up, rubbing her eyes after working two extra hours one afternoon dealing with a flood of signals, grateful that Howard had already slipped into her seat and was adjusting the earphones.

'Madeleine, can I see you in the office for a few minutes?'

Siggie's office was hardly more than a cupboard at the rear of the tender. Madeleine noticed his forehead was deeply furrowed. Oh, dear. Had she missed some important messages? Was she not quick enough at getting the whole message translated? But she knew she was as fast as any of the others. So it was something else. Dear God, don't say he'd had a message that something had happened to one of her family . . . She swallowed hard, her legs trembling.

'Sit down, Madeleine.'

'Siggie, if it's something bad about my family, tell me straight. Don't try to soften it.'

'It's not, and I wouldn't,' he said immediately.

She took in a shaky breath, trying to brace herself.

'I'm being asked to transfer you.'

*Oh, no, not again. It couldn't be.*

'Why?' She stared at him. 'Isn't my work up to scratch?'

'It's not that at all.' Siggie viciously stubbed out his cigarette in the ashtray. 'You're the fastest translator here by far. You probably don't know this, but you're the only one who can translate German into English automatically, even when part of it is encoded. That's a real skill.'

'I don't understand why my way is different. What do the others do?'

'They write the German, and then it's another step to translate it into English – and that's the problem.' He lit a fresh cigarette. 'You've noticed the increase in messages, much of it from the daily battles going on in the skies, and we haven't yet been invaded or London seriously bombed. If one or both happens it will be even more difficult to keep up with the amount coming through. The Air Ministry is desperate to recruit highly skilled and trained people like yourself.' He looked at her. 'You're needed to spot the potential of these people and train them – as fast as humanly possible.' He gave a deep sigh. 'So with huge reluctance I'm going to have to let you go.'

'Wh-where are you sending me?'

Madeleine's stomach clenched, waiting for his reply. But she knew it – oh, she just knew what he was going to say.

Siggie inhaled deeply, then blew a stream of smoke over the top of her head.

'I've been ordered to send you back to Station X.'

# Chapter Forty-One

No, she couldn't go back to the Park. Face Jack. See him for what he was – a deceitful man who would probably come up with a carefully thought-out excuse as to why he hadn't come clean.

Madeleine gripped the edges of her chair, the skin over her knuckles thinning with tightness.

'I'm sorry, Madeleine. I can tell by your expression that you don't relish the idea, but they apparently need you more than *I* do.' He stared at her. 'Mind you, I do think you've been rather upset since that German pilot was shot down.'

'I was, but I know it has to be. And I didn't think after the initial shock that it had affected my work.'

'It hasn't, but I doubt you'd get quite that same intimacy at Station X as you do here, because we see and hear it all as it's happening.' He leant back as far as he could in the hard-backed chair. 'But there's no point in analysing or arguing. There's a war on and we have to expect anything at any time.'

'When do I go?' She felt she was forever asking that question.

'No point in prolonging the agony. Why don't you say

your goodbyes at supper this evening and leave first thing in the morning with Penelope, who'll drop you off at the station.' He opened a drawer in the battered desk and handed her a small brown envelope. 'Here's your railway warrant going through London to Buckinghamshire. Take your time. You might want to pop in and see your parents. They're near London, aren't they?'

'Not far, but they're away at the moment.'

'Well, take in a show or something. You've hardly had a full evening off let alone a day.' He glanced at the calendar. 'Let's see, tomorrow's Sunday. I'll tell them you'll report for duty on Wednesday. That'll give you a bit of a break.'

Madeleine bit her lip. She wanted to beg Siggie not to send her back to Bletchley Park. But nice though he was, he wouldn't appreciate that the last thing she wanted was to face the married man she'd fallen in love with. She had to keep her dignity. Be professional at all times, even though her heart was thumping at the thought of seeing Jack. Then she calmed a little. More than likely he was still away in his secret place. If he was back at the Park, Josie would have mentioned it in her last letter. But even if he was away, he wouldn't surely be gone for the rest of the war. He'd be back sooner or later and it would just put off the evil day.

She suddenly had a thought.

'Siggie, is there a chance I could catch a train to London this evening?'

'I don't see why not.'

'I *would* like to break the journey in London and see two very special people.'

'You do that,' he said. 'I'll run you to the station myself.'

* * *

400

She hadn't been there long enough to make a close friend, Madeleine thought, when Siggie had seen her off on the Hastings platform.

'Give my kind regards to your parents . . . especially Walter.'

'Oh, did you ever find him in the logbook?'

'Oh, yes.' He smiled broadly. 'I recognised his call sign when you told me. We'd spoken quite a few times. I just hadn't realised it was your father.' He studied her. 'Ham radio operators don't necessarily do it for a hobby these days.' He gave her a wink as though to make it clear what he was alluding to.

She gasped. Of *course*. It all made perfect sense. In spite of her father's age, too old to be called up this time, she could have staked her life on it that he was secretly doing his bit for *this* war, too. She couldn't help a glow of pride.

Now in the carriage she sat thoughtfully for several minutes, her book in her lap, thinking about her father buried in his shack, maybe listening in and reporting, just like she was doing. If only she could ask him. Though even if she did, he wouldn't be able to tell her. But fancy him knowing her boss. One day when this was all over, perhaps she'd be allowed to tell him that little piece of information . . . that is, if he didn't know already. She allowed herself a wry smile.

The sun was already low but she shouldn't be too late to pay a surprise visit to the twins. They would just have started back at school for the new year that began in September but she should be there well before bedtime. More than likely the Whites would invite her to stay the night – even two – so she'd have more time with them. The thought cheered her up immensely. Poor little kids.

They must wonder what on earth the grown-ups were doing to one another. She looked at her watch. Coming up to seven.

The conductor told her that if she was going to Ealing she should stay on the train until it came into Charing Cross and then take the tube.

'Bakerloo line, change at Oxford Circus to the Central, love,' he'd said cheerfully. 'That'll get you to Ealing Broadway.'

The train finally belched into London after an unaccountable forty-minute hold-up. She alighted to the sounds of doors slamming shut and shouts through a fog of steam and smoke. Hordes of people were pouring through the station entrance. Frantically, she looked for the Underground sign but instead was swept along with the throng. Her heart beat fast. Where were all these people going? Surely there were too many of them to be boarding the trains. Then to her relief she spotted the escalator leading down to the Underground. It was packed solid but she managed to squeeze in amongst them and to her relief came off the moving step onto the Underground platform.

The noise was deafening from what looked like hundreds – no, thousands of people, swarming to both left and right. She gasped. These people weren't normal passengers. They were carrying bulging bags of food, blankets . . . and *sleeping bags*. What on earth was going on?

And then she heard it above her. Explosions! One after the other. The vibrations shook her body. BOOM! BOOM! BOOM! She threw her head back. Was the roof about to collapse? She grabbed the arm of a passing woman who was holding onto her little girl.

'Wh-what's happening up there?' Madeleine stuttered.

The woman shot her a look of disbelief. 'Don't you know? That's bleedin' Jerry right overhead. They're bombin' us to smithereens. You'd better not go up. You'll be safer down 'ere.'

She couldn't be caught down here. Trapped. Nowhere to rest for the night. Heart thumping with shock and fright, her only thought was to reach the escalator again. Beads of sweat running down her face, she pushed and shoved her way through, apologising as she went. Some families were spreading out blankets, choosing places to sleep. Dear God, the invasion must have started. What everyone had been dreading. London was being pounded. And this time it wouldn't just be soldiers fighting for their lives, it would be ordinary people in the streets.

Somehow she got to the escalator only to find it had stopped working. She'd have to use the stairs. But the staircase was packed with people stumbling towards her. She wouldn't make it. She'd be thrown backwards. She'd have to wait until everyone was on the platform. But even on the ground she could feel the might of the swirl of people all jostling for space. Her lungs felt tight. Her scalp prickled in fear. She felt dizzy with the maelstrom around her.

'Are you all right, young lady?' a tall, well-built man in army officer uniform asked, his face concerned as he came off the last step towards her, people still crowding behind him.

'N-no. I need to get upstairs. Into some air.'

'I'll get you there. Here – let me take your case. Take my arm.'

She did as she was told. Somehow the surge of people turned into individuals who managed to give them a few inches to squeeze past. Still hanging on to him, they reached the top of the stairs and pushed through more crowds carrying bundles, preparing to spend the night in the Underground. Outside, it was dusk and already streetlights and shop lights had been turned off. Her rescuer moved her out of the way of the entrance and under the shelter of a shop front.

'That better?'

She couldn't speak. She could only gasp for breath. The air was thick with the smell of the explosions but to her it was life-giving. And then she saw the dark shadows of aeroplanes above . . . saw bombs hurtling down. Hastings again! She mustn't scream, mustn't faint. But all around her people were shouting and men were shaking their fists in the air and cursing the Germans.

'Where are you heading?' the man said.

Madeleine gulped. 'Ealing. I was just changing when I heard the explosions.'

'Well, your only chance now is to get a taxi which won't be easy with everyone doing the same thing.' He looked at her. 'I think you need a cup of tea. Do you want to stop a few minutes and I'll have one with you?'

She hesitated, hearing the concern in his voice. His friendly, open face was one she was sure she could trust.

'You're awfully kind, but the longer I delay, the worse it might get.'

'That's settled then. I'm going to find you a taxi.'

The blackout didn't help. It was hard to tell if a taxi was available or not. Finally, one stopped to let someone out. A woman immediately jumped in front of them and climbed into the still-open door.

'Hang on a minute,' her rescuer said to the driver. 'We were first. This young lady needs to get home urgently.

'Everyone's urgent at the moment,' the driver said drily. He turned to Madeleine. 'Where're you going, miss?'

'Ealing.'

'Hop in, then. You're lucky. It's close to home. I'll drop the other passenger off first and then you.'

She breathed her thanks, then turned to the officer.

'I can't thank you enough.'

'No trouble,' he said. 'You look after yourself.'

He set her suitcase inside the cab, the other woman grumbling that she now had hardly any space for her own luggage, as Madeleine climbed in. She waved to him as the driver pulled away from the kerb. What a kind man. And she didn't even know his name. But she'd always remember him.

The driver didn't stop talking but in a strange way Madeleine was glad. She didn't have to make any conversation with the woman sitting beside her, who just stared out of the window.

'Well, that street's had it,' the driver said. 'We'll have to do a detour.'

'How long has the bombing been going on?' Madeleine said.

'Started about half an hour ago. No let-up. They must soon run out of any more bombs to drop on us.' He swung into a side road and stopped outside a row of Victorian houses, then leapt out to retrieve the woman's luggage.

'At least you're home now,' Madeleine told her with a smile.

The woman turned and gave a cursory nod before getting out.

'Right, just you now, miss,' the taxi driver said as he pulled away. 'At least we'll both be a bit further from the Smoke.'

No sooner had he spoken than there was a loud bang behind them. Madeleine jerked round to peer out of the narrow rear window. As though she were watching a science-fiction film at the cinema, she saw a building crumple to its knees and burst into flames. Dear God, that was the exact spot where they'd just dropped off the woman. Nausea crawled in her stomach.

'That was a close call,' the driver said. 'If we'd been a minute earlier – well, neither of us would've made it and I doubt that woman did.' He twisted round. 'You all right, miss?'

'Y-yes,' she stuttered, trying to stifle the need to retch. To think that she'd just told the woman that at least she was home now. She swallowed the sour taste in her mouth.

'Don't worry, love, I'll get you home in one piece.'

Madeleine was never so relieved as when she saw the door of the Whites' house. She opened her purse to pay the driver but he interrupted her.

'I'm not charging you.'

When she tried to argue, he said, 'We're all going to have to stick together. And if we can't do a kindness in this bleedin' war, then there's no hope for us.'

She thanked him profusely and he drove off. The house was in darkness, but that was to be expected in the blackout. She walked down the narrow path and knocked on the door. A dog barked. Strange. Did she have the right house? Before she could check the number on the gate the door opened. A figure stood there.

'Jo—' Joseph's name died on her lips.

*Dear God.*

'Madeleine!' Jack said.

# Chapter Forty-Two

It couldn't be. Oh, it couldn't be. What on earth was he doing here? Her head swam. She thought she might pass out. Somehow, she gathered her wits. She had to invoke every shred of acting skill not to let him see how hurt she was. How this was one of the worst moments of her life. Because unless she was very much mistaken, he wouldn't have told the Whites about his wife either, let alone that Madeleine had found out.

'Who is it, Jack?' Madeleine heard Ruth's voice call out from the sitting room.

He half turned to call out to Ruth, 'You'll never guess,' then said to Madeleine, his face split in two with his smile, 'I can't believe it's you. Here, let me take your case. Come on in. You must be exhausted.' He held the door open so she could go ahead. 'Oh, my darling, this is the most wonderful surprise. The twins are going to be over the moon.'

'Where are they?' she managed when he shut the front door firmly behind them.

'In bed.' He looked directly at her in the dimly lit hall and hesitated as though he were about to say something.

She held her breath.

407

But he merely said, 'You know where to go. Just watch out for—'

He didn't finish saying who to watch out for. The sitting-room door opened and a rush of fur and panting tongue flew towards her, jumping up and placing his front paws on her jacket.

'Dexter! Down, boy!' Jack ordered, turning to Madeleine and chuckling. 'He gets rather exuberant when someone new comes to the door. . . especially if he likes the look of them,' he added.

Madeleine bent to pat his head and Dexter immediately licked her hand.

'Back in your basket, Dexter,' he ordered. 'Come on, Maddie. Ruth and Joseph are going to wonder who's causing him to be so excited.'

Madeleine was amused to see the dog practically dragging his three legs, his head twisted round showing a soulful expression to her as he reluctantly obeyed his master.

'Madeleine! I thought it was your voice. This is an unexpected treat.' Ruth half rose from her chair. 'The twins will be thrilled. I expect Jack's told you they're in bed.'

'I'd planned to be here much earlier,' Madeleine said, planting a kiss on the soft skin of Ruth's face.

'Well, this is a wonderful surprise.' Joseph stood and gave her a warm hug. 'But how did you manage to get through London with all the bombing?'

'I'm not sure.' Her voice sounded thin and quavering to her ears as the images danced in front of her. 'It was terrible. But I don't want to dwell on it. I'm here now, and I can't tell you how relieved I am.'

'Just you sit down and I'll make you a cup of tea,' Ruth said, rising to her feet. 'Have you had supper?'

Madeleine shook her head. 'I couldn't eat anything at the moment. But tea would be lovely.'

'A brandy would be more like it,' Joseph put in.

Madeleine shook her head. 'Tea's fine.'

'You're staying, I hope,' Joseph said when Ruth disappeared to the kitchen.

There was an awkward pause. There were only four bedrooms, Madeleine remembered, so if Jack was staying too . . .

'I won't stay the night now Maddie's here,' Jack said, filling the silence.

In the distance they heard the faint sound of several explosions.

'They're still bombing us,' Joseph said, 'so you're not going anywhere tonight, my boy. You'll sleep on the sofa. I'm sure you've had worse.'

Jack glanced at Madeleine with raised eyebrow. She couldn't interpret his expression. Was he play-acting in front of the Whites? But the way he'd greeted her just now at the door, she was sure his pleasure at seeing her was genuine. If that was true, he hadn't ever received her letter. Oh, this was terrible. She'd have to keep up the charade for the evening and first thing in the morning, when she'd catch the first train to Bletchley. But at least it would still give her a chance to see the twins.

'That wouldn't be fair,' she said.

'Not another word,' Jack said, holding up the palm of his hand. 'But you must be wondering why I'm here.'

'Um, yes, I was rather.'

'Dexter misses me when I'm sent away – or so they tell me – and you and I had spoken about the twins possibly having him. Obviously, I wanted to wait and go with you

409

to see how Ruth and Joseph felt about having a dog – but I didn't know where you were or how long you'd be gone. I had a few days off and decided yesterday on the spur of the moment to see how Erich and Lotte were getting on – and introduce them to Dexter.' He smiled at her. 'See what they thought.'

'If you're talking about Dexter,' Ruth said, her mouth twitching with amusement as she came into the room and Joseph took the tray from her, 'the girls love him. But the twins – well, they *adore* him.'

Madeleine couldn't help glancing at Jack. He immediately caught her eye and gave a grin of satisfaction. Before she realised, she was smiling back.

Madeleine's next words were swallowed up by the dog leaping from his basket and barking joyfully as the twins suddenly rushed into the room.

'Maddie!' they screamed in unison.

'You're supposed to be asleep,' Madeleine said as she hugged Lotte.

'I heard you,' Lotte said triumphantly. 'I woke Erich.'

'Maddie, we thought you forget us,' Erich said, throwing his arms around her.

'Why didn't you tell us you were coming to see us?' Lotte demanded. 'Look at Dexter.' She looked up at Madeleine, her eyes aglow. 'He's our new dog.'

'Is that right, Ruth?' Madeleine looked at her.

'Oh, yes. Dexter now belongs to the twins. They will be responsible for him and either look after him together or take it in turns. He'll be thoroughly spoilt – but we already love him,' she added. 'Even Joseph, who isn't normally that keen on dogs.' She threw her husband an affectionate look.

'Dexter knows how to work his way into the hardest heart.'

'He knows I'm really an old softy,' Joseph said, his eyes twinkling.

Oh, how she envied the couple, nearer to her parents' age but so very different from them. Madeleine's heart contracted. Their love flowed from one to the other. They must have gone through such a difficult time when they'd first come to England, maybe putting up with hurtful remarks because their new English name couldn't hide the fact that their accent was distinctly German, and yet they'd come through it all, seemingly without any bad effect.

She sighed softly. Jack, who had been talking to Joseph, shot her a look. She kept her expression pleasant but if he could see into her heart he'd know it was completely out of tune. It suddenly dawned on her that she was going to be sleeping under the same roof as Jack. Oh, it was too bad. She needed to have it out with him as soon as there was an opportunity to talk to him alone. She could feel herself bubbling with anger that he should have allowed – no, *encouraged* her to fall in love with him. Him, a married man. But not here. She couldn't bring any trouble to this family who'd welcomed the twins as their own. No, she'd have to save her fury for when they were on their own. But when would that be? There was little privacy at Bletchley Park – presuming that was now where he was.

After the twins' excitement had died down, Joseph said:

'Time for you to go back to bed, children. You have school in the morning.'

'No, we don't – tomorrow's Sunday,' Erich said.

'It's still late,' Maddie told them. 'Off you go and I'll see you in the morning.'

'How long will you stay with us, Maddie?' Lotte squealed over her shoulder.

Madeleine didn't dare look at anyone as she answered her.

'I'm afraid I have to go back to work in the morning.' She hated to tell a fib but she wasn't going to spend a second night under the same roof as Jack. Out of the corner of her eye she saw Jack raise his eyebrow. 'But I'll try to come the next time I have a couple of days off . . . if that's all right with you, Ruth,' she finished.

'Of course, my dear. Stay as long as you like. You know that. You're always welcome.'

'Will you say goodnight to us like you used to?' Lotte said.

Madeleine was heartened that Lotte still wanted to be tucked in.

'Of course I will, love.'

'And Uncle New Year?' Lotte persisted.

*So Jack was now 'uncle'.* Madeleine sighed. How different this all should have been. How she and Jack would have had a giggle at his promotion. He was gazing at her, a smile touching his lips, as if he were about to say the same thing. But maybe it was all in her overwrought imagination. Wishful thinking. She tightened her mouth.

'I'll let Maddie have you both to herself,' Jack told them, 'as she hasn't seen you lately.'

She drew in a breath of relief. It could have been awkward, even coming down the stairs alone with him. After she'd tucked the excited twins back into bed, she braced herself to go downstairs. Dexter greeted her with a sleepy 'woof' and wagging tail before he settled down in his basket.

412

All eyes were fixed on her. She was acutely aware of Jack's brown-eyed gaze.

'I hope they'll sleep,' she said, for something to say. 'I intended to be here much earlier.'

'They'll be fine,' Ruth assured her. 'But *you*, Madeleine, are not.'

*What did she mean?*

'I'm all right,' she said with not much conviction, even to her own ears. 'It was the shock of all those explosions in London. I'd seen a much milder version when I was in Hast—'

She broke off, feeling the heat rush to her face. Oh, she'd nearly said the whole word. As it was, she was sure Jack knew she was about to say Hastings. She'd signed the Official Secrets Act, for heaven's sake. But then Jack probably had a good idea of where she'd been sent anyway, and the Whites would never breathe a word to anyone about her movements. Sharply, she pulled herself together when she saw the three of them not worrying about where she worked but looking concerned for her.

'Will you have time to see your parents before you go back?' Jack said.

'No. They're away at the moment.'

'Oh, that's a shame,' Ruth said. 'And you're going straight back to work?'

She swallowed. 'More or less.'

'But you have to go through London.' Ruth bit her lip. 'It's not safe if last night is anything to go by.'

'The Luftwaffe have more than likely decided it's safer to bomb us at night,' Jack said, 'but the trains are all going to be up the creek, probably for several days or more, as the bombs will have caused plenty of damage.'

She wouldn't alarm Ruth further by telling her that people were taking blankets and sleeping bags ready to spend the night in the Underground.

Jack turned to Ruth. 'If Madeleine will allow me, I'll take her back.'

'Thank you for the offer, Jack, but it's much too far out of your way.' Madeleine had to keep up the pretence of letting him think she still worked away from BP.

'It's not out of my way at all.' He looked directly at her. 'I believe you're *very* much going my way, aren't you?'

*So he knows I'm due back at the Park.*

This was the last thing she needed – to be cooped up with him in the confines of his motorcar, still not knowing for certain whether he'd received her letter. Him questioning her as to why she was acting so cool towards him. Her venting her fury that he hadn't disclosed he was married. Then a terrible silence to endure for the two-hour drive back to Bletchley. Oh, it was too bad. She was aware of Ruth's eyes widening, as though not quite understanding the sudden turn of the conversation. She caught the glance she sent to her husband, who gave a slight shake of his head as though warning her not to make any further comment.

'Madeleine?' Jack was waiting for her reply.

'Um, it's very kind of you but—'

'No trouble at all,' he said, smiling.

But was she imagining that it wasn't his usual warm smile?

'So it's settled,' he continued. 'We'll start off at nine-thirty. That will give you time to see the twins and say goodbye to them and then we'll be on our way.'

What could she say? She knew he was right about the

414

trains. Even though she had a couple of days in hand she had nowhere else to go and Ruth and Joseph, dear as they were, had enough to cope with without two extra people who clearly had things to work out between them. She was trapped.

'Thank you, Jack,' she said. She couldn't find any more words to add.

Madeleine slipped between the bed sheets of Ruth and Joseph's guest room, feeling a spike of guilt that it should be Jack lying there, not herself. She could smell the scent of him, a little musky . . . and very masculine. It was almost as though he were here, lying beside her in the dark. Her cheeks burnt with the image. She lay there, trembling as much from that thought as she was from thinking about the day and the surprise attack on London. Just how prepared were the British in defending the island? she wondered.

'Please let the war end soon,' she said out loud. 'Lives are too precious to be thrown away over that megalomaniac.'

If only she could do more. She set her chin. Being back at the Park and doing what was considered an important job was the only thing to concentrate on now. With that thought in mind, she crept further down under Jack's sheet and pulled the blanket high around her shoulders, then closed her eyes. But twenty minutes later she was still awake. All she could think of was Jack. She might as well admit she still loved him with all her being. He was only a staircase away from her. All she had to do was tiptoe downstairs and into the sitting room. Then she'd confront him. But what was the good? He was probably tired and had just fallen asleep and wouldn't take it kindly that she'd woken him. The 'old' Jack wouldn't have minded in the least, but she didn't know how this Jack was going to react when they finally had some privacy and she'd know for certain whether he'd received her letter finishing things or not. Hot tears ran down her face when she thought how kind he'd been to think of the twins and all they had been through – all they still might have to face – and had given them his dog to comfort them and bring them some happiness. She swallowed hard. It could have all been so different. She let the tears fall onto her pillow, not bothering to wipe them away.

Another hour passed before Madeleine's restless thoughts diminished and she could finally fall asleep.

# *Chapter Forty-Three*

Madeleine cautiously opened her eyes that felt like slits. Where was she? Her gaze fell on the flowered curtains at the window – curtains she didn't recognise. And then it all came flooding back. The tube station. The man who'd found her a taxi. Then the last person she expected to see. She couldn't help it. She held the top of the sheet to her nose and breathed in the scent of him. He'd seemed so normal yesterday evening. So genuine. Was he play-acting, the same as she was, because they were guests in someone else's home?

Vaguely she heard a dog bark. Dexter. Jack's dog. Now he belonged to the twins. She smothered a yawn. What was the time? It was pitch-dark in the room but that was because the blackout blind was firmly pulled down. She half sat up and switched on the lamp beside the bed. That was better. She picked up her watch and peered at it. Twenty to eight. She was surprised she couldn't hear all the children. But everywhere was quiet. But of course. Today was Sunday.

She glanced round the modest room, restful in the gentle blue-painted walls the Whites had chosen. There was a single wardrobe, a neat chest of drawers in walnut, a small

417

sink with mirror above and braided rugs covering a parquet floor. She threw the covers aside and hopped out of bed to wash her face, then glanced in the mirror above the basin. Her eyes were still sore from last night. She splashed cold water on them, hoping the puffiness would go down, then shook her head and ran her hands through her hair.

There was a light tap at the door. It wouldn't be the twins. They'd knock, then come bouncing in. It must be Ruth. Quickly, she got back into bed and called 'Come in.'

A tray came round the doorway. Carrying it was Jack. Oh, why did it have to be him? She looked a sight.

'I've brought you a cup of tea,' he said, setting the tray on the bedside table. The smell of toast wafted into her nostrils. He put the cup and saucer in her hands. 'Did you sleep well?'

'Better than I thought I would.' She took a sip of the hot tea, grateful for something to do, so aware of his nearness. She saw how his eyes crinkled with what looked like concern as he stared at her.

'Your eyes look sore as though you've been crying. Have you?'

'N-no. It was a bit windy yesterday when I left. I expect that's what's done it.'

'The stiff sea breeze of the coast, no doubt.'

She shot him a look but his expression was bland. She put the teacup to her lips.

'I brought you a couple of slices of toast with real butter and marmalade,' he said. 'You'd better eat it or I'll be in trouble, what with the rationing.'

She crunched her way through the toast, aware of the noise she was making in the silent room, aware of him watching her from the bedroom chair. In her nervousness

418

she picked up the cup to finish her tea but instead slopped some of it in the saucer.

When she'd finished he took the crockery back and set it on the tray.

'May I sit on the bed?'

She nodded. It was hard to speak. He picked up her hand, studying it.

'You have beautiful hands,' he murmured. 'Smooth, with slender fingers and pretty nails. Lovely enough for an artist to paint.'

She couldn't go on pretending a moment longer. She'd have to say something.

'Jack, did you ever receive—'

There was a crash outside the door, then it flew wide and two dark, tousled heads dived in, with Dexter barging his way in front, giving short, excited barks.

'Maddie, Maddie, look who we've brought to help you wake up.'

'Dexter'd wake up the devil,' Jack chuckled. 'I think Maddie is well and truly awake now.' He threw a glance at Madeleine. 'I'll leave you with this mob.'

He picked up the tray and was gone from the room. Madeleine gave a sigh of relief.

'I can tell how improved your English is, both of you,' she said, ruffling the twins' heads. 'You must both be doing well at school.'

'I came fith in class,' Lotte said.

'It's fifth,' Erich corrected his sister. 'It has two "f"s.'

Madeleine gave an inward smile. He was still in charge of his twin's pronunciation.

'Can you think in English now?' she said.

'Yes,' they answered together.

419

'I can dream in English,' Lotte said, throwing herself off the bed and doing a handstand up the wall.

'Maddie, have you heard from Mutti and Papa?' Erich's face was serious. Suddenly Madeleine could see anxious adult eyes staring at her through a child's face. 'We still have not received a letter.'

'Nor have I, my love,' Madeleine said, hating to give him such an unsatisfactory answer.

Lotte had stopped playing about and came to sit quietly on the bed.

'I miss Mutti,' she said. 'And Papa.' Her eyes filled with tears.

'I know you do, darling,' Madeleine said, hugging her. 'I miss them, too. But we have to hope that we see them soon after the war ends.'

'But the war is getting worse,' Erich said. 'They dropped a lot of bombs yesterday. It is all in Uncle Joseph's paper this morning.'

A ten-year-old shouldn't be reading such news. It must be terrible for him and his sister to be aware that their own country was dropping bombs on the country they were now sheltering in. She gave a deep sigh. Even in the short time she'd seen them yesterday she'd noticed a change in them. They were forced to grow up rapidly now their childhood had been snatched from them.

She needed to see the newspaper. How much damage had been done. She couldn't bear to think further of how many injuries – or worse – the explosions had caused.

'I'm going to have to shoo you both out,' she told them. 'I need to get up.' She looked at the dog, lying quietly, his head on his paws, but his brown eyes alert, bizarrely reminding her of Jack's. 'Yes, and you, too, Dexter, there's a good boy.'

420

Bathed and dressed, Madeleine went into the dining room, her stomach rumbling. The toast had just tided her over. Jack looked up from the table and smiled at her. Her heart squeezed at the familiarity of his smile – warm, loving, concerned.

'Morning, again, Maddie. You look more like yourself now.'

'Not like someone who's been dragged through a hedge backwards.' She smiled back.

'You never look like that. You always look beautiful.'

'Thank you, kind sir, even though we both know it's not true.'

They'd slipped back to their bantering. How had that happened, she wondered, when she was supposed to be so furious, so hurt . . .

'There's fresh tea in the pot,' Jack said, as she sat down opposite him. 'No one's about. The children have taken Dexter for a walk. Ruth's in the kitchen making porridge.'

Was he letting her know they were on their own? That she could continue what she had started to ask him yesterday? Whether he'd received her letter. But now was not the time. Ruth could come in at any minute.

The silence was awkward.

'I think I'll go and see if Ruth needs any help.'

Ruth looked up and smiled as Madeleine went into the kitchen.

'Good morning, my dear. Did you sleep?'

'When I finally drifted off,' Madeleine said.

Ruth sent her a sharp look, then attended to the saucepan.

'The porridge will be ready in a few minutes.' She turned the gas burner low and put the lid on the saucepan. 'Let's sit down while we have a few moments on our own.'

421

Ruth sounded serious, Madeleine thought. She screwed up her courage.

'Have you heard from—'

'No – nothing. But I'm afraid that's to be expected now. We won't hear – unless it's very bad news.'

Madeleine gulped.

'It's not that, love,' Ruth continued. 'Something's not right with you and Jack. I can't put my finger on it. He seems more or less the same, though a little wary . . . perhaps cautious is a better word . . . when you're speaking to him. As though he senses – as I do – that you're not quite so happy, the pair of you.' She looked directly at her. 'Am I right?'

'Yes, you are,' Madeleine said miserably.

'Do you want to tell me about it? You know I wouldn't dream of letting it go further – not even with Joseph.'

'I know you wouldn't. But it's—' She broke off, biting back the tears. 'It's something serious, Ruth. I've had to break it off with Jack. You see, he's been deceitful—'

'What!' Ruth sat stock-still, her jaw slack.

'He's married!' Maddie tried to control her trembling voice. 'That's the thing. I know about it but I don't think he realises I know.'

Ruth stared at her incredulously. 'I don't believe it! How did you find out?'

'S-someone wrote me a note.'

'Who was it from?'

'There was no name,' Madeleine said miserably. 'She just stuck the note in the writing case Jack gave me.'

'And you haven't discussed this with him?'

'No. I haven't had a chance. I only found out when I was transferred to . . . the coast.'

'So you believe an anonymous note from someone without the gumption to come clean and tell you to your face, rather than use your instincts and common sense to know that someone with the integrity of Jack would do no such thing. You're talking about Jack, who you told me got you out of a sticky moment on that train, and I imagine it was he who arranged for the twins to have false passports so they could come here safely – am I right?'

Madeleine nodded.

'Well, that would be at risk to his job if he'd ever been found out.' She looked directly at Madeleine. 'He came yesterday to give the twins his dog so they have something to love of their own – and, incidentally, I can tell he loves that dog to bits.' She broke off to take a breath. 'And *you*, Madeleine – well, anyone with half an eye can see he adores you. No, I would never believe he's been deceitful.'

Ruth's outburst took her aback. Madeleine bit her lip hard to stop an angry retort when she looked at her friend's clear brown eyes. Wise eyes which had witnessed the beginnings of atrocities against her own people in her own country that had prompted her and Joseph to emigrate to England, leaving relatives and friends and their life and home behind. Could she possibly be right?

'Do you have any idea who this person might be?' Ruth said, getting up to check the porridge.

'Yes, I'm sure it was the woman who had the next bed to me in the hostel near where Jack and I worked. She worked at the same place. You see, she said she'd been going out with him but he'd left her for another woman whom he married.' She appealed to Ruth. 'Why would she say that if it wasn't true?'

'Hmm. Sounds like a classic case of jealousy to me. She's

seen how happy you and Jack are and she wants to dig her claws in.' Ruth put down the wooden spoon and turned to face Madeleine. 'Take some advice, my dear. Don't accuse him of any deceit. Just tell him about the note and how upset you've been. You need this conversation on your own, with proper time to work it out. It's no good telling him in the car on your way back to work. He needs to concentrate on the road.' She ladled out the porridge in four bowls. 'Is it set in stone that you have to be at work today? I mean, with all the bombing in London, they surely can't expect everyone to move around as normal.'

'I don't actually have to be at work until Wednesday,' Madeleine admitted.

Ruth gave her a sharp look.

'Then there's no reason why you couldn't stop along the way for a couple of days, is there?'

# *Chapter Forty-Four*

After breakfast and Madeleine had packed her things, not only the twins but Ruth and Joseph's three daughters asked when Madeleine was coming back.

'And Uncle New Year,' Lotte shouted as all the children trooped in from playing with Dexter in the garden. 'We want to see him, too.'

Dexter was the only one displaying any joy, with his wagging tail and panting tongue.

'If it involves people, he thinks we're talking about him and his next adventure,' Jack said, chuckling and giving the dog a good pat.

'Remember what I told you, Madeleine,' Ruth said quietly when she kissed her goodbye. 'He's a good man – I know it.'

'I'll try to remember.' Madeleine almost choked on the words. She turned to Joseph, kissing his cheek. 'Thanks for everything, Joseph.'

'You're welcome here anytime,' he said gruffly.

'Don't forget to write to me, you two.' Madeleine gave the twins a tight hug, holding back her tears. She could tell by Lotte's red eyes that the little girl had been crying, but as though the dog knew, he pushed his nose into Lotte's hand. 'And look after Dexter.'

'We will,' they said in unison as Lotte bent down to pat Dexter's silky head.

Jack saw her settled in his motorcar before getting into the driving seat, having already packed their luggage in the boot. He started the ignition and pulled away from the kerb, giving a quick toot of the horn. Madeleine twisted her neck to give the final wave, then glanced at Jack's profile as he put his arm out of the window to signal he was passing a horse and cart. When he was safely by, he said:

'The twins seem a lot better now than when we had to give them that awful news, don't they?'

'Yes,' she agreed. 'They've responded to Ruth and Joseph's love and kindness.' She turned to him. 'But I think much of it was down to your giving Dexter to them. They've now got something of their own to love and he is more than happy to show his love in return.'

She wondered if she sounded sentimental, but Jack merely nodded. It was several minutes before he spoke again.

'Maddie . . .'

*Oh, no. Here it comes. I'm not ready to have it out with him at this minute.*

She sat up straighter, trying to give herself courage.

'. . . what do you think about having a little detour?'

Had he been talking to Ruth?

'What sort of detour?'

'Well, we're very close to Churchill's old school at Harrow-on-the-Hill. I wondered if you'd like to see it. I've never been but it might be interesting. We'll only be able to look at the outside, obviously.' He paused. 'What do you think?'

'I'd like to,' she said immediately. At least they'd be amongst people. 'How far is it?'

'Not more than half an hour. Actually, it's on the way, so not a detour at all.'

Jack didn't say much else until they arrived at Harrow. He parked close to the school gates outside Druries, one of the Harrow houses, just as a class of boys and their tutor emerged.

'Don't the boys look smart in their uniforms?' Madeleine said, admiring their grey trousers and dark-blue jackets topped by boaters set at jaunty angles on their heads. 'And it's an impressive group of buildings.'

'It is,' Jack agreed. 'Going back to the seventeenth century, though it was added on to in Victorian times.' He looked at her. 'Why don't we walk into town.'

He held out his arm. She hesitated. But she had to take it because if not, it would kick off the row, and this was definitely not the right time. He gave her a quizzical look but made no comment. Her hand in the crook of his arm felt right. Comfortable. Safe. He smiled at her and she weakly smiled back.

'Oh, dear, look at that.' Jack tilted his head as he pointed to a cinema with half the top storey gone. 'I did hear Harrow took a bomb or two last month but thankfully no one was killed.' He sighed deeply. 'Terrible thing is, this is only the beginning. I think we'll have more horror to put up with.' He stopped and turned her towards him. 'Maddie, I don't know quite what's up with us but I do know we need to talk.'

So he *did* realise something was amiss. And he knew it was serious enough for a private discussion. It made her feel a little better. Her accusation wouldn't come completely out of the blue. But then she stopped her flow of thoughts. What had Ruth said? Something about not accusing. Just tell him about the note. Then let him speak. Unconsciously, Madeleine bit her lower lip.

They strolled on a little further until they came to a café.

'Why don't we stop here and have a cup of coffee?' he said.

They took one of the tables by the window and Jack ordered two coffees, but when they came, and after the first swallow, Jack grimaced.

'This tastes terrible. It's worse than the ersatz coffee that we get served at the Park sometimes.'

'Not only that, but look at my cup.' She showed him a trace of lipstick on the rim.

'That's it.' He threw down some coins and they pushed the chairs under the table and were back on the street.

'Let's try over there.' Jack gestured to a hotel on the opposite side. 'They usually do coffee even if you're not staying there.'

He opened the door to let her through to a foyer which was almost empty and walked up to the reception desk. The woman nodded and told them to take a seat. Minutes later they were sitting on a sofa in their own quiet corner buttering homemade scones and drinking what Jack called 'a decent cup of coffee'. For the first time since arriving at the Whites' door, Madeleine felt able to relax a little in his company. But there were still people wandering around. She daren't start the conversation – the questions – that were bursting from her.

As though Jack had tapped into her thoughts he said:

'Now, then, darling, I need to know what's going on. Why you've somehow changed towards me when I feel exactly the same towards you.' He looked directly at her. 'Have you met someone else?'

The words startled her. She took a swallow of hot coffee too quickly, burning her throat. But at least she could reply to his last question.

'No, I haven't met anyone else.'

Jack leant back. 'Well, that's something, I suppose. But it's not all, is it?'

'No,' she said miserably.

'It sounds serious. We've been apart for a long time and all I'm longing to do is to kiss you and hold you and tell you how much I love you. But we've not had the chance.' He glanced round the room. The receptionist was talking on the phone, a few more people were coming in. 'We need some real privacy which we're not going to get when we're back at the Park.' He looked at her. 'When are you due back?'

'Wednesday – so I have to be back Tuesday night.'

He nodded. 'Good. I managed to get a couple of days and this seems a very nice hotel.' He looked directly at her. 'What about staying here and sorting this out? Give ourselves a little break. We've never had the chance before.'

She hesitated. Was this his underlying motive? To get her into bed?

*How can you say that?* her inner voice whispered. *You know perfectly well Jack loves you. You've based everything lately about him on an anonymous note. He deserves the chance to give you an explanation. And there must be one.*

'Maddie?'

Still she hesitated.

'We can have separate rooms . . . if that's what you're worried about.'

429

His eyes met hers. Appealing to her. An overwhelming sense of exhaustion seeped through her. Through her head, her limbs, her insides . . . to just be with Jack, let him take over . . . too much had happened . . . Her mind fragmented.

'Will you let me arrange it, darling?'

'All right,' she said.

He didn't smile, he didn't look triumphant, he just nodded. Somehow that reassured her. She watched him as he walked up to the desk, her heart beating furiously at her decision and what might become of it. He was back within minutes.

'They either have rooms on different floors or they have a double with a single room off it, I imagine for children. I'd prefer to take that option.' He looked at her. 'I don't want us to be on different levels. It's too worrying now the bombing has well and truly started.'

'All right,' she said feebly. It was as though the same two words were all she was capable of.

'I'll go and fetch our luggage.'

She half rose but he stopped her.

'Just relax, darling. You look tired out. I'll be back in a jiffy. Here's the key if you want to make sure the room is to your liking. And don't worry. I'll take the single.'

Numbly, Madeleine picked up a magazine and leafed through it without taking anything in, her thoughts flying. For goodness' sake, she was twenty-two but she was acting like a nervous virgin. She jerked up, the magazine falling to the floor. It hadn't registered at the time, but tomorrow was her birthday. She'd be twenty-three! There was a war on. The threat of invasion was still a dark cloud hanging over the country. If the unthinkable happened it would mean imprisonment or worse for anyone who disobeyed the Nazis. Or a bomb could drop, killing anyone at any time, whatever their age. Jack had said he wanted them to be on the same floor if there was an air raid. She shuddered, imagining a direct hit on the hotel. Well, she'd rather die in Jack's arms than alone and she was sure he'd feel the same. Her pulse quickened. Because no matter what explanation Jack came up with, she still loved him. It was no use thinking she might meet someone else. Even if she did, she would never love him the way she loved Jack – with all her heart. She swallowed hard, thinking of him on the sofa at the Whites'. *No*. She shook her head for emphasis. She would *not* allow him to be in a single bed in the next room. Her resolve deepened. She was going to lie in the same bed right next to him whatever the outcome.

She shot to her feet and picked up the key Jack had left on the table.

It was a large double room on the second floor with a high-beamed ceiling and its own bathroom. She wouldn't bother inspecting the single room next door as here everything looked spotless. Her heart missed a beat when she pulled back the bedcover to find crisp white sheets and pillowcases ,imagining what might take place there now she'd made her decision. In the bathroom she caught sight of herself in the mirror above the washbasin. Jack was right. She looked every bit as tired as she felt. Quickly, she brushed her hair and gripped it back with her combs, then touched up her faded lipstick. There – that looked tidier. She smiled and the face in the mirror smiled back.

There was a light tap at the door and Jack came in with their luggage. He glanced round.

'This is nice.' He looked at her. 'Is it okay for you?'

'Yes,' she said. 'It's charming.'

As he made for the door leading to the single room she said:

'No, Jack. I don't want you in a separate room. I want you here with me.'

He flashed a look of surprise then said softly, 'Are you sure?'

'I'm very sure.'

'Then come here.' He took her in his arms and she rested her head on his shoulder, taking in the familiar smell of him – clean, masculine, a hint of tobacco. She wanted this man with all her being. She tilted her head up ready to be kissed. But instead he gently put her away from him. She stumbled back a step but he caught her firmly.

'Not yet,' he said. 'I want to kiss you more than anything in the world, but then I won't be responsible for my actions. I need to know what's gone wrong between us first.'

'But I don't,' she blurted, wondering where the words had sprung from. 'I need you *now*. And then we'll talk.'

Before she could say another word, he gathered her back into his arms and kissed her. Jack's magical kiss. The tip of his tongue. Then deepening. A nervous thrill caused her to catch her breath as she knew he was going to make love to her. *They* were going to make love.

'May I undress you?' He didn't wait for her answer but took off her jacket, unbuttoned her blouse and removed it, letting his hand brush her breast before undoing her skirt, then the slip, tossing them onto a nearby chair, until she stood before him in her bra and cami-knickers. 'Beautiful,' he said softly, pulling the combs from her hair and letting it fall free, running his fingers through the shiny strands. He kissed her bare shoulder, then put her gently away from him, looking deep into her eyes. 'I love you, Maddie, and I always will.'

'That makes two of us.' Madeleine smiled back, the misery and doubt she'd gone through these last months draining away. 'And now it's my turn to do the same,' she said with a mischievous grin, as she unbuttoned his shirt.

They would work something out, was her last thought as he entered her.

## Chapter Forty-Five

She awoke, still in his arms. It was very early. She could tell that by being awake half the night, so aware had she been that Jack was here beside her. How extraordinary. She traced his sleeping face with her fingertips. Over his eyebrows that nearly met. Ran them down his nose, along his jaw. It was when her fingers touched his lips that he suddenly kissed them, making her jump.

'I thought you were asleep.'

'No, and I wasn't going to tell you – I was enjoying every second.'

'Jack, now we're alone—'

'I should hope we are.' Jack's chuckle seemed a little forced as though he knew what was coming.

'No, listen. We must talk.'

'But before that I want to talk about something else,' Jack said, and pulled her tightly towards him. 'Tell you how much I love you and want you again.'

She pulled away, adjusting the sheet so it covered her breasts. She faced him, wishing she could still her racing heartbeat.

'Please, Jack, don't. This is much too serious and it's driving me crazy.' She sat up and looked down at him, his dark hair tousled, his eyes suddenly anxious. 'I want you to tell me the truth.' She felt her chest tighten. 'I'll know if you're lying.'

'I've never lied to you,' Jack protested, 'so what's given you that idea?'

'An anonymous note I found when I went to Hastings. It was hidden in the writing case you gave me.' She watched his expression carefully. 'Why didn't you tell me you were married?'

There. It was out. Everything rested on his answer. She felt her insides quake as she waited for his reply.

He was silent. She could hear his breathing. What was he thinking? How to tell her in the least cruel way? To give excuses as to why he hadn't told her?

A shadow passed over his face.

'Is that what this *anonymous* note said?'

'Yes.' She stared at him. 'It's a simple yes or no, Jack.'

'The simple answer is "yes".' He paused. 'But . . .'

Oh, it couldn't be true. Not after she'd fallen in love with him. Not after what had happened last night. Her face burnt at the memory. She flung the bedcovers off, then realised she had no clothes on. Her dressing gown was still in her suitcase. Oh, this was terrible.

'No buts, Jack. No excuses. I want to go.'

She snatched her clothes from the chair and rushed into the bathroom, her anger vented on herself as much as him. The anonymous writer was telling the truth. He'd just verified it. Quickly, she dressed, not caring that her blouse wasn't tucked in properly, her skirt round the wrong way. She stormed back into the room where Jack was sitting up, two pillows supporting him, and his hands behind his head. He sighed when he saw her.

'You wouldn't let me finish,' he said.

'There's nothing to finish,' she shot back. 'You're married. That's the end of it.'

'No, it isn't – if you'll just let me speak.' There was a sharp edge to his voice that she hadn't heard before. 'Just sit down a minute.' He gestured to the bed. She glared at him but sat in the chair.

'You asked me why I didn't tell you I was married,' he said. 'The answer is that I *was* – but no longer.'

She bit her lip. 'So you're divorced?'

'No. I'd call myself separated from my wife.'

Oh, how she hated to hear that word 'wife'. What sort of woman would he have picked to be his wife? Had it been *her* fault – or Jack's?

'You see, I lost her. She died. In a motor accident.'

She stared at him, open-mouthed. This was dreadful. She felt the heat rise up her face. Her cheeks felt as though they were on fire. She'd never thought—

'Wh-what happened?'

'I was driving,' he said dully. 'That's the worst part. I didn't see the lorry until it was too late. It was pitch-dark. Kathy was asleep. If not, she probably would have seen it because it was on her side. It came out of a side street with no lights and I smashed into it.' He paused and looked away. 'I've never stop blaming myself for her death.' His voice cracked. He put his head in his hands. 'And our unborn child.' His voice was muffled but she heard those shocking words.

Dear God. Jack raised his head. He looked stricken as though he were living the accident again. She ran to his side, sat on the bed next to him and held him while he wept.

'I'm sorry,' he said gruffly, clearing his throat. 'I haven't felt that bad for a long time. I never talk about this to anyone.'

'I'm sorry, too.' Her voice was choked with tears. 'But why didn't you tell me – when we first said we loved each other?'

'I wanted to – so many times. But I thought you'd blame me. It would just be my word what happened. Even if you believed me you wouldn't dare sit in a car with me at the wheel.' He took a handkerchief and blew his nose loudly.

'You're a wonderful driver. I wouldn't have thought anything of the kind.'

'That's now. But you didn't know me then – and you'd have had doubts about it not being my fault. I was scared to lose you . . . I couldn't risk it. I was so stupid to doubt your love wouldn't be strong enough.' He looked at her. 'I know who would've written that note.'

'Cora,' Madeleine said.

His head whipped up. 'How do you know?'

'She's been very odd with me since the day I arrived. She's seen us together. I caught her reading the letter Ruth sent me about the twins' parents . . . and her bed was next to mine in the dormitory so she had easy access to my personal belongings – such as the writing case.'

'Yes,' Jack said. 'It was definitely her. No one else would have known anything about my private life.'

She met his gaze. 'So you *did* know her before you went to the Park.'

He nodded. 'And before you ask –' he blinked '– I went to school with her brother, who introduced us. We went out a few times but I was never in love with her . . . or made love to her. I realised pretty soon the kind of

437

possessive person she was. I'd already ended it when I met Kathy and knew that she was the one for me. Cora was bitter and threatened to make trouble . . . and she bloody well almost succeeded.' He looked directly at her. 'When I saw her at the Park I couldn't believe it. I just hoped by now she'd have put this all behind her. . . met someone else. I never guessed she would turn on you.' He shook his head almost in wonder. 'My God, what a dreadful woman.'

It was Madeleine's turn to be silent. Recriminations bounced through her head. How could she not have guessed that Jack might be a widower? She drew in a jagged sigh.

'When did it happen?'

'Three years ago.'

'It must have been terrible for you – unbearable.' She didn't know what else to say.

He didn't answer.

'And you never met anyone else?'

She tried to prepare herself for something she preferred not to hear. She shouldn't have asked such a question.

He shook his head.

'No, no one who came even close to what I'd found in Kathy. That is, until I set eyes on *you*.' He took her face in his hands. 'But what I don't understand is, why did you trust whoever you thought wrote the note that they were telling the truth?'

'Because –' Madeleine faltered '– because she said she knew you before. She made it sound as though she knew you intimately.'

'Not in the way she must have implied. And she obviously hadn't heard about the accident.'

'She didn't only imply that,' Madeleine said after a few

moments. 'She said your work wasn't all you purported it to be, or words to that effect.'

'WHAT!' Jack shot up, the exclamation still shaping his lips.

'She more than hinted you were a spy.'

Now, even saying the words, she realised how ridiculous it sounded.

Jack threw his head back and laughed. Then he suddenly stopped, his face serious. 'But you believed it?'

Madeleine brought her lips together in a tight line.

'Cora's just made a malicious stab in the dark,' Jack said. 'She hoped *that* accusation would finally make you drop me . . . and she was bloody well near successful.' He gazed at her. 'You know, Maddie, I can tell you very little, if anything, about what I was doing in Berlin. But what I can tell you is that the cultural attaché title was a cover for my real work, which was mainly finding out information from the Germans about their forthcoming military strategies and reporting it to the right people.' His brown eyes probed hers. 'And we have never had this conversation.'

Madeleine felt the warmth rush to her cheeks. 'No, of course not. I understand.'

How brave Jack was, she thought, to be involved in – well, it could only be called spying, but on behalf of the British. She felt a surge of pride.

There was a minute's silence between them. Then Jack said:

'But there's one important thing I want to ask *you*, Maddie. Why on earth didn't you write and ask me yourself about whether I was married? It could have saved a whole lot of grief.'

This was it. This was what she should have done if she'd

had a grain of sense in her. But the overwhelming hurt and misery had clouded her judgement.

'I did write,' she said in a small voice. 'But not what you'd want to hear.'

He raised his eyebrows. 'Really? What did you say?'

'I said I never wanted to see you again. But then you wrote two or three times more and I realised you hadn't received it. And then you were sent away yourself – but you suspected something, I could tell.'

'Yes, because you never answered my last three letters.'

'How could I? I'd told you not to contact me again, and then you said you were being sent away where you couldn't send or receive letters.' She paused. 'Where were you?'

'In Scotland. Sent to train personnel. It was all very hush-hush – still is.' He gave her a direct look. 'By the way, what did you do with the last three letters I sent when you were so furious with me?'

'I almost tore them up.'

'Almost?'

'Yes.' She bit her lip. 'But I couldn't – don't ask me why.'

'So what did you do with them?'

'I put them in your mother's writing case with all the others.' *Even the anonymous note.* But she didn't tell him that.

'Oh.' He gazed at her. 'I wonder what made you hang on to them. But whatever the reason, I'm glad you didn't just chuck them away.' Before she could comment, he said, 'There's one more thing. Why didn't you ask me if I was married last night before we made love? Then if I still was, you could have rejected me – sent me to the single room.'

If she were honest, she hardly knew herself. The worry of being hit by a bomb now seemed purely an excuse.

'Maddie?'

'I don't know. I suppose I must have felt instinctively that you hadn't kept something so important from me. Or that you could be so deceitful.' The words tumbled from her lips as though someone else was saying them. Someone wiser than she. 'That there had to be an explanation. Also—' She stopped abruptly. Should she confess? 'Also,' she repeated, lightening her tone, 'if it *were* the truth, then I wasn't going to miss the chance of making love with you just the one time . . .'

'. . . before telling me to get lost,' Jack finished, grinning. 'Come here, you forward hussy. I'm going to show you just what you've been missing since we woke up this morning.'

'As it's my birthday, I'll allow you.'

'What!' He looked at her in astonishment. 'Your *birthday*! Why didn't you tell me? I haven't got you a present.'

'I disagree,' she beamed, pulling him close. 'I have the best birthday present in the world right here in my arms.'

# Chapter Forty-Six

*Bletchley Park*
*Christmas 1940*

'I ain't dirty!' Madeleine squawked, her expression one of self-righteous indignation. 'I washed me face and 'ands before I come 'ere, I did.'

Charles, now Professor Higgins, curled his lip in disgust. Madeleine bit back a giggle. He was a good actor, she had to admit.

'Sit down, Eliza,' he ordered. 'Now listen carefully, then repeat after me – "In *Hert*ford, *Here*ford and *Hamp*shire *hurr*icanes *hard*ly ever *happen*".'

'In '*Ert*ford . . .' *Ere*ford and '*Amp*shire . . .' *urr*icanes . . .' *ard*ly . . . *hever appen*.'

The audience guffawed.

'No, no, Eliza. Again! And no more chocolates until you pronounce it all correctly.'

When at the very end of the play Professor Higgins, his back to her, leant practically horizontal in his armchair, his stockinged feet crossed at the ankles, his hands clasped behind his head and asked Eliza where on earth his slippers were, Madeleine decided the clapping and whistling were

442

every bit as enthusiastic as at any West End play. For a fleeting moment she wished her mother could have been in the audience, clapping along with everyone else, proud of her daughter. But it wasn't fair of her to blame her mother for everything. It couldn't have been easy for her to watch the family business disappear down the drain and know from then on everything depended upon her as the breadwinner. Madeleine resolved to be more understanding in the future.

There was no curtain in the ballroom, but that didn't matter as Charles grabbed her hand and the whole cast stepped forward in unison and bowed to a roar of approval. Cecil ran alongside the seating until he reached them and took a bow to even more clapping, then gestured for Madeleine and Charles to come forward as the two leading characters to take an extra bow.

Madeleine caught Jack's eye in the front row. He gave her his special smile as he joined in with more fervent clapping.

Cecil waited until the noise had died down, then stepped forward.

'I've been wanting to do Bernard Shaw's *Pygmalion* for several years,' he said, then glanced at Madeleine. 'But no one ever seemed the right person to take the role of Eliza Doolittle. That is, until I saw Maddie in *Private Lives* when she stood in and played Sibyl. I immediately had her down for Eliza. But that's when the powers that be decided to send her away. But the gods sent her back just in time to rehearse for the Christmas play.'

There were some shouts of 'Bravo' and more whistles.

Madeleine beamed as she nodded to the audience, noticing as she did so that Cora was wearing the same pink dress with the plunging neckline she'd worn in *Private Lives*. Next to her was Daniel Strong. The woman threw her an icy look. *She's never forgiven Jack, and she's never forgiven Cecil for casting* me *as Eliza Doolittle*, Madeleine thought.

'So let's hope she'll do many more shows.' Cecil turned to look at Madeleine. 'Will you, Maddie?'

'If you'll have me,' Madeleine replied, a little husky from all her singing, her gaze fixed on Jack. He grinned and sent her a wink.

A sudden warmth surged through her. One day this war would be over – please God let it be soon – and she would see whether she was talented enough to fulfil her dream of becoming a professional actress. But whatever was in store for her and Jack, just like the song of the moment said, 'I'll Get By As Long As I Have You', and so would they.

# *After . . .*

There was a sudden knock at the door. Dexter pricked up his ears and barked, then jumped from his basket.

'Can you get it, dear?' Ruth called from upstairs to her husband.

Joseph reluctantly laid down the newspaper recounting the Royal Navy's latest triumph and scrambled from his chair, shutting the dog in the sitting room. He went down the hall, unbolted the front door and opened it. A tramp stood there, well back from the entrance. Long, scruffy beard and scraggly grey hair, wearing a baggy pair of corduroys topped by a nondescript jumper. No jacket, even though it was a crisp morning.

The two men silently studied one another. The tramp's bloodshot eyes staring at Joseph from his bony face unnerved him.

'Water,' the tramp managed through cracked lips.

'I can't offer you much,' Joseph said, 'but you may step in for a minute. I'll make you a cup of tea and a piece of toast if you're hungry.'

He could have bitten his tongue out. Of *course* the poor devil was hungry. He was as thin as a stick.

'That's kind of you,' the tramp mumbled as he edged his way in and followed Joseph to the kitchen.

Joseph ran the water into the kettle and turned on the gas, all the while aware of the tramp watching his every move. Was he looking about him seeing if it was worth taking anything? He shouldn't have invited him in in the first place. Oh, why didn't Ruth come down to see who was at the door? She was so sensible – she always knew what to do.

He needed a cup of tea himself. Might as well make a large pot. He took from the shelf a large teapot, their good one, normally used for special occasions, but it was the only one which would give the unexpected visitor two or three mugs of tea and one for him and Ruth. Her parents had given it to them on their first wedding anniversary. He heated the pot, then put in three level teaspoons of tea and filled it to the brim.

He heard footsteps coming down the stairs. Thank goodness. There was something about the tramp that he wasn't comfortable with. The old boy was looking around the room in a vague manner. Joseph wondered if he'd escaped from prison and was eyeing up their modest possessions. He shouldn't have let him in. Ruth would have thoroughly disapproved.

At that moment the door swung open and Ruth came in.

'Who was it at the door, dear?' Then she stared at the stranger and froze. 'Dear Lord, it can't be!'

'Yes, dear Ruth, it is,' the old man replied in German.

446

At his words Joseph swung round, his jaw dropping in astonishment.

'*Mein Bruder*? Can it *really* be you?'

'Ruth recognised me straightaway.' Hermann Weinberg gave a weak chuckle after he'd fortified himself with a fried egg and toast Ruth had made him. 'But my own brother didn't.' He paused. 'I suppose I must look different from when you last saw me.'

*Only thirty years older,* Joseph thought, *though it's only been eight years. He was taller than me, but no longer. And lost half his weight. And his voice . . . it's so thin. He's so different from my clever, confident brother I always worshipped. Poor man. Whatever had they done to him?*

He turned to his wife. 'But *you* were able to recognise him, Ruth.'

'Woman's intuition.' Ruth laughed it off.

Joseph looked at the ghost of his brother.

'We heard you and Renate were sent to concentration camps and we feared the worst.'

'Yes. Renate was sent to a different one. It broke my heart to be separated.' Silent tears ran down Hermann's cheeks and fell into the long beard. 'Conditions were so terrible, I planned to escape the first week.' He lifted his head with what seemed like an effort. 'Do you know, rat meat became a delicacy.' He closed his eyes. 'We were all starving and disease-ridden, then had to put up with the cruelty of the guards, some of them even Jews, can you believe? And other prisoners you tried to help died before your eyes if they weren't marched off to the gas chambers. I knew it would soon be my turn.'

447

Joseph momentarily closed his eyes and heard his wife gasp in horror. So the rumours were true.

'No, I'll never forget it until my dying day.' Hermann stopped to cough into a filthy rag. 'I can't imagine what my poor wife is going through. But the camp those bastards have sent her to, she's probably no longer alive. If it's true, it's for the best. Dying is preferable than living through that hell.'

The long speech seemed to have taken what little spark of life the breakfast had given him. He leant back in the ladder-backed chair and covered his face with his hands. He gave a loud sob. Joseph put out a steadying hand on his shoulder.

'Take it slowly, Hermann,' he told his brother. 'You have all the time you need.'

'Joseph's right,' Ruth said. 'You're home now. You're with us. And I know two little people who will be overjoyed to see you – but not in that condition. You're going to have a bath, put on some clean clothes, and Joseph will trim that unruly beard, and get another meal inside you, before they come out of school.'

'It was the twins who kept me going through all those hundreds of miles,' Hermann said, looking up and blinking. 'I kept thinking every step was bringing me closer to them. It's taken me a long winter and several more months. I only made it because some very kind people along the way helped me. Two Belgian fishermen risked their lives to get me across the Channel.' He looked up with watery eyes. 'But it'll be worth every painful footstep when I set eyes on my children.'

'Well, you will in just a few hours,' Ruth told him. 'Meantime, I'm going to run that bath, and then I have an important letter to write.'

There was no let-up in the war although the bombing in London had considerably eased. The one recent victory was the Royal Navy sinking the German's prize battleship – the *Bismarck*. Rumour had it that the Navy had been tipped off from information sourced at Bletchley Park. Madeleine couldn't help feeling a glow of pride, even though she'd had nothing at all to do with locating the ship's whereabouts.

Josh Cooper had immediately taken her back as one of his official cryptanalysts, working with Tom and Percy to crack Luftwaffe codes, the messages of which she now knew were rushed in from various listening stations. That must include Fairlight as well, she told herself with a certain amount of satisfaction.

'Do you mind if I open Ruth's letter?' Madeleine said, as she and Jack were having a cup of tea one afternoon in Hut 2. 'I haven't heard from her for a while so I hope everything's all right.'

'Of course I don't mind. Read it out if it's nothing personal.'

She smiled at him.

*My dear Madeleine,*
*It was wonderful news to hear you and Jack are engaged.*
*When is the happy day? I imagine you're going to have a*
*quiet wedding if the war's still on. The twins were so excited*
*when I told them the news. Lotte wants to be your*
*bridesmaid!*

*'Maddie's going to marry Uncle New Year,' Lotte kept repeating and made Erich dance with her around the table – he said it was embarrassing but I know he was very pleased, too.'*

She and Jack grinned at one another. Madeleine read on.

*'Now, my dear, you must brace yourself for what I'm about to tell you.'*

Her stomach turned.

'Oh, Jack, I hope this isn't the news we've been dreading. I couldn't bear it.' She handed him the sheet of paper. 'Will you finish reading it?'

He nodded and cleared his throat.

*'You are never going to believe this but an hour ago, who do you think turned up on the doorstep? Hermann Weinberg, Joseph's brother!'*

Madeleine's hand flew to her mouth. It wasn't possible. How on earth had he got from a concentration camp in Germany to England?

'Oh, Jack—'

He put his hand up. 'Let me read on, darling.'

*'Poor Joseph didn't recognise him. He thought he was a tramp and took pity and invited him in for a cup of tea. He's aged terribly and has lost a lot of weight but he's going to stay with us and I'm sure he will soon improve. He escaped from the camp and walked all the way to the*

*Belgian coast, then crossed the Channel with the help of a father and son who were fishermen. It's beyond belief.*

*He has no news of Renate, his wife, but is convinced she's no longer alive. A shocking thing to say but he's told us of unimaginable cruelty and says death is preferable. It was only the twins that kept him going. Joseph is going to get him spruced up as much as he can so they don't have too awful a shock, although they will be horrified when they first set eyes on their father. But when it sinks in they'll be ecstatic. Then, of course, they'll want to know about their mother. But we have to face that when it comes.*

*Dexter somehow knows and has been very calm around Hermann. No barking or jumping up which is a blessing as he is wary of any dog now. He said the Nazis used them in the camp to terrify their prisoners.*

*Anyway, my dear, I wanted you and Jack to be the first to know. I'll write to Fran tomorrow and tell her. I can't wait for the twins to come home and see their papa. I'll write more on this later when things have settled a bit and we know more.*

*All our love,*

*Ruth.'*

Jack looked up and gazed at Madeleine. A tear trickled down her cheek and he took his forefinger and gently wiped it away.

'It's more than anyone could have dared hope,' she said, as he handed back the letter. She noticed *his* eyes were bright with unshed tears. 'The twins must have been so thrilled to see their papa though they were bound to be shocked at the change in him.'

'Ruth will soon fatten him up,' Jack said, smiling.

Madeleine took the letter and folded it, then tucked it into her handbag. She looked at Jack's dear face. This reunion was all because of him. If he hadn't pretended she was his fiancée on the Berlin train all that time ago, which led to her divulging their situation, the twins would never have got British passports so they could travel safely to England. They would very likely have ended up in the concentration camp like their parents and might not have survived. She gulped. It was too awful to contemplate. Thank God Jack had never received that cruel letter she'd written, telling him she didn't want to set eyes on him ever again. He could so easily have accepted her instructions – given up.

Jack caught her eye. As though he knew what she was thinking, he picked up her hand and kissed it.

He wasn't about to keep secrets from her, his darling Maddie. Except one. He'd made up his mind never to tell her he'd received that terrible letter saying she didn't want to set eyes on him ever again. The postboy had handed it to him just as he was leaving for Scotland, apologising and explaining the delay had been because it was put into the wrong post box. He'd been so thrilled to finally hear from her but instead the letter had shocked him to the core, leaving him angry and frustrated that no correspondence would be allowed until he returned to England – and who knew how long that would take, he'd thought, his mouth set in a hard line. All he could do was hang on to the dream that one day he'd have a chance to explain in person and that she'd understand. Thank God his dream had come true. He smiled at her, his beloved girl who had promised to marry him.

Madeleine remembered how Jack had once said: 'No

matter what happens I will always come back to you.' Even though she'd lost faith at one point, he'd kept his promise.

Warmth radiating through her, she beamed back at him. No matter how much evil existed in the world, there was the unbelievable news that Herr Weinberg had managed to find his family and had finally been reunited with his children. For a few moments she pictured Erich and Lotte's excited faces – and their joy at seeing their father. Not able to contain her happiness, she leant over the table and kissed Jack soundly on the lips, ignoring some nearby chuckles, then grinned as he winked at her.

Meanwhile, she and Jack had important work to do – right here at Bletchley Park. There was a war to win.

# Acknowledgements

I can't say too often that it takes many people to produce the books that you read. First and foremost is my lovely friend and literary agent, Heather Holden Brown of HHB agency and my super editor at Avon HarperCollins, Rachel Hart. I'm blessed with both of them, not to mention the entire award-winning team at Avon who are always so enthusiastic about my latest book and work hard to make it look stunning so that it stands out amongst all the other hundreds on the shelves.

But there are several other people close to me that deserve a mention. I belong to two very special writing groups, the Diamonds and the Vestas – four in each – one of which I founded and one of which I muscled in on! Besides being dear friends and published in different genres, they have a variety of talents for spotting anachronisms, tautologies, continuity issues, filling in plotholes (my computer insists they are 'potholes' but there's not much difference!), info dumps . . . the list goes on when we read out our wobbly chapters. And when we're told unanimously by the rest of the group that we're pitch perfect, well, that's a reason to celebrate!

The other three Diamonds are Terri Fleming, Sue

455

Mackender and Tessa Spencer. We meet every month for the whole day, and anyone who steps into the room and hears us screaming with laughter would think we weren't taking our writing seriously at all. They might be surprised to learn that we really concentrate on the reason why we meet – to improve our own and one another's writing.

The three other Vestas are Gail Aldwin, Suzanne Goldring and Carol McGrath. They are more far flung so we meet for several days, usually twice a year, sometimes in a cottage in Port Isaac and a house in the Mani district in Greece – sometimes in one of our UK homes. And even though it's like a fun-filled holiday when we work in a shady area overlooking the bay or sip a glass of champagne while watching the sun set over the Mediterranean, we still work hard on our writing.

Last, but definitely not least, there's Alison Morton, author of the award-winning Roma Nova series, and my good friend and critique writing partner who resides with her husband, Steve, in France. She's been amazing on my Bletchley Park series, correcting my German as well as a few historical slip-ups where her military experience and master's degree studying the German women's point of view in the Second World War occasionally caused her red pen to go berserk. And for this novel Steve advised me on the role of the ham radio operator (he was one himself for many years) as well as other details of signal intelligence in the war. Thank you both so much.

A new friend in the village, Clair, who is writing a first novel based on her own family, offered to take me to the listening station at Fairlight, near Hastings. There's little left to see now except the radar tower, but nevertheless it brought to life the remote spot where the men and women, and scores of others dotted around the country in various Y stations, were taking messages from the mouths of the enemy itself, most of which went directly to Bletchley Park. Of course, we ended up with a delicious lunch at the same guest house as those who'd worked at Fairlight all those decades ago, bringing them closer.

But there comes a time when the writer has to be alone with her pen or computer and actually produce the work. Thankfully, I love the routine of my writing days with gaps to do some more research. For the Bletchley Park series I've visited the Park twice since starting to write the novels, and three times many years ago, so I've been able to tap into a rich source of material. On the last visit with Heather we arranged to meet one of the historians based at the Park, Dr Thomas Cheetham, who kindly filled in some answers to questions I couldn't find in my large number of research books and even more generously agreed to read some of the more techy pages. So if there are any mistakes after all these checks, then they're all mine.

And a final acknowledgement to you, dear reader, for picking up this book. I do hope you enjoy this glimpse into the characters' lives and the work they did during this turbulent period as much as I've enjoyed writing about them. Thank you.

# *Historical Note*

In this series I've enjoyed mixing my imaginary characters with a handful of the remarkable figures who worked at Bletchley Park. In *Wartime Wishes* I've given Professor Josh Cooper a small but pivotal role in my story. He was one of the cryptographers at the Park as well as being head of the Air Section and I've endeavoured to follow his eccentric character in my brief portrayal of him.

Brinley Newton-John who was quite a well-known actor at the Park gets a passing mention in the novel after I discovered that in real life he was Olivia Newton-John's father!

I am always very careful to be faithful to historical events and accurate with the dates they happened as I weave them into my story. When war was declared on 3rd September 1939, the Nazi government really did order thirty-nine diplomats to remain in the British Embassy in Berlin to wait for the thirty-nine German ambassadors to return to Germany, and the British really did have a mascot dog who also had to stay behind during that time.

Literally out of the blue, the Germans dropped 11 bombs on Hastings, mostly on the cricket ground at 7.15 a.m. on 26 July 1940, as I described. As for the Blitz on 7th

September 1940, I used the actual hour it started on the evening when Madeleine gets caught up in the Underground at Charing Cross.

My father was a ham radio operator, building his own radios and subsequently our first 9-inch television! I wanted to use his call sign G3HXM which I've always known off by heart, but learnt that it was not a wartime call sign as it had more than three letters and numbers. I never realised until I did the research for this book that ham radio operators played quite a significant part in the war, particularly men who had served in the Great War and were too old or maimed to play an active part in the Second World War, which is what Maddie's father, Walter, was doing. (It did make me wonder if my own father was doing the same in his spare time.) Walter would have been one of the Volunteer Interceptors, vetted for security but wouldn't know the full impact the messages were having when picking up German intelligence in the field, including traffic from the Abwehr, and even tracking down German spies. These VIs were told a band of frequencies and if they spotted anything unusual, to pick up any messages on their private sets and send the logs to Box 25, Barnet. This led to a substantial house called Arkley View, and here the staff would read the logs and return them to the Volunteer Interceptors with comments such as 'MORE TRAFFIC PLEASE'; 'VERY GOOD'; 'NOT WANTED'; 'OK COVERED THANKS'; 'STILL WANTED' and 'TRAFFIC RETAINED FOR INFORMATION FOR WHICH MANY THANKS'.

The guest house called The Cove at Fairlight village was real and it really *was* vegetarian. Apparently, when the crew at Fairlight Y station were billeted there they were not at all pleased with a strictly vegetarian menu, so they had meat delivered, much to the kitchen staff's disgust! The guest house still exists and has retained the name, though when I recently visited as research for my story, I saw it now offers meat and fish, though still has a good variety of veggie dishes which pleased me.

I am a great fan of the TV programme: *The Repair Shop*. One day a woman and her adult daughter came into the barn with a battered leather writing case. It was a strange pale pinky-coral colour which the woman said used to be bright scarlet. It was her mother's case when she worked at Bletchley Park and kept her father's love letters in it. As soon as I heard that snippet, I immediately knew the writing case had another journey to make – in my novel – and that it would have a crucial bearing on the story. Needless to say that Suzy, the leather expert from *The Repair Shop*, handed a beautifully restored scarlet writing case, complete with insets, back to the two women who were amazed and tearful. So was I. But I feel thrilled that as well as Suzy, I've given the scarlet writing case a new and active lease of life! I only hope the original owner would have approved.

# Reading List for *Wartime Wishes at Bletchley Park*

*The Enemy is Listening: The first woman in British history to be commissioned as an intelligence officer* by Aileen Clayton

*The Secret Listeners: The men and women posted across the world to intercept the German codes for Bletchley Park* by Sinclair McKay

*They Listened in Secret* edited by Gwendoline Page

*Bletchley Park's Secret Source: Churchill's Wrens and the Y Service in World War II* by Peter Hore

*Secret Days: Codebreaking in Bletchley Park* by Asa Briggs

*The Women Behind The Few: The Women's Auxiliary Air Force and British Intelligence during the Second World War* by Sarah-Louise Miller

*Failure of a Mission* by Sir Nevile Henderson

Now you've finished Maddie's story, why not go back to where it all began in the first Bletchley Park Girls novel . . .

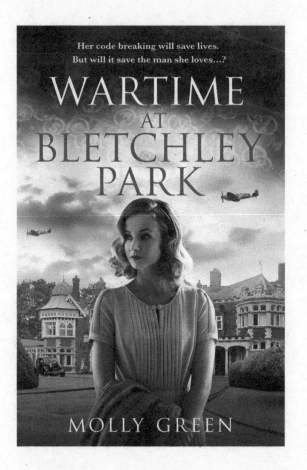

Available in paperback, eBook and audiobook now.

Then follow up with Rosie's story
in the second Bletchley Park
Girls novel . . .

Available in paperback, eBook and audiobook now.

And why not check out Raine's wartime tale of hope and friendship in the Victory Sisters series?

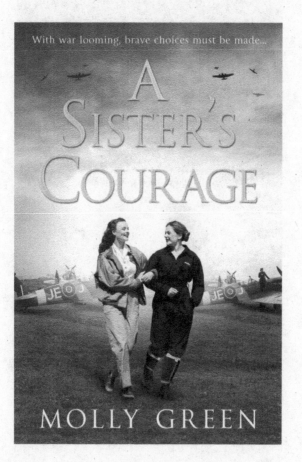

In the darkest days of war, Suzanne's duty
is to keep smiling through . . .

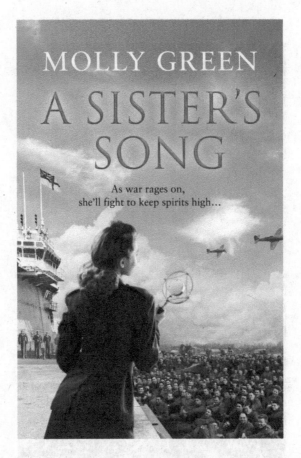

Ronnie Linfoot may be the youngest sister, but she's determined to do her bit . . .

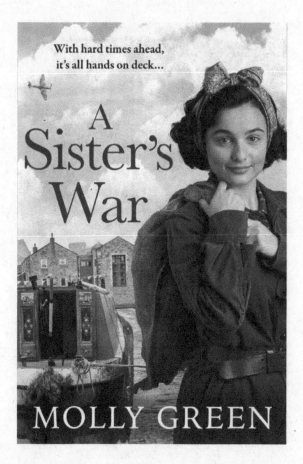

Available in paperback, eBook and audiobook now.

Or why not curl up with Molly Green's heart-warming Orphans series?

Available in paperback, eBook and audiobook now.

War rages on, but the women and children of Liverpool's Dr Barnardo's Home cannot give up hope . . .

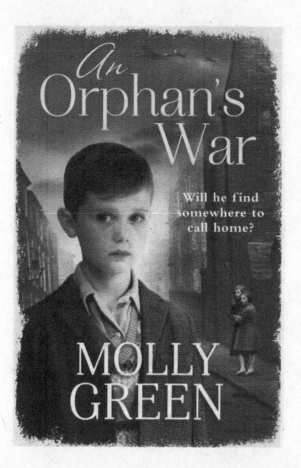

Available in paperback, eBook and audiobook now.

Even when all seems lost at Dr Barnardo's orphanage, there is always a glimmer of hope to be found . . .

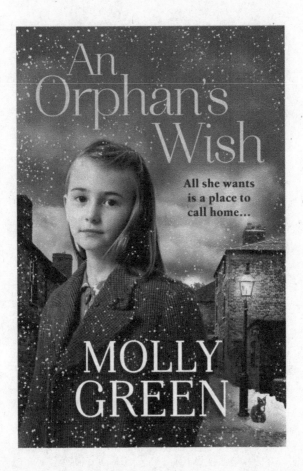

Available in paperback, eBook and audiobook now.